Secret Feelings

ISBN-13: 9798509513763

Cover design by: Pauline Adolfsson

Prologue

I never meant for this to happen, I swear I didn't. How it managed to do so anyway, I had no idea. It didn't only happen in a day, though. It had come creeping on me during the last couple of years. Ever since puberty, I believed, but I *swear*, it wasn't supposed to happen. I never meant to fall for one of my best friends.

But I did anyway.

The worst part of it was that I was sure he didn't feel the same way. Louis Tomlinson, falling for a guy? Pfft, yeah, sure. He was a ladies' man, and he was great with them too. He never failed to hook up with one at a party and then take them home for the night. He was the best of us all.

So why did I have to fall for him out of all people? I couldn't tell how many times I had asked myself this. Too many, that was for sure. Every day was like torture, having to be around him while hearing him talk about all his flings. If only he knew, though. If only he knew how much I wanted to be the one he talked about.

The good thing about having feelings for Louis in particular was that I got to see him every day. However, I wasn't really sure it was a good thing considering it was hard to be around him without showing how much I liked him. I knew I couldn't do that. He would think I had gone crazy or something. I mean, Louis, Niall, Liam, and Zayn didn't even know I was bisexual. They thought I was just as big of a ladies man as they were. If only they knew.

Even if my four closest friends didn't know about the fact that I liked boys as well as girls, I had been with some of them during my teenage years. It was never anything serious with either of them, but then again, I had never had anything serious with a girl either. I had never felt as though I wanted to be in a relationship with someone until my feelings for Louis blossomed.

He made me feel something I had never felt before. The way my heart fluttered whenever someone just said his name. The way my breath hitched in my throat when he, for example, would take off his shirt in the locker room. The way he made goosebumps appear on my skin whenever he touched me, and the way he made butterflies erupt in my stomach whenever he smiled. I had never experienced that feeling before. He made me realize what really liking a person felt like.

So, it was pretty safe to say that I, Harry Styles, was crushing on my best friend, and sadly, there was nothing I could do about it other than keep it a secret.

Chapter 1

High school. A place where I had spent almost three years now, or two and a half to be specific. After these years, I had yet to conclude whether I liked it or not. Sure, it was nice to hang with your friends all day, but I was starting to grow tired of studying. It felt like I didn't know what a world without having school work was like, and I could already tell that the last semester wouldn't be better.

It had almost been a month since I was there, though. After summer break, Christmas break was the best time of the year because that meant no school work. Usually, at least.

However, that also meant I hadn't seen the guys in a while. Sure, we hung out outside of school as well, but it wasn't like being at school where we were together every second of every day. The last time I had hung out with the guys was last weekend at Niall's house. We didn't even have soccer practice during the break because apparently, we needed a break from that as well.

This meant I hadn't seen Louis in a week. That was a week too long. I missed hearing his melodic laughter that always made my heart flutter, and the crinkles by his eyes that would appear whenever he was truly happy. Not to mention those crystal blue eyes, or that cute, button nose. I missed everything about him.

However, it was Monday today, also the first day back at school after Christmas break. To say I was excited would be an understatement. It was just sad that it was only because I couldn't wait to see a specific person and not because of the other parts that came along with high school.

Did you notice my dilemma yet? Why I still couldn't decide whether I liked high school or not? If it wasn't for Louis, I was pretty sure I would have wished to be finished with it already, but now I wasn't so sure. Louis and I were friends, but what would happen when we finished high school? Where were we all heading after this?

I thought of all this while sitting on the school bus, looking out the window. Sadly, I was the only one out of me, Louis, Niall, Liam and Zayn that lived on the south side of the town, which meant I always rode the school bus alone. Honestly, I couldn't wait to get my driver's license because I was so tired of always having to get on time to these buses. Luckily, my eighteenth birthday was in only two weeks, so hopefully, I wouldn't be riding this bus much longer.

After school, when I didn't have soccer practice and when I didn't hang out with the guys, I usually worked at a diner in town to save up money for my future, but also a car once I got my license. You see, my dad left us when I was eleven, and ever since then, we'd had it pretty difficult with money. Mom didn't want to leave the house, even though she made just enough money to pay for it each month. That meant she never had enough to buy other stuff, let alone anything for her children.

Therefore, my sister Gemma and I had gotten ourselves jobs to make our own money, and I never complained about it because I liked to have money I had made myself and not received from my parents. I knew I was one of very few people at my school thinking that way, though, because I knew for a fact that neither Niall, Liam, Zayn nor Louis had ever had a job. They thought I was lame every time I had to tell them I couldn't hang out because I needed to work. I didn't care, though.

The school bus finally came to a stop outside of school, so I grabbed my bag from the seat beside me before getting up, slinging it over my shoulder. It was cold outside, being the middle of January and all, so I made sure to hug my arms around myself to keep warm as I walked across the schoolyard towards the entrance.

As soon as I was inside, I unzipped my black winter jacket and ran a hand through my chocolate brown curls while my feet brought me further towards my locker. It was located pretty far from the entrance, so I had to walk for a while to get there. That meant I passed by a lot of students who all seemed more talkative than usual, which wasn't surprising considering it was the first day back at school.

Some of them glanced my way when I walked by them, but I didn't turn to meet their gazes. I wasn't the most unknown student around here considering I played soccer on the school's team, and being friends with Liam, Niall, Zayn, and Louis didn't make matters worse either, but I didn't like to brag about it.

Once I arrived at my locker, I unlocked it to get rid of my bag and jacket. I then started thinking about what my first class was, having totally forgotten about it during Christmas break.

"Harry, my man!"

I turned around only to see a blonde-haired guy walking up to me, one of his arms already out to bring me into a side hug.

"Niall," I smiled, happy to see him. As I mentioned before, I wasn't used to be away from them for an entire week. "Feels like ages ago."

He nodded in agreement. "I know right? I'm fucking happy we're back at school. Soccer starts again, and I get to see you guys every day."

I couldn't help but smile at his words. "I love you too, man," I joked, making him chuckle.

"Have you seen the other lads? I just arrived here," Niall wondered, and I shook my head.

"Nope, I just arrived here as well. Maybe Louis overslept or drove off the street," I shrugged, a hint of humor in my voice.

Louis was a year older than the rest of us. He had to repeat a year because of his lack of presence during middle school. I bet he was mad at himself for it now, seeing as his old friends graduated last year, but I didn't exactly complain about it. If he never repeated that year before we met, I may not have known him like I did today.

Seeing as he was older, it meant that he already had his driver's license. Or, he had gotten it two weeks ago considering his birthday was on Christmas Eve. He had received a car from his parents as a birthday and Christmas present, and only a week later, he had been able to drive it alone. Honestly, I had been surprised that he got the license so fast considering he wasn't much of a studying type of guy, but I was happy for him. I bet Liam and Zayn were as well considering they lived close to him and could now ride with him to school. Those lucky bastards.

Niall's lips twitched. "Yeah, probably. So, how's it going with your driver's license, eh? Your birthday is coming up," he smirked, making me roll my eyes.

"I don't know, Niall. I hope I'm going to make it, but we'll see."

He patted my shoulder in reassurance. "I'm sure you will, mate. I'm sure you will."

Right then, three guys came walking towards us in the hallway. One with chocolate brown hair styled in a quiff with brown eyes, one with short, raven hair, a nice stubble on his cheeks and sparkly brown eyes, and then the last one, the one that always took my breath away.

I instantly did a double-take because damn, a week really was a long time. It felt like an eternity since I last saw Louis, and I could tell my body felt the same way judging by my pounding heart and my shaking hands. God, I was a mess.

Judging by the smug smile on Louis' face, I could tell that he had driven here. He had been so proud of himself for getting that driver's license, and I understood why. When or if I would get mine, I would be proud of myself too.

"Morning, guys," Zayn greeted, walking over to wrap an arm around Niall's shoulders. Louis and Liam stopped in front of us.

My eyes were stuck on Louis, taking in his appearance. He was wearing a black jacket with a white t-shirt underneath along with a pair of black, ripped skinny jeans. His feathery brown hair was styled perfectly to the side, that smile still prominent on his face. I found it hard to believe that he hadn't caught me staring yet.

"So, you didn't drive off the street then?" Niall laughed, looking at Louis whose mouth fell open.

"Well, of course not. Who said that?" He wondered, faking offended although I wondered if he actually was a little hurt.

I bit my bottom lip when Niall turned to me. "Harry did. But I mean, you guys hadn't shown up yet, and you are kind of a reckless driver, Louis," he shrugged, making Louis huff.

His blue eyes turned to me, his rounded eyebrows raised. "You thought I was going to drive off the street, huh?" He asked, ignoring the fact that Niall had just talked shit about his driving as well.

If it weren't for the fact that I could hear the challenging tone in his voice, I would've been nervous. I mean, the last thing I wanted was to have Louis being mad at me. However, Louis and I usually bickered with each other, so I should know that he didn't take me seriously.

"I mean, it was only two weeks ago you got that driver's license," I shrugged, the corners of my lips twitching.

He rolled his eyes, shaking his head. "You are definitely not getting a ride from me, Curly. You'll have to wait until you have your own driver's license."

I let out a whine. "Heey, that's mean."

He frowned. "You were mean first."

"Alright, guys. If you're quite finished, I wanted to tell you that Coach is going to pick a new captain of the team today," Niall interrupted.

My gaze snapped to the blonde-haired guy as my eyebrows shot up. "Really?"

The other guys seemed surprised about the news as well. "Finally, man. Ryan is the shitiest captain we've ever had. It was about time," Louis said in relief, and honestly, he was right. Ryan was the most selfish player on the team, and therefore not a worthy captain at all.

Liam and Zayn nodded in agreement. "Who do you think will be the new captain?" Niall continued, and it didn't take a second for us to make our minds up, all of our gazes landing on the feathery-haired boy.

Louis looked a bit surprised, but I could tell he was flattered at the same time. "What? You guys are great as well. I'm sure it's going to be a tough fight."

Liam shook his head. "You're a year older than us and Coach really likes you. Besides, you're a great teammate and a hell of a scorer," he said truthfully.

A smile formed on Louis' lips. "Thanks, mate. I appreciate it."

My eyes flicked between the two of them during their conversation, my eyebrows furrowed. I wanted to be the one who complimented Louis and made him smile like that. Why did Liam get the honor?

"I'm pretty sure class starts in a few minutes, so I've gotta go. See you later, guys," Niall announced, taking Zayn's arm off his shoulders before walking away.

"I should probably go too. My class is on the other side of the building," Zayn sighed. "Bye, guys," he said before taking off as well.

Liam placed a hand on Louis' shoulder. "Thanks for the ride, mate. I really appreciate it. See you guys later, yeah?"

I nodded while Louis gave him another smile. "Of course, mate. I'll be sure to drive you whenever you want because apart from some other people, you didn't insult my driving skills."

My mouth fell open at his words, and I could tell by the smirk on his face that he knew exactly what he was doing. Liam let out a chuckle before disappearing as well. I remained on my spot, staring at Louis.

"Where's your class?" He wondered, looking at me expectantly.

I was still a bit taken aback by what he just said, so it took a while until my brain started working normally again. "Uh, down that hallway," I replied, nodding in the right direction.

"Cool. Mine too."

I know, I know, I know, I wanted to tell him. I even knew that he had drama class the first thing in the morning. If only he knew that I cared so much that I had learned so many things about him. I mean, I remembered all of his classes, but I couldn't even remember what I had first thing in the morning.

We started walking down the hallway after Louis had grabbed his books from his locker across the hallway. My heart was racing in my chest because I was spending alone time with him. I rarely got to do that considering the other boys were always around otherwise.

"You do know I was only joking about your driving, right?" I couldn't help but ask because, for some reason, I was afraid that he had taken it seriously after all.

He shook his head, looking at the side of my face. "Of course, Harold. However, I am aware that you actually do mean it, so I'm still making you pay for it. I'm not driving you anywhere."

I pouted my lips, although a smile was on my face. "Well, good thing my eighteenth birthday is coming up then," I said smugly, happy that he wasn't genuinely mad at me.

"Good for you, Styles. Good for you," he smirked, shaking his head in amusement. "Here's my stop. I'll see you later then, mate, yeah?"

I came to a halt, turning to look at him. "Of course. Bye, Louis."

"Bye!"

There was only one word repeating itself in my brain during the rest of the walk to my classroom.

Mate.

Would I ever get to hear him call me something other than that?

Chapter 2

My first class was Economics, something I found okay at least. The only downside was that neither of the guys was in it, so that meant I was alone. However, I had befriended a few other people in this class, and one of them was the girl sitting in front of me, Emily. Or, I hadn't really befriended her. She was more of an acquaintance, but anyway.

I was doodling in my notebook, not really listening to the teacher when Emily turned around to face me. She had long blonde hair that reached below her breasts and green eyes. A hopeful smile was on her face when she looked at me. I instantly got suspicious.

"You have something on your mind, Emily?" I asked, and her eyebrows shot up.

"Is it that obvious?" She wondered.

I tilted my head to the side, letting out a laugh in amusement. "Yes, it is."

She rolled her eyes. "Alright, fine. You win. I was wondering if you wanted to come to my party on Friday?" She asked with the same hopeful smile on her face as before.

I narrowed my eyes at her. "How many people have you invited?"

She let out a laugh. "I'm not a nerd, Harry. I know a lot of people."

A smirk made its way to my lips. "I was just kidding. I'll be there, and I'm bringing the guys if that's okay?"

"I didn't expect anything else," she smirked. "And you can tell Louis that he is specifically invited."

A lump formed in my throat at her words, and I could feel my heart sink in my chest. I nodded my head with a frown between my eyebrows. "I... uh, I'm sure he'll be glad to hear that."

"Awesome," she grinned before turning back around in her seat.

I looked up at the teacher who hadn't seemed to notice my and Emily's conversation with the frown still evident on my face. This was one of the situations I hated when it came to having feelings for Louis; Every time a girl openly showed her attraction to him right in front of me. I just wished he was with me so I could throw it in their faces that he was taken.

During the rest of the lesson, I listened to what the teacher said while continuing doodling in my notebook. If my thoughts wandered to different ways of how I was going to keep Louis away from Emily at the party, then it was only up to me.

The second the bell rang, I gathered my books and exited the classroom. When I got to my locker, the guys were already there, chatting with each other. Niall was leaning against the lockers, Liam standing in front of him. Zayn was standing beside Niall and Louis was in front of him. Both Liam and Louis had their backs towards me.

"Hey, Harry," Niall greeted with a wide smile on his face, making both Liam and Louis turn around to face me as well. "How was class?"

My locker was right beside Zayn, so I walked over to toss my books into it. "It's my favorite class, so it wasn't that bad," I shrugged, slamming my locker shut before turning to them. "How was yours?"

He pursed his lips. "Same old nonsense, I guess."

I couldn't help but chuckle. "I see. Actually, there's something I wanted to tell you guys. I talked to Emily in my class, and--"

"Oh, you've got a little fling?" Louis smirked, cutting me off.

I wanted to snort at his comment, but I just shook my head. If only he knew that it wasn't each other we were interested in but him. "Not really. She asked me if we wanted to come to her party on Friday."

Louis pursed his lips. "Who is this Emily girl?"

No one you have to know about.

"She's a nice person with a lot of friends, so it's going to be a party we don't want to miss," I shrugged.

Why did I tell Emily we were going to this party to begin with? Right, because it would be weird if I declined her offer. I mean, we never declined going to parties.

"Sounds awesome!" Niall burst out with a genuine smile on his face.

The three other guys agreed with a nod of their heads. "Yeah, you can tell her we'll be there. Do you think there will be a lot of girls? It's been way too long since I got laid, man. I mean, when was the last time we were at a party? Before Christmas? God, it's been so long," Zayn muttered.

Louis' lips twitched at his words. "I agree, mate. We could definitely use some partying to get some girls," he chuckled, making me swallow hard.

Liam rolled his eyes, probably because he had already settled down. He was happy together with a girl named Alice, and they had been together for almost a year now. Before her, Liam had been just like the rest of us, finding different girls to hook up with every weekend, though.

However, what neither of them knew was that lately, I had been starting to step down on hooking up with people. I found it more and more difficult to be with them the more my feelings for Louis grew. However, Liam, Zayn, Louis, and Niall didn't need to know that, so I always made sure to be seen with someone at every party anyway.

Before any of us could say something else, the bell rang, and we all grabbed our books before walking away in different directions to get to our separate classes.

The first day of school was over much quicker than I first expected it to. I bet that was because it had been a long time since we were last here and since we saw each other. I didn't complain, though.

I was currently standing at my locker, grabbing my black winter jacket to shrug it on when Liam and Louis joined me. All of our lockers were located in the same area, which was great since we all always met up between classes.

"You're coming to soccer practice later, Harry, right?" Liam asked when he had grabbed his jacket and bag. There were only five lockers between mine and Louis', so he barely had to move to get where we were standing.

"Of course. I wouldn't miss it for the world. It's been too long of a break," I replied, grabbing my bag and shutting the locker before turning to them.

Liam nodded in agreement while Louis tilted his head to the side. "So, you don't have to work after school today, then?" He teased, stuffing his hands in the pockets of his jacket.

I rolled my eyes, shaking my head. "I don't work when we have practice, Louis."

A smile made its way to his face. "Good for you. Wouldn't want to miss the chance of becoming the new captain, eh?" He winked, making my heart flutter in my chest, although I knew he didn't mean anything flirtatious with it.

"It's not like I stand a chance, but I don't want to miss out when the new captain is getting picked," I shrugged. "On another note, you should stop teasing me about my job, Louis. I'm at least making some well-deserved money apart from some other people."

His mouth formed the shape of an 'o' while I flashed him a smug smile. I thought it was clever to use the same monologue he had used on me earlier. "Watch it, Styles," he said with narrowed eyes. "If you ever want a ride in my car, you should be careful with what you say."

I rolled my eyes. "I think I'll survive."

He shrugged his shoulders. "Suit yourself." He then turned to Liam who had fished his phone from his jeans pocket and was now typing away on it. "You coming, Liam?"

The brown-haired boy looked up from his phone. "Oh, yeah, sure. Is it okay if Alice joins us? Apparently, her school bus is running late due to the weather conditions."

A cocky smile formed on Louis' lips. "Of course. There's plenty of room in the car for her," he said, his eyes locked on me.

"Awesome."

With that said, the two walked away, leaving me to stare at their backs. I just shook my head with a smile on my face. There was just something about my and Louis' playful banter that I loved. As long as we were both on the same page with the jokes, I could do it all day.

Zayn and Niall had finished school earlier, so I made my way through the hallways by myself. It wasn't that bad, though, since I usually walked through them alone in the mornings and to my classes.

When I got outside, I instantly noticed what Liam meant by 'weather conditions'. The snow was pouring down from the sky, leaving a slushy mess on the ground.

The corner of my lips turned downwards as I made my way to the bus stop, making sure to pull the hood of my jacket over my head. It was only a few minutes later I noticed that Alice's bus wasn't the only bus that was delayed. All of them were. We were several students standing in the pouring snow, stamping our feet repeatedly due to the cold.

It was then I really started regretting telling Louis all those things about his driving skills. I could kill to get away from this awful weather right now, and I would have been home now if it weren't for my stupid mouth. Fuck me.

After thirty minutes, the bus finally showed up around the corner, causing the people to sigh in relief, and I was one of them. The second I got onto the bus, I pulled the hood off my head while looking down at my wet jeans. I really hated the snow. It was both freezing and wet, two things I didn't like.

Fifteen minutes later, the bus came to my stop, and I got off before practically sprinting to my house. I was careful not to slip, though. I didn't want to get more drenched than I already was.

Once inside the old, blue house, I quickly got rid of my jacket, bag and shoes before sprinting into the bathroom that thankfully was located close to the entryway. With a lot of difficulties, I got out of my clothes before stepping into the warm shower, letting the hot water hit my cold skin. I didn't even care that I was going to have to shower twice that day. All I wanted was to feel my limbs again.

I turned off the shower a good ten minutes later, stepping out to the now foggy room. Running a hand through my wet curls, I bent down to pick up my wet clothes that I had thrown on the tile floor earlier to toss them in the washing machine.

With a towel around my waist, I went to my room across the bathroom to get changed into my soccer gear. It felt weird to put it on when I had just been in the shower, but I didn't really have a choice. Practice started in only half an hour, and I had yet to eat something.

My room was pretty small, but I actually quite liked it. There was a bed in the right corner of it with a nightstand beside it. Then I had a body length mirror in the left corner of the room, and my closet was just beside the door. The walls were navy blue, and the floor was of hardwood. To be honest, there was nothing not to like about it besides the fact that I could use a TV. That was one of the things I wanted to buy after I had gotten my driver's license and bought myself a car.

When I was standing at the counter in the kitchen ten minutes later, making a ham sandwich, I could hear the front door swing open.

"Harry?" A voice called out, and I instantly recognized it as Gemma's.

"In the kitchen!" I called back, bringing the sandwich to my mouth to take a bite of it before I had even sat down at the kitchen table.

My sister made an entrance only five seconds later, looking at me with raised eyebrows. "Are you in a hurry?"

I pulled my eyebrows pulled into a frown. "What makes you think that?"

"Well, you're eating a sandwich while standing, and your shirt is inside out," she said, crossing her arms over her chest.

I looked down at my chest, noticing that she was right. With a pout, I shrugged my shoulders. "It wasn't my fault the school bus was delayed, but just because of that, I'm now starting to run late for practice."

A brilliant idea popped up in my brain then. "Could you pretty, pretty please drive me there? I won't make it in time otherwise," I pleaded because I was sure that if I rode the bus to practice, I was not going to get there on time.

She tilted her head to the side as if contemplating it. However, the smile on her face told me otherwise. "I don't know. What would I get in return?"

My mouth fell open at her words. "Are you for real? Gemma, I *never* ask you to drive me. Can't you just be a nice sister just this once?"

Her smile widened for a second until it broke into laughter. "I'm just kidding, brother. I'll drive you, but hey, don't expect it to become a routine. I'm nice, but not that nice," she smirked, making me roll my eyes.

"Honestly, I didn't expect anything else," I chuckled.

She let out a gasp. "Hey, I'm offended."

"Well, you were the one just implying that you aren't nice all the time, so blame yourself," I shrugged with a cheeky smile on my face.

She rolled her eyes at me. "Touché, little brother, touché."

I couldn't help but give her a wide smile at that. I loved my sister to bits. There was nothing about her that was not to like. Well, except for when she acted like a hormonal bitch. It could be for stupid things like if I had taken one of her hair ties to put my curls in a bun, or if I had borrowed her brush or something like that. I didn't see any problem with it, but she certainly did.

Other than that, we were always there for each other when we needed help. Today was one of those cases, and although she liked to act as if she actually didn't want to help me, we both knew that she always did anyway.

Once I had finished my sandwich, I made sure to fix my shirt so it wasn't inside out anymore before making my way back into my room to get my bag with my cleats, water bottle, shin pads, a towel, some shampoo and a change of clothes. I found Gemma sitting on the grey couch in the living room when I was finished. "I'm ready."

Her gaze turned from the television to me, a frown making its way to her face. She took off her hair tie from her wrist and reached her hand out. "You have to put your hair up. Otherwise, you'll get it in your face," she said, a natural expression on her face.

My eyebrows shot up. Did she really just offer me to take her hair tie? Well, I was not going to decline that. "Thanks, sis," I smiled, walking over to take it from her extended hand.

"You're welcome."

I gathered my hair on top of my head and put it in a bun while Gemma got up to put her shoes and jacket on. Once we were both ready, we got out in the stormy weather. I pulled the hood of my jacket over my head again, shielding my face from the snow while practically running to Gemma's car.

The second we had shut the doors behind us, we both breathed out sighs of relief. "This damn weather is not to play with, fucking hell," Gemma muttered.

I shook my head. "It sure isn't."

During the car ride - which took twice as long as it would have if it weren't for the weather - we talked about school, work and friends. She asked me if it was nice to see the guys again, and I asked her how work had been.

She didn't know I had feelings for Louis. I hadn't told anyone because I didn't trust them well enough. I mean, Gemma was that kind of person who could easily throw a secret like that out if she saw me staring at Louis while the guys were over or something like that, and I could not take that risk. However, she and mom did know that I was bisexual, though. They were the only ones who knew except for the few guys I had been with during my life.

"And we're here," Gemma announced when she had pulled over outside the gym. Fortunately, our practices were indoors during the winter. Otherwise, I would not have attended them. At least not on a day like this, that was for sure.

"Thank you, Gems. Will you come pick me up too?" I pleaded, giving her the best puppy eyes I could muster.

She rolled her eyes. "Fine, but only today, brother. Remember, this won't become a routine. You'll have to find some other way to get here when the weather is shitty until you've got your own driver's license."

I flashed her a smile. "I will, thank you."

"Bye, H."

"See you later, Gems," I called out while getting out of the car.

I slammed the door shut behind me before sprinting towards the gym entrance. The first thing I was met with when I opened the doors was a long hallway that led to different locker rooms and the gym. I made my way through it, focusing on listening to what room the guys were in. I had to make it all the way to the last locker room until I found the right one.

"Harry, there you are, man!"

Every guy on the team was already there, dressed in their gears with their cleats and shin pads on. They all looked ready to go out and start practice. I pursed my lips. "The weather is being a bitch," I muttered, taking my place beside Niall on the bench.

He instantly noticed that my hair was damp. "Why is your hair all drenched? You didn't walk here or something, did you?" He asked, worry lacing his voice.

I shook my head, grimacing. "No, I had a shower."

Laughter could be heard in the locker room then, and I turned around to see Ryan, Tristan and Derek looking at me with mocking faces. I shot them a glare before my eyes fell on the person whose opinion always mattered most to me. Louis.

He was looking at me from across the room with a cheeky smile. "You shouldn't have talked shit about my driving skills, Styles," he smirked, and my heart instantly fluttered in my chest, just like it always did when he paid attention to me.

I just shook my head with a smile on my face. He was the only person that could make my mood change so drastically from being down to happy. "Who says it was due to the weather I had the shower, eh?"

He shrugged his shoulders. "Well, it was either that or because you needed to get rid of a boner. If it wasn't any of those options, I would find you a weird guy, Curly. No one showers before practice."

I let out a huff while Ryan, Tristan and Derek burst out laughing once again. "I bet he did because he just felt like it," Ryan laughed, hitting himself on his knee repeatedly.

"Oh, shut up," I snapped at him. Now, I could tolerate Louis making fun of me because our banter was mutual, but Ryan, Tristan and Derek just liked to make fun of people in general, and I did not accept that.

"Alright, Louis. You're right. Maybe I wouldn't have needed to wait in the pouring snow for thirty minutes until the bus came so I had to take a hot shower when I came home if I didn't talk shit about your driving, but hey, I don't regret it because that shower was pretty damn nice, and I don't like to lie to people," I smirked, making his mouth fall open.

Neither of us had time to say anything else until Coach joined us in the locker room. "Alright guys, Christmas break is over, and it's time to get serious again. Let's go out today and do a hell of a practice!"

Chapter 3

Practice went surprisingly well, and by surprisingly, I meant because things had been pretty shitty after school when I had to wait for the bus outside in the storm, and then I had almost run late to practice. I didn't expect my day to make a turn for the better again, but it did.

We were all currently sitting in the locker room. We had just finished practice and were taking off our cleats, socks, and shin pads when Coach entered the room. He was a bald man with dark brown eyes in his early forties. When he made an entrance, everyone shut up and turned their attention to him.

"Alright, I know rumors about me selecting a new captain today have been going around. It's true, and I'm here now to tell you who I have picked," he announced, making a low chattering erupt in the room.

"Coach, can I ask why you didn't tell us you were selecting a new captain today before practice?" A guy named Trevor asked.

"I didn't want you to know because then I knew you were going to think about it during practice, and I want you all to be at your best all the time, not only when you are trying to impress me. That's why. Oh, and for those of you who already had your suspicions, I hoped that it would leave your minds if I didn't mention anything before practice. Seeing how you all played like I'm used to seeing you play, I'm positive I succeeded."

I wondered if that was because most of us who knew beforehand were people who didn't really care if we became captains or not. The only thing that mattered was that it was someone who was a great leader and player.

"So, who have you picked?" Derek wondered.

Coach glanced at him before flicking his gaze between everyone of us. "I have chosen someone who always tries his best, who is a great teammate that always wants what's best for the team, and who I think would make a great captain..." He trailed off, his gaze stopping at one specific person.

"I've chosen you, Louis. I think you are aware of what good leadership is, and I'm sure you'll make a great captain."

Cheers erupted in the locker room, people walking over to pat him on the shoulder and congratulate him. Louis' entire face was lit up in a beautiful smile, the crinkles by his eyes showing. I could only gape at him because damn, was it even possible to look that pretty? I mean, the fact that he was sweaty as well only added to his beauty. I was in awe.

"Harry!"

I snapped back to reality, looking at the person who had called my name. It was Coach. "Uh, yeah?" I asked with a scowl on my face.

"You're going to be the new alternate captain. Whenever Louis is off the field, if he gets injured or if he just needs backup, you're going to be there, alright?"

My eyebrows shot up in surprise. "For real?" I almost gasped. I was not expecting that at all.

"Yeah, you've been showing me that you have power in you lately, and I'm curious to see where it's going to take you. Besides, you are a good teammate. I'm sure Louis is going to be happy to have you as his backup," he explained, giving me a polite smile, and honestly, that was probably the best compliment I had ever received from someone regarding my soccer skills, or just in general.

"Thank you, Coach."

I could feel a hand slap my shoulder, and when I turned to my side, I could see Niall giving me a toothy grin. "Congrats, mate. You really deserve it, man."

He was one of the few people who were acknowledging me after what Coach just announced, most of them still circling Louis. I didn't mind, though, because I didn't need their attention. Just knowing that I was going to be the alternate captain of the team during the last semester of high school made my heart swell with pride for myself. I never thought *I* was going to come anywhere near a title like that.

"Thanks, man."

The only one who wasn't cheering or talking in the room was Ryan. He was sitting on the bench, typing on his phone with a grumpy look on his face. Well, seeing as he had just been kicked from his title of being captain, I understood why. However, I didn't feel any sympathy for him considering I knew that he hadn't made the title justice. One evidence took place just earlier when he mocked me for taking a shower before practice. I mean, he wasn't even part of the conversation, he just had to intervene anyway.

I snapped myself back to reality, where the rest of the boys were now sitting on the benches again to get out of their sweaty gears. My eyes found Louis' across the room, and the second they met, a cheeky grin formed on his lips.

I rolled my eyes with an evident smile on my face. What were the odds that Louis became captain and I his backup? Just the fact made me so happy. It felt like we had just gotten closer to each other somehow.

Coach was now gone, making the chatter in the room erupt once again. I didn't bother joining any conversation, though. I just got out of my stinky clothes and went into the shower for the second time that day, bringing my towel.

Once I was dressed in a pair of black joggers and a black hoodie, I pulled out my phone from my bag to make sure Gemma was ready to pick me up. By now, a lot of the guys had started leaving the locker room.

Something came up, so I can't come pick you up, brother. I'm sorry. I hope you'll figure it out x

Oh, for the love of God. Was she kidding me? How on earth would I find someone to drive me home on this short notice? I mean, the busses were most certainly running late or not going at all, so what was I supposed to do?

Letting out a sigh, I ran a hand through my wet curls. "What's the matter, Harry?" I could hear someone say from my right.

I looked up to find Niall's eyes on me, watching me curiously. "Gemma can't pick me up, so I'll probably have to walk home in this weather," I muttered.

His eyes widened. "Oh, but why don't you ask Louis if he can drive you? I mean, Liam, Zayn and I are going with him anyway," he suggested.

Letting out a snort, I looked over to the feathery-haired boy across the locker room who was just in the action of putting on a pair of grey joggers. He wasn't wearing a shirt, fuck.

Swallowing hard, I averted my gaze back to Niall. "I'm sure he wouldn't agree to that after the way I've been insulting his driving skills all day," I grimaced, but I also realized that it may be my only resort. How else would I get home?

Niall rolled his eyes. "Nonsense. You are his friend. You just have to ask him, and I'm sure he won't say no."

Letting out a flat laugh, I shook my head. I needed a strategy to make Louis agree to this because if I just walked over and asked him, I was sure he was just going to make fun of me. The question was; Could I even get away with this without him making fun of me? I wasn't so sure about that.

When only about ten guys remained in the locker room, I walked over to Louis who was now sitting on the bench fully clothed, talking to Zayn. The second he noticed my presence, he turned his face to me.

"Hi there, Curly."

I rolled my eyes at the nickname. "Hey," I greeted. "Congrats on becoming the new captain," I told him, flashing him a genuine smile.

He raised his eyebrows in surprise, probably not expecting me to say something nice to him. He instantly caught on, though. "Well, congrats to you too, I guess. It's going to be a lot of fun being the leader of the team," he smirked, making me chuckle.

"Well, as long as you don't get injured or play so badly that Coach doesn't want you on the field, then sure. Otherwise, I'm going to be the leader of the team," I winked, making him roll his eyes.

"It's not going to happen," he promised me.

I shrugged my shoulders. "Never say never. Oh, and besides, you might actually want my help too sometimes."

He shook his head with a smile on his face. When he didn't say anything, I opened my mouth to continue talking. "So, I heard you're driving the boys home," I said, looking at Zayn who was watching my and Louis' conversation.

The feathery-haired boy tilted his head to the side. "Oh, I see now. I knew you didn't just come over here to congratulate me. You want me to drive you home, don't you?" Louis predicted, looking at me knowingly.

I bit my bottom lip, reaching up to scratch the back of my head. "Maybe? But only because my sister told me she can't pick me up, and I don't want to walk home in this weather."

He watched me with a smug look on his face. "I thought you said you would manage just fine without me driving you since I'm such a reckless driver, eh?" He teased, making me let out a groan.

"I know what I said, Louis."

He pursed his lips and narrowed his eyes as if thinking about it. "What makes you think I would drive you when you insulted my driving skills?"

I tossed my head back in frustration. "Oh my God, Louis. Can't you just be nice and drive me home without being an ass about it?" I huffed, making him chuckle.

"Only if you never insult my driving again," he smirked.

"If you prove me wrong, then fine," I reasoned, and he agreed. "Fine."

There was no question that I had strong feelings for Louis, but man, he could really frustrate me sometimes. I secretly wondered if that was one of the reasons I actually did feel so strongly for him. I loved how we always teased each other, even if he got on my nerves sometimes. I bet I got on his sometimes as well, though.

I walked back to Niall to retrieve my bag, and I didn't miss the smile he sent me. "What?" I wondered.

"I told you he would agree to drive you."

I rolled my eyes, slinging my bag over my shoulder. "Come on, let's go."

He got up from the bench, and together, we walked over to Louis and Zayn, who had now been accompanied by Liam as well. "Ready to go, lads?" Niall questioned.

Louis and Zayn got up from the bench, Louis nodding his head. "Yeah, better get going before the weather gets even worse," he grimaced.

Niall and I walked ahead of Liam, Louis, and Zayn out of the gym. We didn't really talk, though, because as soon as we were outside, we all started jogging towards the parking lot. The snow was still pouring down, but instead of transforming to slush once it hit the ground, it had now started creating a white layer on it. It was better this way because then it was easier not to get wet, and I bet it was easier to drive as well.

We all hopped into Louis' black sports car before slamming the doors shut behind us. For some reason, I managed to end up in the middle of the backseat, which was not a benefit since I was sure I was going to be the first one to be dropped off.

The first thing Louis did when he had gotten behind the wheel was to turn on the radio. Instantly, loud music started blasting through the speakers, almost burning holes in my ears. "For the love of God, Louis!" I shouted, covering my ears with my hands.

He turned down the volume a little, looking back at me. "Sorry, princess. Forgot I had a child in the backseat," he chuckled, rolling his eyes.

I shot him a glare. "Oh, shut it. Such high volume is not even healthy, Jesus," I muttered, shaking my head.

Inside, my heart was beating like crazy because did he really just call me princess? I mean sure, it may not have been in the way I wanted it to be, but a man could dream, couldn't he?

Louis let out another laugh before pulling out of the parking lot and driving off. I conversed with Liam and Niall in the backseat during the fifteen minutes it took for Louis to drive to my place, talking about soccer and being back at school.

Surprisingly, Louis drove pretty safely, keeping the speed limit and the car on the right side of the road. I wondered if that was because he knew I was in the car and wanted to prove to me that I had been wrong about his driving skills, or if it was because of the bad road conditions. Because I knew for sure that he didn't drive this well otherwise. I had been in the backseat when he drove before he got his driver's license, and the differences were significant.

When he pulled over outside my blue house, he turned around in his seat to look at me again. "So, are you going to stop insulting my driving now?" He asked with a smug smile on his face.

I couldn't help but smile back at him, but mine was more genuine. "If I knew you weren't trying so hard to drive well, then maybe. I'll think about it, though," I promised, flashing him a smirk.

His mouth fell open at my words, but I didn't keep my eyes on him for more than five seconds until I told Niall to get out of the way so I could get out of the car. He let out a whine when he realized he had to get out as well and get wet in the process. Well, it wasn't my idea to make me sit in the middle seat in the first place.

"Thanks for the ride," I called out to Louis before taking off towards my front door, not looking back to see if he heard it.

Before I had time to open the door, though, I could hear how he sped off towards Niall's house, the tires of his car screeching against the ground. He definitely only drove so safely because I was in the car. I was sure of it.

Chapter 4

The next day during lunch break, Liam, Louis, Zayn, Niall, and I were sitting together at a table in the cafeteria, talking about the upcoming party on Friday. Zayn, Louis, and Niall were super excited about it. Liam and I were too, but not on the same level as the three of them were. They couldn't stop chatting about how fun it was going to be to get drunk and hook up with girls again.

I didn't really feel the same need to do that, but I could admit that it was going to be nice to party and get some alcohol in my system. As mentioned by Zayn, it had been a long time since we last were at a party.

"So, who can host the preparty?" Zayn asked, looking at each of us hopefully.

I bit my lip, raising a hand in the air. "Mom is working late, and I'm quite sure I can get Gemma out of the house."

Mom worked as a nurse and therefore, she always had different shifts. On Friday, I knew that she was going to work late, so it was a perfect opportunity to throw a preparty at my place. As long as we didn't break or get something dirty, I was sure she wouldn't mind. Especially not if we cleaned up after ourselves.

"Really? That would be awesome!" Niall burst out, looking at me with wide, excited eyes.

I shrugged my shoulders. "Of course."

There was just one problem, though. Whoever arranged a preparty always fixed the alcohol, and I was sure Gemma wouldn't do me one more favor this week. As she mentioned before, she was nice, but not that nice. She had a limit. Why couldn't my birthday be this week instead of in two weeks?

"I've got a problem, though," I said, grimacing a little.

Zayn looked at me, tilting his head to the side. "What problem?"

"I'm not eighteen yet, and I've already asked Gemma for more favors than she is willing to accept this week, so I don't have anyone who can fix the alcohol."

Liam raised an eyebrow, looking over at Louis. "Louis' eighteen, so how about you two fix it together?" He suggested.

I swallowed hard, looking over at the feathery-haired boy who was sitting on one side of Niall. I was sitting on his other. He shrugged his shoulders, turning to meet my gaze. "Well, why not? Might as well buy some alcohol now that I'm allowed to. How about before practice tomorrow?"

I nodded my head slowly, feeling my heart race in my chest. "It works for me."

"Then it's settled," Zayn said excitedly, clapping his hands together.

Before any of us could say something else, Liam's girlfriend Alice walked over with three of her friends. Alice was a pretty girl with short, brown hair and shiny, brown eyes. I understood why Liam liked her so much. She was both beautiful and nice.

She leaned down to kiss him on the lips sweetly. "Is it okay if the girls and I sit here?" She asked, her gaze flickering between us.

"Of course," Louis smirked, patting the backrest of the empty seat beside him. "You're more than welcome."

One of the girls who had long, blonde hair and ocean blue eyes sat down beside him while the two other girls sat down on the empty seats next to her and beside Zayn on the other side of the table. The blonde girl instantly started talking to Louis, twirling a strand of hair around her finger.

I rolled my eyes at the scene. I should have gotten used to seeing Louis flirt with different girls by now, but somehow, I always wanted to go find the nearest bathroom to throw up whenever it happened. The sad part about it was that I couldn't look away. My eyes were stuck on the pair, taking in their entire encounter.

It wasn't until a few minutes later I noticed that someone was staring at me. My eyes left the pair to look for the source, and it didn't take long until they stopped at one of the girls who were sitting beside Zayn. She had black hair that reached her shoulders and the bluest eyes I had ever seen. They were even bluer than Niall's, and wow, she was pretty, there was no denying it.

The second my eyes settled on her, a smile broke out on her face. I couldn't help but return it with a bright smile of my own. Was I the reason she was smiling? Unbelievable. As far as I knew, I had never talked to this girl before.

During the rest of the lunch break, I could feel her eyes on me every now and then, making me squirm in my seat. It always made me nervous whenever people checked me out, and this was not an exception.

When we exited the cafeteria and started heading to our lockers, she walked up to me. "You're Harry, right?" She wondered, looking at the side of my face.

I turned my head to meet her gaze. "Yeah."

"I'm Evelyn."

I nodded my head, flashing her a small smile. "Cool."

"So, are you attending Emily's party on Friday?" She questioned hopefully.

"Yeah, that's the plan. Are you?" I asked in return, not wanting to seem like an asshole. I mean, she was nice, so I didn't see a reason not to be nice to her in return.

"Yeah, the girls and I are going. I'm excited about it. I hope it's going to be a lot of fun," she said dreamily, making me chuckle slightly.

"It's been a while since you partied as well?" I couldn't help but ask.

She turned to me again, a smile on her lips. "You can tell?"

"Yep. The look on your face and your excitement give it all away," I smirked, making her shake her head in amusement.

"Damn, I have to work on that. Can't go around knowing I'm that easy to read."

A laugh escaped my lips. "Well, in this case, I don't think it made matters worse. I'm quite excited to party as well," I shrugged.

By now, we had arrived at my locker. The guys were walking in front of us, the blonde girl still by Louis' side. She was a little too close if you asked me. The fact that she occasionally leaned in to whisper something in his ear didn't make me feel any better. If anything, it only made me feel worse.

"Great," Evelyn said, beaming at me. "So, I'll see you at the party then?"

I nodded my head, tearing my eyes off Louis and the blonde girl. "Definitely."

We said goodbye to each other before I turned to my locker. It wasn't until I had grabbed the books for my next class I noticed that the blonde girl and Alice had followed Evelyn, so it was now only the five of us lads left.

"Damn, guys. You can't wait until the party to chat up with the girls?" Niall asked, shaking his head while looking between me and Louis.

I rolled my eyes but didn't say anything. Louis seemed amused by his comment, though. "You're just jealous, Niall. I'm sure you'll find some girl at the party as well," he winked, making the blonde-haired boy pout.

"I'm not jealous."

I let out a chuckle, walking over to wrap an arm around his shoulders, my books in my other one hand. "It's okay, mate. I'll help you find someone on Friday, I promise."

Niall turned to look at me, his lips still in a pout. "I'm out, guys. See you after class," he announced, reaching his hands up before taking my arm off his shoulders and walking away.

We all exchanged a look with each other, our eyebrows raised. "He must be so sexually frustrated," Liam laughed, shaking his head.

"Tell me about it," Zayn chuckled.

"Poor man," Louis said, looking in the direction that Niall walked off.

"Just because you got a girl's attention," I muttered, rolling my eyes.

His head snapped to me, his eyebrows raised. "You said something, Curly?"

I shrugged my shoulders. "Just saying."

"Well, you had a girl by your side as well, didn't you?" He pointed out.

I shot him a look. "Yeah, but I didn't say anything. Besides, it's not like I was flirting with that girl as it looked like you were doing. We were just getting to know each other."

Louis let out a snort. "Why does that even matter?"

I bit my bottom lip, mentally facepalming myself. What on earth was I saying? I sounded like a jealous bitch, which I was, but he couldn't know that. "I'm just saying," I said again while shrugging, hoping I managed to make it look like I didn't care.

He narrowed his eyes at me suspiciously, but before he could open his mouth to say something, the bell rang. I mentally let out a sigh of relief as I turned around to start walking in the direction of my next class.

That was a close one.

I had work that afternoon, and I was honestly excited about it. It had been a few days since I was last there and I already missed it. I worked at a diner, not some fancy restaurant, but there was something about the place that I loved. I worked with people I got along with, and most of the customers were great as well. There was really nothing to complain about it.

I was currently entering the backdoor to the diner after taking the bus there. Thankfully, the weather was better today than yesterday. It was colder, so the snow had made a white layer on the ground. However, it was still pretty slippery, so it was a good thing that they had salted the streets.

The first thing I was met with when I entered the kitchen was Richard, my boss. He was a tall man in his late fifties with a nice greyish beard and short greyish hair. He was standing at the stove, stirring in some stew. "Good afternoon, boss," I greeted.

He looked up from the pot, his aging face lightening up in a smile. "Harry! Nice to see you, lad."

That was another thing I liked about this place. My boss treated me like a close friend and not like someone he was ready to snap at in any second, and honestly, I thought those were the best bosses. Sure, it was necessary to have respect for your boss as well, but it was also important to have a great relationship with them. Otherwise, things could get quite tense in some situations. Besides, it was easier to enjoy the workplace if you got along with your boss.

"You too, Ricky. I'll be out in the diner to serve the customers," I winked, to which he shook his head in amusement. He knew I was popular with the customers.

"Do what you're best at, young man," he chuckled before I disappeared into the diner.

My co-worker, Lucas, was standing at the cash register, charging the customers when I got there. He was a guy my age with short, blonde hair and blue eyes. He was pretty skinny as well, but he was rather attractive. I wouldn't mind hooking up with him if I ever got so drunk that my thoughts on another specific guy slipped my mind.

Lucas turned around when I entered the room. "Hi, Harry," he smiled. "How are you doing?"

"I'm doing great. School has started again, and I'm looking forward to graduating soon," I shrugged. "What about you? How are you doing?"

He glanced down at the watch around his wrist. "I've been here since nine in the morning. I'm honestly just looking forward to getting home and lying down on the couch in front of the TV," he chuckled.

"I know the feeling," I smiled. "So, when are you getting off?"

"In an hour, so at seven. I hope I'll manage."

"I hope so too," I laughed, walking over to grab one of the aprons we were obliged to wear at work.

The next following hour, I served the customers who entered the diner, doing my best to make them all feel welcomed and pleased. Judging by the thankful smiles and little tips I received every now and then, I was positive I was doing a good job. Well, at least I'd like to think so.

At around seven-thirty - a while after Lucas had gotten off his shift - two familiar girls entered the diner. It was Louis' younger sisters, Lottie and Fizzy. My eyes widened at the sight, and I didn't hesitate to walk over and join Jade who had taken over Lucas' place to work the cash register.

The two girls walked over to the counter, their faces brightening when they caught sight of me. "Hey, Harry," they greeted in unison.

Lottie was fifteen and Fizzy was thirteen. Yes, I was aware of this fact because I knew a lot about Louis Tomlinson, alright? "Hi there, girls. How come you're here all alone?" I wondered, secretly wanting to know who had driven them here because I was sure they hadn't gotten here by themselves.

"Dad's in the car. We're just picking up our dinner," Lottie explained.

I nodded in understanding. "I see. I thought Louis would have wanted to drive whenever there's an opportunity now that he's gotten his driver's license, though?"

Fizzy shook her head. "Mom doesn't trust him with driving us around, says that he's not a good enough driver just yet."

I couldn't help but let a smirk form on my lips. "Is that so?"

Lottie nodded her head. "Well, it's that, and he doesn't want to do any favors either. He would probably never do anything our parents ask him to," she said with a grimace.

I had never really witnessed how Louis was around his parents. Whenever we were at his place, the girls were usually the only ones around. However, I could imagine that he was a typical teenager who would always go against his parents' will because that was what his personality showed off. Well, at least the way he acted towards me.

"Sounds like Louis," I chuckled.

Lottie's lips formed a smile. "So, Harry, when are you coming over next time? Feels like ages since you last were at our place," she pouted, making Fizzy let out a groan.

"Stop flirting, Lottie. Harry's too old for you anyway."

I did a double-take at her words. Wait a second. Had Lottie taken an interest in me? I had never picked up on that.

I turned to the blonde girl with an amused smile on my face. Her cheeks had now turned a light pink. "I don't know. Louis usually doesn't offer to hang out at his place, so you'll have to ask him when next time will be," I smiled, making Lottie's cheeks go even redder.

"Uh, yeah, sure. I'll make sure to do that," she mumbled.

Right then, another of my co-workers walked over to place a white plastic bag on the counter beside me. "Chicken stew with rice?" He asked Lottie and Fizzy who nodded their heads.

"That's us."

Lottie paid for their food while Fizzy took the bag in her hands. Once they were finished, they both turned to me. "Bye, Harry. It was nice to see you."

I reached up to wave at them. "It was nice seeing you too. Make sure to say hi to the rest of the family from me," I smiled, to which they nodded before exiting the diner.

Chapter 5

After meeting Louis' sisters, I thought a lot about our encounter. I thought about the fact that Fizzy had exposed Lottie's attraction to me, but I also thought about the way they had described Louis. As mentioned earlier, his behavior didn't come as a surprise to me. I mean, I was sure he would never do me a favor if I asked him either because he was always a pain in the ass to me. The fact that he was willing to fix alcohol for me had caught me by surprise. However, Liam was the one who had asked him, not me. Maybe that was the reason.

To be honest, I had never put much thought into why my and Louis' relationship was different from the ones we had with the other lads. Sure, we all liked to tease each other every now and then, but not on the same level as me and Louis. We practically couldn't go a day without doing so.

Thinking about my and Louis' relationship made butterflies erupt in my stomach. I loved the way we always teased each other because whenever he did to me, I always felt so special as if I was the center of his attention. Having his eyes on me made me feel like I was on cloud nine. However, I bet he didn't even know what effect he had on me.

Alright, back to the fact that Lottie had taken an interest in me. During the times the guys and I had been at Louis' place, she had always been there, chatting a little with us, but I never noticed anything. Maybe I was just overthinking this. Maybe she just had a little crush on me, which she had developed recently. Either way, it was kind of cute.

It was now Wednesday, and I was sitting in the last class of the day, waiting for the bell to ring so Louis and I could finally go buy the alcohol. Or, more like so *he* could do it since I would have to stay in the car because if I went with him and they asked for my ID as well, we would both be in trouble.

My thoughts were interrupted by the bell, snapping me back to reality. The students around me started getting up from their seats while I still had a hard time trying to register what was going on.

Eventually, I got up as well, gathered my stuff, and left the classroom to head to my locker. The first thing I noticed was that Louis and Liam were already there, chatting with each other at Liam's locker.

"Hey, guys," I greeted, flashing them a smile while I went over to my locker to get rid of my school books and grab my jacket and bag instead.

They both turned to me. "Hi!" Liam said.

"Ready to go buy some alcohol?" Louis smirked, making me chuckle.

"Of course."

"See you at practice, Liam," I told the brown-haired boy who had now turned to his locker.

He turned his head back to look at me. "Sure. See you then," he smiled.

With that, Louis and I started walking through the hallways towards the exit. We didn't say anything during our walk to the lot where his black sports car was parked, but it was okay because it didn't feel necessary.

The weather was pretty much the same as yesterday but a little colder, and it wasn't snowing. Although I didn't like the cold, I was happy that I didn't have to get wet the first thing I did when I stepped outside.

Louis unlocked his car before we both got in. I placed my bag at my feet while he put the key in the ignition, turning both the car and heat on. "Damn, it's so fucking cold," I muttered, looking down at my lap.

"Tell me about it, Curly."

To my surprise, he didn't decide to turn on the radio on full blast, which he didn't hesitate to do the last time he drove me in his car. I was secretly thankful that he had decided to listen to me this time. Or, he just wanted to be able to talk during the ride.

"So, I met your sisters yesterday," I told him, looking at the side of his face.

His eyebrows shot up in surprise. "Really? Where?"

"At work. They came to fetch the food you guys had ordered," I explained, my eyebrows pulling together.

Was he so unaware that he didn't even know they had ordered food from the diner I worked at? Jesus.

His mouth formed the shape of an 'o'. "Right! They didn't talk shit about me, did they?" He chuckled while shaking his head.

I tilted my head to the side, pursing my lips. "Well, if telling me that you never do anything that your parents ask you to and that your mom doesn't trust you in driving your sisters around count as nothing, then no, they didn't talk shit about you," I said, giving him a smug smile.

His mouth fell open. "They didn't."

I nodded my head. "Oh, yes, they did," I grinned, making him run a hand over his face.

"I swear, I'm going to murder them when I get home," he muttered.

I let out a gasp. "Hey, they haven't done anything but tell the truth, Louis. You can't blame them for that."

He turned to me, his eyes narrowed. However, he didn't say anything. He just averted his gaze back to the road, and I took that as my cue to continue talking. "I knew you were just pretending to drive well when you drove me home after practice Monday," I said in amusement, turning to look at the road as well.

He let out a snort. "If you're going to bring up my driving skills again, I won't hesitate to throw you out the window."

"Are you offended?" I couldn't help but ask, my eyebrows raised.

His eyes turned to look at the side of my face. "No. I'm just tired of hearing it. I proved to you that I can drive safely, and I am doing so right now too, aren't I?"

To be honest, I hadn't even thought of the fact that the car was moving, so I guess that was proof enough that he could be a good driver if he wanted to.

Biting my lip, I shrugged my shoulders. "I suppose."

My comment made a smug smile form on his pink lips. When I noticed this, I turned to him quickly. "Why that face?"

The smile widened on his lips. "I like winning arguments."

I let out a huff, crossing my arms over my chest. "Shut up," I muttered.

"What was that? Couldn't hear you," he chuckled, cupping his hand around his ear to make me repeat myself.

I shook my head, not saying anything. I wouldn't give him that pleasure.

A few minutes later, Louis parked his car outside Tesco, turning off the engine. "So, what do you want me to buy?" He asked, raising an eyebrow at me.

I pursed my lips, thinking about it. "Uh, a few beers, one vodka and maybe one Jägermeister?"

He nodded his head. "Sure. See you later, Mr. I'm-too-young-to-buy-my-own-alcohol-so-I'll-let-my-friend-do-it," he winked before slamming the door shut behind him.

I could only gape at his figure as he strode over to the entrance. Did he really just say that? If there was anyone murdering someone today, it was going to be me murdering him... or, maybe not. I liked him too much for that.

While I was waiting for Louis to come back, I decided to occupy myself by going through my social media on my phone. I scrolled through my entire Instagram and Twitter feed before he finally turned the door handle on his side of the car.

"Here you go, mate," Louis said, placing the plastic bag on my lap. It was so heavy that it almost hurt.

"Damn, how much did you buy?" I gasped, opening the bag to check the inside of it. He'd bought at least 24 beers.

"We're five teenage lads, Harold. We're gonna need all that," he said firmly, putting his hands on the wheel.

I crossed my arms over my chest. "I'm not paying for all of this. I told you to buy a *few* beers, not these many!" I grumbled, making him chuckle.

"Relax, man. I can pay for it," he smiled.

I raised my eyebrows. "What? I mean, it's not like I can't afford it. It's just that... you know I'm saving up for a car, and I really want to be able to buy one once I get my driver's license," I explained, biting my bottom lip.

He rolled his eyes. "I know, Curly. So, let me pay for it this time. I don't mind, honestly."

Why did my stomach erupt with butterflies at the thought of Louis buying something for me? It shouldn't, considering he didn't exactly buy *me* it, but it did anyway.

"Thank you," I told him honestly, making the corners of his lips twitch.

"No problem, mate."

He dropped me off at my place a few minutes later, saying goodbye and that we'll see each other in a bit. He didn't offer to pick me up for practice, and I didn't expect him to either. Honestly, he had done way more things for me today than he had ever done for me in total, and I was more than happy about that. Besides, the busses were going as usual today, so it wouldn't be a problem.

I slung my school bag over my shoulder, holding the plastic bag with the alcohol in my right hand as I walked over to the porch. Behind me, I could hear Louis speeding off down the street, and I couldn't help but roll my eyes at the fact. He was definitely a wild driver, whether he wanted to admit it or not.

"Gemma?" I called out once I had shut the front door behind me.

Since the door was unlocked, I figured she was home. Moreover, her car was in the driveway. "In the living room, brother!" She replied.

I toed my shoes off, shrugged off my jacket, and placed the two bags on the floor before joining my sister in the living room. She was sitting on the couch, her legs propped on the coffee table with the TV-remote in her hand.

"Where have you been? Thought you got off at three today?" She wondered, checking the time on her phone. I knew it was around four-thirty.

"Louis and I were just buying some beverage for Friday," I shrugged, sitting down on one end of the couch.

She raised her eyebrows at me. "Right, he's already turned eighteen. Good thing for me. Now I don't have to do those favors for you anymore."

I rolled my eyes at her. "Well, my birthday is only in a week and a half, so it's not like you would've had to do it many more times anyway," I chuckled, making her glare at me.

"Whatever," she muttered. "So, what's happening on Friday? Are you guys attending a party?" She wondered.

I nodded my head. "Yeah. This girl in my Economics class is throwing a party at her place, and she invited me and the guys."

She pursed her lips. "I see. So, it's a big one?"

Shrugging my shoulders, I bit my bottom lip. "Don't know, to be honest. I know a lot of people who are going, though, so I think so. The guys are excited, at least."

Gemma raised her eyebrows at me. "But you aren't?"

I ran a hand through my curls. "Well, of course I am. Maybe not as excited as they are, but yeah, it's going to be fun to party again."

She narrowed her eyes at me. "Harry, are you hiding something?"

I mentally panicked at her words, but I tried my best not to show it. The only reason I wasn't as excited as the other guys were about it was that I didn't have the same desire to hook up with someone as they did. The only one I wanted to hook up with was one of them. Besides, I wasn't too excited to see Louis flirt with some random girl either. I was going to do my best not to think about it, though. I mean, it wouldn't be the first party we attended since I realized my feelings for him.

"No, I'm not," was the only thing I said.

I was positive she noticed that she shouldn't push it any further by the tone I was using. Instead, she placed her feet on the floor, putting her hands on her thighs. "Alright, I'm going to get something in my system. You're welcome to join me in the kitchen, H."

With that said, she got up from the couch and walked by me to get to the kitchen. I let out a sigh, getting up myself because I knew I would have to eat something before practice. Besides, my stomach was starting to churn, so it was probably for the best.

Gemma was standing at the counter when I got there, putting two slices of bread in the toaster. "Can you put two in for me too?" I asked, walking over to the fridge to grab the butter, a package of ham and the milk.

Through the corner of my eye, I could see her doing as I asked her to. Meanwhile, I put the items on the kitchen table before sitting down on one of the chairs. "Look, I'm sorry for being so curt earlier, Gems. I didn't mean to," I apologized, biting my bottom lip.

She turned around, her lips twitching. "Don't worry, brother. I didn't take offense. I understand that you don't want to talk to me about everything. You'll tell me when you want to... if you want to," she said with a light chuckle.

I shook my head with a smile on my face. "Thank you, Gems."

The toasts popped then. Gemma grabbed all four of them before sitting down in the seat opposite me, passing two of the slices over to me. "So, I assume you want me to be away on Friday?" She predicted, raising an eyebrow at me.

I rolled my eyes. "Well, I can't force you to, but yeah, I do. Unless you won't be a bother, that is," I smiled.

She rolled her eyes. "Now that I think about it, I'm quite sure I don't even want to be home anyway. Watching five teenage boys get drunk together? No thanks."

I couldn't help but laugh at her. "We're not that bad, Gemma."

She shrugged her shoulders, clearly amused. "I'll find a way to be somewhere else anyway. It's better that way, isn't it?"

Nodding my head, I smiled. "Yeah, probably. For both of us."

"For both of us," she agreed.

Chapter 6

Thursday flew by, so it didn't take long until Louis, Niall, Liam, Zayn and I were standing at our lockers on Friday afternoon. The last bell of the day had just rung, and we were all ready to go home and start the weekend.

"So, what time can we come over, Harry?" Niall asked, leaning against the locker beside me.

I shrugged my shoulders. "Whenever you want to, I guess. Mom's working all evening and Gemma's going to be out, so just come when you're ready."

Niall's face lit up in a smile. "Well, then I'm just going home to get changed first, then I'll be there," he chirped, clapping his hands together in excitement.

"With that excitement, I'm afraid you're not going to make it to the party tonight, Niall," Zayn chuckled, shaking his head.

"Hey, what's wrong with being excited? I can take it easy on the alcohol if that's what you're worried about," the blonde guy huffed, crossing his arms over his chest.

Zayn rolled his eyes. "We'll see about that later."

Niall sent him a glare.

"I'll be there at around seven if that's okay? Mom wants me to do some chores before I'm allowed to go out," Liam grimaced, scratching the back of his neck.

Louis scrunched his nose up. "I feel sorry for you, man. I'd be pissed if my mom forced me to do any chores, especially on a Friday evening."

I rolled my eyes at his words. "You'd never do any chores even if your mom forced you to, Louis."

The feathery-haired boy raised his eyebrows at me. "How can you be so sure of that?" He wanted to know.

"Inside information," I said, flashing him a knowing look. "Besides, your personality gives it away. You're a lazy arse."

"I'll have to agree with Harry on that," Liam butted in, wrapping an arm around my shoulders. "You'd never do any favors for your parents."

Louis looked between the two of us, his mouth agape. "What is this? Some kind of teaming up against Louis thing?" He huffed.

"It doesn't matter. This is just proof that we know you so well that we can tell stuff about you without really knowing it," Liam shrugged.

Actually, I did have proof that it was true. Louis' sisters had just told me the other day what a lazy arse he was, but I didn't feel the need to mention that for some reason.

"Whatever," he muttered.

My eyes remained on him while the other guys continued talking. I couldn't help but examine his beautiful appearance. He was wearing his big, black jacket and a pair of black, tight, skinny jeans. His fringe was swept to the side, as usual, and I could almost see the crinkles by his eyes forming in front of me even if he wasn't smiling. I just knew they would be there if he did. Then it was his sharp jawline that I wanted to run my fingers along, and those pink, thin lips that I wanted to touch with my own. Don't even get me started on those beautiful, ocean blue eyes that were framed by his brown lashes. He was living proof that beauty existed.

"Harry?"

I snapped back to reality, turning to Zayn who was talking to me. All of them were looking at me, though, even Louis. "Yeah?" I wondered, scratching the back of my neck awkwardly.

"You zoned out. I was saying that I'll be at your place whenever Louis' ready because he's my ride."

"Oh, yeah, sure. When are you planning on coming then, Louis?" I asked, clearing my throat.

The blue-eyed boy shrugged his shoulders. "Maybe at five? We'll see."

Before we had time to say anything else, a girl walked up to us. Liam had dropped his arm from my shoulders, but it was now replaced by the girl's. "Hey guys, you're coming tonight, right?"

I turned my head to look at the side of Emily's face. "Hey, Emily. We were actually just talking about it, and--" I started, but was rudely cut off.

"Of course we'll be there," Louis told her, making my eyebrows pull together.

Emily's face lit up in a smile, probably because Louis had talked to her. "Awesome!"

She dropped her arm from my shoulders to walk away, but she made sure to stop at Louis on her way to whisper something in his ear. I could feel my blood boil at the sight. Couldn't she just lay off? I got that she found him attractive, but did she have to throw it in my fucking face all the time?

A smirk made its way to Louis' lips as she talked to him, and it didn't drop once she had walked away. His eyes then found mine. "Why didn't you tell me she specifically wanted me to come to the party?" He asked, raising his eyebrows.

Because I didn't want you to know.

"I don't know. It didn't feel like a big deal, I suppose," I said, shrugging my shoulders in disinterest.

He scoffed. "Well, it is. Now I know I'm definitely going to get laid tonight," he said, licking his lips.

I swallowed hard, looking away from him. Thankfully, neither of the guys seemed to notice my actions. They were too caught up with studying Louis to do so.

"Fuck, man. Now I'm definitely jealous," Niall grumbled, pouting his lips.

Zayn, Liam and Louis smiled at him in amusement while I couldn't be bothered. Instead, I fished my phone from the back pocket of my skinny jeans. "I've gotta go, guys. My bus is here any second," I lied. It wasn't supposed to be here until another ten minutes.

With that, I left them without waiting for a response, making my way through the hallways towards the exits. I didn't get there until Niall caught up with me, though. "Hey, man. Why did you just walk off like that? We always walk to the bus together when we finish school at the same time," he whined.

I turned to look at him, biting my bottom lip. "I'm sorry, Niall," I apologized. "I was just nervous about missing the bus."

He pulled his eyebrows together, probably knowing that it wasn't the truth, but he didn't say anything. I was more than happy about that. "So, what did you and Louis buy for tonight?" He asked instead.

My lips twitched at the mention of Louis' name, even though I still couldn't get the image of him having sex with Emily out of my head. "A lot of beer, one vodka, and one Jäger."

Niall nodded his head, obviously impressed. "Sounds good, man. You know it won't be long until I'm knocking on your front door, right?" He chuckled, making me roll my eyes.

"I know, Niall. That's why I'm in such a hurry," I joked. "I need to clean the place before you get there."

An amused smile made its way to his face. "Knowing us lads, it won't be necessary," he laughed, and I knew he was right.

Niall didn't joke around when he said he was only going home to get changed before coming over to my place. He knocked on the door only half an hour after I had gotten home. Honestly, I barely had time to get changed myself. However, I did end up in a black button-up with three buttons undone from the collar and a pair of black, skinny jeans.

Thankfully, Gemma had already left the house when Niall got there, so it actually didn't matter that he came over on such short notice. The only thing it did was stress me out a little bit.

While we waited for Zayn and Louis to show up, we occupied ourselves by playing some Fifa. It was our all-time favorite video game, which we always ended up playing when we all hung out together. The only sad part about it was that I never seemed to know how to win a match against any of the guys.

"And Nialler wins again! Who's the king of this game? I repeat, who's the king of this game? That's right! I am!" He exclaimed when he won the second match against me.

I let out a sigh and was just about to open my mouth to reply when another voice interrupted me. "You are not the king of Fifa, Niall. You just happen to be playing against someone who's shit at it."

I turned to the doorway, seeing Louis leaning against it with a smirk on his face. My heart suddenly started racing in my chest. Damn, he looked hot. He was dressed in a white, short-sleeved button-up and a pair of black, skinny jeans that were unfolded at the ends. They also made his bum look amazing, and I could tell this because he was sticking his hip out.

45

His words made me let out a whine, though. "Heey, that's mean!"

Louis rolled his eyes at me, walking over to take a seat on the couch beside Niall. "Well, we both know it's true," he smirked.

I let out a huff, crossing my arms over my chest. Zayn joined us in the living room not even a minute later. "Don't you guys know how to knock on a door?" I muttered, making all three of them laugh.

"You're just grumpy because you don't want to admit the truth about being shit at Fifa," Louis said in amusement.

I picked up a pillow from the couch beside me and threw it at him. It hit him right in the face since he wasn't expecting it. "Look who's grumpy now," I said when the smile dropped from his face.

"Oh, I'm not grumpy. I'm furious," he muttered, picking up the pillow to throw it back at me, but Zayn caught it before he could do so.

"Easy there, Louis. We don't want to cause any fights this evening," he warned, placing the pillow beside him again.

Louis just looked at him for a few seconds before turning to me, his eyes narrowing slightly. "You're not getting away with that, Styles."

I chuckled at him. "It was a pillow, Louis. Calm down. Besides, I'm not scared of you," I smirked.

He shot me a playful glare. "You should be."

He leaned back against the couch again, crossing one leg over the other. "Give me the controller, Niall. I'm gonna beat Curly's ass to prove a point," he said, and Niall handed him the controller with an amused smile on his face.

"We'll see about that," I said smugly, although I was pretty sure he was telling the truth. I would try my best to win, though, but I wouldn't admit that if I ended up losing.

While Louis and I started playing, Zayn went to the kitchen with Niall to fetch the alcohol. "You can bring the bowl of chips and the one with popcorn as well!" I called after them.

"You already have it prepared?" Louis asked, raising an eyebrow at me.

I shrugged my shoulders. "Yeah, why not?"

He rolled his eyes before turning his attention back to the game. Niall and Zayn joined us only a minute later, Zayn carrying the alcohol and Niall the two bowls of snacks.

"If I didn't know better, I'd take this as a typical lads night," Niall said, sitting down on the same spot beside me that he sat before, after placing the two bowls on the coffee table.

"Yep, except Liam's not here," Zayn butted in, sitting down next to Louis.

"True."

Zayn placed four beer cans on the table, and Niall didn't hesitate to pop his open and take a large swig of it. Zayn was quick to follow. "Come on, can't you just lose now, Curly? I wanna drink too," Louis whined.

"Oh, shut up. It doesn't matter whether I lose or not. The match won't end faster anyway," I said matter-of-factly. "You can always forfeit, though."

I could feel his glare from the corner of my eye.

Somehow, I ended up winning the match. I was pretty sure it was because I tried my very best to show him that I could be good if I wanted to. And, if he wasn't grumpy before, he sure was when the match was over. He crossed his arms over his chest with a pout on his lips while I flew up from the couch to do a little pirouette.

"I told you I wasn't shit at it, Louis," I beamed from ear to ear.

He grumbled something under his breath, not making eye contact with me. When I sat down again, Niall patted my knee. "I'm actually proud of you, mate. Never seen you play so well before," he complimented.

I smiled at him. "Well, I guess that if you really want to, you can always win," I said, making Louis let out a huff.

I turned to look at him. He had grabbed a beer can from the table and was now popping it open. "You shouldn't have any preconceptions about me, Louis. You never know how things will end up when I'm involved," I smirked.

"Watch your mouth, Styles. Otherwise, the pillow is going to hit *your* face this time," he muttered.

Before I could open my mouth to reply, there was a knock on the door.

"Thank God Liam's here. He'll have to help me keep the two of you from jumping on each other," Zayn sighed in relief.

He had no idea how much I actually wanted to jump on Louis, just not in the way he thought.

A few beers, vodka, and Jäger shots later, we were all laughing while talking about awkward situations that had happened in our pasts. Niall had just told a story when he had made a girl join him in the locker room after a game when all the other guys had left. They had been going at it in the shower when Coach suddenly showed up, clearing his throat to tell them that he had to lock the place.

We all doubled over in laughter. It was actually really awkward. Honestly, I wasn't sure if I would be able to look Coach in the eye again if that were to ever happen to me.

"Danny's going to be here in five minutes. We should probably get ready," Louis informed us once we had all calmed down and he was looking at his phone.

Danny was one of Louis' old friends who he had gone to school with when he still went with the students the same age as him. That meant Danny had turned eighteen and was able to drive us to the party tonight.

"Awesome!" Niall called out, getting up from the couch.

Being the responsible son that I was, I got up to take the empty beer cans to the kitchen along with the shot glasses. Since I couldn't take them all in one go, Liam decided to help me.

"Thanks, man," I told him once the glasses were in the dishwasher and the cans were in a paper bag on the floor.

"No problem."

We were about to exit the kitchen when he pulled me back by grabbing my forearm. "How come you're not as excited to go to this party as the other guys?" He asked bluntly.

I raised my eyebrows at him. "What? I am excited."

He narrowed his eyes at me in suspicion but didn't say anything about it. "Evelyn has been talking about you," he told me instead, changing the subject.

My mouth formed the shape of an 'o' at the mention of her name. Not to be rude, but she had slipped my mind completely. "She has?"

"Yeah. Alice told me she's been talking non-stop about meeting you at the party."

Shit. I was rude, wasn't I? I mean, she seemed like a really nice girl. She really did. It was just that my mind was always busy thinking about someone else. No other person was able to get my attention the way Louis was. "I'll make sure to talk to her tonight then," I promised him, to which he nodded with a smile on his face.

Five minutes later, we were all sitting in Danny's car. Niall was sitting on Liam's lap while Louis was sitting in the front beside Danny, and I was in the middle... again. I didn't know how I always ended up sitting there, but I didn't like it.

It didn't take long until Danny pulled over outside a big, white wooden house. "Thanks for the ride, man," Louis said to Danny, patting him on the shoulder in appreciation.

"No problem, Louis. Have fun!"

We all got out of the car, Niall wobbling a little from all the beer he'd had. Otherwise, I would say we were all pretty okay. None of us was that drunk... yet.

Chapter 7

We all went our separate ways once we were inside the house. The music was on full blast, blaring from the speakers. It was easy to tell that there were quite a few people here judging by the jackets that were thrown in a pile in the hall. Also, people kept passing by when I was in the process of taking off my own jacket.

I went into the living room, which wasn't hard to find since you just had to follow the music. A lot of people were dancing, some of them already making out and groping each other. It was strange how fast I had weaned myself off parties because this almost felt like a foreign place for me to be.

Therefore, I took my eyes off the dance floor to try and find where they were serving the drinks and beer. If I was going to survive this night, I most definitely needed some more alcohol in my system.

I made my way through the crowd of people, bumping my shoulders into most of them until I found a table with beer cans and a big punch bowl along with some empty plastic cups. I decided to grab a beer and was just about to pop it open when I could feel someone tap my shoulder.

Turning around, I was surprised to see the black-haired girl I had talked to Liam about earlier. I hadn't expected to see her this early into the party. "Evelyn, hi!" I shouted over the music, plastering a smile on my face.

She was nice. There was no reason for me not to be polite to her, I tried to remind myself. I mean, she hadn't even tried flirting with me yet, so why should I not be polite? God, I sounded like such a girl who was afraid that some nasty guy was going to hit on me. She was pretty too, so there really wasn't any reason for me to be impolite. Then why was I even debating this?

"Hi, Harry. So, you did show up after all," she smirked, reaching around me to grab an empty plastic glass. She filled it with some punch before bringing the cup to her lips.

"I told you so, didn't I?" I chuckled, making her smile widen. "How long have you been here?" I wondered.

She grabbed my forearm to pull me out of the crowd and into the kitchen that was a lot less crowded. It took some time because there were so many people on the dance floor, but eventually, we managed to get there. Only five people were in the kitchen, chatting with each other. Evelyn didn't stop pulling me forward until we were standing beside the fridge, leaning against the counter.

"I've been here for half an hour, I think? What about you?" She asked, taking a sip of her punch.

"I came about fifteen minutes ago. I walked right up to that table when I got here," I said, taking a swig of my beer.

She raised her eyebrows. "So, you went straight to the beer?" She laughed, nodding towards the can in my hand.

I shrugged my shoulders. "A man gotta have his alcohol, you know?" I joked.

She shook her head with a smile on her face, clearly amused.

"So, a bird told me you've been going around talking about me," I said, raising my eyebrows at her, the corners of my lips twitching.

Her cheeks turned light pink as her eyes widened in surprise. "Who tol-- Alice! Ugh, I knew I shouldn't have trusted her," she grumbled, looking down at the cup in her hand in embarrassment.

I opened my mouth to reply when the kitchen door suddenly flew open, catching all of us in the room off guard. In came a quite drunk Louis, looking around the room as if searching for someone. My heart instantly picked up its pace and butterflies erupted in my stomach. He always had this effect on me when he showed up without my knowing.

His gaze landed on me, the only face he must have really recognized in the room. "Curly, you haven't s-seen Emily, have y-you?"

My heart dropped at the sound of her name, but what was more important at this second was how he had managed to get this drunk so fast. We had been here for what? Twenty minutes, and he had already managed to get this intoxicated?

I pulled my eyebrows together as I shook my head slowly. "No, but Louis, wha--" I didn't get to finish that sentence until he had slammed the door shut behind himself and left the room as quickly as he had shown up.

Ouch.

I turned back to Evelyn who seemed shocked by the scene that had taken place judging by the look on her face. "Wasn't that Louis, your best friend?"

I nodded my head, grimacing.

"Wow, it was quite rude of him to just cut you off like that," she frowned, biting her bottom lip.

I shrugged my shoulders, averting my gaze from her. "He's usually like that to me when he's drunk."

"Really? And you're okay with it?"

Honestly, I would have wanted Louis to enter the room, walk up to me and wrap his arm around my waist to claim me as his. I would have wanted him to pull me away from Evelyn just to show her that I wasn't available, that I belonged to him and him only. I doubted that would ever happen, though.

"That's the way he is, I guess," I said, trying to make it seem like it didn't bother me. I mean, I was used to the way he wouldn't acknowledge me as much as I wanted him to, especially when we were at parties. For some reason, he always treated me this way then.

Evelyn narrowed her eyes at me in suspicion, but she didn't say anything. Instead, she changed the subject and started talking about school.

We stayed in the kitchen for at least an hour, chatting with each other. It didn't bother me as much as I first thought it would. I was hesitant about her at first, but only because I was afraid she just wanted to get into my pants. She wasn't like that, though. She was honestly a sweet girl.

"Do you wanna dance?" She suddenly asked, making my eyebrows shoot up.

"Eh, yeah, sure," I accepted, flashing her a smile.

Honestly, I wasn't much of a dancer, but tonight, I really felt like letting loose a little. It had been almost a month since I last did, after all.

She took my hand in hers this time - instead of grabbing my forearm - and together, we walked back to the dance floor that was still as occupied as it had been when we left it. Actually, it seemed like there were even more people dancing now than before, which I found almost impossible considering I thought it was already packed with people then.

Somehow, I managed to catch sight of Niall and Liam in the crowd. Niall was dancing with a brunette, his hands on her hips while his lips were attached to her neck. I couldn't help but smile at the sight. So, Niall got his girl eventually after all.

Liam was dancing with Alice, his arms around her waist while hers were around his neck. They were making out with each other, but not in a nasty way - which you would have assumed at a dance floor - but in a sweet and caring way. They looked like a power couple, and it made my stomach twist because damn, I wanted that too.

Speaking of which, Louis hadn't been present in my mind since he left the kitchen earlier, and I took that as a good sign. The less I thought about him, the fewer images of him hooking up with some girl flashed through my mind. It was probably best if I kept my attention to Evelyn. She was a good distraction.

It was funny how my first intention when I got here was to get drunk, but now an hour later, I had only downed one beer. I blamed Evelyn for that. Or, maybe I should thank her because being hungover was something I could definitely live without tomorrow. It was much better this way.

Evelyn and I started dancing, my hands on her hips while she had her arms around my neck. She leaned her head on my shoulder after a while, hugging herself closer to my body. I was just about to do the same thing to her when I swore I heard a bang.

I knitted my eyebrows together, looking at my surroundings to see if anyone else had noticed the sound. Neither of them seemed to be reacting the same way I did, so I decided to take matters into my hands and investigate what was going on. The noise had come from the entryway.

I excused myself to Evelyn, telling her I needed to use the bathroom. She nodded in reply, and I soon found myself pushing through all the sweaty bodies in the crowd. After a while of struggling, I finally managed to get out and make my way to the entryway.

The sight in front of me made me almost take a step back in surprise. Louis was sitting on the last step of the staircase, one of his hands pressed to his forehead and his nose scrunched up in pain. His brown feathery hair was disheveled as if someone had run their hands through it almost too aggressively. Honestly, it looked like he had sex hair.

"What was that noi-- Louis?" A voice from the top of the staircase called out.

My eyes snapped to the source and settled on none other than Emily. Of course.

I swallowed the jealousy and shock down and finally put my muscles into action, walking over to where Louis was sitting on the step, groaning in pain.

I ignored Emily as I kneeled down in front of him, feeling how my heart was racing in my chest because I had no idea what I was doing. My muscles moved thanks to the feelings I had for him. I did it without thinking.

Placing my hand on his knee, I managed to get his attention. His eyes fell on me, his face softening a little. "H-Harry?"

That must be the first time I heard him call me by my real name in ages. I didn't even remember when he last called me that.

"What happened, Louis? I just heard a loud bang," I asked, noticing how Emily disappeared out of the corner of my eye. Thank you.

He scrunched his nose up again, and I couldn't help but find it cute, despite the circumstances. "I uh... I think I f-fell?" He mumbled, his eyebrows furrowing together.

I took his hand away from his forehead to look at the damage, noticing that he had a swelling going on along with a red bruise. Biting my bottom lip, I searched his face to see if he had hurt himself somewhere else too. When I didn't find any more bruises, I pressed my forefinger and middle finger against the swelling lightly. "Is this the only place where you got hurt?" I asked him, looking into his blue eyes.

He nodded his head slowly. "Yeah. It wasn't th-that bad. I just fell on the last s-step and hit my head against the w-wall," he explained, pointing at the white wall beside us.

I let out a sigh, mentally rolling my eyes because of course he wouldn't admit that it was bad, even if he was as drunk as he was now. "You should be lucky it wasn't worse, Louis."

He didn't say anything. He just let out another groan before leaning his head against the wall, closing his eyes. I realized he was too drunk, too tired, and too hurt to stay here, so I reached out to wrap my hand around his wrist. I got up to my feet before pulling him up with me, wrapping his arm around my shoulders.

He let out a loud grunt in resistance, trying to sit back on the step, but I forced him to stand up. "Louis, come on. We have to get you home," I muttered.

He shook his head. "No, no. You sh-should go enjoy yourself, H-Harry. Don't m-mind me."

"Don't be stupid. You can't fend for yourself," I sighed, trying to find our jackets in the huge pile on the floor. It was difficult because almost all of them were black, and ours were too. Moreover, I was trying to hold up a drunk guy in the process.

After almost five minutes, I finally found them. I shrugged mine on while Louis leaned his entire body against the wall, his head slipping further down it every second. I managed to catch him before he dropped to the floor and wrapped his jacket around his shoulders before pulling my phone out of the back pocket of my jeans.

I called the first person I could think of. I just hoped to God that she hadn't consumed any alcohol tonight.

"Gemma?"

"Harry, why are yo--"

I cut her off before she could finish the sentence. "Can you please pick me up at the party? Louis has hurt himself, and I can't wait for a cab to pick us up."

She was quiet on the other end for a while before she let out a sigh. "Fine, but I'm only doing it because of Louis. How bad is it? Does he have to go to the hospital?"

I was surprised by how worried she sounded. I didn't think she cared so much about my friends. Glancing at Louis' face, I noticed that he was starting to fall asleep on me. "No, I think he's fine. He's just had a bit too much to drink, so he's starting to fall asleep on me," I explained.

"Alright. I'll be there in ten," she said and hung up on me before I could reply to her.

I slipped my phone back into my pocket before turning back to Louis. He had scrunched his nose up again. "You stink, H-Harry," he mumbled, looking at me through his long eyelashes.

If he didn't look so fucking beautiful right now and if he wasn't hurt, I would have gotten back at him for that, but I couldn't. "Now is not the best time to joke around, Louis."

"I'm not j-joking... Eww."

I shook my head at him with a smile on my face. "You're unbelievable."

He just stared at me, and for a second I didn't see any trace of the Louis I had gotten to know. This Louis looked so much softer. It made me want to squeeze him into my arms. Damn. I had never felt that way about him before. Usually, I wanted *him* to be squeezing me into *his* arms. This Louis was something to remember, though.

Right then, I could see the lights of a car flashing by through the window in the entryway, and I instantly knew it must be Gemma. "Come on now, Louis. Let's get out of here."

Somehow, I managed to bring him to Gemma's car without falling over. He wasn't very cooperative, so it was a good thing that he wasn't heavy. He was both shorter and lighter than me, which had me wondering how he always made me feel smaller than him otherwise. I assumed it was thanks to the power that always radiated from him.

I got into the backseat together with Louis, and Gemma instantly turned around to look at us. "How's he doing?"

I studied his face, noticing that he had closed his eyelids once again. "I mean, he still knows how to insult me, so I'm sure he's okay."

An amused smile formed on her face before she turned around to drive off. During the ride, Louis' head fell on my shoulder, and I realized he must have gone to sleep completely now. Damn, I couldn't take him home in this state.

"Gemma, I think it's best if we take him to our place. He's fallen asleep on me," I mumbled, making her turn around to look at me again. Her eyes flickered to Louis for a few seconds before she nodded at me.

Once she parked the car in our driveway, I got out of the car on the side where Louis wasn't sitting before making my way around the vehicle to open his door. I leaned down to take him in my arms so I was carrying him bridal style, and wow, he really was light.

Gemma walked ahead of us to unlock the front door while I walked behind her, trying my best to carry him without falling over thanks to the slippery ground. When I finally got inside, I kicked the door shut behind me before bringing Louis to the living room, gently laying him down on the soft cushion of the couch. I then propped a pillow under his head and draped a blanket over his body so he wouldn't get cold.

Gemma entered the living room a second later with a bag of frozen peas. "You said he hurt himself, didn't you?"

I flashed her a smile. "Thank you, Gems," I said when she'd thrown the bag of peas to me.

"No problem, H. Make sure he's okay before you go to bed, yeah?"

I nodded my head. "Of course. Goodnight."

"Goodnight, Harry."

She left the living room, and I didn't waste another second until I kneeled down beside Louis and pressed the bag of peas against the bruise on his forehead. He inhaled a deep breath and grimaced at the touch in his sleep, but it didn't take long until he relaxed. I stayed there for a couple of minutes, pressing the bag to his skin until I was positive it was long enough.

I examined his features and couldn't stop my heart from fluttering in my chest. How was it even possible to look so beautiful? I wished I could touch him, show him how much I liked him. I wished I could tell him how beautiful he was, how badly I wanted to kiss him. I just wished I could do all this without him finding it weird.

With a sigh, I got up to my feet and started making my way out of the room. I stopped at the doorway to get one last look at him, though.

Yeah, I really did wish he was mine.

Chapter 8

"What am I doing at your house, Curly, and why was there a bag of melted peas on the coffee table?"

I let out a loud yawn, reaching up to rub the sleep out of my eyes. I hadn't even opened them yet. Louis had just bashed into the room while I was still asleep, but he had definitely woken me up now. "Would you be quiet? I'm trying to sleep," I groaned.

Even though my eyes were still closed, I could practically see him roll his eyes. "Wake up, Curly. My head hurts like a fucking bitch."

I guess we were already back to the nicknames...

I opened one eye to peek at him, noticing that he was standing at the end of my bed, looking down at me. He was dressed in the same clothes he had been wearing yesterday, and his hair looked even more disheveled today than it did when I found him sitting on the stairs. He also had a big, swollen bruise on his forehead where he had hit himself in the wall, and I couldn't help but grimace at the sight.

Opening both of my eyes, I sat up against the headboard, revealing my naked chest. "I'm quite sure that's due to the alcohol you had last night, but also because you hit your forehead in the wall on your way down to the first floor at Emily's place," I explained, nodding towards my mirror to indicate him to look at his reflection.

He pulled his eyebrows together in confusion, walking over to body length mirror. His eyes widened when he caught sight of his forehead, and he instantly lifted a hand to run his fingers over the bruise.

It wasn't until then it registered in my brain that Louis was actually here, in my room alone without the other guys anywhere in sight. It had never happened before, and this fact made my heartbeat quicken in my chest. It just felt so private for some reason.

"Why don't I remember any of this?" He asked, turning to look at me.

I shrugged my shoulders, biting my bottom lip. "What's the last thing you remember?" I couldn't help but question even though I probably didn't want to know because I remembered how his hair looked when I found him and that Emily had been standing at the top of the stairs.

He thought for a while. "Um, I'm pretty sure I walked upstairs with Emily, but I don't recall more than that."

I nodded my head, trying to hide the grimace on my face. "Well, you tripped on your way down the stairs and hit your head. I heard when you fell, so I helped you. I was supposed to take you home, but then you fell asleep on me, so I figured it was best to take you here."

He pursed his lips, turning back to look at himself in the mirror. "That explains the bag of melted peas," he mumbled. "Thanks, though."

He said the last part so quietly that I barely heard him, but I did register it, and I couldn't help the smile that formed on my lips. "No problem," I said louder, making him snap his face to me.

It took a few seconds until he opened his mouth. "I should go home now. Mom and dad are probably worried about me," he muttered, averting his gaze to the floor.

I nodded my head curtly, looking down at my lap to hide my disappointment. Was he able to drive already, though? I mean, he most likely still had alcohol in his system. On the other hand, I didn't want to argue, so I pulled the blankets off my body and got out of the bed to get dressed.

Louis was still standing by the mirror, and I could see through the corner of my eye that he was looking the other way. I pouted my lips as I grabbed a black t-shirt from my closet along with a pair of black, skinny jeans.

When we exited my room, we ran right into Gemma who had just walked out of her own room. Her eyes widened when she caught sight of us. "Oh, good morning, guys. How are you feeling, Louis?" She asked, the same genuine concern written on her face as last night.

I could see how Louis' mouth fell open in shock, clearly not expecting Gemma to know anything about what happened yesterday. "Uh, my head hurts like a bitch, but otherwise, I feel okay, I guess," he confessed, biting his bottom lip.

Gemma nodded her head in understanding. "I'll get you a glass of water and some pain killers then," she smiled and was just about to walk to the kitchen when I stopped her.

"Actually, Louis was just--"

"Going to use the bathroom. I'll be back in a minute," he said, cutting me off.

I gaped at him as he walked by me to go into the bathroom. What made him change his mind?

Gemma sent me a questioning look, but I just shook my head in dismissal and followed her to the kitchen. I couldn't talk to her when we were standing right outside the bathroom.

She pulled out a glass of water and filled it while I grabbed two Advils from our medicine cabinet. "Why did you look so shocked by what he said?" Gemma wondered, turning to me with raised eyebrows.

I shrugged my shoulders. "Before we walked out of my room, he told me he was going home. That's what I was about to tell you when he cut me off."

"Really?"

I nodded my head. "Yeah. I wonder what made him change his mind," I said, my eyebrows furrowed.

"Maybe it was because I was the one who offered to help him?" She suggested jokingly, making me shoot her a glare.

"Don't you dare, Gemma. He's my friend," I muttered, secretly afraid that she was right. What if Louis did have a crush on her? I mean, Louis' sister apparently had a crush on me.

She let out a chuckle, shaking her head. "I'm just kidding, brother. Calm your tits."

The same second I shot her another glare, Louis entered the kitchen. "Why didn't any of you tell me my hair looked like shit? It looked like a cat had clawed in it," he pouted, taking a seat at the kitchen table.

I raised my eyebrows at him. "You were staring at yourself in the mirror in my room for almost five minutes earlier. Didn't you notice then?" I asked, making him turn to look at me.

"No, I was busy staring at the big, fat, swollen bruise on my forehead that I don't even remember how it got there," he muttered, placing his arms on the table so he could lean his head against them.

I grabbed the glass of water from Gemma's hand and walked over to Louis with it along with the pills in my other hand. "Here you go," I said, placing them in front of his arms on the table.

He looked at them for a few seconds before taking the pills in his hand and popping them into his mouth. He then grabbed the glass of water and chugged the whole thing down in one go.

"So, I was just about to prepare some breakfast. Do you want some, Louis?" Gemma asked, and Louis turned to meet her gaze.

With a faint smile on his face, he shrugged his shoulders. "Sure, if I'm not a bother."

Gemma shook her head. "Of course not. Just stay there. Harry will help me make it," she smiled.

My mouth fell open. "Hey, I never said anyth--" I cut myself off when she shot me a death glare and let out a defeated sigh.

I could see Louis smirk faintly through the corner of my eye, and somehow, it made my heart flutter. I loved it when he acknowledged me, absolutely fucking loved it.

Gemma and I fixed some toasts and pulled out the juice, milk and cereal along with glasses, bowls and spoons, and placed it all on the table.

"So, where's your mom?" Louis asked when we were all sitting down, eating.

"She's asleep. She got off her shift at three in the morning," Gemma explained, to which he nodded.

"What about your mom? Have you heard anything from her? You told me your parents were going to be worried about you if you didn't go home earlier," I wondered, looking at him curiously.

I realized we'd had pretty civil dialogues today, where we talked like two normal people without insulting or making fun of each other. Honestly, it felt better than I expected it to. It was nice to be able to really talk to him and not just joke around, even if I liked doing that too.

"I haven't checked," he mumbled, shrugging his shoulders in dismissal.

I pursed my lips as I nodded my head. Maybe I was the only one out of the two of us who liked talking without joking around? Judging by his short answer and his lack of interest in keeping up a conversation, I assumed so at least.

When we had finished eating breakfast, Louis excused himself again, saying that he had to go home. So, I walked him to the entryway where I had placed his shoes and hung up his jacket last night. He opened the front door and was just about to leave when he turned around to flash me a small smile.

"Thank you for helping me yesterday, really. Please don't tell the other guys what happened, though, yeah? It's already too embarrassing as it is."

I nodded my head without thinking twice about it. I wouldn't tell them if he didn't want me to. "Sure. See you on Monday then?"

He sent me another faint smile, and I knew it must be because of all the pain he was in. "Yeah."

With that said, he shut the door behind himself, leaving me to stare at it for almost half a minute until I turned around to go into my room.

What just happened?

The rest of that day and Sunday went by pretty quickly. I had work on Sunday, which made the time pass by even faster than I knew it would have if I didn't. So, it wasn't long until I was sitting on the bus, on my way to school on Monday morning.

Other than the party on Friday, it had been a relaxed weekend. Mom didn't work on Saturday, which usually meant we had family dinner, and this Saturday was not an exception. Mom cooked Chicken Alfredo, a favorite of mine, which we all ate while chatting about what had happened during the week. After that, we all settled on the couch to watch a movie. I had my head on mom's lap and my feet on Gemma's while mom played with my curls. Believe it or not, but this was also a tradition.

Gemma would always question why I got to be the one always lying down. I figured it was because I was the youngest and the only guy in the family. "He's the most vulnerable out of us," mom always said, though, and I would have disagreed if it weren't for the fact that I enjoyed having her fingers carding through my hair so much.

The relaxed weekend also gave me time to think about the party and what happened after it. I couldn't take my mind off the way Louis had been so much quieter than he usually was. However, he had been in a lot of pain, so that was probably the reason why.

The second the school bus came to a halt, I grabbed my bag from the seat beside me and slung it over my shoulder before exiting the vehicle. The snow was now gone, which meant that the ground was only wet with water. As long as the busses were still going, I didn't care whether there was snow or not. I just couldn't wait until the summer when you could go outside without a jacket on.

Walking through the hallways, I noticed that the students had gone back to their normal routines after a week. They weren't as talkative as they had been last Monday morning, but most people were still chatting quietly with each other.

After avoiding eye contact with the people looking my way, I finally made it to my locker. Only Niall was there so far, and he was just about to pull out his school books when I got there, but when he heard the presence of another person, he turned around.

"Harry! Good morning, mate," he greeted with a wide smile on his face.

My eyebrows shot up in surprise. "Morning, Niall. What's got you so happy?" I asked as I got rid of my bag and jacket, putting them in my locker.

Through the corner of my eye, I could see him shrugging, still with the same smile playing on his lips.

I narrowed my eyes at him, trying to figure out what he was getting at when it suddenly hit me. "You got laid at the party, didn't you?" I could help but laugh. This was funny.

He shrugged his shoulders, the smile turning even wider if that was possible. "Maybe."

Rolling my eyes, I shook my head. "I saw you dancing with that brunette. Was she the lucky girl?" I chuckled.

When he didn't say anything, I took that as a yes. Letting out another laugh, I stuck my hands in my jeans pockets. "I'm happy for you, mate. You deserved some good ol' intercourse," I smirked.

He shot me a playful glare. "What about you, Harry? I didn't see you at the party after you disappeared with that black-haired girl. Did you take her home, eh?" It was his time to smirk at me now.

I shook my head, opening my mouth to answer him when I could suddenly feel an arm go around my shoulders, pulling me to its body. "Harold here took a cab home with me. We both got sick of the party. Isn't that right?"

Louis was now looking at the side of my face, and I couldn't breathe. He was standing so close and he had his arm around my shoulders. Did he know what he was doing to me? I couldn't even begin to explain how fast my heart was racing.

When I came to my senses, I furrowed my eyebrows. What did he expect? That I would tell Niall what really happened when I told him just the other day that I would keep it a secret? I wasn't that kind of person, especially not when it came to the person I liked.

"Uh, yeah. I wasn't really feeling it, and I found Louis who told me he felt the same way, so we went home together," I shrugged.

Niall turned to Louis with raised eyebrows. "I thought you were staying at Emily's? You went away with her, so we all just assumed that you stayed the night."

Louis bit his bottom lip, shaking his head. It wasn't until then I remembered that he had hit his forehead that night. Glancing at his face, I was amazed that the bruise was barely visible anymore. It was a little red, but he had covered it up well with makeup. The swelling was all gone, though.

"No, I went home."

He then turned to meet my gaze, obviously feeling my stare. The glare he sent me when he noticed that I was looking at his forehead made me avert my gaze abruptly while biting my bottom lip. Honestly, it stung a little that he couldn't even tell Niall that he had slept at my place, but I guess he didn't want any following questions as to why he hadn't just gone home to his own place instead. Either way, I couldn't stop my heart from sinking a little.

"Coach wants us to meet him before practice starts today, Styles. He said it was about something important," Louis muttered under his breath.

I turned my head to meet his eyes again, swallowing hard. "Sure, I'll be there."

I had honestly no idea how I would manage to get there earlier, though. The busses didn't go that frequently, so I would have to be there at least forty-five minutes earlier.

Louis noticed that something was bothering me. "What's the matter?"

I shrugged my shoulders. "It's just that the busses don't go that frequently in the afternoon, and I don't want to be forty-five minutes early. To be honest, I don't know if I'll even make it to that bus considering we get off school at three-thirty," I said sheepishly.

Louis rolled his eyes. "What about Gemma?"

I shook my head. "She's working today."

He pursed his lips. "I'll pick you up then. If you want to ride with me, that is," he laughed, shaking his head in amusement.

I thought he didn't want to bring his driving up again? Oh well, I wasn't the one to blame this time, so I guess I would just go with it. "It's okay as long as you drive the way you have been the last few times I've ridden with you."

He sent me a smirk. "Then I'll pick you up at five, Curly. Be ready."

Chapter 9

Louis left me and Niall after a short while to go to his class. The first thing Niall did when he was gone was to raise his eyebrows at me.

"What?" I asked him, having no idea what was on his mind whatsoever.

"Did you and Louis just have a conversation without bickering with each other?"

I pulled my eyes together, thinking about it. I mean, sure, we didn't exactly bicker like we usually did, but he did glare at me and he was more quiet than usual. I assumed he was still a little on edge since what happened on Friday night, though, judging by the way he interrupted my and Niall's conversation like that just now.

"I don't know?" I said stupidly, biting my bottom lip.

He looked at me strangely. "You actually agreed with each other on something. I've never seen you get along like that before."

I avoided making eye contact with him. Why was keeping a secret so hard? I wanted to tell him that Louis had slept over at my house after the party. I wanted to tell him how much it all meant to me, that it felt like we had gotten closer somehow, even if we hadn't really talked much. Spending time with Louis alone just made me feel closer to him.

"Actually, the fact that you two went home together after the party is a little off as well. I mean, you guys don't usually hang out just the two of you otherwise, right? And now he's even offering to drive you to practice. You didn't even have to ask him," Niall said, thinking out loud.

Thankfully, the bell rang right then, and I instantly took the opportunity to say bye to him before heading to Economics. On my way there, I couldn't stop thinking about why I had felt so uncomfortable in the situation. I mean, nothing had changed between me and Louis, so why couldn't I just explain that to Niall?

Maybe because I wanted me and Louis to have grown closer.

When I got home from school that day, mom was sitting at the kitchen table, writing what I assumed was a to-do list. The second I entered the kitchen, she looked up from her papers, a smile forming on her lips. "Hey there, sweetie," she greeted, pointing to the seat opposite her.

I sat down on the chair, letting my arms rest on the table just like Louis had done two days ago, only that I wasn't in pain. I was just tired after a long day of school. Just the thought of having to go to practice made me yawn.

"I thought you had a late shift today," I mumbled, thinking about the fact that Louis was going to pick me up because he thought I didn't have anyone else to drive me.

She shook her head, the smile still prominent on her face. "I was supposed to, but my boss called me last second to tell me I could have the day off. I thought I might as well get some stuff done then," she explained, referring to the to-do list on the table in front of her.

I pursed my lips. "I wish I could have the day off as well," I sighed, leaning down to rest my head on my arms.

I could see her giving me a sympathetic smile through the corner of my eye. "Is my baby feeling tired?" She cooed, making me roll my eyes.

"I'm not a baby, mom," I groaned, burying my face in my arms. "But yes, I am tired."

She let out a light chuckle. "You should get something to eat. I'm sure you'll get a boost of energy then. I can make you some pancakes if you want?" She suggested, and I snapped my head up to look at her.

"Really?" I asked incredulously.

"Of course."

With an appreciating smile, I got up from my chair to give her a kiss on the cheek. "You're the best, mom. I'm going to change into my gear. I'll be back in a minute," I promised her.

She rolled her eyes at my affection as I made my way out of the kitchen to my room. I already felt more alert, and then I hadn't even had something to eat yet. Just the fact that mom was making pancakes made me happy. I loved it when she was home on weekdays because she would always do small things to both me and Gemma that meant so much. That was her way of showing how much she loved us. She didn't have to buy us loads of expensive things for us to know that.

Once I had changed into my gear, I went back to the kitchen where mom was now standing at the stove, frying the pancakes. When she heard me entering the room, she turned around to face me. "What time does practice start?"

"Louis' picking me up at five. Apparently, Coach wants to talk to us," I said, biting my bottom lip when his name rolled off my tongue.

She looked a little surprised by that. "Louis, you say? I haven't met him in a while," she pointed out, pursing her lips.

"He was actually here the other day," I said, feeling how my heart was racing in my chest because we were talking about my crush, which she didn't know, but anyway.

"When I was at work?"

I shook my head. "No, he stayed the night on Friday after the party. You were still sleeping when he went home Saturday morning," I explained.

Her mouth formed the shape of an 'o'. "I see. How is he doing?" She wondered, turning back to face the stove so she could flip the pancake in the pan.

Louis had told me not to tell the boys what happened at the party. Did that also include my mom? I mean, they barely ever talked, so it wasn't like he would ever find out she knew anyway. Besides, she would never make fun of him or anything like that if so.

I shrugged my shoulders, although she couldn't see me. "He's doing good, I think," I mumbled. "He hurt himself at the party, though, and he's been acting a little different since then."

She turned around so I could see the frown on her face. "Why is that?"

I bit my bottom lip, sitting down at the kitchen table. "Honestly, I don't know, but I think he was in pain Saturday morning, which was why he wasn't as high on life as he usually is. He didn't want the boys to know what happened at the party because it's already too embarrassing as it is, he said. So, he was acting a bit weird at school today too."

Mom nodded her head slowly. "I don't know what's going on inside that boy's head, but I think you should listen to him."

Of course I listened to him. I liked him so much, so if I ever were to disappoint him or let him down, I would never be able to forgive myself. I didn't know why he wanted everything that happened to be a secret, but if that was his wish, I was going to keep my promise.

"Of course, mom. I'm not stupid," I muttered.

She let out a chuckle, walking over to place the pancake in the pan on the plate in front of me. "I've raised you well, my son."

I rolled my eyes at her comment before digging in to the delicious pancakes. I ate so many of them that I thought I was going to throw up if I even tried to get up from my chair. How on earth was I going to be able to play soccer now?

"Mom, you're the reason I won't be able to go to practice today," I whined, massaging my full stomach under my shirt.

She was sitting in the seat opposite me again, an amused smile on her face. "You shouldn't have eaten so many of them, honey."

Letting out a groan, I buried my face in my arms on the table. I didn't have time to think of how I was going to accomplish my situation until I could hear a car honk outside, though. My head instantly snapped to the kitchen window, looking out only to see Louis' black sports car. Fuck.

"Is it Louis?" Mom wondered, looking at me.

I nodded my head as I let out a sigh. "He's going to kill me if I don't go out there, but I can't fucking move."

Mom let out a chuckle. "I don't think he's going to kill you, honey."

She clearly didn't know him because I was one hundred percent sure he would be pissed at me if I didn't go out there now. I could hear his words from this morning on repeat in my head; 'I'll pick you up at five, Curly. Be ready'.

As if reading my mind, I could hear the front door swing open in the entryway right then. "Harold Styles! Didn't I tell you to be ready at fi-- Oh, hi, Anne."

Louis was now standing in the doorway of the kitchen, scratching the back of his neck awkwardly upon seeing my mom at the table with me.

Mom turned around in her seat to get a look at him. "Louis, my dear. How nice to see you again. It's been way too long," she smiled, making Louis' lips twitch a little, but he was still hesitant.

"Uh, yeah. I uh, I didn't expect you to be here? Harry never mentioned anything about it," he explained, his cheeks a little rosy.

I found it absolutely adorable. I liked this guy so much that I couldn't even begin to describe it. The way he was standing there, his black winter jacket on over his soccer gear with his hair perfectly swept to the side even if the weather wasn't the best. How did he always manage to look so good?

"He didn't know either. He was just as surprised as you to see me here, darling."

This time Louis' lips curled into a genuine smile. "I see. Well, Coach wants the two of us to get to the gym a little earlier. So, Harry, will you come with me?" He asked, raising his eyebrows at me expectantly.

I found it a little funny how he called me by my real name just because my mom was in the room. I wondered if he was afraid she was going to point it out if he called me by one of his nicknames because I was sure he would have never called me 'Harry' otherwise.

"I wish I could, but unfortunately, I can't move," I grimaced, making his eyebrows knit together.

"What on earth are you-- I mean, what are you talking about?" He wondered, clearing his throat in the middle of the sentence because the first part came out a little too harshly.

I pouted my lips. "I ate too many pancakes."

He rolled his eyes at me, looking at my mom. "Do I have your permission to pick him up, throw him over my shoulder and take him to my car?"

Mom let out a loud bark of laughter. "Yes, you have."

I let out a loud gasp, looking at mom with wide eyes. "Mom, how could yo--"

The air was suddenly knocked out of my lungs when my chest collided with Louis' back, causing the interruption of my sentence. "Louis, I'm going to throw up on you!" I shrieked in warning, hitting him just above his bum.

If it weren't for the fact that it felt like the pancakes in my stomach were going to come right back up, I would have enjoyed the situation much more. I mean, his ass was right in front of my fucking eyes, and he was touching me, even carrying me. Could it get better?

When he didn't answer me, I let out a loud groan, trying my best to keep from throwing up at him by covering my mouth with my hand and swallowing the arisen bile down. When I could feel cold air hit the skin on my lower back where my shirt had ridden up, I let out a squeal.

"My jacket, Louis! My shoes and my bag!"

We made it to his car successfully - thank God for that - and he put me down in the passenger seat. "I'll get your stuff. Stay right there."

As if I could go anywhere even if I wanted to. If I had been feeling sick before Louis decided to throw me over his shoulder, it couldn't compare to how I was feeling now. I put my palms over my face, inhaling deep breaths to make the sickness go down. It only helped a little.

Louis came back a minute later, tossing my jacket at me, my shoes on the floor at my feet, and my bag in the backseat before climbing in behind the wheel. I could feel him stare at me where I was sitting, hunched over with my hands over my face.

"What?" I groaned, turning my head and parting my fingers so I could peek at him.

"Nothing."

With that, he turned on the engine and drove off towards the gym. We were quiet for at least three minutes until we started talking, and when the silence broke, it was because of him. I didn't even know if I could speak normally yet. I was too afraid of throwing up.

"How many pancakes did you eat?"

I pulled my eyebrows together, taking one last deep breath before opening my mouth, hoping that it wouldn't turn out a disaster. "Five, I think?"

He let out a chuckle. "Your stomach couldn't handle five pancakes?"

"Heeey," I whined. "I was just finished when you got there. If I had just gotten a few more minutes, my sickness would have gone down, but you decided to turn me upside down."

He rolled his eyes. "It was the only way for us to get to the gym on time."

I shot him a glare. "You could have carried me bridal style, or at least piggy back, but no. Now I definitely won't be able to practice," I groaned, running my hands through my hair. Great, now I didn't have a hair tie either.

"It's going to go down until then, trust me."

Well, I sure hoped so.

We were quiet for another while. I was now sitting upright in my seat, looking out the window while biting my lip. Thank God he was driving safely. Otherwise, I would probably be throwing up right now. However, my sickness was going down by the second, and the reason behind that was most likely because he was actually driving really well.

"I have to give it to you. You can be a good driver when you want to," I admitted sincerely, looking at him through the corner of my eye to see his reaction.

The corners of his lips twitched a little, but only a little. "Didn't I tell you that already, Curly?"

"Sod off," I muttered.

Couldn't he just take a compliment from me and be happy about it? No, he just had to make a joke out of it, didn't he?

When he noticed I was still looking out the window without saying anything else, he opened his mouth to speak. "I uh, thank you, I guess? I don't usually get many compliments, so I don't really know how to handle it."

I knitted my eyebrows together. What did he mean by that? I mean, just the other day, Liam complimented him about being a great teammate and leader. Coach did too, and then he was handling it well. So, what was he getting at?

"You don't? I mean, you received quite a few of them when Coach chose you to be captain. Liam also told you what a great captain you would be that day in the hallway," I pointed out, still frowning.

He shrugged his shoulders. "That was basically just about my soccer skills. It doesn't feel that personal to me, you know?"

I pursed my lips, nodding my head thoughtfully. "Well, I think you're a great guy, Louis. At least when you want to be," I chuckled, making the corners of his lips twitch.

"Should I even take that as a compliment?"

Nodding my head, I sent him a smile. "Yeah, you should."

The smile remained on his face for at least two minutes until he spoke up again. "So, how did things go between you and that girl at the party? It seemed like you were pretty close," he smirked cheekily.

I bit my bottom lip, looking down at my lap. "Evelyn's a great girl. She's really nice, but we didn't... do anything. I uh, I heard you fall in the stairs when I was dancing with her," I shrugged.

Louis hummed quietly. "I'm sorry about that. I didn't mean to interrupt anything for you."

I shook my head vigorously. "No. No, you didn't. I uh, I wasn't about to do anything with her anyway. I just wasn't... feeling it, you know?" I muttered.

Why was this so difficult? Well, maybe because I was talking to my crush about a girl that didn't really matter to me because he was all I could think about.

He raised his eyebrows at me. "Oh, I see."

Letting out a sigh, I reached up to run a hand through my curls. "What about you and Emily?" I asked although I didn't want to know. It felt mean of me not to ask him about her when he had asked me about Evelyn, though.

He shrugged his shoulders. "She wasn't really good, to be honest. Way too obedient."

I swallowed hard as I nodded my head. "So you remember what happened now?"

He looked at me for a second before looking back at the road. "Yeah, a bit more, at least. I remember falling on my way down the stairs and hitting my head. Then I remember you coming to my rescue."

I bit my lip to prevent a smile from forming on my lips. We didn't have time to talk more about it, though, because right then, Louis was sliding into an empty spot in the parking lot outside the gym.

"You feeling better now?" Louis asked when I opened the door to get out of the car. I had slipped my feet in my shoes and put on my jacket.

I nodded. "Yeah, the nausea is gone, but I'm still feeling full."

He let out a chuckle, getting out of the car. "I could always carry you over my shoulder again if you still aren't able to walk," he chuckled.

I let out a snort. "I think I'll manage."

We grabbed our bags from the backseat and headed towards the gym entrance. Coach was already sitting in the locker room when we got there, a folder on his lap. He looked up at us when we joined him, a smile forming on his lips.

"Hi, boys. Thank you for coming in earlier."

Louis and I nodded in acknowledgment. "Can I ask what you wanted to talk to us about?" Louis wondered, raising his eyebrows at Coach.

He nodded. "It's about two things. One, I'd like you two to fix a lineup, what players you want to start playing at the upcoming games and what positions they should have. Second... and this is a bit more serious. They called me from the Arsenal Football Club Academy a few days ago, and they would like to give the best player on our team a scholarship."

Both Louis and I let out loud gasps.

"But it can only be one player, and it's between the two of you, so you are going to have to fight for it."

Chapter 10

Fight against Louis for a scholarship? If it had been anyone else, I would have been so excited about it, but I wasn't sure if I was able to compete against him. I wanted him to be just as happy as I wanted myself to be in life. Sure, the scholarship would be a great opportunity, and I would be thrilled if I got it, but I would feel incredibly awful for Louis if I took that chance away from him.

I was so shocked by Coach's words that I was gaping at him. Meanwhile, Louis let out an excited gasp. "Are you serious? A scholarship for Arsenal Football Club Academy?"

Coach nodded his head. "That's correct. Oh, and please let this stay between the three of us. We wouldn't want any bad blood between you and the other players, yeah?"

Louis and I nodded our heads, me a little slower than him because I was still in shock. Coach flashed us a wide smile before getting up from the bench. "Alright, guys. I hope to see you two play at your very best during the rest of the season, and good luck to both of you."

He patted our shoulders on his way out of the locker room, leaving me and Louis alone. The second Coach shut the door behind himself, Louis turned to me. "The game is on, I see," he said cheekily.

I let out a chuckle. "I guess it is."

A few minutes later, the rest of the guys on the team started slipping into the locker room. Louis and I were sitting beside each other on the bench, tying our cleats and pulling on our shin pads when Niall entered the room. He looked at us curiously while making his way over.

"So, what did Coach want to talk to you about?" He asked us as he had placed his bag on the bench beside me.

I cleared my throat, deciding to be the one to reply. "It actually wasn't as important as he made it out to be. He wanted me and Louis to come up with a lineup for the upcoming games this season," I shrugged. The best part about it was that I didn't have to lie, I just left some parts out.

"Oh, I see. I hope the two of you put me and the guys on the field," Niall said, fluttering his eyelashes.

Louis let out a chuckle. "Of course, mate. Wouldn't dream of anything else," he chuckled before turning to me.

"By the way, when do you have time to fix the lineup, Curly?"

I shrugged my shoulders, biting my bottom lip. "Uh, I can't tomorrow."

He rolled his eyes. "Let me guess. You have work tomorrow, don't you?"

"Yes, Louis, I do. And didn't I tell you to stop teasing me about my job? I don't have rich parents who can afford to buy me whatever I want," I huffed, crossing my arms over my face with a pout on my lips.

The cheeky smile on Louis' face faltered a little by my words. "How about on Wednesday before practice, then?"

I was a little surprised that he decided not to argue with me on that. He liked teasing me, and I thought nothing I said was going to stop him from doing so. Now, he was probably going to bring up my job again in the future, but the fact that he decided to drop it now caught me off guard.

"It works for me."

Right then, it was time to go out to the gym. Louis got up to leave the locker room, and so did I. However, before I had reached the door, I was pulled back by an arm on my shoulder. I turned around in confusion only to see Niall standing behind me with raised eyebrows, a knowing look on his face.

I just shook my head because honestly, if Niall thought things were different between me and Louis, he was wrong. Things weren't different and they would probably never be.

Training went alright, even though I had eaten so much I nearly threw up earlier and didn't have a hair tie to put my hair up in a bun with. We practiced penalties and long shots, which made Liam have to work a lot since he was the goalkeeper. He was a good one too and managed to save a lot of penalty shots.

So far, Louis hadn't shown any sign of competing against me. He kept playing like he usually did during practice, even when we played a game at the end of it and the two of us ended up on different teams. I thought he was going to try slide tackling me or something, just to make a point and show Coach who deserved the scholarship the most, but he didn't.

Maybe he wanted to get the scholarship only if he deserved it? I mean, blackmailing or distracting me wouldn't make him get it fairly, not by hurting me either. I wondered if that was his thought on it, or if it was simply because he would never do something like that to get what he wanted. He wasn't an ass, after all.

When we were back in the locker room, I slipped off my sweaty gear before grabbing my towel and shampoo bottle. I then headed into the showers. Honestly, showering directly after practice was one of the best feelings, especially when it was cold outside. The gym was pretty cold as well, so the hot water felt amazing against my skin.

"Curly, can I borrow some shampoo? I forgot mine at home."

My eyes widened at the angelic voice, making my breath hitch because shit, I was in the shower, which could only mean one thing. He was in the shower as well. I turned my head slightly to the right to see Louis standing under the spray next to me. Quickly shutting my eyes, I inhaled a deep breath before opening them again.

Keep your eyes on his face, Harry. Keep your eyes on his face.

"Uh, sure."

He reached his hand out, expecting me to hand the bottle to him. I grabbed it from the floor and extended it to him, but when he pulled it out of my grasp, I still held my hand out expectantly. He cocked an eyebrow at me. "Wha--"

"You only said you wanted to borrow it," I shrugged, my lips twitching into a cheeky smile.

He let out a snort. "Aren't you funny, Harold?" He said, rolling his eyes.

I dropped my hand, my entire face beaming. "But sure, you can *have* some if you want," I said, making him shake his head in amusement while opening the bottle.

While he squirted some shampoo into his hand, I tried my best not to peek at his ass. I mean, it looked amazing with clothes on, so I could only imagine how it looked without any. Shit, what the hell was I thinking? I should not be thinking about this while I was in the showers with him.

"Here you go."

I shook the thoughts out of my head and snapped back to reality, where Louis was standing, the bottle of shampoo extended in his hand. I grabbed it, putting a smile on my face. "I expect you to lend me some next time."

He looked at me with amusement. "Don't you mean *give* you some, eh?" He said, making my mouth fall open.

Laughing, Louis turned off his shower, grabbed his towel and left. I let out a huff, turning my shower off as well before wrapping my towel around my waist. I couldn't believe I let him use my joke on me.

He was still laughing when I got back to the bench, but this time it was for something Zayn had said or done. The black-haired boy was sitting on the bench opposite us along with Liam and a few other guys. "What's going on?" I wondered, my eyes on Louis although the question was more directed at Zayn.

Zayn slapped his hand on his knee, pointing at Niall who had a grumpy look on his face. "Oh my God. You should have seen his face," he laughed.

Furrowing my eyebrows together, I sat down beside the blonde-haired boy. "What did he do?" I asked Niall since Zayn seemed too busy laughing to explain.

Before he had time to say something, Liam opened his mouth. "He grabbed Niall's towel while he was undressing, so when he was supposed to wrap it around his naked body, it was gone," he explained. He was not as amused as the other guys, but the corners of his lips were threatening to curl.

Zayn let out another bark of laughter when he heard the story all over again.

"Shut up, Zayn. It's not funny," Niall grumbled, who now had the towel wrapped around his waist.

The other guys in the room found it amusing as well, but they had now gone back to mind their own business. I placed a hand on Niall's shoulder. "Don't mind Zayn, Niall. He's just being an ass," I reassured him, making the corners of his lips twitch.

"So, Harry, your birthday is coming up. You have anything specific planned for it?" Zayn asked, changing the subject when all laughter in the room had died down.

I shook my head slowly. "No, I haven't really thought about it, to be honest," I confessed, reaching into my bag to get out the black sweater I had packed.

Partying hadn't really been on my mind lately, but throwing an eighteenth birthday party had always been something I wanted to do in life. There were still a few days left to prepare for it, though. No need to rush things, right?

"Well, your day is getting closer, Harry. I sure hope you're going to come up with something unforgettable," he smirked, making me shake my head in amusement.

"Don't worry, Zayn. I'm only turning eighteen once in my life."

"That's what I wanted to hear," he chuckled, getting up from the bench to head into the shower.

Niall and Liam followed suit, leaving me and Louis alone with the other guys that hadn't been paying attention to our previous conversation. Louis was pulling a forest green Adidas hoodie over his tousled, brown hair, and I couldn't help but look at him. I loved that hoodie on him so much. He looked so sexy in it. I just wanted to wrap my arms around his body and cuddle into him.

"You planning on throwing a big party then, yeah?" Louis wondered, raising his eyebrows at me.

I cleared my throat, trying to get back to reality by blinking my eyes and focusing on his face. His eyes were really dreamy, though. I could stay lost in them forever. "Uh, yeah. I guess that's the plan."

"You guess?" He chuckled.

I shrugged my shoulders. "As I mentioned, I haven't really thought about it yet."

He raised his eyebrows at me. "Your birthday is next week. You should have started thinking about it a long time ago."

I knitted my eyebrows together, pulling my own sweater over my head. "You didn't even *throw* a party when you turned eighteen," I pointed out.

He shook his head, the corners of his lips twitching. "My birthday is on Christmas Eve, Curly. No one wanted to celebrate someone's birthday then."

I rolled my eyes. "It doesn't matter. I don't need a month to prepare for a party. I just need a couple of days."

Louis shrugged his shoulders, a smile on his lips. "If you say so."

We both got dressed, and it didn't take long until Liam, Zayn and Niall reemerged from the showers after that. Niall was hitting Zayn across his head - probably for something he had said - while Liam was walking behind them both, shaking his head in amusement.

"Do you guys need a ride home?" Louis asked them when they had sat down on the benches.

All of them shook their heads. "Dad's picking me and Zayn up," Liam replied.

"Greg is picking me up," Nialls said, smiling.

Louis turned to me then. "I guess that means it'll be just you and I again, Styles," he smirked, making me swallow hard.

Alone with Louis again? That had happened so many times lately that I was starting to lose count. Honestly, it rarely happened at all before. How did that change so drastically? It felt like someone either wanted me to suffer, or to prove me something.

"I guess so," I mumbled, shoving the remaining things in my bag before zipping it closed.

"Hey, Louis, what have you done to your forehead?" Zayn spoke up, making every muscle in my body freeze.

Everything was going so well. Louis had acted normal the entire afternoon thanks to the fact that the incident at the party hadn't been brought up. Why did Zayn have to mention it now? Right, because the makeup covering Louis' bruise had been removed in the shower. Fuck.

Louis pulled his eyebrows together but didn't say anything. I took that as my cue to open my mouth and start explaining. "Louis and I practiced soccer during the weekend, and I managed to knock his forehead with my elbow when we both jumped to head the ball at the same time," I explained, making Zayn's eyebrows shoot up.

"You spent time together just the two of you?"

Why was that so hard to believe? Sure, it hadn't happened too many times in the past, but they made it sound like it was completely out of the question.

"Without killing one another?" He continued, still shocked.

"I know right? That's what I said when they told me they went home together after the party too," Niall piped up.

"Oh, shut it. Louis and I don't bicker all the time," I muttered, glancing at the feathery-haired boy.

Louis looked deep in thought, pulling at his bottom lip with his thumb and forefinger. When he noticed that all of us were watching him, though, he looked up. "What?"

Zayn rolled his eyes. "What are you thinking about, Tommo?"

He shook his head, pursing his lips. "Nothing. Are you ready to go, Harold?"

I nodded my head, getting up from the bench and slinging my bag over my shoulder. "Bye, guys."

I could feel their stares at our backs when we left the locker room, and I bet Louis could too. It was impossible not to because it was obvious that they were both curious and suspicious.

Louis and I didn't say a word until we were sitting in his black sports car. I turned to him, expecting him to say something, *anything* really because he had been quiet for so long that it was making me frustrated. Louis was never this quiet otherwise. It seemed like it only happened whenever the incident at the party was brought up.

"Alright, you need to tell me why it's so necessary to keep what happened at the party a secret from the guys," I told him, staring at the side of his face.

He was looking down at his lap while fiddling with his fingers. It took at least ten seconds until he let out a deep breath and turned to meet my gaze. "You know that Zayn's parents work with mine, right?"

I nodded my head slowly, trying to work out how that had anything to do with it. "Yeah?"

He took another deep breath, running a hand through his hair. "I just don't want my parents to find out what happened, alright?" He explained, looking at me in a way that made me not question him any further. There was something that told me it was a topic that he didn't want to talk about, so I dropped it with a nod of my head.

Louis turned on the engine of the car and drove off towards my house. "Thank you for saving me there, though," he mumbled after a few minutes of silence.

I glanced at him, the corners of my lips twitching a little. "No problem."

Once Louis pulled over outside my house, he turned off the engine and turned to look at me. "About the scholarship. I want this to be a fair competition between us. I don't want it in any way other than because I deserve it. I hope you feel the same way about that too."

"Well, of course."

A smile made its way to his face by my words. "Then I guess I'll see you tomorrow at school, Curly. Oh, and don't forget about Wednesday. Coach won't be happy with us if we don't come up with that lineup soon."

"I won't, Louis," I smiled. "I won't."

Chapter 11

Tuesday turned out to be rather uneventful. I didn't talk to anyone other than the guys at school, and no new, funny customers had entered the diner during the evening either. It was nice to meet Lucas again, though, since it had been a while since the last time.

Before I knew it, Wednesday rolled around. The lads and I were currently sitting in the cafeteria at school, chatting about... girls. It wasn't exactly my favorite topic, but it wasn't like I could do anything about it. Guys our age usually talked about girls, I assumed.

"So, Zayn. Did you get laid on the night of the party?" Louis asked him with raised eyebrows.

A smirk formed on the black-haired guy's face. "Oh, yeah, for sure. And damn, it was nice."

Liam rolled his eyes while Niall laughed.

"What about you, Tommo?" Zayn asked in return, ignoring Liam and Niall's reactions.

This was one of those moments I wanted to press my fingers against my ears to block their voices out, but unfortunately, I couldn't do that now. Instead, I had to bite my tongue and pretend that whatever words escaped Louis' mouth wouldn't affect me.

Louis looked down at his lap for a few seconds before looking up with a smile on his face. "Yeah, but it was only a quicky, though," he smirked.

Niall and Zayn 'ohed' at him, Zayn even wiggling his eyebrows. "Who was it? Was it the girl who hosted the party? What's her name again? Emma?"

"Emily," I said flatly, making all their eyes fall on me. "She's in my Economics class."

"Right," Zayn said, clearing his throat. "Was it her?"

Louis shot me a questioning look before turning back to Zayn when he noticed I wasn't going to meet his gaze. "Eh, yeah. Honestly, I don't remember much of that night, though. I had a lot to drink," he grimaced.

He sure did. I mean, he did fall asleep on me in Gemma's car, after all.

"What about you, Harry? I saw you and that black-haired girl getting it on, eh?" Zayn said, wiggling his eyebrows at me this time.

"Her name is Evelyn," Liam piped up. His eyes were locked on me, seeming curious about what happened between us at the party.

I shrugged my shoulders. "We just got to know each other, that's all. She's a lovely girl, though," I explained honestly, making Zayn furrow his eyebrows together.

"Right."

As if on cue, we were accompanied by Alice and her friends only a couple of minutes later, and Evelyn was one of them. Sadly, the girl who had taken a liking to Louis last time was with them as well, and she didn't hesitate to sit down on the empty chair beside him.

"Hey, boys," Alice greeted with a smile on her face, leaning down to peck Liam on the lips.

Evelyn took a seat next to me, turning to give me a wide smile. "Hi, Harry."

"Evelyn," I smiled back, glancing at Louis through the corner of my eye. He seemed too busy chatting with the blonde girl to even acknowledge me, or any of the other guys either for that matter. I mentally let out a deep sigh.

"I haven't seen much of you since the party, where you suddenly disappeared too," she pouted, looking at the side of my face.

I turned to meet her gaze again. "Oh, right. I'm sorry about that. Something came up and I had to go home. It wasn't anything personal, though, I swear," I promised her, giving her an apologizing look.

She shook her head with a smile on her face. "It's okay, Harry, although I was a little disappointed. I thought things were going great between us."

I swallowed hard, nodding my head slowly. "Yeah, I'm sorry," I apologized again.

We fell into a conversation about what I had missed at the party after I had gone home. Some guy had apparently lashed out at another guy because he had talked to his girlfriend, which had caused chaos. Then a girl had thrown up on the dancefloor, thus creating a mess. Honestly, I didn't feel like I had missed out on anything.

Lunch break was soon finished, and we separated from the girls. The second we were standing at our lockers, Zayn turned to me with raised eyebrows. "Just getting to know each other, huh? From the looks of it, you and that Evelyn girl seem to have gotten quite close."

I rolled my eyes, opening my locker to get my school books out. "It's nothing, Zayn."

He let out a snort. "If that's the case, make sure she knows about it too because she obviously thinks there is something more going on."

Pulling my eyebrows together, I bit my bottom lip. Did Evelyn really like me that much? In that case, how come I hadn't noticed it? I wasn't too caught up in Louis to have missed it, right?

Before I could reply to him, Louis shut my locker right in front of my face. I turned to him questioningly, only to see that he was looking at me with narrowed eyes. "Is that what you call 'getting to know each other' and 'not feeling it'?" He wondered, nodding in the direction of the cafeteria.

I swallowed hard, feeling a bit confused about what he was on about. There was something about him that was so intimidating that I couldn't look away from his blue eyes, though. "What are you talking about?"

He rolled his eyes. "Whatever."

With that said, he walked off without so much as looking back. I turned to Zayn who had no idea what was going on either judging by the shrug of his shoulders. Letting out a deep sigh, I decided to drop it.

If something was bothering Louis, he was going to tell me about it, right?

Once the last bell of the day rang, I gathered my books on the desk and pressed them to my chest before exiting the classroom. On my way back to my locker, I caught a few glances from people I met, some of them even greeting me by my name. And although I didn't know their names in return, I smiled back at them because I didn't want to seem rude.

Louis and Liam were at the lockers when I arrived, too busy getting out their jackets and bags to acknowledge my appearance. "Hey, guys," I greeted to gain their attention.

They both turned to me then, Louis with a hand on his hip. "Alright, Curly. School's over. Where are we headed?"

I had not forgotten about the fact that we were going to meet up to make the lineup today. Honestly, I hadn't been able to stop thinking about it since we agreed on it. Being alone with Louis? Yes, please.

"Um, how about your place? It's been a while since we were there," I suggested.

He shook his head firmly. "No. My sisters are home, and they are always a pain in the ass," he muttered.

I raised my eyebrows at him. "Well, speaking of your sisters, Lottie told me she wanted me to come over soon."

He let out a snort. "Yeah, whatever."

"She also told me she has a crush on me."

Technically, she didn't admit it herself, but it didn't really matter how I found out about it. Louis' reaction was priceless, though. He took a step towards me, pointing a finger at my chest. "Don't you dare try anything with her, Styles," he warned me.

I shook my head in amusement, which he didn't find funny at all. If only he knew she wasn't the Tomlinson I was after, though. "I mean it."

"I would never," I said with a cheeky smile on my face. It was fun to play with him a little because to me, it was so obvious that I would never try anything with Lottie. He didn't need to know just how obvious it was, though.

He let out a growl, taking another step towards me. He was so close that it was almost impossible for me to breathe normally. Shit. "Harold Styles, I swear to God. If you ever touch my sister, I won't hesitate to--"

"As long as you don't try anything with Gemma, I won't go near Lottie," I reasoned, cutting him off.

Even if I had forced myself not to think about it, I couldn't help but be a little bothered by the way he had acted around Gemma the day after the party. I mean, he had changed his mind about going home when she had offered to help him, and he had gladly accepted to eat breakfast with us when she asked him. That couldn't just go unnoticed.

His body visibly relaxed, and he took a step back, running a hand through his fringe. "You think I'm interested in Gemma?"

I shrugged my shoulders, avoiding eye contact with him. "Well, seeing as you practically like every human being with boobs and a butt, I wouldn't be surprised," I muttered, feeling how my heart sunk in my chest at my own words because damn, they were so true. "Besides, you didn't really seem to *not* like her when you were over."

He rolled his eyes, shaking his head. "How about we just stay away from each other's sisters, alright?"

I extended a hand for him to shake, and he took it without hesitation. "Deal."

For some reason, our conversation made me happy. It didn't seem like Louis had any problem with staying away from Gemma, so maybe I had just gotten it all wrong? Either way, I knew I wouldn't have a hard time keeping my promise because the only Tomlinson I was after was him.

Moreover, the fact that I got to hold Louis' hand didn't make me any less happy. I felt electricity shoot through my entire arm just by his touch, and I loved it. It made butterflies erupt in my stomach.

"Alright, guys. Now that you've called a truce, I just wanted to tell you that I'm heading home," Liam announced, making both Louis and I turn to him.

"Oh, right. See you at practice, Liam," Louis replied with a smile on his face.

I said goodbye to him as well before he walked off. Louis and I started making our way through the hallways too once I had fetched my jacket and bag from my locker. "So, we never decided where we are heading," he reminded me.

I shrugged my shoulders. "Let's just go to my place then. I don't think either mom or Gemma is home anyway."

He nodded his head curtly, pulling his bottom lip between his teeth.

Once we got to his car, we threw our bags in the backseat before getting inside. It was still cold outside, so the first thing Louis did was to turn the heat up once he had started the car. We didn't talk much during the ride to my house, but he did make sure to drive safely and not put the radio on a high volume. It seemed like he had actually listened to me for once.

The second he pulled into my driveway, we got out of the car and I got my bag from the backseat before walking over to unlock the front door. As I had suspected, neither Gemma nor mom was home, which meant it was only going to be me and Louis.

We got out of our jackets and shoes before heading to the living room. I sat down on one end of the grey couch while he sat down on the other. "So, what players do you think are worthy to play from the start of the game, Curly?" Louis wondered.

I thought about it for a while before replying. "Well, obviously, I think Liam, Niall and Zayn should get to play. Then I guess Trevor and Tristan are worthy of it as well. What about you?"

"Liam, Niall and Zayn are a given. But Tristan, really? Then we might as well put Ryan in the lineup too," he snorted.

I rolled my eyes. "Just because I don't really like them as a person doesn't mean they aren't good players. We can't not have them in the lineup only because we don't like them," I told him.

He crossed his arms over his chest. "So you do want Ryan in the lineup?"

I shrugged my shoulders. "He's not a bad player, Louis."

He scoffed, shaking his head. "His ego is so fucking big it drives me mad. He's going to fuck things up on the field if he gets to play."

Looking away from him, I bit my bottom lip. "Coach is not going to like us if we don't put him on the field, Louis. I mean, he must have been captain for a reason, right? He's not a bad player, and therefore, he should get to play."

"I can't believe you're even saying this," he muttered. "I mean, after the way he's been treating you, I thought you would never want him to play."

Honestly, I didn't know why I thought Ryan should be in the lineup either. I didn't like him, and I hated his ego, but that didn't make him a bad player. We needed him on the field to be the greatest we could be.

"It doesn't matter how he treats me. What matters is whether we are going to win or lose the games," I mumbled, still not looking at him.

"So, you don't think we'll win if he's not on the field?"

His words made me snap my eyes to him, and I shook my head. "That's not what I'm saying. What I'm saying is that we should play with our greatest players on the field."

He rolled his eyes. "I still don't like the idea, though."

We fell silent for a while before I spoke up again. "I think this is going to take a while. Do you want something to eat before practice?" I asked, making his eyebrows shoot up.

"Are you really offering me food, Curly, or am I imagining this?" He wondered, squinting his eyes at me.

I let out a chuckle. "Just because we usually bicker with each other doesn't mean I'm rude, Louis. I know *I* can't go to practice without getting food into my system, though, so it's up to you," I shrugged.

He didn't seem convinced about the fact that I was being serious, so I tried again. "Didn't I take care of you at the party?" When he didn't say anything, I continued. "Yes, I did, which means you should know that I can be kind."

He rolled his eyes. "Alright, fine. What do you have to offer, Curly?"

With a smile on my face, I got up from the couch and walked to the kitchen. Louis followed suit, leaning against the counter while I got out some groceries from the fridge.

"How about some sandwiches?"

"Works for me," he said, shrugging his shoulders.

I made us some ham sandwiches while Louis watched my every move. It honestly made me nervous, so nervous that I almost dropped one of the sandwiches to the floor. Louis noticed this and let out a bark of laughter, covering his mouth with the back of his hand to stifle it.

I pouted my lips while putting the groceries back in the fridge. "You know, I can eat your sandwich too if you're only going to make fun of me."

He raised his eyebrows at me. "I'm not so sure about that. Last time you ate too much, you couldn't even walk. I don't think you're willing to put yourself in that situation again," he winked.

Crossing my arms over my chest, I let out a huff. "Shut up."

We sat down at the table and started eating our sandwiches in silence before Louis spoke up. "So, have you come up with any ideas regarding your party yet?"

I shook my head slowly. "No, not really. But it seems like you care a lot about this party, so do *you* have any ideas?"

He shrugged his shoulders, a cheeky smile forming on his lips. "Maybe I have a few."

I narrowed my eyes suspiciously. "Is this because you never had a birthday party of your own?" I couldn't help but ask him.

When he only pursed his lips, I tilted my head to the side. "Alright, so what do you suggest I do for *my* birthday party, then?"

The cheeky smile returned to his lips. "Well, I think you should start everything off by inviting a lot of people. You can't have a birthday party without any people there. Then, I suggest you rent a facility because not to be rude, but your house is too small for a big party. You should also buy a lot of alcohol, and by a lot, I mean *a lot*. After that--"

"Alright, alright. I think I get it. There's just one problem, though."

He looked at me as if I had grown a third eye, which caused me to glare at him. "I don't have the money, Louis."

He furrowed his eyebrows together, biting his bottom lip. It took a few seconds until he opened his mouth to reply. "Well, since I never had a birthday party of my own, I am willing to pay for yours. I'm not letting you miss out on it just because you can't afford it."

I wanted to grimace at the fact that I couldn't afford it, but I was too busy trying to handle the feelings that welled up inside me. Louis was willing to pay for my birthday party? No, I must have heard wrong. There was no way he just said that.

"You what?"

He shrugged his shoulders. "I mean, it's not like I have an issue with money," he said as if it wasn't a big deal. But it was. It was a huge deal to me.

"I don't know if I can let you do that. I mean, what have I done to deserve that from you? Sure, I took care of you when you got hurt, but it definitely wasn't enough for you to do this for me," I rambled.

He rolled his eyes, shaking his head. "See it as a birthday present. Plus, I know what it's like to miss out on your eighteenth birthday party. I don't want you to do it as well."

Had I misunderstood Louis all along? Maybe I didn't know him after all these years? Because this person sitting in front of me right now was foreign to me. Louis had never done something like this to me before. Hell, I couldn't even recall that he had done a favor like this to anyone before.

So, how come that had suddenly changed?

"There is just one catch," he said. "If I'm paying for it, you're going to let me help you arrange everything."

Chapter 12

That was how Louis and I ended up hanging out with each other basically every day after school that following week. If we had practice, we went to my place to discuss things before Louis drove us to the gym. If I had to go to work, he drove me home after school to discuss things with me during the ride. Then he would wait in the car while I got changed before driving me to my job where he dropped me off.

To say I was happy would be an understatement. Louis and I had never spent so much time together before, and although we didn't share the same thoughts all the time and would bicker with each other occasionally, we did have a lot of fun. We mostly just teased each other, which made my heart flutter in my chest every time it happened because I couldn't help but love it. The mere fact that we got along somehow made me all fussy inside.

It was now Thursday, the day before we had planned to have the party, and I was sitting in the car with Louis after school, discussing what alcohol he was going to buy after dropping me off at work. My real birthday wasn't until Sunday, but we figured Friday would be the best day to throw the party on. Everyone was in the mood to go out once the school week was over to celebrate a little.

"So, how many vodka bottles do you think will be necessary?" I wondered, sitting in the passenger seat with Louis' phone in my hands. I was typing everything down so he would be able to check it if he forgot something later on.

"Um, we've invited about sixty people, so you are surely going to need at least fifteen."

When he saw my eyebrows shoot up, he rolled his eyes. "Remember, we are teenagers, Curly. Teenagers are practically alcoholics."

I let out a snort. "Fifteen bottles seem a lot, though. I mean, vodka is *one* of the things we're going to be serving, not the only one. I think ten will be more than enough," I tried to reason, but he wouldn't have it.

"Look, this is going to be a party that I, Louis Tomlinson, have participated in arranging. We are not skimping on the alcohol. Besides, if it all doesn't go to use, we could just have it on another occasion. There's no harm in buying too much alcohol, but it'll be quite embarrassing if we buy too little," he stated, his gaze on the road.

Alright, maybe he did have a point. It was just the fact that he was paying for everything that made me want to step on the pedal. It just felt wrong to make him pay for everything when it was my party.

"It's just... It feels so wrong, you know? I'm not used to getting all I want and be able to go crazy on buying a lot of stuff, so I guess this is just what I would normally think. Besides, it feels wrong to make you pay for all of this. Everything is going to be so expensive. It already is expensive enough, and we haven't even bought the alcohol yet. We've basically only rented the facility so far," I mumbled.

He rolled his eyes. "Haven't I already told you not to think about that? I have money, Curly. Don't worry about it."

I furrowed my eyebrows. "How can I not think about it when I work every other day to make my own money? Maybe money isn't valuable to you, but it is to me. I cherish every pound I have on my bank account," I huffed.

He went quiet then, gripping the steering wheel tightly. It took at least one minute until he opened his mouth to reply. "Do you know how lucky you are, though? I would switch places with you any day."

Now that caught me off guard. Did he actually know what he was talking about? Who wouldn't want to have so much money that you didn't have to worry about it? "Are you making fun of me?" I asked with a scowl on my face.

He shook his head. "No. No, I'm not."

The tone he was using caught me off guard as well. He sounded so honest that I lost the ability to talk. What could I say? I had no idea what was going on inside his head right now, and I didn't want to say something that would upset him.

Thankfully, we arrived at the diner right then, so I didn't have to come up with something to say. However, to my surprise, Louis pulled over and turned off the car. Usually, he would just pull over at the sidewalk and drop me off, but this time, he parked the car in an empty spot.

I turned to him in confusion. "Wha--"

"I'm hungry," he cut me off with a faint smile on his face while shrugging his shoulders.

His reply made me even more confused. "I thought you were going to buy the alcohol?"

He scrunched his nose up in a way that made my heart race in my chest. "That can wait. I have the entire evening to do that."

I pursed my lips. "Well, then. I'll be in the diner in just a few minutes. I'm just going to go through the backdoor and put on my apron," I smiled before opening the car door and getting out.

When I had shut the door behind me with my back turned to him, I couldn't help the wide grin that broke out on my face. Louis was going to enter the diner while I was there working. As far as I could remember, that had never happened before, and then his family had ordered take away quite a few times in the past. Was it weird that I had butterflies in my stomach?

I greeted Richard quickly once I had shoved my jacket into my locker and switched my shoes. I noticed that Lucas was working the cash register when I entered the diner and decided to stop there considering I knew it was the best place to be when Louis entered the building. I could see the door clearly from here.

"Good afternoon, Lucas," I greeted, the wide grin still prominent on my lips.

My mood caught the blonde-haired guy by surprise. "What's causing that huge smile on your face, my friend? Are you that happy to see me?" He joked while chuckling.

"Of course, Lucas. Who wouldn't be happy to see you?" I smirked, playing along.

He shook his head, clearly amused. "Well, I'm glad then."

I was just about to make another comment when the door was pushed open by the feathery-haired boy I had the honor to call one of my best friends (although I wanted him to be more than that). He was in the action of swiping his brown fringe to the side when his eyes fell on us, a crinkle forming between his eyebrows.

He made his way over, and during every step he took, I could feel my heart beating faster and faster. How did he do that?

"Hello, there. How can I help you?" Lucas asked him politely, even though Louis wasn't paying attention to him. He was too busy looking at me.

"Curly here will help me, won't you?" Louis said, raising his eyebrows at me expectantly.

"I'm sorry, but Harry's job does not incl--"

I cut him off by raising a hand. "It's okay, Lucas. He's a friend," I explained, giving him a smile.

Lucas' mouth formed the shape of an 'o' before he turned back to Louis with a warm smile on his lips. "Well, then. It's nice to meet you..."

"Louis."

Lucas gave him a nod. "I'm Lucas, Harry's co-worker."

Louis looked him up and down quickly before his eyes found their way back to me. "I can see that."

I cleared my throat, sensing the tension in the air. Was Louis usually like this when he met new people? For some reason, I doubted that. This must be an exception.

"So, what would you like, Louis? Some chicken stew maybe? Or the steak?" I wondered, and the muscles in his face visibly relaxed.

"What do you recommend, Curly?" He questioned, wiggling his eyebrows.

I couldn't help but chuckle at his facial expression. "Um, I think I'd say the chicken stew. It's probably the best one I've ever had," I told him truthfully.

His eyebrows shot up. "Oh, it is now? Well, then I should probably choose something else. Something's telling me you have a horrid taste," he teased, making my mouth fall open.

"I do not!" I gasped, turning to Lucas. "Tell Louis I'm not joking about the stew!"

He was amused by my and Louis' conversation. "Well, actually, it's not one of my favorites, but it's not bad," he shrugged, making Louis let out a loud bark of laughter.

"See! I told you so, Curly," he said smugly.

It was hard not to like either of Lucas or Louis, so I knew the two of them would get along if they wanted to. Louis probably just had a hard time warming up to some people, which must be the reason behind his behavior.

I rolled my eyes, placing a hand on my hip. "Alright then. What do *you* recommend, Lucas?" I asked, raising my eyebrows expectantly at him.

He shrugged his shoulders. "My favorite is the steak with fries and barbecue sauce. You just can't go wrong with that."

Louis nodded his head slowly, seeming impressed. "That's actually true. I think I'll take that one."

I let out a huff, crossing my arms over my chest. Louis noticed this and turned to me with an amused smile on his face. "I'm sorry, Curly. I promise I'll try the chicken stew next time," he smirked.

Next time? Did that mean he was going to eat here again? Or was he talking about the next time his family would order takeaway from here? I couldn't help but hope for the prior.

I pouted my lips as Lucas charged Louis and sent the order to the kitchen. Once Louis had paid for his food, he turned to me again. "So, what table do you suggest I sit, Harold?"

I couldn't help but let my lips form into a smile at the simple fact that he was asking me this question. "I'll show you."

I took him to a table in the corner by the windows. I loved that table because no one really paid attention to it, and that meant you didn't have anyone who stared at you while eating.

"Here it is," I announced, crossing my arms over my chest.

He nodded his head with a thoughtful look on his face. "It's actually not that bad. I like secluded tables."

I smiled to myself, happy that I had managed to please him. "Great. I'll be back with your food in a little bit."

When I made a move to leave, he grabbed my wrist to stop me. Confused, I turned around to face him again. "There aren't that many customers right now. Do you have to go already?" He asked, almost sheepishly.

It took me by surprise. Louis was never that person who was unsure of what he said. However, looking around the diner, I noticed that he was right. So, I shrugged my shoulders and sat down in the seat opposite the one he was about to take. If I needed to go back to work, they would just call me, right? Besides, I wasn't the only waiter working this shift, so I was positive they wouldn't even notice.

"I just don't want to look like a complete fool who's sitting here all by myself, you know?" He grimaced, making my heart sink a little. So, it wasn't because he wanted my company specifically?

I nodded curtly without saying anything.

He took that as a sign to start a new conversation. "So, how come you've never mentioned you have such close friends at work?" He asked, raising his eyebrows at me.

"Um..." I trailed off, biting my bottom lip. "I don't know. Lucas and I aren't that close. We just talk to each other when we are here," I shrugged.

Maybe I hadn't mentioned anything to him because before we started arranging my birthday party, we didn't really speak to each other as we did now. Honestly, mentioning that I had friends at work would have never crossed my mind to tell him back then.

The real question was; would it even have done so now? Because truth be told, I had no idea where Louis and I were standing right now. What level of our friendship were we on? Did we even talk about personal stuff with each other? Not really, so why would it have crossed my mind to tell him about Lucas?

I shook my head to myself, looking down at the surface of the table. I wish things were different. I wish I could tell him anything. I *wanted* to be able to tell him everything that was going on in my life. I wanted him to know every single detail of it, but no. Louis wasn't interested in having that relationship with me.

"What are you thinking about, Curly?" Louis asked, snapping me back to reality.

I looked up at him, furrowing my eyebrows together. "Nothing," I muttered.

He was quiet for a while, searching my features before letting it drop. "Alright, so Lucas isn't someone you'd want to come to your eighteenth birthday party?"

"I've already invited him."

Louis seemed surprised by this. "Oh, and you didn't think of mentioning that to me either?" He huffed. "Is there anyone else you've invited that I don't know of, huh?"

I rolled my eyes. "Last time I checked, it's my birthday party. Don't I get to decide who's going to be there then?"

He muttered something under his breath as he averted his gaze. "I just thought since I'm helping you arrange the whole thing that I should be informed of how many people there are going to be there. Don't you agree with that?"

I looked down at the surface of the table, secretly wondering why this mattered so much to him. Why did he care that I had invited someone that I hadn't told him about? It wasn't like it was going to make a difference anyway.

"It's just Lucas I have invited apart from the other ones, so you don't really have anything to worry about," I told him, looking him in the eyes.

With that said, I got up from the chair, knowing that his food was going to be ready any minute now. "I'll be back with your food in a sec."

When I got back to Lucas at the counter, he turned to me. "You and Louis fighting over something?" He wondered, nodding in the direction of the mentioned boy. He was now sitting with his phone in his hands, typing away on it.

I shook my head. "No. Things are just... complicated."

Lucas hummed. "How so?"

Letting out a sigh, I turned to look at him. "It's hard to explain. I don't think I could even if I tried," I grimaced.

A small smile made its way to his face then. "I see."

There was something about his smile that told me he suspected something. I didn't have time to question him about it, though, because right then, I was called to the kitchen.

Richard handed me Louis' food along with another plate with some fried chicken and fries. I took them and went back to the diner to serve the chicken and fries first before walking over to Louis, who was still typing on his phone.

"Bon appetite!"

Louis looked up from his device, locking eyes with me for a second before taking a look at the food in front of him. "Hmm, looks nice," he mumbled, placing his phone on the table.

I was about to walk away from him when he stopped me this time as well. "I'm buying the alcohol after this, then I'll come back to drive you home once you get off your shift. Alright, Curly?"

My eyes widened in shock. Was he being serious?

"Uh, sure."

"Great," he smiled.

Chapter 13

Once Louis had dropped me off at home later that evening, the first thing I noticed when I entered the house was that Gemma was in the living room. She had her legs propped up on the coffee table just like the last time, but she had a bowl of popcorn on her lap now as well.

The second she saw me in the doorway, she grabbed the TV-remote and pressed pause. "Baby brother, come sit for a sec," she ordered, patting the couch beside her.

"I'm not a baby, Gems," I muttered, rolling my eyes. However, I did as she said anyway and walked over to sit down beside her. "As a matter of fact, I'm turning eighteen in three days."

She tilted her head to the side. "You'll always be my baby, though," she smiled.

I pouted my lips, making her chuckle. "On another note," she said, clearing her throat. "I've noticed that Louis' been around a lot lately."

I could feel how every muscle in my body froze to ice, and I instantly went rigid. "He has?" I chuckled dryly, playing dumb.

She snorted, shaking her head. "Yeah? I mean, sure, he's one of your best friends, but I never thought you spent so much time with him just the two of you. It's always been Niall you hang around with when the other boys aren't here as well."

"He's been helping me arrange my birthday party," I explained, feeling how my body relaxed by the second because I could tell her the truth this time without having to lie about it. Usually, I always had to dodge it whenever Louis was brought up in our conversations because I didn't want her to find out about my feelings for him.

Her eyes widened in surprise. "Oh, really? How come Louis' helping you out of all people? I didn't think you were that close. I mean, sure, you took care of him after that party, but I thought that was just a one-time thing?"

She was right. We weren't that close, but that didn't mean I didn't want us to be.

I shrugged my shoulders. "He offered to help me one day. I think it's mostly because he never had a party of his own when he turned eighteen."

To be honest, I wasn't entirely sure why he offered to help me with my party this much. I mean, he was paying for *everything*, and he literally didn't get anything in return except for helping me arrange it. He must be so delighted.

However, he did mention that he didn't want me to miss out on my eighteenth birthday party since he knew what it felt like to do so. Who knew, maybe the main reason was that he was simply empathetic?

"That's nice of him. I've always had a feeling he's a great guy," she smiled warmly.

"He is," I said, and I couldn't help but let my lips curl into a smile of my own.

"So, when is this party, and why haven't you mentioned anything about it to me?" She wanted to know, raising her eyebrows at me.

I shrugged my shoulders. "It's tomorrow, but I don't really find it a big deal, which is why I haven't mentioned anything, I guess. Sure, it's my eighteenth birthday, but I haven't really put too much thought into it," I explained.

"You're not excited about it. Is that what you're trying to say?"

I pulled my eyebrows together, shaking my head. "No. I am excited. I'm actually very excited, especially now after Louis' help. I don't think I would have ever come near a party like this if it weren't for him. I guess the reason I pushed it to the side before he offered to help was just that I don't look forward to being the center of attention, and I don't want people to feel like they have to celebrate me," I grimaced.

Plus, I didn't want to witness Louis being with yet another girl, but I decided to leave that part out.

She tilted her head to the side, shaking her head with a smile on her face. "You're putting yourself down, H. I'm sure there are a lot of people who want to celebrate you. I get what you mean, though. We've been taught not to be full of ourselves. Mom made sure we would never become stuck up assholes, but in this case, I think you should serve yourself, H. You deserve to have a big party and be the center of it. People want to be there for you because even if you might not believe it, I'm sure you have a lot of people caring about you."

I bit my bottom lip, looking away from her. Maybe she was right. Maybe I should serve myself and let myself be in the center without feeling weird about it. You only turned eighteen once after all, and if people didn't want to be there for me, they wouldn't show up, right? And so what if Louis was going to find a girl to play around with? I had seen that before, and I wasn't going to let it bother me. Not tomorrow.

"You may be right," I mumbled, my eyes finding hers again.

"I know I am," she smirked, patting me on the thigh. "Besides, Louis has helped you arrange this party, so you should not let him down."

The corner of my lips twitched. "I won't."

During the lunch break the next day, the lads and I were sitting at a table in the cafeteria, chatting away like usual. Only today, the main topic was my party that I was throwing this evening. Alice was there as well, along with the blonde girl who had seemed to find a strong liking of Louis. I could tell because this wasn't the first time she had tried flirting with him, and she was literally sitting as close to him as possible, their arms even brushing together.

It was bugging me, even after my attempts at trying to persuade myself into thinking that seeing Louis with another girl wasn't going to bother me today. The plan was already backfiring, and the party hadn't even started yet. I was telling myself that I was not going to let it bother me tonight, though.

At the moment, however, it was bugging me so much that I couldn't take my eyes off of them, even if the lads were talking about my party. Honestly, it was difficult to grasp what they were saying specifically because the only thing I could focus on was Louis and that girl.

"So, who's going to be there tonight, Harry?" Zayn asked, his eyes directed at me.

I averted my gaze from the two of them to look at Zayn. "Um, I have invited the guys on the soccer team and quite a lot of other people," I replied.

"Are there going to be a lot of girls?" Niall asked excitedly, making me want to roll my eyes.

I didn't know what made me do what I did next, but I wanted to take Louis' attention away from that girl, so what came out of my mouth wasn't really thought-through. "I don't know. Louis, have we invited a lot of girls?" I asked, raising my eyebrows at the feathery-haired guy questioningly.

Louis snapped his head to us at the mention of his name, his eyes widening slightly when he noticed I had revealed the fact that he was involved in the arrangement of the party.

We hadn't told any of the boys about this. They didn't even know that we had been hanging out after school the entire week. They only thought Louis had driven me home to drop me off, not to hang out, and that fact alone had made Niall suspicious.

"Louis?" "We?" Niall and Liam let out in unison, and they exchanged surprised looks together with Zayn. Alice looked a bit surprised as well.

Louis flashed me a pointed look, and I could tell he wondered why I had mentioned it now when we hadn't brought it up during the entire week. I didn't have anything to hide, though. So what if the guys found out Louis had helped me arrange the party? They were probably going to find out about it anyway. Besides, what did we have to hide?

"Um, yeah. I've helped Curly here arrange the party," Louis shrugged as if it wasn't a big deal.

Niall's mouth fell open, and so did Liam's.

"You mean that you guys have managed to arrange something together without getting on each other's nerves? Is that even possible?" Zayn asked incredulously.

I rolled my eyes at his comment, but before I could reply to him, Niall beat me to it. "Why would you even want to help him arrange it? I mean, not to be rude or anything, but I didn't think you were that close?" He asked Louis.

"Why not?" Louis asked, knitting his eyebrows together. "It seemed like Harold here wasn't about to start preparing the party, so I thought I might as well help him get started. Then I ended up helping him arrange the whole thing," he explained.

I didn't know why he decided not to tell the entire truth, but I didn't question him about it. Maybe he just didn't want to bring up everything about his own birthday party that never took place? I mean, I knew he didn't want to seem weak in front of other people, and feeling sad about missing out on a birthday party might seem weak.

They were still shocked when I turned to Louis, raising my eyebrows at him. "You never answered my question."

He let out a chuckle, turning to the blonde girl sitting beside him for a second before looking back at me. "You know just as well as I that we have invited quite a lot of girls now, don't you, Curly?"

And here I was, hoping that my question was going to take his attention away from that blondie. It wasn't working very well, it seemed. With a huff, I crossed my arms over my chest, ignoring the big smirk on Louis' face.

"I'm still shocked by the fact that you managed to arrange something together without hating on one another," Zayn said, shaking his head in disbelief.

It seemed like Niall's interest in how many girls there were going to be at the party had slipped his mind because he nodded his head in agreement.

"That, and that they managed to do the whole thing without one of them calling it quits along the way."

Louis and I went to the facility as soon as we had finished school. The lads had yet again shaken their heads in disbelief when we left school together, this time knowing that the two of us were going to spend time with one another.

Honestly, I thought they were exaggerating. I never really got mad at Louis, even if we bickered sometimes. It was all just fun and games, nothing serious. So, I didn't understand why they were so shocked by the fact that we had managed to arrange the party together. Maybe they had different opinions on our relationship than I did.

As soon as Louis had parked the car outside the big, white building that was located in the center of the town, we got out to walk over to the big, black door. It was still cold outside, being late January and all, but it was manageable. The ground wasn't covered in slush as it had been the first day of school, but a white layer of snow was covering it beautifully again.

Louis reached into the pocket of his black jeans to get out the key we had received from the owner of the facility. He then fit it in the lock and turned it. The second he yanked the door open, a big room with long tables and a crazy amount of chairs made of wood was revealed. There was even a stage in there, right in front of the tables.

My eyes widened in surprise. "Wow, this is amazing!" I breathed.

Louis had a smug smile on his face when I turned to look at him, his arms crossed over his chest. "I've been to a wedding party here once, so I knew what it had to offer."

I couldn't help but roll my eyes at that. Of course he knew what he was getting into when he decided this was the facility he was going to rent. He would never choose a place he didn't know anything about.

"I'm not surprised about that."

He tilted his head to the side, raising his eyebrows at me. "Why's that?"

I shook my head with a grin on my face. "You'd never just choose any facility. You would make sure it'll live up to your standards," I chuckled.

He pursed his lips. "Well, we can't throw a party in a shit hole, now can we?"

I rolled my eyes again, taking a step inside the building. To my surprise, Louis placed a hand between my shoulder blades to guide me forward. The gesture caught me off guard although I knew it didn't mean the same thing to him as it did to me. It even made me halt in my steps, which resulted in me having to force muscles to start working again in case I didn't want him to notice anything. Nothing could stop my heart from racing, though.

He showed me the kitchen that was on the left side of the building, telling me where we should keep the alcohol and snacks. He also showed me where the toilets were before turning to me with a smile on his face. "Now, all we have to do is make this look like a place where it's going to be a party, and not just some big, boring room."

I nodded my head in agreement. "Let's do this."

Thankfully, Louis had already bought the decorations, which he kept in his car, so he went out to go fetch them. Meanwhile, I took another look around the room. I couldn't understand why Louis wanted to do this for me. It was so hard to believe because I had never had anyone do something like this for me before, so the fact that it was him out of all people made it feel like I was dreaming. It was just surreal, like a dream come true.

"Alright, Curly. Let's get started!"

It took an hour for us until we were finished decorating the place, but hell, it was worth it because it really looked like someone was arranging a party in here now. There were lights, there were glasses, there were silver balloons, bowls, snacks and more.

"I'll just have to pick up the cake on my way back here later," Louis smiled smugly.

"Cake?" I asked, turning to him in confusion. We hadn't spoken about a cake when we had discussed the party.

He rolled his eyes. "We can't have a birthday party without a cake, duh," he said matter-of-factly.

I shook my head, letting out a sigh. "This is already too much, Louis. I can't believe you wanted to throw your money on all this in the first place."

He crossed his arms over his chest. "As I said, Curly, money is not an issue for me. Besides, I can't have you miss out on your eighteenth birthday party because of the lack of money," he explained. "And, I didn't expect I would say this, but it's actually been quite fun arranging this party with you. At first, I kind of wanted to come up with all the ideas myself, but I'm happy it turned out like this. It honestly feels like this is partly my birthday party as well."

I couldn't help the smile that formed on my lips. "I'm glad you feel that way, and I'm sorry you never had the opportunity to celebrate your own birthday like this," I grimaced.

He waved a hand in dismissal, although I could see that it was bothering him. "Don't think about it. Let's just party like we never have before. I think we both deserve it."

I nodded my head, feeling how a thought slowly came to mind, and I was suddenly smirking at him. "Just make sure you don't drink too much, though. We wouldn't want you to fall and hit your head again now, would we?" I said, raising my eyebrows at him in a joking manner.

He instantly caught on, shaking his head in amusement. "Make sure you don't eat too much of those snacks, then. I don't really feel like carrying you home in the middle of the night just because you're too full to walk, alright?" He winked, making my mouth fall open.

How did he always manage to have the last word and make me speechless? It was a mystery to me, and I did not like it. Not one bit.

Chapter 14

I was standing in front of my mirror, examining myself when Gemma burst through the door. I turned to her abruptly, my mouth falling open. "Gemma, you can't just barge in like that!" I gasped. "I could've been naked for all I know!"

She rolled her eyes, placing a hand on her hip. "Are you ready?" She asked, ignoring what I just said completely.

I took a look at my reflection in the mirror again. I was wearing another black button-up than the one I had at Emily's party along with a pair of black, skinny jeans that were ripped at the knees. I had my black boots on my feet, and my curls were hanging loosely down the sides of my face, reaching just below my earlobes.

"Yup, I'm ready."

I could see her tilting her head to the side skeptically through the mirror. "No, you're not. You are not wearing that to your eighteenth birthday party."

I looked down at my outfit before looking back at her with a frown on my face. "What's wrong with this?"

She just shook her head, walking over to my closet. "This is your party, Harry, not anyone else's. You're going to be the center of attention tonight, so you can't wear plain black," she explained. "Here."

She tossed me a polka dot marron button-up shirt. "It's not the best, but it's better than the black one," she confirmed, crossing her arms over her chest.

I rolled my eyes at her dominant manner as I unbuttoned the black shirt I was wearing. Once I had switched it to the polka dot button-up, I turned to her again, spreading my arms out. "Is this okay, then?"

A smile formed on her lips as she nodded her head. "Yep, much better. You look hot, brother."

I let out a snort, turning around to look at myself in the mirror again. "I really don't, and you should stop with your incest comments. It's kind of creepy, you know?"

She let out a loud bark of laughter. "Oh, shut up. You know you love it," she winked, making me roll my eyes.

"Can you drive me to the party now? The lads are probably waiting for me to get there."

Louis, Liam, Zayn and Niall were supposed to show up about an hour before all the guests were invited. We wanted to have a small get-together with just the five of us before the real party started.

"Sure."

The second Gemma and I were sitting in her car and she had pulled out of the driveway, she turned to me with a small smile on her face. "So, is there anyone specific you're trying to impress tonight?" She asked, wiggling her eyebrows.

I was a bit confused by her question, so I decided to joke it off. "You're acting like a mom to her ten-year-old child," I commented, making us both burst out into laughter for a couple of seconds.

When we had calmed down, she shook her head. "Alright, maybe I was being a little childish, but I am genuinely curious. Is there anyone you like at the moment?"

I couldn't help but swallow hard. I wasn't expecting her to ask me that question. "Um, there might be someone, but I'm not telling you more than that."

Her mouth fell open in both shock and disappointment. "I can't believe you haven't told me about it! Why can't I know who it is?"

Because you would tell him about it either intentionally or accidentally.

"Because I want to keep it a secret. It's never going to be us anyway," I said, trying to make it seem like it didn't matter to me by shrugging my shoulders. It did matter, though. I really wanted me and Louis to be together, even if it was never going to happen.

She furrowed her eyebrows together. "How can you be so sure about that?"

I didn't know how to answer her without saying too much, so I just stuck to something simple. "It's just someone I am sure will never be attracted to me."

Gemma let out a snort. "Impossible. You're putting yourself down again, H. I'm sure that whoever the person is will find it hard not to like you if you just show them how you feel," she promised me.

I bit my bottom lip, looking out the window without saying anything. When she noticed that I wasn't going to reply, she opened her mouth to speak again. "Can I ask if it's a girl or a boy?"

When I turned to look at her, I could see that she had knitted her eyebrows together as if she was thinking deeply about something. With a sigh, I looked down at my lap. "It's a guy, and he's straight. So, now you know," I confessed, avoiding her gaze.

She was quiet for a while, still thinking deeply, I assumed. However, her silence made me nervous, so nervous that I was fiddling with my fingers on my lap while patiently waiting for her to say something, anything about what I had just admitted.

"You know, even the straightest people are a little bit gay. Haven't you heard of that?" She asked me, and through the corner of my eye, I could see her looking at me with a smile on her face.

Her attempt at lightening the mood succeeded because I could feel the corners of my lips twitching at her words. I shook my head, a little chuckle escaping my lips. "I have heard of it, but I don't think it's true."

She let out a snort. "I'm sure that everyone can be a little bit gay for you, though, H. Something's telling me you're quite irresistible."

For some reason, her words made me laugh. "You seriously have to stop with those incest comments, Gems. You really are making me uncomfortable."

When we arrived at the facility, Louis, Zayn, Liam and Niall were already there, waiting for me. By the looks of it, they hadn't been there for too long, though, because otherwise, they would be freezing their asses off right now. It was pretty cold outside, after all.

The second Gemma stopped the car, I said goodbye to her before getting out. The lads turned to me when I had shut the door behind me, wide smiles breaking out on their faces.

"Happy birthday!" Niall exclaimed, being the first one to take a step forward and wrap his arms around me.

I rolled my eyes at the comment. "It's not my birthday, Niall. Besides, you have already met me today," I chuckled, reciprocating the hug.

When we pulled away, he flashed me a crooked smile. "We're still celebrating you today, though, so might as well call it your birthday," he shrugged.

I shook my head to myself, the corners of my lips twitching. My eyes then fell to the other lads who were waiting to greet me as well. It honestly felt a little weird having so much attention directed at me already. I wasn't used to it. Well, at least not when it came to my closest friends.

Once I had hugged Liam and Zayn, I turned to Louis who had a smirk on his face, which didn't really surprise me. "What are you smirking at?" I asked, raising my eyebrows at him.

He was dressed in a pair of blue jeans along with a tight, grey button-up with black dots that was unfolded at the sleeves. His hair was perfectly swept to the side, making him look really, fucking hot. I just wanted to go over and bury my hands in his hair and-- No, that was not going to happen.

Louis shook his head, letting out a little laugh. "I see you made it."

I placed my hand on my hip, sticking it out. "Of course I did," I said, flicking my hair nonchalantly.

All of them laughed at me, Louis' smile widening.

"It seems like you actually did manage to fix this party together. I'm beyond proud of you," Zayn commented, looking between me and Louis impressively.

Louis decided to wrap his arm around my shoulders, bringing me close to his side. I tried my best to act normal about it, although my heart instantly started racing in my chest. Let's not begin speaking of the way goosebumps rose on my skin. I was so gone for this boy that it wasn't even funny. "I did most of it, though, didn't I, Curly?" He teased, looking at me with feigned expectancy.

I rolled my eyes at him. "It may have been your plan to do it all by yourself, but I didn't let you," I smirked, making him let out a loud bark of laughter.

He turned to the other guys, shaking his head. "If Harry had gotten to decide, we would be running out on alcohol in like an hour, no doubt about it. There wouldn't be these many people attending either, I'm sure," he pointed out.

There wouldn't even be a party without his help. He was paying for everything, after all. If I had arranged it all by myself, we would have been at my house, which in itself would have resulted in fewer people and less alcohol, so he was right. I wasn't going to give it to him, though.

The lads seemed amused by my and Louis' banter because they were all smiling at us.

"Heeey, I'm not used to throwing big parties, is all," I whined, sticking my bottom lip out in a pout.

Louis tapped my shoulder lightly. "It's okay, Curly. I was here to help you," he joked, making the corners of my lips twitch.

The fact that he was standing so close made it easy for me to get lost inside his blue irises. I loved his eyes. They were just the perfect shade of blue, and they were framed by these long, golden eyelashes. I could look into his eyes for an entire day without getting tired of it.

"Alright, shall we go inside?" Liam suggested, nodding his head towards the grey door. "It's freezing out here."

We all agreed and started making our way towards the entrance. Sadly, Louis dropped his arm from my shoulders, leaving me colder than I already was. I tried not to think too much about it, though. This night was supposed to be one of the greatest nights of my life, and I was not going to let anything ruin that.

I turned the door handle, preparing myself to see the huge, decorated room. However, what I was met with caught me completely off guard.

"Happy birthday, Harry!"

Everyone was already here, gathered right in front of me. They were all smiling as they shouted out the greeting, their arms thrown in the air. I was so shocked that I almost fell backward. If it weren't for someone catching me, I would have. I couldn't believe my eyes. Were they all here because of me?

The feeling that exploded in my chest couldn't be described. I mean, this was probably the greatest thing I had ever experienced. "Oh my God," I breathed, reaching my hand up to cover my mouth in shock.

I could feel a pat on my back before people started walking forward to greet me personally. They hugged me, laughing when they saw my face.

"You didn't expect this, did you?" Lucas smiled at me when he walked over to greet me.

I shook my head, looking behind me to see if the guys were still there. They were, but they were busy talking to other people. "Did they plan this?" I asked, and Lucas nodded his head.

"Yeah. I don't know whose idea it was, but I'm positive Louis was the one who spread the word around. He helped you arrange all this, didn't he?"

I couldn't help the smile that formed on my lips. "Yeah, he did."

Was that why Louis wanted to know what people were invited to the party? So he could inform them that they were going to surprise me?

Before Lucas could say anything else, I felt a hand on my shoulder. "Took you by surprise, didn't it?" Louis smiled, raising his eyebrows at me in amusement.

"It sure did. Was it your idea?" I couldn't help but ask. I really wanted to know this for some reason.

He tilted his head to the side. "Yup, it was. My idea, and my idea only," he said proudly, making me chuckle. It also made my heart swell because damn, he had done all this for me? That fact made butterflies erupt in my stomach.

"I'll see you around, Curly," he smiled before dropping his hand and walking away.

I turned back to Lucas who was looking in the direction Louis just disappeared. "He really cares about you, doesn't he?"

I could feel my cheeks heat up as I shook my head. "No. I'm sure it was all just to make the party as great as possible."

Lucas raised his eyebrows at me for a few seconds before shrugging it off. "You want to go find something to drink?" He asked, changing the topic.

A smile formed on my lips. "Sure."

Louis and I had pushed the long tables to the walls so the dance floor would take up most of the room, which was a good thing because damn, there were really a lot of people in here. I also noticed that it was a good thing that I had helped set it all up because now I knew exactly where the drinks were, so I didn't have to search for them.

Did we really invite all these people? I wasn't sure if I even knew these many teenagers. Louis must have invited people that I didn't even know.

On our way to the table, someone grabbed my hand from behind, making me halt in my steps. Lucas, who was walking on my other side stopped as well, and we both turned around to face the person.

"Happy birthday, Harry!" Evelyn beamed, not hesitating to bring me in for a tight hug. It didn't last too long, though.

My lips formed a smile at the sight of her. "Thank you, Evelyn. I'm glad you could come," I told her honestly. Zayn's words about her liking me entered my mind, but I decided not to care about it. She was sweet, and as long as I made it obvious that I didn't have feelings for her, there was nothing to worry about, right?

"Well, of course! I wouldn't miss it for the world," she said, tilting her head to the side.

It wasn't until then she noticed I wasn't alone. Her eyes found Lucas but only stayed on him for a few seconds until she was looking at me again. "Who's your friend?" She asked.

Lucas being the outgoing person that he was, extended a hand for her to shake. "Lucas," he greeted, a smile breaking out on his face.

Evelyn's eyebrows furrowed as she looked down at his hand before taking it in hers hesitantly. "Evelyn," she replied, looking at me in confusion.

I couldn't help but let out a chuckle. "Lucas is my co-worker," I explained, throwing an arm around his narrow shoulders.

Her mouth formed the shape of an 'o', the puzzle pieces falling into place in her head, I assumed. "Nice to meet you," she grinned at Lucas, who nodded his head in acknowledgment.

"Likewise."

Lucas then flicked his gaze between the two of us. "And the two of you...?" He trailed off with a questioning look on his face.

"Oh," I said, feeling stupid that I didn't introduce him to Evelyn in return. "Evelyn and I know each other from school. She's also friends with my best friend's girlfriend," I explained.

"Louis?" Lucas asked in confusion.

I shook my head vigorously, feeling my cheeks heat up a little. "No. Uh, my other friend, Liam."

His features turned into a look of realization. "Oh, I see. Didn't think of the fact that you might have more than one best friend," he chuckled, shaking his head as if he was being stupid.

I patted him on the shoulder before dropping my arm from him. "It's okay, Lucas," I joked.

When I turned to Evelyn, she shifted her weight from one foot to the other. "Do you want to go get something to drink? We were just heading to the table," I asked, raising my eyebrows at her questioningly.

A bright smile formed on her lips as she nodded her head. "Sure."

That was how I found myself enjoying the night together with two people I liked. Evelyn was such a sweet and nice girl who you couldn't help but laugh and have fun with, and Lucas was just Lucas. Being bored didn't exist when you were around him.

I was clutching my stomach from laughing so hard probably an hour later - I didn't keep track of time - in a more secluded place in the building that was now echoing with music. It was pretty safe to say that I was intoxicated. I had downed at least four cans of beer, two vodka shots and one tequila. Maybe it wasn't that much, but I was a lightweight, I would admit that.

"Alright, everybody!" A voice suddenly spoke up, the music dying down in a matter of seconds.

My eyebrows furrowed in confusion as I tried to look for the source of the voice. It didn't take long until I saw none other than Louis standing on the stage, talking to everyone in the room.

"I think it's time to sing for the birthday boy, don't you agree?"

My eyes widened in shock, my mouth falling open. Sing? For me? No. He must be kidding.

"Curly, where are you?"

And suddenly the lights were on me, and so was everyone's attention. I instantly felt my cheeks heat up, my heart beginning to pound in my chest. Why was he doing this to me?

The second his eyes fell on me, I suddenly found it hard to breathe. The way his lips turned into that beautiful smile that made the crinkles by his eyes appear... I wanted to go up there and kiss him. God, I wanted it so badly that I had to force my feet not to move.

However, the second he started singing and got all the other people in the building to join him, the thought left my mind and was replaced by a feeling of embarrassment. I really didn't like having so many people looking at me at the same time.

I breathed out a sigh of relief when it was over, turning to take a large gulp of my opened can of beer. I needed more alcohol, and that was now.

It didn't take long until I could feel someone throwing their arms around my neck from behind, bringing me to their chest. I knew it could only be one person.

"Harry, my man! I haven't seen you in ages!" Niall called out, turning me around in his hold so I was facing him.

My lips twitched into a smile. "Heeeey."

"Are you feeling eighteen yet?" He asked, wiggling his eyebrows. There was no denying that he was drunk. He turned even more outgoing than he usually was whenever he had gotten alcohol into his system.

I rolled my eyes. "I thought we were over this, Niall. My birthday isn't until Sunday."

He waved a hand in dismissal. "You at least got something to drink? You look way too sober, mate," he accused me, pointing a finger at my chest.

Letting out a chuckle, I nodded my head. "I'm great. Thank you for caring, though," I chuckled, making him huff.

He shook his head, taking a hold of my upper arm. "We're taking shots together. I am not letting you be this sober on your eighteenth birthday."

I let out a loud laugh, following him to the table of drinks. I didn't know if Evelyn and Lucas were following or if they left, but at the moment, I didn't really care. I was happy to spend some time with Niall.

Three tequila shots later, I knew that I was definitely intoxicated. My vision was blurry, and I couldn't walk straight even if I wanted to. "Now we're talking!" Niall let out, patting me on the shoulder proudly.

Once he left to probably go find some girl to hook up with, I got this sudden urge that I wanted to talk to Louis. I hadn't talked to him since we got here, and that was a long time ago. I wanted to confront him about the singing, and I wanted to hug him and kiss him and--

I started making my way through the crowd of people, almost falling into them in the process because I was not stable. At all. Some of them even grabbed a hold of my arm to save me from falling, but that didn't make me stop. My eyes searched the room, trying to get a glimpse of the feathery-haired boy. Unfortunately, being drunk didn't exactly help with that.

It took at least ten minutes until I finally caught sight of him, but I wished I didn't because he wasn't alone. He was in one of the corners of the room, pressing that blonde girl who had been flirting with him during lunch for over a week now. That wasn't the only thing, though. They were making out. Her arms were around his neck with her fingers in his hair, and his hands were under the back of her top, tracing her skin.

The sight made a knot form in my stomach, and I instantly wanted to look away, but I somehow found it impossible. My gaze was glued to them.

"Harry, there you are!"

It was the sound of Lucas' voice that finally made me tear my eyes off the two kissing people, and I didn't hesitate to grab a hold of his upper arm. He flashed me a look of surprise when I started pulling him forward.

It wasn't easy to drag him with me since I couldn't walk straight, but eventually, we finally got to the kitchen. I shut the door behind us and instantly pressed him against the wall. His eyes widened in surprise once again.

"Harry, wha--"

I didn't let him finish that sentence because right then, I leaned in to crash my lips against his, shutting him up completely. He let out a gasp - probably not expecting me to kiss him - but relaxed in a matter of seconds and reached his arms out to bring me closer to him.

To be completely honest, I had no idea what I was doing. I only knew one thing, and it was that the plan of not letting Louis's actions get to me tonight had flown right out the window. I was bothered, beyond bothered. I just wanted to get the image of the two of them kissing out of my head, and that was now. I needed a distraction, and Lucas was the perfect distraction.

I didn't know if I was imagining it because I was too busy thinking about everything that was going on at the moment to acknowledge my surroundings, but the sound of a door shutting hit my eardrums.

I was probably imagining it, though. I was drunk, after all. Way too fucking drunk.

Chapter 15

I woke up the next day with a killer headache. Honestly, I didn't want to open my eyes because I knew that it was only going to make matters worse. So instead, I let out a groan and rolled over to the other side of the bed, hugging the blankets closer to me.

"Harry, sweety. Are you awake? It's one in the afternoon." If I opened my eyes, I was sure mom was going to be standing behind my door, poking her head inside the room.

On another note, I was surprised that it was already lunchtime. Had I really slept for that long? "No, 'm not," I muttered, burying my face in my pillow.

I could practically see her rolling her eyes at me. "How much did you have to drink last night, honey?" She sighed, walking into the room. I could tell by the sound of her footsteps and also by the sound of the door clicking shut.

The mattress sank down at my feet, indicating that she was now sitting at the end of my bed. The fact made me let out another groan. "Mooom, can't you just leave me alone? I wanna sleep."

"I want to talk to you."

The seriousness in her voice caught me off guard. It made me furrow my eyebrows together and slowly peek an eye open. She was sitting at my feet - as expected, her legs crossed while looking down at my figure with her lips pressed together.

"What is it?" I asked, reaching up to rub the sleep from my eyes.

She didn't start talking until I was sitting up against the headboard, both of my eyes open and directed at her. "Do you remember anything that happened last night?" She wondered.

Her question made me even more confused because truth be told, I didn't remember much at all. I did recall Louis getting everyone to sing for me and Niall coming over to do shots, but that was about it. Everything after that was blank.

The look on my face probably spoke for itself because she shook her head disapprovingly. "Do you know that Liam brought you home last night? Or more like in the morning. It was three am, and you couldn't even walk by yourself."

I bit my bottom lip, scrunching my nose up. Was that true? I mean, I didn't remember anything that happened after doing those shots with Niall, so it could be. Shit, I wondered if I had done something I was going to regret.

The disapproving look on her face didn't falter as she shook her head. "I'm not proud of you, Harry. We both know that I raised you better than this. I thought you were responsible, but I guess I was wrong," she said in disappointment, averting her gaze.

I felt a knot form in my stomach by her words. If there was something I hated, it was disappointing my mom, and that was exactly what I had done last night. It was my birthday party and all, but I had crossed the line. It was something that rarely happened, but apparently, yesterday was an exception.

"I'm sorry, mom," I mumbled, looking down at the blankets.

She let out a sigh, turning to look at me again. "I know it was your birthday party, and I am happy that you seemed to enjoy yourself, but anything can happen to you if you drink so much that you don't know what you're doing, alright? I am not lecturing you or anything, I'm just trying to look out for you."

I grimaced at her words, nodding my head. "I know. It was stupid of me. I just got carried away, I guess."

She flashed me a small smile. "I get that. I was young and stupid once in my life too, you know?" She chuckled lightly. "I just don't want you to do things that you'll regret, yeah?"

I nodded my head again, feeling how my skull was literally pounding against my forehead. "Shit," I muttered, reaching up to rub the throbbing spot.

Mom flashed me a look of concern. "I'll get you some pain killers and a glass of water. I'll be back in a minute," she said, getting up from the bed to leave the room.

Meanwhile, I reached out to grab my phone from my nightstand, noticing that I hadn't put it to charge last night. Great, only five percent left. However, that wasn't the first thing that caught my attention. I had received quite a few messages, and they were all from the same person.

Lucas?

Narrowing my eyes to get a better view of the screen, I tried reading what they said. The throbbing in my head made it difficult, though, so I eventually decided to unlock my phone to see if that would make it easier to read the messages.

Lucas: I'm so sorry about what happened yesterday, please don't hate me!

Lucas: Harry?

Lucas: It wasn't supposed to happen, I swear, but you pulled me in and I couldn't stop, fuck.

Lucas: Do you hate me?

Lucas: I guess I'll see you at work on Tuesday...

What was he talking about? What did he mean by 'you pulled me in and I couldn't stop'? And why did he think I hated him? As far as I knew, we had just hung around and had a couple of drinks together with Evelyn yesterday.

Hold on for a second.

After doing those shots with Niall, I went to search for Louis, didn't I? And when I finally found him, he was making out with that blonde girl who had been flirting with him for two weeks now. Then I could swear someone had called my name. Was it Lucas?

Then it hit me like a slap in the face. I kissed him. I was so upset about witnessing Louis kissing that girl that I had just lost it. Fuck.

Running a hand over my face, I let out the loudest groan yet. What the hell was I going to do?

Before I could think more about it, mom entered the room again. This time, she was holding a glass of water in one hand and two Advils in the other. She was just about to hand them to me when she saw the look on my face. "Did something happen?" She asked, her eyes widening slightly.

I squeezed my eyes shut, shaking my head. "You were right, mom. I definitely should have been more responsible last night."

She furrowed her eyebrows together, sitting down on the edge of my bed before finally handing me the glass of water and the pills. I took them, popped the Advils into my mouth, and swallowed them down with the water. I downed the whole thing.

"Did you just remember something?" She asked, tilting her head to the side.

I nodded my head, letting out a sigh as I ran a hand through my curly mess on top of my head. "I hope things will be okay, though."

She flashed me a small smile. "As long as you didn't get anyone pregnant, sleep with someone that's already in a relationship, or murder anyone, I'm sure you'll be okay," she joked in an attempt to lighten the mood. It worked.

The corners of my lips twitched at her words, and I shook my head as a chuckle escaped my lips. "I think I'll be fine then."

"Good," she smiled, taking the glass from my hand.

She was just about to leave the room when she stopped at the doorframe to turn around and face me again. "Do you have anything planned for your birthday tomorrow?"

I pursed my lips, shrugging my shoulders. "The lads and I have been talking about going out to eat somewhere, why?"

She shook her head, the smile never leaving her face. "I just wanted to know that you won't be spending the day alone since I have a shift tomorrow," she explained and didn't wait for an answer before continuing. "You coming down to watch a movie with me later? Something's telling me this is going to be a day where you'll be staying inside. Might as well spend some time with your moma then, yeah?"

I let out a chuckle. "As long as you promise to massage my scalp and card your fingers through my hair, then yeah, I'm definitely in."

The day turned out just like mom expected it to. I didn't step out of the house, and I spent the entire afternoon watching movies with her. It was actually nice. I enjoyed spending time with her because believe it or not, but we were very alike. We had the same sense of humor and it was easy to just talk to her. Now, I didn't tell her everything that was going on in my life because of obvious reasons, but I knew I easily could if I wanted to.

It was now Sunday, and I was preparing myself to go out with the lads. It was almost lunchtime, and we had decided to go to the best burger place in town. It was everyone's favorite, especially mine, and since it was my birthday, I got to decide.

Since Louis was still the only one out of the five of us who had gotten his driver's license, he was picking us all up. Liam and Zayn lived in the same area as him, so I knew it was going to take a while until they would be here, which was why I still hadn't gotten changed. I was working on it, though.

Looking through my closet, I let my fingers wander over my button-ups and shirts until they stopped at a red, checkered material. I grabbed the button-up from the hanger and put it on, leaving the three top buttons undone. I then ruffled my curls in an attempt to make them not stick out in every direction before pulling my black, skinny jeans that were ripped at the knees on.

I was just about to take a look at myself in the mirror when a car honked outside, making me come to a halt. Instead of walking to the mirror, I stopped at my window, looking out to see Louis' black sports car pulled over outside the house.

Knowing how mad he usually got when I wasn't ready on time, I hurried out of my room and jogged to the entryway to slip my black boots on. I then snatched my winter jacket from the hanger before leaving the house, locking the front door behind me since Gemma wasn't home.

I jogged over to the car, barely having time to open the backseat door until they all yelled out; "Happy birthday, Harry!"

I let out a chuckle as I slipped in beside Niall, who had a wide smile on his face. "Now you can't correct me anymore because today is your actual birthday," he pointed out, making me roll my eyes.

"I guess it is. Just don't remind me too much, yeah?" I chuckled.

The other lads were turned to me as well, all of them except for Louis. He was staring out the windshield even though the car wasn't moving yet. I found it a little off, secretly wondering if something had happened.

"You ready to eat some burgers, eh?" Zayn asked, wiggling his eyebrows at me.

I tore my gaze away from Louis to look at Zayn in the passenger seat while nodding my head. "Yup, I'm starving."

Louis let out a snort but still didn't turn around. Instead, he turned on the engine and drove off, accelerating like a madman. The action made my eyes widen, and I instantly felt the need to grab the seat in front of me. "Jesus Christ," I breathed, looking out the window where the trees were passing by way too quickly.

"What? Is this too fast for you, Curly?" Louis asked, his voice emotionless.

It made me furrow my eyebrows. What was going on? Why was he acting so weird?

The other lads didn't seem to notice anything, though, since they didn't say a word about it. Instead, Niall and Liam started asking me how it felt to finally turn eighteen and if I was getting close to get my driver's license. I replied to them even if my focus stayed on the boy in the driver's seat. He didn't turn to us once during the entire ride, though.

The second Louis parked the car in an empty spot outside the restaurant, we all got out and headed for the entrance. "I'm paying for your meal today, Harry," Niall said, patting me on the shoulder when the waitress had shown us to a table.

Louis' gaze shot up, looking between the two of us with a crease between his eyebrows. He sat down beside Zayn, opposite me, Niall and Liam at the table, instantly fishing his phone from the pocket of his jeans. Now I was really starting to get confused.

It was my birthday and we had barely even talked to each other. I thought we had moved past this? I thought we were finally starting to really get to know each other. But now it felt like we were back to square one again... or not even that because he had never treated me this coldly before. He wouldn't even look at me, nor tease me the way he usually did.

I couldn't help but feel sad about it. It was my birthday - not that I really cared about that, but I had hoped he was going to give me more attention than usual today. I assumed that wasn't going to happen, though.

The waitress came back a few minutes later to take our orders. I didn't pay much attention to her, though. I just muttered out what I wanted to have while staring at the surface of the table. The second she had walked away again, I felt a nudge in my side.

"Dude, that girl was totally checking you out," Niall pointed out, wiggling his eyebrows at me.

I frowned, turning to the direction where the girl just disappeared in. "Really? I didn't notice."

Louis let out a scoff from the other side of the table, rolling his eyes. "Of course you didn't," he muttered barely audible. This made the crease between my eyebrows grow even deeper. What was he getting at?

Zayn broke the silence that had occurred by turning to me with a smile on his face. "So, I just have to say that the party was amazing. You definitely did a great job with it," he complimented.

My lips twitched at his words, and my gaze wandered to Louis quickly. He was part of the reason it had turned out the way it did, but he was staring at his phone again, not even caring that Zayn hadn't included him.

"Thank you, but it was all thanks to Louis," I said, not even caring about the fact that he had barely acknowledged me since I got into his car earlier.

Louis' head snapped up at the sound of his name, and he flicked his gaze between me and Zayn before pulling his lips together in a flat line as he nodded his head curtly.

Letting out a sigh, I turned to Zayn who shrugged his shoulders. "Well, it was a great party nonetheless. You should be proud, mate," he said, and Liam and Niall agreed with him.

"Thank you," I mumbled, my lips forming a small, almost forced smile.

A few minutes later, the waitress came back with our food. This time, I did notice that her gaze lingered on me for a little longer than the other lads, and she also fluttered her eyelashes flirtatiously when I met her gaze. I returned the smile politely, thanking her for the food.

When she left again, they were all looking at me, Louis included. "What?" I asked, raising my eyebrows at them.

"Dude, you acted as if you didn't even notice the way she was trying to flirt with you. Are you okay? Should I get a doctor? I mean, you're literally missing out on a great opportunity here, mate," Zayn said, looking at me in disbelief.

My eyes weren't focused on him, though. As usual, they were on Louis, and he was giving me an unreadable look. I couldn't tell what was going on inside his head, but damn, I really wanted to.

"I'm okay," was the only thing I said as I flashed him a smile.

He raised an eyebrow at me before shaking his head. "If you say so."

During the time we ate, the lads talked about the upcoming school week, how they had a lot of tests to do and essays to write. Louis wasn't participating in the conversation, though, which made me distance myself as well. I knew something was wrong, and I could tell that it was because of me. Otherwise, he wouldn't have been ignoring me like this.

When we were all finished, Liam's phone started ringing. He fished it from the pocket of his jeans and brought it to his ear. "Hello?"

After a minute, he put the phone down to his shoulder. "It's Alice. There's a get-together at Rebecca's place and she's wondering if we want to come," he asked, his gaze wandering between all of us.

Niall's eyes instantly lit up. "Of course! I'm in!"

Zayn nodded. "Sure, why not?"

Liam's gaze flicked between me and Louis then. "Louis and Harry, what about you guys?"

Louis furrowed his eyebrows. "Actually, I think I'm just going to head home. I'm not really feeling it today, to be honest," he admitted, grimacing a little.

We were all surprised by his answer because Louis Tomlinson never missed a chance of going out and meet people. It made me start wondering how bad whatever had happened actually was.

"O-kay. And you, Harry?"

I shook my head. "I think I've celebrated this day more than enough already. I'm actually still a little out of it since the party too."

Liam nodded his head with a small smile on the face before bringing the phone back to his ear. When he was finished, he shoved it in his pocket. "She and her friend will be here in three minutes to come pick us up, so you don't have to drive us there, Louis," he explained, looking at the feathery-haired boy.

Louis opened his mouth to say something, and I was positive he wanted to protest because he realized he would have to sit in a car alone with me, but nothing came out. Instead, he closed it again and just nodded his head curtly before looking down at his lap.

I was definitely going to take advantage of this opportunity because I needed to know what was going on, why he was acting the way he was. Something was wrong, and I was going to find out what.

Chapter 16

We all walked out of the restaurant together when Alice and her friend showed up. Niall didn't hesitate to wrap his arms around me before leaving, giving me a tight hug. "Happy birthday again, mate. I love you, man," he said into my ear, patting me on my shoulder blade.

I couldn't help the wide smile that formed on my lips at his gesture. "Thank you, Niall. I love you too."

He pulled away, flashing me a grin before jogging off towards the white car that belonged to Alice's friend. Zayn and Liam said goodbye too, fist-bumping both me and Louis before walking to the vehicle as well.

As soon as they were gone, Louis started heading in the direction of his own car. He didn't say a word when I followed him and slipped into the passenger seat next to him. He just turned on the engine and pulled out of the parking spot, making sure to speed up as soon as we were out on the streets.

I wanted to say something. I wanted to ask him why he was acting this way, and I wanted to stomp those fucking brakes because I couldn't take this anymore. It wasn't until he turned on the radio at a ridiculously high volume that I actually reacted, though.

"Alright, that is fucking enough," I snapped, reaching out to slam my hand against the power button to the radio.

Louis looked a bit taken aback by my outburst, but he didn't say anything. Not a single word, and it made me even more frustrated.

"What's going on?" I asked him, staring at the side of his face. My entire body was facing his figure as I watched him, my eyes boring into his skin.

"What? You can't handle some music and fast speed, huh?" He asked, raising his eyebrows at me.

The words made my jaw clench. "You know that's not what I'm talking about."

He clenched his jaw as well, turning his head to stare back at the road. When he didn't say anything, I crossed my arms over my chest. "Tell me," I demanded, still watching him.

Louis frowned, gripping the wheel tightly. "There's nothing to say."

I snorted. "Bullshit. You've barely even looked at me today. The only thing you've done is to give me snide remarks. Other than that, you've just been on your phone and kept quiet, and you are never quiet," I pointed out.

He rolled his eyes. "Everything is not about you, Curly."

Letting out a huff, I shook my head. "Of course everything is not about me, but you've been treating me like shit today. Have I done something? Is that it? What have I done?" I pleaded, and I almost reached out to grab his arm in desperation.

I couldn't have him hate me, especially not for something I didn't even know what I had done wrong. I liked him so much that the thought of him hating me made me want to cry. My mission was to make him smile, make him like me in return, not the opposite.

He was quiet for another few seconds, just staring out the windshield until he finally opened his mouth to explain. "I just... Why have you never mentioned that you like guys?" He asked in a mutter, not turning to meet my gaze, but the entire atmosphere suddenly changed in the car.

My eyes practically bulged out of their sockets as my mouth dropped open in shock. Did he just say what I thought he said? How on earth did he find out? "I... *What*?"

He rolled his eyes without a trace of humor on his face. "I saw you and Lucas at the party. Don't act like you don't know what I'm talking about."

I had to inhale a deep breath as I slumped back in my seat, my head hitting the headrest. "I was drunk," I said in an attempt to cover it. He saw through me, though. I could tell by the way a humorless smile crossed his face.

"You were way too into it not to be enjoying it. It was obvious that was hardly the first time you kissed a guy either for that matter."

I swallowed hard, turning to look out the window where the trees were now passing by slower than when he had driven us to the restaurant earlier. I didn't know what to say, what to do, or how to react. Was he going to judge me if I told him the truth? Was he going to be grossed out?

So many thoughts were spinning around in my head that I barely registered that Louis had opened his mouth to start talking again. "Why did you never say anything?" He sounded so calm, yet so confused and... disappointed? Did it really matter that much to him?

I turned to him with a frown on my face. "Why would I?"

He looked at me as if I was crazy. "Because we are best friends maybe? And close friends can tell stuff like that to each other."

The crease between my eyebrows only deepened. "From what I've come to know, you and I aren't that close, though," I huffed.

I didn't know why I was acting this way. I just didn't know what to do. The only thing I was sure of was that I didn't want him to find out who the guy I actually had feelings for was. Then I knew for sure that he would never want to speak to me again.

A frown formed on Louis' face as his eyes locked on the road with a tight grip on the wheel. "What about the other guys then? Do they know?" He muttered, his Adam's apple bobbing up and down as he swallowed hard.

I bit my bottom lip, averting my gaze from him. "No, they don't," I mumbled. "Are you... are you going to tell them?" I couldn't help but ask, secretly afraid that he was going to out me to everyone.

He shrugged his shoulders. "If you don't want me to, then no, I won't. I mean, you kept a secret for me," he told me, most likely referring to the incident when he hit his forehead on his way downstairs at Emily's party.

I nodded my head, letting out a sigh of relief. He wouldn't tell anyone. But wasn't it already bad enough that *he* out of all people knew about it? He was the main reason I didn't want people to know that I was bisexual because I was sure it would be so obvious that I had feelings for him. I found it weird how Louis hadn't noticed it himself yet by the way I so easily got lost inside his eyes.

"Do you... mind?" I asked hesitantly, feeling how my heart was pounding in my chest. This was the moment I had been dreading ever since I realized I liked him.

"That you're bisexual?" He asked, turning to raise his eyebrows at me.

I nodded my head slowly, barely daring to look at him.

A small, genuine smile formed on his lips as he shook his head. "No, I don't mind. Love is love, right?"

My lips twitched into the widest smile I had pulled the entire day. I felt so relieved. He wasn't disgusted. He didn't mind. He didn't actually mind that I was into guys. Holy shit. This must be the best birthday present I could have asked for... besides actually getting together with him, of course.

"I guess."

We drove for another few minutes until he broke the silence again. "Are you and Lucas...?" He trailed off, glancing at me through the corner of his eye.

I raised my eyebrows at him in surprise. "Dating? No. God, no. We're friends, just friends," I explained quickly.

He nodded his head slowly, his eyebrows furrowed. "And you don't have feelings for him?"

I looked at him as if he just asked me the stupidest question of all time because I really didn't want him to think I liked Lucas like that, which was the truth. I did only see Lucas as a friend, even if I had mentioned that I found him attractive. However, he couldn't compare to the guy sitting right next to me. If only I could tell him that.

"No. I didn't know what I was doing that night. I was drunk and..."

Mad at you for kissing that girl.

"And?" He asked, raising his eyebrows at me.

I knitted my eyebrows together as I shook my head. "Nothing."

He let out a sigh, running a hand through his feathery locks as he looked out the side window.

I bit my lip as I watched him. Something was telling me that more things were going on inside his head. He wouldn't have declined to go to Rebecca's place only because I never told him about my sexuality, right?

"Is there... is there more to it? The reason behind your actions, I mean?" I asked him hesitantly, not wanting him to feel like I was trying to intrude on his life.

He turned to look at me for a second, his face emotionless. "No. I just don't have a good day in general," he told me, and honestly, I didn't know what to believe. Was he lying to me or was he telling me the truth?

"Okay," I said, looking down at my lap while biting my bottom lip.

By now, Louis had pulled over outside my house and turned off the engine. I turned to him with a hesitant smile on my face. "Um, I guess I'll see you tomorrow then?"

He nodded his head, watching me as I climbed out of the car. I was just about to shut the door behind me when he stopped me. "Wait!"

I leaned down to look at his face. "Yeah?"

"Happy birthday."

I thought things would go back to normal after that, but I was wrong. During the next couple of days, Louis was still distant. He barely joined my and the boys' conversations during lunch break, or any break for that matter. During our soccer practices, he was being a more formal and strict captain than the laid back and open-hearted one we all knew him as. We knew that Louis wasn't like that in general either, so there was no doubt that something was still bothering him. I just wondered what.

Something was telling me I wasn't the reason behind his behavior this time, but I wasn't completely sure. He hadn't made any snide remarks as he did at the restaurant, which was the reason behind my assumption. To be honest, he had been looking at me more than he usually did. Sometimes, I could even feel his eyes on me when we were sitting in the cafeteria, but whenever I turned to meet his gaze, he looked away.

I wondered what that was all about, especially since he wouldn't talk. Things would be so much easier if he just opened his mouth and said something, *anything*. Then I would at least have something to go on.

On another note, Lucas and I had talked through what happened at the party when I arrived to work that Tuesday. We were both on the same page, which was a huge relief. The last thing I wanted was for him to think we could be more than friends. I was not looking for that, even if I really liked him as a person.

He had apologized the first thing he did when he caught sight of me, his eyes pleading as he grabbed my arm. When I asked him why he was apologizing (since I had been the one to kiss him in the first place) he told me that he knew I was drunk, so he was afraid I thought he had tried to take advantage of me. It wasn't my thought of it at all, though. Even if I was drunk, I knew what I was doing. I had been insanely jealous, that was why it had happened in the first place.

After our talk, we went back to normal. There was no tension or awkwardness between us, just banter and laughs like always. Oh, how I wished things were that easy with Louis too. It had only been a week, but I already missed the way he would include me in a conversation just to tease me.

It was now Wednesday, a week and two days after my birthday, and I was supposed to be in the locker room to get changed for practice, but I was running late because I had just passed my driving test. Yes, I had gotten it on my first go. I was so happy. The second the man had told me the news, I had let out a high squeal and almost flung my arms around him. I was pretty sure nothing could take away the exhilaration I was feeling.

Gemma drove me to the gym without even a second thought. She was happy for me too and said that the least she could do was drive me there.

I slammed the door shut behind me after saying goodbye to her, sprinting towards the entrance of the gym. The second I swung the door of the locker room open, the biggest smile was on my face.

The guys looked up at the sound of my arrival, their eyes widening in surprise when they saw my face. "Harry, what's gotten you so happy, man?" Trevor asked, his eyebrows raised.

My eyes weren't on him, though. They were searching the room for the person whose opinion meant the most to me. The second I found Louis sitting on one of the benches, my heart fluttered in my chest. He was looking at me too.

"I just got my driver's license!" I cheered, making hollers erupt in the entire room.

"That's awesome, mate!" I could hear Niall yell out.

"That's how you do it, man!"

"Congrats, mate!"

"Knew you would get it, lad!"

Some of them even got up to pat me on the shoulder in congratulation, making me even happier than I already was. I couldn't believe they all cared about me so much. "Thank you, guys," I said, my eyes looking around to find Louis' gaze again.

My heart almost stopped beating when I saw his face. He was smiling. He was actually *smiling* at me. An entire week had passed where he hadn't so much as shown one emotion on his face, but right now, his lips were twitched upwards and the crinkles by his eyes were even prominent.

Would anyone catch me if I fainted? Because I could feel my vision getting blurry. This was too much for me to handle, Jesus.

My breath hitched in my throat as I desperately tried to return the smile, but thanks to the chaos going on inside me, it probably turned out more like an ugly grimace. He didn't stop smiling at me, though.

I felt this sudden urge to go over and talk to him. I mean, during the week before my birthday, we had hung out *every* day after school to prepare for the party, and I missed talking to him. I even thought we were getting closer to each other at that point, but I wasn't sure if he felt the same way.

Instead of doing what I wanted, however, I sat down on the bench to put my shin pads and cleats on. I didn't want to pressure him because I knew how he had been acting this past week. If I just walked up and talked to him, his smile would probably drop and he would find a way to get out of the situation, and I didn't want that. Take it slow, that was the right way to deal with this... I hoped.

Today's practice was all about getting ready for the upcoming game this Saturday. Coach wanted us to show him what we'd got during our first game, that we really wanted to win the league this season, so all of us were really focused on performing during practice as well.

We were currently playing a match, and I was dribbling the ball past one player to another. Unfortunately, it was suddenly stolen from me by someone with quick and gracious legs, practically snitching it at my feet. I let out a gasp, looking up to find Louis heading in the opposite direction with the ball right in front of him.

Pulling myself back together, I started running after him towards our goal, but Ryan caught up with him before anyone else could. Louis swung his leg back to kick the ball towards the net, but before his foot could hit the ball, he was slide tackled right to the left foot, causing him to fly forward and land into a heap on the ground.

"What the hell?!"

My mouth fell open in shock as my feet stopped moving. Shit, that must have hurt.

It turned out that wasn't the end of the situation, though, because Louis sprang up to his feet without even acknowledging the pain that must be shooting through his foot at the second. His jaw was clenched tightly, and so were his fists at his sides.

By now, the match was off and everyone was staring at the scene in front of them. The look on Louis' face told me that he was about to do something he was going to regret, so I pulled my limbs into action and hoped I would get to him before it was too late.

Louis was walking up to Ryan, his face red with anger as he swung his fist back and--

"Louis," I said with a calm voice although I was a little out of breath from running, catching his forearm before he could swing, my eyes boring into the side of his face.

My touch must have sent him completely off guard because his arm instantly went limp in mine and fell to his side. He wasn't facing me, though. He was still glaring at Ryan with his jaw clenched. "You should be happy your face isn't smashed, you fucker," Louis grunted.

I could see Ryan rolling his eyes, snickering slightly at him. It made Louis almost dart for him again, but I assumed the pain was finally starting to kick in because he scrunched his nose up and stopped his movements. "You little shit!" He groaned.

It wasn't until then he noticed that I was still holding his forearm. He turned to me with his eyebrows knitted together before pulling his arm out of my hold. With an angry grunt, he limped off the field towards Coach who was looking in our direction with shock written on his face. Everything had happened so fast that no one had time to react. No one but me, I assumed.

"Louis, you're off during the rest of practice. Ryan, you too. We'll have a talk in the locker rooms later."

Chapter 17

Once practice was over, we all headed to the locker rooms. Coach had wrapped Louis' injured ankle while Ryan sat on the bench with a grumpy look on his face, his arms folded over his chest.

During the rest of practice, I couldn't help but steal glances at the injured boy every now and then, noticing how he had slumped his shoulders while looking anywhere but the field. Even if he had just been injured, he didn't really seem like his usual self lately, and I was getting worried about him.

Coach supported Louis to the locker room with the feathery-haired boy's arm wrapped around his shoulders. You could tell by the look on the younger boy's face that he didn't really want the help, but Coach wouldn't take no for an answer.

When we were all sitting on the benches in the locker room, it was so quiet that you could hear a needle drop to the floor. Everyone was staring at Coach as he paced back and forth, running a hand over his bald head.

"Guys, I am not happy with you. We are supposed to work as a team, not opponents. I do not tolerate what happened out there today. If any of you intentionally try to hurt one of your teammates again, you are off the team. Are we clear?"

His gaze flickered between every guy in the room, waiting for each one to nod their head. "Good. Ryan, I still want to talk to you once you're finished, alright?"

Ryan nodded his head shortly, pursing his lips.

With that, Coach left the locker room, slamming the door shut harsher than necessary. As soon as he was gone, chatter started erupting in the room, but not on the same level as usual. Everyone was still a bit on edge.

"Hey, Louis. How are you doing?"

I looked over to see Liam sitting down beside Louis on the bench, looking at his foot with concern.

Louis shrugged his shoulders almost carelessly as he looked the other way. "Things have been better."

Liam furrowed his eyebrows. "Um, how's your ankle then?" He asked hesitantly.

The feathery-haired boy turned his face to look at him. "I don't know. I'm just mad at Ryan for injuring me so I can't play on Saturday," he muttered, pulling his bottom lip between his teeth.

Liam nodded his head in understanding. "I'd be pissed if I were you too, man. I hope you'll be able to play soon. We really need you on the team, Louis."

The corners of Louis' lips twitched slightly at his words. "Thank you."

Once I had finished showering and changed into a pair of black joggers and a purple hoodie, I zipped my bag shut and was about to sling it over my shoulder when I came to think of something. However, Zayn beat me to say it.

"Hey, Louis. How are you getting home? You can't drive with that injury even if you want to," he pointed out, standing in front of Louis who was sitting on the bench with his leg stretched out.

Louis just shrugged his shoulders, not looking up to meet his eyes. "I dunno. I guess I'll have to catch the bus and leave the car here," he muttered.

"I can drive you," I found myself saying, my eyes widening when I realized what just slipped out of my mouth. Was I really offering to drive him home?

Both his and Zayn's' heads snapped to me, Louis' eyebrows furrowed while Zayn was looking at me as if I had just come up with a brilliant idea. "Of course! Harry got his driver's license today, so he can drive you home," the raven-haired boy cheered, patting Louis on the shoulder.

I could see Louis muttering something under his breath, but he didn't decline the offer, which I took as a confirmation that I was taking him home. What had I gotten myself into? I had officially been allowed to drive a car alone only a few hours ago, and I was already going to drive Louis' car out of all people? What if I was going to crash it?

Feeling myself getting nervous, I rubbed my clammy hands on my sweats as I walked over to Louis and Zayn. Most of the lads were already gone. There were only a few other people than me Louis and Zayn there, so we didn't draw much attention to us as I reached my hand out to Louis. He was wearing his green Adidas hoodie that I liked so much along with a pair of black joggers.

He looked at my hand for a few seconds, his eyes flickering up to meet my gaze before finally taking it in his. Honestly, I was starting to get worried that he was going to leave me hanging. The second our skin touched, my breath hitched in my throat, but I tried my best to act normal. No friends were affected by their hands touching for goodness sake.

I pulled him up from the bench, instantly bringing my arm around his waist to support him while he wrapped an arm around my shoulders. A feeling of déjà vu hit me as I realized this was the exact same position we had been in when I helped him at Emily's party. I had missed it.

Zayn grabbed my bag from my shoulder and scooped Louis' up from the floor before following us out of the gym and towards the parking lot. Once we were at Louis' car, I realized I needed the key to open the vehicle.

"Um, Louis. Where's the key?" I asked hesitantly, not wanting to make him snap. I knew he was sensible nowadays. Just talking to him could upset him.

"It's in my joggers' pocket," he mumbled, nodding towards the pocket that was on my side.

I realized I would have to get it since his arm was still wrapped around my shoulders, and if I let him go, he would most likely fall to the ground. Feeling my cheeks heat up, I bit my bottom lip as I reached out to his pocket. I tried my best to act normal even if my mind was screaming at me.

You're digging through his pocket right beside the most precious part of his body.

The key wasn't hard to find, though, so I snatched it and pulled my hand out without lingering. I couldn't even if I wanted to. I then unlocked the car and walked him over to the passenger seat to help him inside. Meanwhile, Zayn threw our bags into the backseat before slamming the door shut.

"You think you'll be okay now?" He asked me, raising his eyebrows questioningly.

I nodded my head although I wasn't very sure at all. I wanted to be, though. "Yeah, I'll be fine. See you tomorrow?"

"Sure," he smiled, waving to Louis (who wasn't looking) before jogging off to his father's car across the street.

As soon as I got into the vehicle and had slammed the door shut behind me, a tension-filled silence occurred, making me even more nervous than I already was. I started looking for where to put the key until I realized there wasn't even a hole to put the damned thing in. Turning to Louis, I noticed that he was glancing at me.

"You just press the button to your left," he muttered.

My eyebrows furrowed together as I found the button he was talking about. I pressed it, and instantly, the engine started up. High tech stuff really wasn't my thing. What happened to the good old ignitions?

"Um, it's an automatic car, so you don't need to change gears," he explained, looking out the passenger window as if he couldn't care less that he was explaining this to me. I had a feeling he did care, though. Why else would he even help me in the first place?

"Really?" I gasped, my eyes widening. The hardest part about driving was to find traction mode, so I was nothing but thankful that he had an automatic car.

"Are you surprised that I have an automatic car, or did you just not know that these types of cars exist?" He asked, turning to raise his eyebrows at me. Was that amusement? I hadn't seen him act like this for over a week now.

"Of course I know what an automatic car is, duh."

The corners of his lips twitched as he shook his head. "Alright. Let's see how good of a driver you are then."

I pulled out of the parking lot after Louis had shown me how to get the car in reverse. Once I had made it out on the streets, silence filled the car again, and surprisingly, Louis didn't reach out to turn on the radio.

I tried to focus on my driving instead of thinking about the silence in the car. The worst thing about the situation was that I wanted to talk to Louis. I just didn't know how to since I was afraid he was just going to be upset with me.

We made it to a roundabout where I had to hit the brakes to slow the car down. It was just that this car's brakes were a lot more sensible than the car that I was used to driving, so instead of doing a smooth deceleration, we came to an abrupt stop. It sent both me and

Louis flying forward in our seats. Good thing we were wearing seat belts. Otherwise, we would have been thrown against the windshield.

"Holy shit," I gasped, bringing my hand to my racing heart. The abrupt stop had scared the hell out of me.

"And come to think you were the one calling me a bad driver," Louis said, shaking his head.

When I turned to look at him, I noticed that he was smiling faintly while glancing back at me. "It wasn't my fault. I'm just not used to driving this car," I whined, my bottom lip sticking out in a pout.

He let out a light chuckle. "Now you're just trying to save yourself."

I wasn't, but I was too happy to hear him laugh to object. My lips formed a smile in return as I looked at him for a few seconds before turning my attention back to the road. We were quiet for the next couple of minutes.

"Um, how am I going to get home?" I couldn't help but ask. He probably couldn't care less, but I literally had no idea.

He pursed his lips, his eyebrows furrowing. "Okay, let's make a deal," he finally said, turning his body slightly to me.

I glanced at him through the corner of my eye while waiting for him to continue. "Since I won't be able to drive for at least a couple of days now, you can have my car only if you promise to drive me to and from school every day, and practice too. Even if I can't play, Coach probably wants me to work out in some other way," he said, and to say I was shocked would be an understatement.

Was he really offering me to have his car while he was injured and couldn't drive himself? Had he gone nuts while falling when Ryan tackled him? Did he hurt his head too? Because he must be insane for even thinking of an idea like that, especially considering the way he had been acting this past week.

"I uh..." I trailed off.

"I mean, you haven't bought a car yet, have you?" He wondered, raising his eyebrows at me.

I shook my head, my mouth still hanging open from what he had said. "No, I... Of course I'll drive you. I just... isn't this a bit too much to offer?"

He shrugged his shoulders, averting his gaze from me. "If you don't want to, I'll just find someone else to drive me."

I cleared my throat, shaking my head vigorously. "No, I'll do it. I was just surprised you asked me. I mean, you've been slightly on edge the last couple of days. I wasn't expecting you to ask me something like that," I explained to him.

He furrowed his eyebrow together, still refusing to look at me. "Well, I have to get to school somehow, don't I?"

Yeah, but offering me to have your car is something else.

However, I would have to get to him somehow in the mornings if I wanted to be able to drive him, and I knew for a fact that it wouldn't be simple to just ride the bus there every morning. It would be a mess, so having his car at my house was the best solution. I just couldn't understand how he trusted me with something like that. I mean, his car must mean a lot to him.

"I guess..." I trailed off, biting my bottom lip.

By now, we were outside his big, white house that anyone would kill to live in. It always managed to take my breath away.

I got out of the car to help him out, but as soon as I made a movement to support him towards the front door, he flinched away. "I'll manage on my own from here. Um, thank you for driving me, though," he said, his face emotionless.

I knitted my eyebrows together in confusion. Why didn't he want me to walk him to the door? He was okay with me helping him before, so what was different now?

I decided not to object, though, because it finally felt like I had him on my good side, and I didn't want to ruin that.

When he started jumping on one foot towards the front door, I suddenly found myself wanting to stop him. "Louis?"

He turned around hesitantly, his face in a scowl. When he didn't say anything, I took that as my cue to continue. "Are we... are we good?" I couldn't help but ask.

It had been bugging me since he started distancing himself from everyone. I mean, even if he wasn't acting as he did at the restaurant, his change in behavior had occurred right after I confirmed that I was bisexual, so I just wanted to make sure it wasn't because of me.

It took way too long for him to reply, and it made me really fucking nervous. My mind started spinning and I couldn't help but start blaming myself for everything. I was just about to slump my shoulders and walk to the driver's side when he finally opened his mouth.

"Yeah, we're good."

My head snapped up to meet his gaze, and the smile on his lips made my breath hitch. God, he was so beautiful. I wanted to go over there and hug him, bring his body to mine so I could have him close to me.

My lips twitched at the sight as I felt my cheeks heat up a little. "Great."

I wasn't the reason for his behavior. I wasn't the reason he was being so cold and distant. Thank fucking God for that.

I was just about to open the door to the car and get in when the sound of his voice interrupted me. "Thanks for saving me on the field today. I uh... I would have done things that I had probably regretted if you didn't stop me."

My eyes widened slightly, and I couldn't help the flutter in my heart. "I uh... of course. I had a feeling what you were about to do, and now with the scholarship and everything, I figured you wouldn't want to ruin anything by doing something like that. I'm glad I could help, but I'm sorry you had to get hurt. Ryan's a real ass." I said the last part with a grimace, looking down at the roof of his car. I could still see Louis purse his lips, though.

"That's what I've been trying to tell you, Curly," he replied with a faint smile, running a hand through his greasy hair. He hadn't been able to shower earlier thanks to the gauze around his ankle.

My lips twitched at his words, recalling when we had been sitting on my couch to discuss what players should get to start playing at our games. "I guess you were right."

Louis nodded his head curtly. "I'll see you tomorrow, yeah? Seven-thirty." He told me, raising his eyebrows.

"I'll be here," I promised him, my face still performing a smile.

"Don't be late, Curly."

Chapter 18

The second I arrived at home, I slipped off my boots and shrugged off my jacket before tossing my bag on the floor. I was just about to make my way to the kitchen when Gemma emerged from the living room with raised eyebrows. "Did you decide to steal someone's car on your way home from practice, or what?"

My muscles instantly froze to ice. Shit, I hadn't thought about that. Of course mom and Gemma would notice that there was a car parked in the driveway that was neither of theirs. How stupid could I be not to think of that?

Mentally smacking myself on the forehead, I pressed my lips together. "Um, I'm borrowing it from a friend?" I attempted, making her narrow her eyes at me.

"What friend?"

I shrugged my shoulders, averting my gaze from her. She was already suspicious why Louis and I were hanging out so much these days, so I knew she would never shut up if I told her the truth about whose car it was. "It doesn't matter."

This made her narrow her eyes even more. "Wait. Does this have anything to do with the guy you like?" She asked me, making my heart stop beating in my chest. How did she manage to read me so well? What was this? Some kind of superpower she had?

"I... No? Why would you think that?" I asked, trying my best to hide that it was in fact the guy I liked's car that was parked in our driveway, but I had a feeling it wasn't going well.

Before she had time to ask me anything else, mom joined us in the entryway. "Hey, honey. What is Louis' car doing in our driveway? Is he here?" She wondered, looking at me questioningly.

Gemma let out a loud gasp, reaching up to cover her mouth with her hands as she looked at me with wide eyes. My heart had stopped beating in my chest as soon as mom mentioned Louis' name, and I knew I was fucked. I was so fucked that I just wanted to melt into a puddle. Too bad I was inside and there were no puddles in sight. Damn it.

"Louis," she gaped. "You like Louis!"

Mom furrowed her eyebrows, trying to understand what she was on about. "What are you talking about, honey?" She asked Gemma, but her eyes flickered to me.

I didn't know what to do, how to react, or what to say. What *could* I say? I had already been quiet for too long to deny it now, and Gemma just knew. I could tell by the look of realization on her face. It was like the puzzle pieces had fallen into place in her head. She knew that Louis was the one I had been talking about that day of the party in her car.

I still hadn't found the ability to talk when Gemma opened her mouth. "This explains everything! Why you were so caring with him when you brought him home the night of that party when he hurt himself, why you always have that smile on your face whenever you talk about him, and why you were so mad at me when you thought he liked me," she explained, her eyes still widened in surprise.

I opened my mouth in another attempt to explain myself. "I-I..." I trailed off, running a hand through my still damp curls before letting out a deep sigh. "Yeah, you're... you're right. I do have feelings for Louis."

"I knew it!"

Mom's mouth fell open in shock. "How long have you felt this way about him? And why did you never say anything?" She wondered.

I felt so stared out that I had to look down at the floor. My face was burning with embarrassment because I never expected them to find out this way. Honestly, I never planned for them to find out about it at all. I figured my feelings for him would disappear sometime, especially after graduation, and then I would just get away with it that way. I assumed I was wrong, though.

Taking a deep breath, I looked up, flickering my eyes between the two of them. "About three years maybe? And I didn't tell you because he doesn't feel the same way. I'm just... I'm just ashamed that I have feelings for my straight best friend," I explained, biting my bottom lip.

Both Gemma and mom let out deep sighs. "Come on, let's go sit down on the couch," mom suggested, nodding towards the living room.

We all settled down on the grey couch, mom instantly scooting close so she could bring her hands to my damp curls. "How do you know he doesn't have feelings for you?" Gemma asked, raising her eyebrows at me.

I looked at her as if she was stupid. "Gems, you know how Louis is. He's the biggest ladies' man out there. He's literally with a different girl at every party he attends," I muttered, my gaze on the floor.

"Don't you remember what I told you in the car?" She wondered, making me turn my head to look at her. When I gave her a questioning look, she continued. "Even the straightest people are a little bit gay. You can't just know for sure that he doesn't feel anything for you, H. Why are you giving up before you've even tried?" She whined, reaching over to hit me on the leg gently.

I furrowed my eyebrows. "How do you know I haven't tried?"

She raised her eyebrows at me. "Oh, so you're suddenly telling me you have shown him that you like him? H, you literally just told us that you're ashamed of your feelings, so I'm pretty sure you haven't tried anything."

I flashed her a glare, supporting my head with my hands by resting my elbows on my thighs. "Fine," I muttered. "I haven't tried showing him how I feel."

"That's what I thought," she said, rolling her eyes. "But seriously, H. You have what? Three months until you graduate and then you are going separate ways. What are you waiting for? Don't you want to know if you ever had a chance before it's too late?"

I knitted my eyebrows together, biting my bottom lip. To be honest, I hadn't really thought about that. I mean, sure, I did know that we were going separate ways after graduation, but I had always put the thought to the side, thinking we still had a lot of time left and that my feelings for him would have disappeared by then. But three months? Three *months*? What happened to *years*?

"I-I..." I trailed off, not knowing what to say. The realization that Louis and I weren't going to meet every day after these three months hit me like a slap in the face. How was I going to survive? I had already grown fonder of him than I ever thought I would, especially after that week before my birthday when we spent so much time together.

"You haven't thought about it, have you?" She asked, already knowing the answer.

I shook my head, letting out a sigh. "I didn't realize we aren't going to see each other every day anymore once we graduate," I mumbled.

She tilted her head to the side. "See, that's why you have to do something. And, you really don't have anything to lose because you are going separate ways in just a few months anyway. Think about it, H."

Letting out a sigh, I shook my head. "I don't know, Gems. It doesn't feel right to try hitting on him. Our relationship isn't like that. I can't put my finger on it, but it's uh... it's not like anyone else's. We don't know too much about each other in general, but whenever it's just the two of us, it feels like we have this bond. I don't know, I might just be talking bullshit right now," I sighed, running my hands over my face.

Mom stopped moving her hands in my hair. "I don't think you are, honey. I remember when he came here to take you to practice. There was just something about his cheekiness when he asked for my permission to throw you over his shoulder that has stuck to my head," she explained.

I turned to her with a frown on my face. "What are you trying to say?" I wondered.

She shrugged her shoulders. "I'm just saying that I think you two might actually have some kind of bond," she explained to me.

Her words made me shake my head. "You're just saying that to make me feel better, aren't you? Besides, Louis has barely talked to me during the past week, so I'm pretty sure we've both gotten it wrong," I muttered.

"What happened to him?" Gemma asked.

I turned to her, biting my bottom lip. "He's been acting weird since he found out that I'm bisexual. He told me today that his behavior doesn't have anything to do with me, but I don't know for sure. It did really sound like he was telling the truth, though," I sighed.

Gemma pinched her bottom lip between her forefinger and thumb, thinking of what I had just told her. "Okay, so he knows you're bisexual?"

I nodded my head slowly. "He found out at my birthday party, and I confirmed it on my birthday. He was fine with it, though. He just told me that love is love," I explained, my eyebrows pulled together.

"I don't think that's what's bothering him, to be honest," mom implied. "I just have a feeling Louis isn't the type of guy to judge someone. He is good, a sweetheart even."

Mom's description of Louis made my lips twitch. Even if he and I would never be together, it warmed my heart that she seemed to like him so much. I just wished I could call him mine.

"He is, isn't he?" I beamed, feeling relieved that I could finally let my feelings out. I had never expressed my feelings for him openly before, and it felt so good, like a weight had been lifted from my shoulders.

"I refuse to let this chance slip away from you, H. I can see how much he means to you, and if there's even a slight chance he feels the same way, then I think you should go for it. His car is outside our house for some reason, which must mean he cares more than you think, at least."

I inhaled a deep breath as mom placed a hand on my shoulder. "About that, why is his car even here?" She wondered.

Letting out a deep sigh, I ran a hand through my curls. "A guy on the team intentionally tackled his foot during practice, and I think his ankle is sprained, to be honest. However, he couldn't drive home because of it, so I offered to do it. Then he told me I could have his car during the time he'll be injured if I promise to drive him to and from school and practice every day," I explained, and Gemma looked at me knowingly.

"Sounds like someone wants to spend time with you."

I scoffed. "Oh, shut it. He just doesn't have any other way to get to school if he doesn't want to take the bus, which I know he doesn't. Especially not if he's getting crutches."

Gemma let out a chuckle. "Alright, alright," she said, raising her hands in defense.

Shooting her a glare, I looked at mom who was playing with some of my curly locks. "You know what? I think we should invite him over for dinner. Don't you think that would be a great idea? I mean, you say he's not feeling at his best right now, so inviting him would probably cheer him up," she suggested, making me almost choke on my saliva.

"No, absolutely not. That is not happening, mom. Don't you even try," I warned her.

She pouted her lips. "But I want to meet him now that I know you like him."

Letting out a groan, I got up from the couch. "You know, one of the reasons I never told you guys that I like him was because I knew you would tell him somehow, and I don't want you to ruin things for me. Let me just handle my life myself, alright? I don't want you to get involved with this," I explained, crossing my arms over my chest.

Mom and Gemma exchanged looks before turning to me. They both let out sighs, but mom was the one to speak up. "You're right, honey. I just got a little excited about it. I'm sorry," she apologized with a sincere look on her face.

Gemma nodded her head in agreement. "Yeah. I mean, I can't deny that I really want you to do something about the situation, but you are right. This is your life, not ours. We can't control what decisions you decide to make. As long as you do what you really want, then we are happy for you," she told me sincerely. "And I won't tell Louis, I promise."

Mom looked at me, the smile on her face now gone. "Me too, honey. From now on, our lips are sealed."

When I had locked the front door behind myself and walked over to Louis' black sports car the following morning, I couldn't help but feel nervous. It wasn't the fact that I would meet the guy I liked in just a few minutes that caused it, but the fact that I was going to drive his car alone for the second time now. Okay, maybe I was a little nervous to pick Louis up too. We were going to be alone, after all.

After throwing my bag in the backseat, I positioned myself behind the wheel, taking a deep breath before pressing the button to my left. The engine instantly started up with a roaring sound. I then remembered how Louis showed me how to get the car in reverse before pulling out of the driveway carefully. The last thing I wanted was to crash his car.

During the time it took to drive to Louis' place, I tried to get used to the sensible brakes so the car wouldn't come to an abrupt stop when he was in the car with me again. It was quite hard, though, but it got better each time I had to use them.

The second I pulled over outside Louis' white house, the clock read 7:28, which meant I was on time, and I almost breathed out a sigh of relief since I didn't want him to find any reason to be mad at me.

It didn't take long until I could see his figure getting out of the house, and he started hopping on his good foot towards the car. Since it was still cold outside, the ground could possibly be slippery, so I got out of the car to support him the rest of the way to the vehicle. I also did it because I wanted to in general.

"I see you're on time," he mumbled as I wrapped his arm around my shoulders.

"Of course," I said, flashing him a smile. He didn't see it, though, because he was facing forward.

The second we were both inside the car, I turned to him. "How's your ankle?" I asked him, starting up the vehicle with ease now that I had done it three times before.

He shrugged his shoulders, avoiding eye contact. "It's alright. Can't really walk on it, though."

I rolled my eyes, shaking my head. Well, of course he couldn't walk on it. His ankle was probably sprained, and I was sure it hurt like hell even if he didn't want to admit it. "You should probably go to the school nurse and have it checked," I told him. "She'll hopefully give you crutches too because you can't hop around like that all day."

He mumbled something under his breath, staring out the side window. "I've managed just fine so far."

Letting out a sigh, I ran a hand through my curls. "Do you want to get better or not? If you don't get crutches and start walking on it too early, it is going to take much longer until you can play soccer again," I reminded him, which made him shut up.

After a few seconds, he let out a sigh. "I'll go there after first class."

"Great."

We were quiet during the next few minutes, and honestly, I didn't expect Louis to break the silence. He wasn't very talkative these days after all. "I see you took care of my car."

I glanced at the side of his face, noticing that he had cracked a small smile. "Well, of course. You thought I was going to crash it once you weren't in it anymore?" I wondered, raising my eyebrows at him.

Truth be told, that was exactly what I had thought I would do, but he didn't need to know that.

"Judging by the way you were driving yesterday, then yes, I did. It wouldn't have surprised me at all," he told me, an amused look making its way to his face, but it didn't quite reach his eyes.

"Heeey," I whined. "That's not fair. It was my first time driving it, remember?"

He rolled his eyes, nodding his head. "I do remember that, Curly. That's still no excuse, though."

I let out a huff, turning my face to focus on the road. On the inside, however, I was screaming with happiness because even if I could tell something was still bothering him, I just missed this so much, the way he would tease me whenever he got the chance to. Even if it wasn't whole-heartedly, it was at least getting there.

Once I had parked Louis' car in an empty spot, I got out, making sure to get around it quickly to help Louis out before he tried to do it on his own. He let out a grunt when I heaved him up from the seat, gripping his upper arms tightly so he wouldn't fall.

Thankfully, Niall's school bus showed up right then, and I didn't hesitate to call him over because I had no idea how I would manage to support Louis all the way to our lockers while carrying our bags.

The second Niall caught sight of us after hearing my call, his eyes widened in recognition, and he instantly made his way over. "Hey, guys," he greeted, eying Louis. "Damn, how's your foot, man?"

Louis looked down at the ground, avoiding eye contact with the blonde guy. "I'm fine," he muttered carelessly.

Niall looked at me with raised eyebrows, and I just shrugged my shoulders. "Can you please carry our bags, Niall? I don't think I'll manage to do it while supporting Louis," I pleaded, flashing him a small smile.

He nodded his head. "Of course, mate. Are they in the backseat?"

"Yeah."

All three of us started heading towards the school entrance, Louis placing his left foot on the ground lightly every now and then since it was hard not to. He really needed those crutches as soon as possible. Otherwise, I was sure his ankle was never going to heal.

After we had managed to make our way through the hallways that were crowded with people who kept throwing us curious glances, we finally arrived at our lockers. Louis instantly slipped out of my hold to open his and get rid of his winter jacket and bag that Niall handed him. He then shut it quickly before turning around to leave, but I stopped him.

"Louis, what are you doing?" I asked him, my face in a scowl.

He raised an eyebrow at me. "What does it look like I'm doing? I'm heading to class."

I let out a sigh, shaking my head. "You shouldn't put pressure on your ankle," I mumbled so quietly I thought he didn't hear me, but I could tell he did because the next second, he rolled his eyes.

"I'll be fine," he muttered before turning around to leave without uttering another word.

Letting out another sigh, I ran a hand through my curls.

"He's quite stubborn, isn't he?" Niall said, raising his eyebrows at me.

"Tell me about it," I muttered, grabbing my Economics book from my locker. "He just doesn't understand that it will only get worse if he declines the help."

Niall tilted his head to the side, a small smile playing on his lips. "It's actually quite cute how much you seem to care about him."

I could feel my heart stop beating in my chest as my body froze to ice. "He's uh... he's our friend," I tried to cover it, but it only made his smile widen.

"Yeah, but you two seem to have grown closer lately. You don't bicker as much as you used to, you just drove him to school, and now you care about him too. It's cute."

I furrowed my eyebrows, secretly wanting to know what he meant by the word 'cute'. What was *cute*?

"Uh, sure," was all I said before shutting my locker. "See you after class, Niall."

"For sure. Bye, mate!"

Chapter 19

As soon as the bell rang, signaling the end of the first class of the day, I gathered my books and almost sprinted out of the classroom. I wanted to get to my locker as quickly as possible to make sure Louis was really going to the nurse. Knowing him, he could have just told me he was only to make me shut up.

The second I arrived at my destination, I let out a sigh of relief because Louis was there along with Liam, Niall and Zayn. However, he was keeping a distance from them, just like he had done every day this past week. Now that I thought about it, he hadn't even been chatting up a girl during this time that he had been off.

"Hey, guys," I greeted, walking up to my locker to get rid of my books.

"Harry," Liam smiled as Zayn nodded his head in acknowledgment.

"We were just talking about doing something all five of us after school tomorrow. It's been quite a while since we had a guys' night, hasn't it?" Niall informed, looking at me.

I nodded my head. "Sounds nice. What's the plan?"

"We were just thinking of hanging out at one of our places, playing some video games, drinking some beer and whatnot. How does that sound?" Zayn asked, and I couldn't help but look over my shoulder where Louis was standing, his face hidden behind his locker door.

"I'm in," I told him. "What about you, Louis?"

The feathery-haired boy's face appeared from behind his locker door, his lips pursed as he shrugged. "I guess so."

"Great!" Liam cheered, clapping his hands together.

Zayn, Liam and Niall went back to talking about the plans on Friday while I turned my attention to the quiet boy instead. "Have you been to the nurse yet?"

Louis furrowed his eyebrows together, slamming his locker shut. "No."

Letting out a sigh, I ran a hand through my curls. "You should really go there, you know? I'm sure she's going to--"

"Why are you doing this?" He snapped, cutting me off in the middle of the sentence.

I was taken aback by his words, my mouth falling open. "I uh, what... what do you mean?"

"Why do you suddenly seem to care so much? I mean, just the other day you told me that we aren't close, so none of this makes any sense," he explained, avoiding eye contact.

To say I was shocked would be an understatement. I never thought those words would stick to his head. "I... I told you that because I thought that's how you saw us," I mumbled, my eyebrows knitting together.

Louis' jaw clenched and unclenched as he shook his head, a fake smile forming on his lips. "I thought we had grown closer, but clearly, I was the only one thinking so."

I opened my mouth to say something, but I was left speechless. I didn't know he felt that way. Had this been bugging him ever since we had it up all those days ago? Was this part of the reason he had been acting the way he did this past week? But why hadn't he just told me that if so?

Running my hands over my face, I shook my head. "That's not true, Louis. I... I didn't mean to say that. I just... I had to blame the fact that I never told you about my uh... my sexuality on something. Besides, we weren't really close up until a week ago, so I didn't think you would take offense. I'm so sorry," I apologized, pulling my bottom lip between my teeth.

He shrugged his shoulders, looking away from me. "It doesn't really matter. I just wanted to know why you're acting like you care about me. You don't have to pretend, you know? I'm used to having people not caring about me."

Now that made me confused if anything. What was he talking about? But before I had time to question him about it, the bell rang. Louis instantly turned around to start hopping away, but I reached out to grip his upper arm.

"I have no idea what you're talking about, but I am not letting you walk to next class before you have had your ankle checked. I don't care if you don't believe me, but I do care about you," I told him, making him turn around.

He watched me for a few seconds, his eyes examining my features until he let out a sigh. "Fine, I'll do it, but only because I want my ankle to get better sooner," he muttered, and with that said, he turned on his heel again. Only this time, he started heading in the direction of the school nurse instead of his classroom.

It turned out Louis really did go to the nurse because after second class, he came hopping on a pair of crutches with a new bandage wrapped around his ankle. He didn't say a word as he opened his locker to shove the books he had tucked under his arm in it.

He probably noticed me staring, though, because the next second, he turned to me with raised eyebrows. "Something's on your mind, Curly?"

I looked away, biting my bottom lip. "I just... I see you got crutches after all," I mumbled, our last conversation playing on repeat in my head. I couldn't stop thinking about the way he had snapped at me, and the fact that he thought I didn't care about him. If he only knew how much I really cared... he would probably be freaked out.

But thanks to that, I didn't want to come off as too pushy with him because if he thought I didn't care, then he would only get more upset with me.

"I did. It's kind of easier to move now. Don't need to grab everything around me anymore," he chuckled dryly, looking down at his feet.

I nodded slowly. There was a short silence where I realized I wanted to bring up what happened just an hour ago. "About earlier, I didn't--"

He reached a hand up to stop me, a faint smile on his face as he shook his head. "Don't say anything. It's okay. Let's just put that behind us, yeah? Just don't... I'll manage fine on my own, alright?"

I wanted to disagree with him, but I didn't want to make a fuss about it. If he was willing to put that conversation behind us as long as I just took a step back, then I could make him believe I cared in some other way. "Alright," I said, even though every part of me wanted to help him out. "I'll see you at lunch, yeah?"

He nodded his head, the faint smile still prominent on his lips. "For sure."

I was just about to turn to my locker and head to my next class when I saw him struggling to get his books out, and then fumbling with them while using his crutches. I knew he didn't want my help - he had made that very clear - and I knew I shouldn't say anything considering I was sure he was just going to get mad at me, but I couldn't just watch him struggle like that.

"Louis, you don't want me to help you carry--"

He cut me off by turning to me, the smile now gone from his face. "Seriously, Curly. I meant what I said."

I let out a sigh, running a hand through my curls. "I'm sorry."

He muttered something under his breath before finally managing to tuck his books under his arm. He then started hopping away towards his next class.

Why did I have to say that? I knew I shouldn't have offered to help him, but I couldn't stop myself. He had been just fine when I had helped him yesterday and earlier this morning, though, so what made him finally snap at me? Did it all just get too much for him?

During the next hour, I found myself lost in my thoughts, trying to get my head around everything that had happened. I just couldn't stop thinking about how much it hurt knowing that he thought I didn't care about him when I literally couldn't go a day without worrying about how he was doing.

I was happy that he finally told me it had bugged him when I said that we weren't close, though. It had been really stupid of me to say that to begin with because we had grown closer during that week. However, I didn't think he would take it so personally because honestly, I didn't think he thought the same way about it. I guess I was wrong, though.

The second the bell rang, signaling it was time for lunch, I got up from my seat to walk back to my locker. It took some time because the hallways were really crowded during this time of the day, but I managed to get there eventually.

Neither of the guys was there when I arrived, so I quickly got rid of my books, shoving them into my locker. I was just about to turn around when I heard a familiar voice in the hallway, making every muscle in my body freeze to ice because the voice was soon followed by a female's laugh.

When I finally decided to look up, my heart dropped to the pit of my stomach because there Louis was, walking with a brown-haired girl. Or, Louis was using his crutches while the girl was carrying his books.

Okay, so this unfamiliar girl could help him, but I, his best friend, couldn't? Why did that hurt *so* much?

I instantly looked away from them, regretting that I had even mentioned that he hadn't chatted up a girl during the past week. He obviously hadn't changed. I had probably just not caught sight of him when he had been talking to any of them.

With a sigh, I closed my locker and started walking in the direction of the cafeteria. However, I didn't really look where I was going, so, unfortunately, I managed to walk right into someone's shoulder. The impact wasn't harsh enough for either of us to stumble, but it caused our eyes to meet, and God, I really wished I had been aware of where I was going.

Louis' ocean blue eyes scanned my face while I looked back at him, my face probably showing just how hurt I was. He wasn't supposed to see it, but since I was such a klutz, I just had to catch his attention somehow, didn't I?

My eyes trailed to the girl who hadn't noticed what had happened before I looked back at Louis, the muscles in my face hardening. I then turned around abruptly and continued heading in the direction of the cafeteria, not bothering to look back to see if he was still watching me.

Once I entered the crowded room, I bought a cheese sandwich along with a bottle of coke before sitting down at the table where Liam and Niall were already sitting. I greeted them quietly before opening the wrapper of my sandwich although I wasn't planning on eating it. I wasn't really hungry anymore.

It took a few minutes until Louis entered the room, this time without a girl by his side. Instead, he was hopping on his crutches alone towards the café to buy something to eat. The lady behind the cash register eyed him sympathetically as he took both crutches in one hand and the sandwich and bottle of soda in the other, but he didn't notice.

Why was this guy so stubborn? Why didn't he just ask for help? And why couldn't he ask his friends for help instead of people he didn't know? I just didn't understand.

Once he arrived at our table - after hopping on his good foot - he put the crutches to the side before sitting down in the seat next to me, placing his sandwich and bottle of soda on the table. He didn't say a word, nor did he look up to notice that everyone at the table was looking at him.

"So, Louis, how's the crutches working for you?" Niall asked curiously, raising his eyebrows at him.

Louis reached out to unwrap his sandwich before looking up at the blonde-haired boy. "I thought I liked them, but now I'm not so sure anymore," he mumbled, which made me furrow my eyebrows.

His comment made everyone confused. "What do you mean?" Liam wondered.

Louis let out a sigh, looking down at the sandwich in his hand. "I can't fucking carry anything on my own while using them, and I don't like it when people feel the need to help me."

My heart stopped beating in my chest as my muscles froze. Did that mean he never wanted that girl to help him carry his books either?

Niall and Liam seemed a bit taken aback by his words as well. "I'm uh... I'm sure they just want to be nice, though?" Liam said hesitantly.

Louis didn't say anything to that. He just started eating his sandwich while minding his own business. That was until I could feel him glancing at the side of my face. At first, I tried to avoid it, but as he kept doing it, I eventually couldn't stop myself from turning my head to meet his gaze.

"You're not eating, Curly," he pointed out, his eyes flickering to my untouched sandwich on the table.

I shrugged my shoulders. "I'm not hungry."

He shook his head. "Nonsense. We both know you are."

Knitting my eyebrows together, I looked away from him.

"Fine, don't eat then," he huffed, crossing his arms over his chest. "I hope you know that you're still driving me home after school. You do have my car after all," he reminded me.

I opened my mouth to reply, but nothing came out because I was so shocked that he had talked to me like that after everything that had happened today. If I could, I would love to get a glimpse of what was going on inside that boy's head because right now, he was confusing me so much that it was giving me a headache.

Why did he have such a big problem with people helping him, and what on earth did he mean by the fact that he was used to having people not caring about him? Damn, I couldn't wait to find out what the reason behind all this was.

Chapter 20

The second I walked to my locker after the last class of the day, I could almost feel myself getting a little nervous because I was going to be alone with Louis again. Only this time, it felt worse since it was after he had caught me off guard by telling me he thought I was only pretending to care about him this morning.

After lunch, we hadn't really talked to each other, but he had kept glancing at me during the breaks, just like he had done during the last couple of days. It only added to the confusion I felt about every action he made nowadays, but I couldn't help but be a little happy about it as well, considering it meant he was still paying attention to me. As long as he wasn't mad at me, it was all good.

Louis was already there when I got to the lockers, trying to sling his bag over his shoulder while using his crutches. The scene made me almost frustrated because why was he trying so hard? It didn't make any sense. He could easily just ask for help, but he just wanted to do it by himself.

The second he noticed me walking over, he let out a frustrated groan and threw the bag to the floor. "Stupid bag. I'll just leave you there to rot," he muttered under his breath. It made me roll my eyes.

"The bag has done you nothing wrong, Louis. Don't blame it for your stubbornness."

I was almost surprised that those words left my mouth, but I guess I was finally starting to recover from what he had confessed to me this morning. Also, I was growing a little tired of him not wanting any help.

He seemed surprised by my words as well, judging by the way his mouth fell open. He recovered pretty quickly, though. "I don't even like it to begin with," he grumbled. "And I'm not stubborn."

The last part almost made me let out a loud bark of laughter because that must be the biggest lie of the century. However, I settled with raising my eyebrows at him instead. "You're joking with me, right?" I asked him.

But when he looked me in the eye, there was no trace of humor on his face. "I just don't want people to pity me."

Rolling my eyes, I shook my head. "You do know some people might actually *want* to help you, though? I know what you said earlier, but it doesn't really make any sense. Some people do care about you."

I could swear I heard him say 'not the people I want to' but I wasn't sure because he was mumbling. I decided not to question him about it, though, because I knew he wouldn't answer me anyway. Instead, I grabbed my jacket and bag from my locker before closing it.

Without even glancing at Louis, I picked his bag up from the floor and slung it over my other shoulder. "I don't care what you say, I'm carrying your bag no matter what," I muttered, walking past him to start heading towards the exit.

It didn't take long until I could hear the sound of his crutches clinking against the floor behind me, so I knew he was following me despite everything. The second we got to his car, I unlocked it before throwing our bags into the backseat. I didn't help him when he placed his crutches in the car and climbed into the passenger seat. I wasn't so stupid that I was going to repeat the actions I knew would only make him upset with me again.

I didn't start up the car right away because there was something that had been bothering me ever since this morning. Without turning to him, I gripped the wheel while staring out the windshield. "You told me we were good."

Through the corner of my eye, I could see Louis' head snapping to me. He ran a hand through his fringe as he inhaled a deep breath. "We are good."

Yeah, right.

I pulled my eyebrows together, shaking my head. "Then why didn't you tell me it bothered you when I said we weren't close?" I wondered, finally turning to meet his gaze.

He let out a sigh. "Because there's nothing to do about it. I can't go around blaming you for not having the same idea of our friendship as I do."

I opened my mouth to protest, but he held his hand up, signaling me to keep quiet. "You have already explained yourself, it's okay."

I didn't know if that meant he believed me or if he just didn't want to hear me explain myself again. I really hoped for the prior because I couldn't have him think that I didn't want to be close to him. I wanted to be as close as fucking possible. Couldn't he see that?

"Can I ask why you snapped at me? I mean, you were just fine with me helping you yesterday," I mumbled, changing the topic since he seemed to be finished with the previous one.

He let out a sigh. "I have already told you that I don't like it when people pity me, so when you tried to help me so much, I guess something just snapped inside me. I should have just told you how I felt, but I thought you would realize it," he explained.

I pursed my lips, thinking about the fact that he didn't think I cared about him. It wasn't hard to tell that everything was connected. Why he didn't want people to help him, and why he had a hard time believing people cared about him. He told me that he wasn't used to having people caring, but who had he been talking about? Who even put these thoughts in his head to begin with?

"Curly, it's been almost five minutes and we are still parked outside the school. Are you planning on getting out of here anytime soon, or shall I call someone else to pick me up?" Louis questioned, pulling me out of my thoughts.

"Oh, shut it," I muttered under my breath, turning on the engine to pull out of the parking space.

After sitting in silence for a couple of minutes, I couldn't help but ask him about my previous thoughts. "So, you really don't think I care about you, huh?"

Louis turned to me with a frown on his face. "Can't we just forget about that? I already told you I don't really think anyone cares," he grunted.

I ran a hand through my curls, biting my bottom lip. "Does that mean you don't remember how I helped you at the party when you hurt yourself on the stairs? Or how I stopped you from beating Ryan yesterday?"

He was quiet for a long time, so long that I started wondering if he was even going to answer me. "You just did because you felt like you had to."

I let out a snort, shaking my head. "You're unbelievable."

"Can't we just talk about something else instead? I'm sick of having these conversations. Everything is already so fucking depressing nowadays with my injury and uh... other stuff. I just want to forget about it for a second," he muttered, a tired look on his face.

I turned to look at him, my eyebrows furrowed together. "What do you want to talk about then?"

He shrugged his shoulders. "I don't know... um, you maybe? Do you have work today?" He asked me, and it was probably the first time he talked about my job without making fun of it.

I raised my eyebrows before nodding my head, my eyes back to focusing on the road. "I do. It's Thursday, after all."

Through the corner of my eye, I could see him look down at his lap while biting his bottom lip. "Is uh... Is Lucas going to be there?"

I was a little confused by his question. "Yeah, I guess so? I don't really keep track of his shifts, though. Why?" I asked.

He shrugged his shoulders. "I was just wondering," he replied.

His answer made me even more confused, and I was just about to question him about it when he beat me to it. "You know what? I think I might just go with you to try out that chicken stew you told me about the other day. I'm getting quite hungry."

My mouth fell open in shock because what the hell? Where did that even come from? "You what?"

"Why not?" He asked me, looking at the side of my face. "You said it was good, didn't you?"

Yes, but I wasn't expecting you to come up with that idea.
"Uh, I guess."

"Then why not? Unless you were lying about it, that is," he said, narrowing his eyes at me in suspicion.

I couldn't help but let out a light chuckle as I shook my head. "Of course not. I wouldn't lie about that."

"Good."

It wasn't until it fell silent again that I realized just how much I had missed talking to Louis like this. It made my heart flutter in my chest, even if there was a voice in the back of my head reminding me of everything that had taken place before this conversation.

However, I didn't want to think about that now, not when he was acting like this. I mean, before he was injured yesterday, we had gone an entire week without barely even talking to each other, and I had missed it too much.

"I'm assuming I'm not driving you home then?"

He shook his head. "No, you're not. You're driving me to your work once you have gotten changed at your house."

Damn, he actually remembered my routines from driving me to work twice that week when we hung out together. Was that supposed to make my heart burst with joy? Because it did.

I nodded my head, a smile tugging on my lips because I couldn't hold it back.

During the rest of the ride to my place, I learned that the nurse told him he would need to have his ankle bandaged for at least a week because his ankle was in fact sprained. As soon as it didn't hurt anymore, he was going to start putting pressure on it. If everything went as planned, he would be able to walk normally in about a week and a half, but he was going to need rehab afterward in order to no get it sprained all over again.

Other than that, we didn't talk much during the ride to my house and the diner, but it was okay. I was more than happy about the conversation we just had. Between us, it was the closest to normal I had felt in a very long time.

I parked Louis' car outside the restaurant after I had stopped to get changed into a pair of dark blue jeans and a white t-shirt at home. The last thing I needed was to be formally dressed, considering my apron was basically the only thing the customers pointed out about my attire anyway.

Louis got out of the car by himself and grabbed the crutches from the backseat before starting to hop towards the entrance. "I'll see you inside then, Curly."

I nodded my head, smiling at his back as I made my way to the backdoor. I hurried to put my apron on before walking through the kitchen to get out to the diner. Lucas was standing behind the counter when I got there, taking charge of a customer.

"Harry!" He burst out when he caught sight of me, flailing his arms out.

I rolled my eyes, shaking my head. "Someone's happy, I see."

He tilted his head to the side, his blue eyes twinkling from the lights in the room. "I thought we were over this? I am always happy to see you, mate," he chuckled, making me laugh as well.

We were interrupted by someone clearing their throat, causing both of our heads to snap in the direction of the sound. My heart skipped a beat at the sight of Louis, although I knew he was going to show up. He just always managed to have this effect on me.

His jaw was clenched tightly as his gaze flickered between me and Lucas. Lucas didn't seem to notice this because his eyes widened in surprise as he burst out excitedly; "Louis? Wow, it's been ages, man! It's so nice to see you again."

Watching Louis' reaction made a feeling of déjà vu erupt inside me because it was so close to how he had been looking at Lucas the first time he had come here to eat. However, after a few seconds, he composed himself and managed to curl his lips into a smile, although it looked more like a grimace, to be honest.

"You too, Lucas," he nodded in acknowledgment, turning to look at me. "Um, you know my order, right?" He asked, his lips pressed into a tight line as he flickered his gaze to Lucas for a second.

"Of course," I said, a cheeky smile forming on my lips. "My favorite."

His face lit up a little at my words, a light chuckle escaping his lips as he nodded. "I guess."

Through the corner of my eye, I could see Lucas looking at us with raised eyebrows, but he didn't say anything as I found myself getting lost, staring into Louis' blue irises while he was staring back into my green ones. After a few seconds, Lucas eventually interrupted us, though.

"So... Are you handing the order to the kitchen, Harry?" He wondered.

I snapped back to reality, breaking my and Louis' eye contact and clearing my throat. "Um, yeah. Of course," I muttered, turning around to head into the kitchen.

Once I got back to the diner, Louis had hopped away to the same table he sat at the last time he visited. I could feel his eyes on me as I walked over to Lucas who looked up when I arrived. A smile formed on his lips upon seeing me.

"So, what happened to him?" He asked, nodding in the direction of where Louis was sitting, referring to the crutches he was using.

I bit my bottom lip. "Um, a guy on the team intentionally tackled him and hurt his ankle, so now he's on crutches for about a week and a half," I explained.

"Damn, tough luck," he grimaced. "He doesn't really like me, does he?"

I furrowed my eyebrows, knowing he must be referring to the way Louis had replied to him when he arrived, but Louis had never told me that he didn't like him. "He's never mentioned anything about it."

Lucas tilted his head to the side, the grimace never leaving his face. "Harry, I can literally feel him glaring at me at this second. He does not like me. I don't really recall anything I ever did to him, though," he explained, making me even more confused.

I turned around, only to notice that Louis was in fact glaring at us, or more specifically at Lucas. He was right. I didn't recall anything he had done to make Louis dislike him either. So, why was Louis glaring at him?

Lucas had to take care of a customer then, and I was called to the kitchen. When Louis' meal was finished, I grabbed his plate and walked over to him with it. He had now fished his phone from his pocket and was typing away on it.

"Here you go," I said, putting the plate down in front of him on the table.

He looked up from his device at the sound of my voice and placed the phone on the table. "So, this is the famous chicken stew you've been talking about, then?" He wondered, the corners of his lips curling.

"The one and only," I assured him.

He pursed his lips, looking down at it before turning his gaze up to meet mine again. "I can't say it looks very appealing to me."

If it wasn't for the teasing look on his face, I would have thought he meant what he said, but now I knew he was only joking with me. It had been quite some time since he last did, though, so no one could really blame me for thinking he was being serious. "It doesn't get any better, Louis. I can promise you so much," I told him, flashing him a smirk.

He shook his head, a small smile on his lips. "We'll see about that."

Before I had time to reply to him, I was called to the kitchen again, probably to fetch another order I had to serve. I shot him an apologetic look before walking away, hoping I would get to talk to him in a bit again so I could ask him what he thought about the meal.

It turned out I wasn't that lucky, though, because an entire basketball team entered the diner right then, which meant I instantly became caught up with work. It was probably half an hour later that I could finally tear myself away from it, but unfortunately, I could see Louis approach me where I was standing behind the counter then. By the looks of it, he was leaving, which made my heart drop in my chest.

Lucas' shift ended a few minutes ago, so there were only another co-worker and I standing there when Louis stopped in front of me. "Danny's here to pick me up," he announced, nodding in the direction of the exit.

I nodded my head, trying not to show my disappointment. "I'll see you tomorrow, though, right?"

He flashed me a small smile. "Yeah, for sure. You're picking me up at seven-thirty in the morning. I mean, you do have my car after all," he reminded me, making me want to smack myself on the forehead. Right, I was driving his car. How come I had already forgotten about that?

"Right."

He was just about to turn around and leave when he stopped himself. "Oh, and by the way, the chicken stew was good. I can see why you like it so much," he grinned.

With that said, he finally hopped out of the diner, leaving me to smile at the door that closed behind him. I could tell why I liked him so much. There was literally no reason why I shouldn't. He was just... impossible not to like.

The next couple of hours were pretty uneventful. I served boring customers who didn't even as much as try being nice or utter more than a 'thanks' to me. However, that was until a familiar blonde girl walked into the diner. I hadn't seen her in weeks, but the sight of her made my lips curl into a smile.

"Hi, Lottie," I greeted as she walked up to me.

The second she saw me standing behind the counter, her face lit up. "Hey, Harry. Fancy seeing you here."

I let out a chuckle. "It is my workplace after all."

She nodded in agreement, the smile never leaving her face. "So, I don't know if you're the right person to talk to considering I know you're a waiter, but I'm here to pick up another takeaway," she informed me.

That reminded me of something. Didn't Lottie and Fizzy pick up a takeaway of chicken stew the last time they were here? Did that mean Louis never ate with them at that time?

I waved a hand in dismissal. "It's okay," I told her. "Um, can I ask you something?"

She looked at me curiously. "Yes, of course."

"Does Louis eat the food you order from here?" I wondered, making her furrow her eyebrows.

"Um... No, not usually. It's quite seldom he attends our family dinners."

"Why is that?" I couldn't help but ask her, my curiosity blossoming.

She shrugged her shoulders. "It's kind of complicated, and not really my story to tell. However, it's been worse lately, ever since he found out about... something. I understand why he doesn't want to attend them, though," she grimaced, making my mouth fall open.

"Oh."

She nodded her head, looking behind my shoulder. Right then, a plastic bag was placed on the counter next to us by my co-worker. "Pasta Bolognese."

"That's me," Lottie announced, walking over to pay for the food.

I was left in deep thought, thinking about what she had just told me while trying to fit the puzzle pieces together in my head. I was so caught up in it that I almost missed Lottie waving goodbye to me.

"It was nice to see you again, Harry. Bye!"

"Bye, Lottie," I called back, plastering a smile on my face.

During the remaining time of my shift, I walked around the diner, thinking about what I had just learned. Louis usually didn't attend family dinners, and Lottie said he had a good reason not to. Then there was the part that stuck to me the most;

*It's been worse lately, ever since he found out about...
something.*

Could this be the main reason why he had been acting weird the past week?

Chapter 21

When I drove to Louis' place the next morning, I found myself longing to meet him again. The fact that I hadn't been able to speak to him the other day at the diner made me miss him even more than usual, especially since he was finally starting to act like his usual self. Well, if you didn't count the fact that he still got upset when people tried to help him. I knew better than to fall into that trap again, though.

During the last couple of weeks when I had really gotten to know Louis, I had learned that there were a few things that made him upset whenever they were brought up. The first time it happened was after he had hit himself at the party. His entire mood dropped whenever it was mentioned. Then there was whenever someone suggested going over to his house. Even though we had been there before, he was always on edge whenever it was brought up.

At last, it was the way he didn't want anyone to help him. He said he was used to having people not caring about him, which must be the reason behind that. I mean, if you didn't believe people cared about you, you didn't want anyone to look out for you either.

The worst thing about it all was that I couldn't ask him about it. Well, at least not right now because I knew him well enough to know that he would only get upset with me and shut me out once again if I did so, and I didn't want that.

So, as soon as Louis joined me in the car (without his bag, considering it was still in the backseat since yesterday), I promised myself not to bring it up. I wanted to get closer to him, not make him want to leave and get away from me.

"Morning, Curly," he greeted after throwing his crutches in the backseat and clumsily getting into the passenger seat.

I turned to him, a smile on my face. "Good morning, Louis. How're you doing?"

He shrugged his shoulders. "I'm alright. Better than I have been in a while," he admitted, giving me a small smile in return. "You?"

I nodded. "I'm good too. I'm sorry for what happened at the diner yesterday, though. There are usually not that many people there at the same time," I apologized, biting my bottom lip.

Letting out a light chuckle, he shook his head. "It's okay. You were there to work, not talk to customers."

I flashed him another smile before turning on the engine and driving off to school. "So, Lottie visited the restaurant yesterday after you left," I told him, only curious to see his reaction, not to interrogate him about what she had told me.

He raised his eyebrows, looking a little surprised. "Yeah? You didn't try anything with her, did you?" He wondered, sounding suspicious.

I couldn't help but let out a laugh as I shook my head. "No, Louis. We called a truce, remember? Besides, I think I'm more into guys than girls, to be honest."

"Well, that explains why you didn't acknowledge that waitress at the restaurant on your birthday. You should have seen her face when you didn't so much as give her a second glance... She was so disappointed," he said, shaking his head in amusement.

"Really?" I asked him incredulously. I barely acknowledge her actions at all, but mostly because that was the day Louis had started acting weird. It was even the worst day of them all because he hadn't even paid attention to me, and it was all thanks to the fact that he had found out I was bisexual... I think.

"Yeah. It's actually quite funny how you still haven't figured it out. What about that Evelyn girl, though? There's nothing going on between the two of you either?" He asked, looking at me with raised eyebrows.

I shook my head. "Not on my part. Can't really speak for her, though, but I'm trying to show her that I just want to be friends," I shrugged. "But she is a really nice girl."

He pursed his lips, furrowing his eyebrows together slightly. "So, you didn't lie when you told me you were only getting to know her, and that you 'wasn't feeling it' at the party, huh?"

I was confused by his question because what? Did he think I had lied about that?. "Why would I lie about that?" I asked him, glancing at the side of his face.

He shrugged his shoulders. "It just seemed like you two were getting on so well. That was kind of why I was mad at you that time in the hallway if you remember? I just don't like it when people lie to me," he admitted, flashing me an apologetic smile.

I shook my head. "No, I didn't lie, and I never really do either. I've only done it to you once, and to my defense, I didn't even know I was. I mean when I told you that we hadn't grown closer. I just didn't know if you were on the same page as me, and I didn't want to get my hopes up."

He turned to me with a frown on his face. "Get your hopes up? You mean you would actually want us to be close?"

Knitting my eyebrows together, I glanced at him. "Yeah? I thought I had already explained to you that I didn't mean what I said that time."

I remembered the conversation we had yesterday, and I still wasn't sure if he believed me or not, but I really hoped he did now. I didn't mean to hurt him when I said that we hadn't grown closer, but I didn't know any better. I mean, being close to Louis was something I had dreamed of for a very long time. If I knew better, I would have never declined it.

He slumped back in his seat. "I guess I just didn't know what to believe. But yeah, I'd like for us to be close too. As long as you don't deny it again," he said, sending me a cheeky smile. And damn how I loved to see those crinkles appear by his eyes. Especially when it was because of me. I could literally die happy now.

Feeling breathless, I curled my lips in a smile. "I wouldn't dream of it."

Five minutes later, we arrived at school. I turned off the engine and got out of the car to get our bags from the backseat while Louis grabbed his crutches. I was just about to start walking towards the entrance when he held his hand out to me.

"My bag."

I stared at his hand, letting out a deep sigh. "Louis, you have to realize that I'm not carrying your bag out of pity. I'm doing it because I'm your friend, and friends look out of each other, alright?" I said, glancing up at him.

I didn't want him to be mad at me, but I couldn't let him carry the bag when he was using crutches. It would make me look like an asshole in other people's eyes, and I also couldn't see him suffering while trying to carry it.

He bit his bottom lip, furrowing his eyebrows together before letting out a sigh. "Alright, fine, but don't make it a habit. I'm only letting you help me because I don't really know how I would manage to carry it myself all the way to my locker," he huffed.

I rolled my eyes, slinging the bag over my shoulder. "Works for me."

He glanced at me through the corner of his eye, shaking his head slightly before turning the other way. We then walked to our lockers in silence. The guys were already there, chatting with each other when we arrived.

"Harry, Louis," they greeted in unison.

"Hey, guys," I said, handing Louis his bag once he had opened his locker.

Zayn lifted an eyebrow at us, Niall smiling brightly while Liam just seemed unaffected. "Did you guys come here together?" Zayn asked, making me want to let out a frustrated groan. I was getting tired of always hearing how weird it was for me and Louis to hang out with each other. Weren't we already over this?

"I'm driving him to school now that he can't do it himself," I explained, rolling my eyes.

He pursed his lips. "O-kay. So, we were just talking about hanging at Niall's place tonight, sounds good?"

I looked at Niall before nodding my head with a smile on my face. "Sounds perfect. It's been a while since we were there. I kinda miss Maura," I pouted, making the blonde guy scoff.

"Sorry to break it to you, mate, but mom's not going to be home."

"That's too bad," I muttered, flashing him a smirk.

Niall let out a loud chuckle, shaking his head. "Shut up, Styles."

"How are you feeling today, Louis?" Liam asked, turning everyone's attention to the feathery-haired guy who had just shut his locker.

He looked up at us and nodded his head curtly, the corners of his lips curling a little. "I'm good. My ankle's pretty much the same, but otherwise, I'm feeling a little better."

Liam's face lit up, probably happy that Louis replied to him in a way that didn't make him feel like he had asked something wrong. "That's good to hear, mate. We're certainly going to miss you on the field tomorrow," he grimaced, making Louis scrunch his nose up.

"I'm going to miss being there too. I'll be watching, though," he said, his eyes turning to look at me. "Looks like you are going to be captain now, after all," he chuckled, shaking his head in disbelief.

I had only been joking with him that time when I told him I was going to be captain if he got injured. Or, I wasn't exactly joking because I was going to take his post now, but I never really wanted it to happen. Louis was a great captain, and I was sure I wouldn't be able to reach his standards.

Shaking my head, I feigned a smile. I would much rather have him on the field being captain than have him on the bench being injured.

"Hey, Louis."

My eyes snapped up to see the same brown-haired girl who had helped Louis carrying his books yesterday walk over, a bright smile on her lips. Louis' eyebrows shot up, his mouth falling open slightly. "Uh, hi, Chloé."

"How's your ankle?"

Louis pressed his lips in a tight line, and I wondered if it was because he was growing tired of hearing so many questions about how he was doing. "It's okay, I guess. Same as yesterday," he shrugged, looking at me through the corner of his eyes.

I swallowed hard at the scene in front of me because if there was something I didn't like, it was witnessing him flirting with girls, or girls flirting with him. It probably wasn't that hard to understand, though, because I wished I could be one of them.

Chloé grimaced at his words. "So, since we have the same class, I was wondering if I could walk with you?"

Louis shrugged his shoulders, pursing his lips. "Sure, why not?"

Her entire face lit up at his words, and she instantly reached out to take his books from under his arm without even asking him. I could see him furrow his eyebrows, but he didn't say anything as she took them in her hands and pressed them to her chest along with her own.

I was so close to take a step forward and snatch the books out of her hold because no, she did not get to do that without getting told off. I didn't know what came over me, but I had to bury my hands deep into the back pockets of my jeans not to punch something. Maybe I was immature, but I couldn't help the jealousy that flared up inside me.

As soon as Louis and Chloé were gone, Liam and Zayn walked off to their classes as well, leaving me alone with Niall.

"It looks like you're about to punch something, Harry," he pointed out, raising his eyebrows at me.

I turned to him abruptly, my eyebrows knitting together. "I'm not," I muttered, taking my hands out of my pockets, but they were still balled into tight fists.

I could see Niall look down at my hands, and he shook his head while letting out a sigh. "It's about that girl, isn't it?"

The crease between my eyebrows deepened at his words, and I could feel how my heart was starting to pound in my chest. "I have no idea what you're talking about."

He placed a hand on my shoulder, looking me in the eyes. "It's okay, Harry."

I met his blue eyes with mine, staring into them for a few seconds until I let out a deep sigh. "I have to go."

With that said, I grabbed my books from my locker before heading to my class without looking back at the blonde-haired boy.

He couldn't know that he was right, he just couldn't.

Later that day, I drove to Niall's house all by myself in Louis' car. He told me he could ride with Zayn and Liam since they all lived close to each other, and it would only be a detour for me if I came to pick him up. I wanted to disagree with him, but I couldn't since he would probably wonder why on earth I wanted to pick him up so badly.

The second I arrived at Niall's place, the other boys were thankfully already there. After what Niall witnessed that morning, I had done my best to avoid being alone with him. The last thing I wanted was for him to confront me about Louis again because I had a feeling he was suspecting something.

I was wearing a pair of black, skinny jeans that were ripped at the knees, and a purple, checked button-up with the three top buttons undone, thinking I could at least dress up a little. However, I couldn't speak for the curls because I was sure they were a mess, especially considering the stormy weather outside.

Louis, Niall, Liam and Zayn were all sitting on the white couch when I walked into the living room, their eyes instantly turning to me when they noticed I was standing in the doorframe. "Harry!" They called out and instantly scooted over to make some space for me on the couch.

Luckily for me, the empty spot they made room for was beside Louis, so I didn't hesitate to walk over and sit down beside him and Zayn. "What are you guys up to?" I wondered, only then noticing that there were quite a few cans of beer on the coffee table along with two bowls of snacks.

"We just came here like five minutes ago, so all we've done so far is just to talk about some stuff," Zayn explained, shrugging his shoulders.

Louis' crutches were on the floor at our feet, his injured foot propped up on the coffee table in front of him. By the looks of it, he seemed at ease, something I found relieving. The last thing I wanted was for him to have gone back to being uptight.

"What kind of stuff?" I asked, turning to raise my eyebrows at Zayn.

He shrugged his shoulders. "Girls and things like that."

I wanted to roll my eyes because of course they had been talking about girls. What else did these guys talk about? Why did they never chat about soccer with the same passion? I mean, that was something we all loved as well.

"Speaking of girls, have you heard anything from Evelyn?" Liam asked, his eyes set on me.

His question took me by surprise because I hadn't really talked to her since my birthday party, where I had gotten so drunk I barely remembered what happened. "Uh, no?" I said, raising an eyebrow. Was I supposed to have heard from her?

I could feel the muscles in Louis' thigh tense a little, but I didn't turn to see the look on his face.

Liam narrowed his eyes a little. "Apparently, she's told Alice that she wants to ask you out. Maybe she's just not found the guts to do it yet," he shrugged, making me gulp.

Louis fidgeted in his seat beside me, but I was too caught up in my thoughts to put more thought into it. Was Evelyn seriously planning on asking me out? Truth be told, I had not registered those signals from her, but maybe I had just been too blind to notice it?

Zayn let out an 'ooh' sound. "Damn, Styles. Someone wants the 'd'," he joked, nudging me in the shoulder playfully.

I shot him a glare, shaking my head. "She's not like that," I muttered because I knew she wasn't. Evelyn was nice and friendly, and she hadn't shown me any sign of just wanting to get into my pants.

He rolled his eyes. "Whatever, mate. You definitely have her on the hook, though."

I didn't reply to him, and thankfully, Niall decided to change the topic then. "How about we get this party started by drinking some beer, eh?" He suggested.

We all agreed on that, and the tension that had filled the air was soon gone. We all started talking about soccer instead - thankfully. The guys were pretty curious about what players Louis and I had picked out for the lineup, but both of us were pretty reluctant about revealing anything. They would have to wait until tomorrow.

"But Ryan's not playing, though, is he?" Niall asked, arching his eyebrows at the two of us.

Louis shot me a pointed look, and I let out a sigh. I was just about to open my mouth and explain when he beat me to it. "I didn't want him to play, but Curly here insisted."

After everything that had happened between him and Louis, I wasn't sure if I wanted him to play anymore, but we had already made our minds up and handed over the lineup to Coach, so it was too late to make any changes now.

The guys' mouths fell open at Louis' words, making me let out another sigh. "Look, I don't like him, alright? But he is a great player.... when he doesn't injure people," I grimaced, and Louis rolled his eyes.

"Harry, Ryan's a real ass. He doesn't even deserve to be on the team," Zayn pointed out.

"I know," I groaned, running a hand through my curls. "But now he is, and Coach likes him when he's not being a dick."

"Damn, Harry," Liam said, shaking his head in disbelief.

I pouted my lips, looking to my right where Louis was sitting. I was sure he wouldn't give me any look of reassurance because he was the one out of the five of us who hated Ryan the most right now. So, when he patted my thigh when he noticed the pout on my face, I was surprised to say the least.

I looked up at his face, only to notice that he *was* giving me a reassuring smile. It made my heart skip in my chest. I loved seeing him smile, especially when it was directed at me, so I couldn't help but smile back at him, dimples and all on show.

"Alright, guys. How about we play some Fifa?" Niall suggested, snapping me back to reality.

I forced my eyes off of Louis, turning to the blonde-haired guy.

"I'm in!" We all exclaimed in unison.

Niall instantly walked over to fetch the controllers from the drawer under the TV while Zayn started talking about how we were going to play. "We are five people, so two of us have to play together," he said, his eyes flickering between the four of us.

Suddenly, I could feel someone wrap an arm around my shoulder, pulling me close to their body. "I'll play with Curly. He's going to need someone to help him win anyway," Louis chuckled, and it took me at least half a minute until it registered in my brain what was happening.

I could feel my jaw drop, but I tried to pick it up as quickly as possible. I was surprised that he had just said that, but that was not going to stop me from getting back at him. "Says the one who was beaten by me the last time," I snorted, sticking my chin out.

This time, it was Louis' mouth that fell open in surprise, but he composed himself pretty quickly and reached out to flick me on the nose with the hand that wasn't around my shoulders.

"Heeey," I whined, reaching up to rub the sore spot. "What was that for?"

He tilted his head to the side. "That, my dear friend, was for more things than you can imagine."

Chapter 22

I drove Louis to the game the next day. Coach wanted his help to coach the team now that he couldn't be on the field himself, and I was going to take his place as a captain, something I was quite nervous about, but I didn't let it show.

We were currently warming up, the entire team standing in a circle and passing the ball to each other while one of us was in the middle, trying to catch it. If you did, you got to switch places with the one who had passed the ball.

The warm-up went on until the referee blew his whistle, calling me and the captain of the opposing team over to the centerline. After tossing the coin - which I won - we walked back to our separate teams that had now gathered at the side of the field to have a talk before the game would begin.

Coach and Louis had joined the circle when I got there, Coach talking about what we should think about and what our priorities were. Before we all separated, I opened my mouth to say the last words.

"Alright, guys. Let's go out there and kick some asses!"

And that was exactly what we did.

After the first half of the game, we were winning with 3-0. Liam hadn't let the other team score, and our defenders were doing a great job at keeping their attackers away from the goal. Other than that, I had scored two of the goals and Niall the other one.

I wasn't going to lie, it felt amazing. I didn't recall the last time I had felt this pumped for a game. The adrenaline was practically seeping through my veins, and I could tell I wasn't the only one feeling this way judging by the atmosphere among the team.

We were now all sitting in the locker room, chatting about the first half of the game and how we were going to keep up the good work when Louis plopped down on the bench beside me, placing his crutches on the floor.

"You're doing a great job out there, Curly," he complimented.

I turned to him, a toothy grin forming on my lips. "Thank you, Louis."

He nodded, returning the smile half-heartedly. I could tell he was sad that he couldn't play, and I felt really sorry for him. I knew better than to say anything about it, though, because he didn't like it when people sympathized with him. Instead, I patted his thigh twice to show him that I knew what he was thinking and that we all wished he could play.

"We're missing you out there, you know?" I told him honestly.

He cracked another smile, shrugging his shoulders. "I'll be back soon, though."

I nodded my head in agreement.

After that, it was time to head back to the field. We all left the locker room and got ready to play the second half of the game, which we were all just as excited for. The adrenaline was noticeable by the entire team, not just a few of us.

That was certainly what made us win the entire game. It ended 5-1, Zayn and Ryan scoring the last two goals. Coach was so happy with us, it wasn't hard to tell when we were all sitting in the locker room ten minutes after the game.

"You did amazing out there, guys. Everyone watching should be proud of you because I know I am," he smiled, looking between all of us with a bright smile on his face.

"Coach is right," I said, nodding. "We were missing our captain today, but I am proud of you guys for managing so well without him. I did the best I could, but I am sure I'm not only speaking for myself when I say that we all missed him out there with us today."

I turned to Louis who was sitting on the bench opposite me, sending him a smile. He flashed me a small one in return, shaking his head as if I was being a sappy mom. I didn't care, though. I thought he should know because it was the truth.

The other guys let out hums in agreement, the two guys sitting beside Louis patting him on the shoulder. "Thank you, guys, I appreciate it. I'll be back to kick ass soon enough," he chuckled, avoiding the glare Ryan shot him.

"Alright, guys. Off to the showers!" Coach said, clapping his hands together before leaving the locker room.

The second he shut the door behind him, chatter erupted in the room, making it impossible to make out what anyone was saying.

Niall was sitting beside me, in the process of stripping off his sweaty gear.

"You were great out there, Harry," he complimented, turning to look at me sincerely.

I shook my head with a smile on my face. "Thanks. You too, mate."

He rolled his eyes. "I meant you were great at being captain, dumbhead."

I looked down at my lap. "Louis' the better captain," I said, furrowing my eyebrows.

Niall looked over at the feathery-haired boy who was talking to Zayn and Trevor. "Louis' great, but you're good too. Coach should have made you co-captains."

I shook my head, looking up at him. "No. I'm happy being alternate. Louis wouldn't be happy if he had to share the post anyway."

"Nonsense," he scoffed. "I don't know what is going on between the two of you, but something has changed, and I'm pretty sure Louis wouldn't mind sharing anything with you anymore. I mean, you're even sharing his car now," he chuckled, rolling his eyes.

I nudged him in the side, feeling my cheeks heat up a little as I looked over at the blue-eyed boy across the room who was now glancing our way. "That doesn't..." I trailed off, my eyebrows knitted together. "That's not true."

Niall let out another chuckle, tilting his head to the side. "Whatever you say, mate. Whatever you say."

During the next few days, Louis and I talked more than what we had done in what seemed like forever. It finally felt like it had done before my birthday party, before whatever happened that made him distance himself from everyone other than the fact that he had found out I was bisexual. This meant he always lingered in the car after I had driven him home after school, it meant that he insisted on joining me to my work another time, and it also meant that he made sure to include me in conversations he had with other people.

It felt amazing, I wasn't going to lie. However, I had not forgotten what Lottie had told me at the diner that day, nor what Louis had admitted about thinking no one cared about him. I had made sure not to bring it up, though, because I knew he would only get reserved if I did. I figured I would have to wait until I was sure he trusted me, and he wouldn't get up and leave as soon as I asked him about it.

It was now Friday, a week after we had hung out at Niall's place, and Louis was finally allowed to take off the bandage and start using his foot without the help of crutches again. He was ecstatic about it. The second he came back from the nurse, walking - but limping slightly - with both of his feet, he was practically beaming.

And his good mood was there to stay the entire day. When we met up at our lockers after the last class as per usual nowadays, he grabbed his bag from his locker and slung it over his shoulder, giving me a knowing look.

"See? Perfectly capable of carrying my own bag," he said, making me roll my eyes.

"I'm sure it's happy about that considering how badly you've been treating it the last couple of days," I chuckled, shaking my head.

He let out a snort, closing his locker. "I didn't lie when I said I never liked it, so I'm sure it's used to the way I treat it."

I wanted to hit his arm because did he really just say that? However, I settled with letting out a loud bark of laughter. "I can't believe we're actually talking about a bag. It's not like it has feelings," I laughed.

He shrugged his shoulders, and even if he remained serious, his lips threatened to twitch. "Who knows? This bag might have," he smirked, making me shake my head in amusement.

Before I could say anything, the lads joined us at the lockers. "What are you guys laughing at?" Zayn wondered, raising his eyebrows at us.

By now, they had all finally accepted the fact that Louis and I had grown closer and didn't question us about it any longer. Niall was still suspicious, though. I could tell by the way his gaze always followed us and lingered a bit every now and then. However, I tried not to think about it.

"Louis claims his bag has feelings, but I'm not too sure about it," I said, muffling another laugh with the back of my hand.

Louis rolled his eyes while the three guys looked at us as if we were stupid. "Damn, I'm starting to wonder if you two growing closer was a good idea," Liam sighed, shaking his head, but an obvious smile was playing on his lips.

Louis snorted, grabbing my bicep arm. "Come on, Curly. I don't have time talking to these idiots."

"Speak for yourself, Tommo. We're not the ones claiming a bag has feelings," Zayn called after us, making both me and Louis laugh.

However, we didn't get very far until Louis halted in his steps and had to slow down due to his limp. I slowed down as well so I was walking beside him, making sure I didn't pressure him into walking faster.

As soon as we got to his car, he placed a hand on his hip while extending the other one to me, his palm facing upwards. I cocked an eyebrow at him, making him tilt his head to the side, a wide grin on his face.

"I want my car back now that I can drive again."

My mouth fell open because damn, I hadn't even thought about that. I had gotten so used to joining him to his car that I didn't even think about the fact that he could drive now, much less that he might not even want me here. What if he didn't want to drive me home? I lived on the other side of town after all.

I quickly fumbled in my back pocket, fishing the car key up before handing it to him. When he noticed that I wasn't making eye contact, he narrowed his eyes a little.

"What crawled up your ass and died, Curly?" He wondered, his hand still on his stuck-out hip.

I shrugged my shoulders. "I uh, I guess I should head to the bus stop," I mumbled, nodding in the direction of it, but didn't make any move to leave.

He let out a scoff. "Nonsense, I'm driving you. You've been driving me for more than a week now, so that's the least I can do," he said, crossing his arms over his chest.

I furrowed my eyebrows together. "But I've been driving your car, Louis," I pointed out, looking up at him.

He tilted his head to the side, shaking his head. "It doesn't matter. You've been paying for the gas. Besides, I'm not letting you take the bus anyway. Come on, Curly, just get in the car," he told me, limping over to the driver's seat.

I bit my bottom lip, thinking about it for only a few seconds before letting out a sigh and walking over to the passenger seat. I put my bag on the car floor before getting inside, shutting the door at the same time as Louis.

He turned on the engine with a bright smile on his face. It wasn't hard to tell that he had missed driving his car because his entire aura showed it. He reached over to turn the radio on, and instantly, loud rock music started blaring through the speakers, making me press my fingers to my ears.

"For God's sake!" I groaned, making him let out a loud laugh before turning the volume down.

"Sorry, princess," he winked. "Forgot there's a sensible person in the car."

I let out a huff, crossing my arms over my chest. He let out a chuckle at my actions before pulling out of the spot and driving off to my house.

"So," he said after a couple of minutes. "Have you found any car you're interested in yet?" He asked, glancing at the side of my face.

I bit my lip, shrugging my shoulders. "There are a few, but I haven't looked too much into it," I admitted. Honestly, I hadn't really thought about it now that I had driven Louis' car. However, I was sure I was going to miss being able to drive anywhere I could now, so I knew I needed to really get to grips with it.

"Been too busy drooling over mine?" He assumed, raising his eyebrows at me.

I couldn't help the smile that formed on my lips. "Maybe."

"I know. It's hard not to fall in love with it," he said nonchalantly, making me shake my head, still with the smile on my face.

"You're such a bragger."

He closed his eyes for a few seconds, his lips curling. "Oh, but you love it, Curly."

I bit my lip to prevent myself from smiling any wider. I was actually starting to think that he was right. These feelings I had for him were growing so strong that I was sure other people would have probably defined them as love.

I decided not to answer him, though. Instead, I let my gaze wander out the window, looking at the bypassing trees and houses outside.

"Can I ask you something?" Louis wondered after a while, glancing at the side of my face.

I turned to meet his gaze. "Sure."

Furrowing his eyebrows, he bit his lip. "Um, how did you cope when your dad left? I mean, wasn't it hard to process the fact that he just left without caring about staying in touch with you?"

To be honest, I never expected him to ask me something like that. I rarely talked about my dad because he was in the past. He wasn't a part of my life anymore because he had made it clear that he didn't want anything to do with it.

I shrugged my shoulders. "Of course it was tough in the beginning, but I guess you learn to live with it after a while. My mom has done an amazing job at raising me and Gemma by herself, and she's never made us feel like we needed that father figure again after he uh... he left," I explained. Although it was a long time ago, the subject was still touchy, and it was probably always going to be.

Louis nodded his head, cracking a small smile. "I see."

"Why are you asking?" I couldn't help but wonder, raising my eyebrows at him.

He shook his head. "No reason. I was just curious."

I hummed, turning my head to look out the window again. We stayed quiet for the rest of the ride, which only lasted for about five minutes. The second he pulled over outside my house, I could feel myself getting reluctant about getting out of the car. I didn't want to leave him yet. Things were so great between us now that I never really wanted to be apart from him.

He turned to look at me, raising his eyebrows at the expression on my face. "Something's on your mind, Curly?"

I met his gaze, biting my bottom lip. "You don't want to come inside? I mean, I'm not working today and we don't have soccer practice," I asked him, feeling my stomach fill with nerves. Even if Louis and I had gotten closer, we still hadn't hung out just the two of us since before my birthday.

The corners of his lips twitched at my request. "Sure, why not?"

"Great," I smiled, unbuckling my seatbelt before opening the car door, now feeling much more willing about leaving.

It wasn't until then I noticed that Gemma's car was parked in the driveway. I hoped to God she wouldn't torture me about Louis now that she knew I had feelings for him. It was going to be the first time she met him since she found out about it.

With my bag slung over my shoulder, I walked to the front door of my house, Louis following close behind. I decided to stay quiet when we entered the building in hopes of not having Gemma show up and greet us.

After tossing my bag to the side, shrugging off my jacket, and getting out of my boots, I turned to Louis who was waiting for me to take a step into the house. "Hungry?" I wondered, raising my eyebrows.

An amused smile made its way to his face. "Are you offering me your sandwiches again?" He chuckled, making me pout my lips.

"There's nothing wrong with my sandwiches. They're delicious, but we can always have something else if you don't like them," I huffed.

We started walking to the kitchen, Louis nudging me in the side playfully. "I'm just kidding, but I want to show you how real sandwiches are made."

I turned my head to look at him, my eyebrows arched. "You, making sandwiches?"

His mouth fell open. "Hey, what gives you the impression that I don't know anything about food?" He gasped, faking offended.

Rolling my eyes, I shook my head. "Wouldn't take you as a cook, is all," I shrugged, earning another nudge in the side, this one a little harsher than the first.

He opened his mouth to reply, but cut himself off at the sight of the girl sitting at the kitchen table, sipping on a cup of tea. She had looked up at the sound of our entrance, her eyes widening at the sight in front of her.

"Oh, Louis," Gemma gaped, her eyes flicking to me in surprise.

I bit my bottom lip, averting my gaze from her.

"Hi, Gemma," he greeted, a smile forming on his lips.

"Hey," she replied, composing herself. "It's been a while since I last saw you. Where have you been?"

Louis furrowed his eyebrows together, his eyes darting to the floor for a second before moving back up. "Um..."

"He's been injured, Gemma, and being injured makes your life shitty," I explained, finishing off for him. I could tell he didn't like the topic, and I knew why considering the way he had been acting that week.

He shot me an appreciating smile before turning back to Gemma, whose mouth had formed the shape of an 'o'. "I see. Well, it's nice to see you again," she said, her eyes flicking to me to send me a wink.

I inwardly groaned at her actions, feeling myself getting frustrated about the situation. I always knew it would be a bad idea that she knew about my feelings for Louis.

"You too," Louis smiled, seemingly not having caught the wink.

I shot Gemma a pointed look, and she let out a sigh but got up from her chair reluctantly. "I'll see you around, boys."

On her way out of the kitchen, she made sure to bump my hip with hers behind Louis' back, and yet again, I wanted to hit her. She needed to just lay off.

"So, where do you have the good stuff?" Louis hummed, walking over to the fridge curiously.

During the next half hour, Louis tried to assemble two sandwiches, and no, it didn't go very well. First, he managed to drop the ham to the floor, which he blamed on me for being in the way. Then, he squirted way too much mustard on one of them, which he blamed on 'the damn bottle'. At last, he just put so much stuff on them that they didn't even look edible. You literally couldn't cut them without everything falling out.

"And you told me the chicken stew didn't look appealing," I said, scrunching my nose up at the sandwich in front of me.

Louis rolled his eyes. "Don't knock it till you try it."

The sandwich wasn't good, just as I had assumed, and I made sure to let Louis know about it. Maybe, it would stop him from bragging so much, although I doubted it. I wouldn't let him think it was good, though. No one deserved to have that made for them.

"It wasn't that bad, though, Curly," Louis told me once we were finished eating (I left half of mine), and we were walking to my room.

"Yes, Louis, it was," I said, letting myself fall back first on my bed.

He let out a huff, walking over to the shelf beside my closet, letting his eyes wander over the picture frames and books on it. "Is this you?"

He was holding a picture of me as a kid, hugging a teddy bear to the side of my face.

I let out a loud groan. "No, stop, Louis."

He chuckled lightly, placing the picture frame back on the shelf. "It's cute, though. I didn't know you used to have straight hair," he smiled, striding over to sit on the edge of my bed, at my feet.

I got up in a sitting position, scooting over so I was sitting next to him. "It turned curly when I was twelve," I mumbled, looking down at my lap.

Louis let out a hum, nodding his head.

We were quiet for the next few seconds, and it was then it actually hit me that he was here, alone with me in my room, sitting on my bed. I had probably pictured this in front of me a couple of hundred times before, but I never thought it would happen in real life. It made me nervous, but I tried to remind myself that this was Louis, the Louis I had grown comfortable being around.

"Can I ask you something?" I wondered. Somehow, this felt like a good opportunity to ask him about what Lottie had mentioned at the diner. I didn't feel like he was going to run away right now.

He knitted his eyebrows together, thinking for a few seconds until he answered. "Only if I can ask you something first."

His words caught me by surprise because what could he possibly want to ask me about? "Uh, sure," I shrugged, getting more and more aware that our thighs were pressed together.

He bit his bottom lip as he turned to look at me. "How did you realize you were bisexual?"

My mouth fell open in shock. That was not what I had expected him to ask at all. It took a few seconds until I found the ability to talk again. "Um, I don't know? I guess I just knew at some point that I was attracted to both girls and boys," I shrugged, making the crease between his eyebrows deepen.

"You just knew? You never felt the need to like... try out your theory or something?"

The question that kept repeating itself in my head was; why was he asking me this? But I just couldn't ask him about it. "I uh... I may have gotten this urge to kiss a guy when I was thirteen, and I may or may not have kissed him when I brought him home to my house one time," I admitted, biting my lip.

The nerves were suffocating me, and talking about kissing people with Louis just felt like an awful idea because I could feel myself getting the same... no, *worse* urge to kiss him as I did with the guy five years ago.

"Yeah?" He breathed, his face inching closer to mine, making my heart race in my chest. He was so close that I could almost feel his breath on my lips, and it was making it hard for me to breathe. "And you knew you were bisexual after kissing him?"

Swallowing hard, I nodded my head curtly. "I... yeah, I guess so."

He let out a hum, and the crease between his eyebrows was so deep now that I was sure it couldn't get deeper. He was looking me in the eye, and he was so close that I could barely see his entire face. I inhaled a deep breath in an attempt to stop my heart from racing, but it was to no avail. It didn't make matters better when he reached out to run his fingertips along my cheekbone, so feathery light that I could barely feel it.

His eyes dropped to my lips for a second before looking back into my irises. The action made me stop breathing altogether because I could feel it; he was going to kiss me. The Louis Tomlinson that I had been head over heels for for more than three years now was about to kiss me. Was this some kind of dream that I was going to wake up from the second our lips touched or what was it?

Before I could think more about it, Louis shut his eyes and leaned in to close the small distance between us. His soft, pink lips nudged against my own, making me release a soft gasp, a tingling sensation making its way through my body. I didn't know how to react at first, so I sat there, frozen in place as his lips moved gently against mine, almost massaging them.

The second I snapped back to reality, I started moving my lips with his, feeling a new sensation run through my body. This feeling was something I had never experienced before. It was like my entire body was on fire, yet it was basically only our lips that were touching.

I was just about to reach out to place my hand on the side of his neck when he pulled away, so quickly that I could feel my heart drop in my chest. When I fluttered my eyes open, Louis was staring at me wide-eyed, his mouth formed into the shape of an 'o'. "I-I... shit. I shouldn't... fuck, I shouldn't have done that."

He got up from the bed abruptly and started limping backward towards the bedroom door. I shook my head frantically, feeling a stab in my heart with every step he took. "Louis, wai--"

He instantly cut me off. "I'm sorry, Harry," he mumbled, looking at me with this apologetic glint in his eyes that made me want to crawl into a ball and cry my eyes out.

With that said, he opened the door and walked away, leaving me sitting on my bed with a broken heart.

Chapter 23

I had no idea how long I sat there on the edge of my bed, staring at my closed door. I felt numb, absolutely drained of emotions. It felt like it had all been some kind of dream that I had now woken up from to realize it never happened. Except, it did happen. Louis did kiss me. He kissed me just to pull away and tell me he shouldn't have done it.

It wasn't until the entire scene played out in my head all over again that I first felt how my heart was aching in my chest. I had never felt so psychically hurt before, yet so happy at the same time. Louis had *kissed* me. I never expected that to happen in real life, but at the same time, it felt like someone was stabbing me in the heart over and over again because he regretted it.

I couldn't help the tears that started rolling down my cheeks.

God, I was so pathetic. I was crying over a boy, a boy I was now certain I was in love with, who had also just broken my heart. He honestly couldn't have told me that he didn't feel the same in a better way. It was like a slap to the face. Was it okay to cry over that? That the one you loved didn't love you back?

Things had been going so well. Louis and I were finally close again, even closer than we had been before. Why did that have to be ruined? Why did he have to kiss me? Sure, kissing him was something I had dreamt of doing for a very long time now, but if these were the consequences that would follow, I didn't want it to happen. I'd rather have Louis in my life somehow than not have him at all.

I knew things were going to be different now. I knew he was going to start ignoring me because that was how he dealt with things in life. On the other hand, I wasn't sure if I would be able to look him in the eye after this either. It felt so embarrassing because that kiss was no doubt the best kiss of my life, and Louis didn't even enjoy it. How *could* I look him in the eye after that?

After sitting there on my bed for a while, there was a gentle knock on my door. "H, are you in there?"

It was Gemma. I didn't want to talk to her, but I knew she wouldn't stop bugging me if I didn't reply to her.

"Yeah," I breathed, pulling my knees up to my chest so I could lean my chin on my kneecaps.

A second later, she opened the door and walked into my room, letting out a deep sigh at the sight of me on the bed. "I heard Louis leaving quite urgently earlier, so I assumed something had happened. Are you okay?"

She sat down next to me, reaching out to wrap a loose arm around my waist to show me that she was there for me. It was sweet, but I was so busy thinking of what had just happened that I barely registered it.

I looked up at her, wiping my dampened cheeks with the back of my hand. I hadn't shed many tears, but still many enough for my skin to get wet. "I don't know," I frowned because I didn't. I had no idea how I really felt. I just knew that my heart was hurting really bad.

She sent me a small smile, pressing her lips together. "Do you want to tell me what happened?"

Looking away from her again, I stared at the shelf where the picture of myself as a kid that Louis had shown me earlier was placed, staring me right in the face. I swallowed hard, leaning down to rest my chin on my kneecaps again. "He kissed me," I mumbled.

I could practically hear how her jaw dropped, but she stayed quiet, waiting for me to continue.

"But he... he pulled away after only a few seconds and told me he shouldn't have done it. Then he left," I grimaced. It hurt to even explain what happened, and it didn't make matters better that my lips were still tingling from the gentle touch of his.

Gemma let out a sigh, squeezing my hip in reassurance. "I'm sorry, H."

Shaking my head, I pressed my forehead against my knees. After taking a few breaths, I looked up at her, feeling tears pricking my eyes. "It just... it hurts so much," I breathed. "Things were going so well."

She leaned down to rest her head against my shoulder. "Yeah, I saw that. You two were in your own little world when you walked into the kitchen," she mumbled.

I didn't say anything. Instead, I exhaled a deep breath, hugging my knees closer to my body. "We'll never be like that again."

She lifted her head from my shoulder to look at me with a scowl on her face. "You don't know that."

I let out a snort, flashing her a fake smile. "Yes, I do. He always ignores his problems no matter what, so I'm sure he is not going to talk to me, Gems. I know he won't," I muttered.

Gemma bit her bottom lip, the crease still prominent between her eyebrows. "I'm quite sure you mean more to him than you think. I don't know what's going on inside his head at the moment, or why he told you the kiss shouldn't have happened, but he likes you, H. I mean, I do have eyes."

I pursed my lips, just then remembering what he had asked me just before he leaned in to kiss me. "He asked me how I realized I was bisexual," I said, furrowing my eyebrows together. "Why did he do that?"

She cocked an eyebrow. "He did that?"

I nodded my head. "Yeah, just before he kissed me."

Her eyes widened. "Do you think... do you think he's questioning his sexuality?"

I bit my bottom lip, thinking about it. Could that be it? Was that why he had kissed me? To know whether he liked guys or not? Well, in that case, he must have found out that he didn't, considering he told me it shouldn't have happened and then left.

"Then he must've realized that he didn't. He left, after all," I muttered.

She let out a hum, reaching up to pinch her chin with her forefinger and thumb. "Or, he liked it but didn't want to admit it."

Letting out a snort, I shook my head. "Don't say that just to get my hopes up. It's rude."

She rolled her eyes. "I'm not. It could be the truth, H. I mean, we don't really know now, do we?"

No, but he did leave me with a broken heart, and nothing can change that.

"I guess not."

Things turned out exactly how I expected them to. On Monday morning when I got to school after taking the school bus, Louis didn't even look at me as I arrived at my locker. All the boys were there, everyone acknowledging me when I showed up apart from him. Instead, he slammed his locker shut, muttering a goodbye before walking off, leaving the boys confused, and me just very sad.

Looking down at the floor, I put my combination in and opened my locker, shoving my bag into it carelessly. I could feel the guys' gazes on me, boring holes into the side of my face, but I didn't turn to meet them.

"Did something happen between you two?" Liam asked, and I mentally sighed.

I didn't want to explain what happened. I didn't want to talk about it. Hell, I didn't even want to *think* about it. I just wanted everything to be normal. I wanted Louis to greet me with a smile on his face, the crinkles by his eyes showing and his eyes sparkling just upon seeing me, just like he had done the last couple of days.

Shutting my locker, I eventually turned to meet their confused gazes. "No, everything's fine," I said monotonously, walking past them to head to my Economics class.

I didn't pay much attention during that hour, but I was pretty sure Emily tried to catch my attention at some point, although I didn't really acknowledge it. However, she must have noticed that I wasn't in the mood to talk because she turned back in her seat to keep working in a matter of seconds.

When the bell rang, I gathered my books and left the classroom, walking to my locker while facing the floor. I could feel eyes on me the entire way there - more than I was used to - but I tried not to think about it as I dragged my feet along the floor.

Only Niall and Liam were standing at the lockers when I arrived, chatting closely with each other. When I got there, however, they both turned to me with small, hesitant smiles on their faces.

"Hey, mate," Liam greeted.

"Hi," I said, cracking a smile of my own.

Niall let out a deep sigh as I walked past them to open my locker. "Look, Harry. We don't want to seem nosy, but both you and Louis are acting strange. You have barely talked to us today, and that's not typically you. Besides, you won't even look at each other. I mean, Louis was just here but left as soon as he saw you approaching us."

I could feel my heart drop in my chest at his words. Louis left as soon as he saw me? I shouldn't be surprised, but it still hurt. So much.

Biting my bottom lip, I looked down at the floor. "It's nothing, really. You don't have anything to be worried about," I tried to reassure them, but the concern didn't leave their faces.

Liam opened his mouth to say something but was interrupted by his girlfriend who took him by surprise by hugging him from behind. "Morning, babe," she greeted, leaning in to press a kiss to his cheek.

An immediate smile broke out on his face as he turned around, giving her a hug and a peck on the lips. "Hey, love."

Their affection made me feel sick to my stomach, but only because it was too much for me to handle after what happened Friday afternoon. Otherwise, I was practically in love with their relationship. They were just the perfect couple, always showing off just how much they loved and cared for each other. I wished I had that.

They left us only a minute later, leaving me alone with Niall who was watching my every move. After a few seconds, he inhaled a deep breath, looking at the side of my face. "Is there something going on between you and Louis?" He asked bluntly, catching me off guard completely.

I turned to him wide-eyed. "What?"

Niall shrugged his shoulders. "I don't know. I just... I have seen the way you look at him, Harry," he explained, flashing me this knowing smile. "It's like he's your entire world. I mean, I could only wish for someone to look at me like that. So, when you guys grew closer, I just assumed..." He trailed off, glancing at me.

I didn't know what to say or what to do. I was shocked. I had no idea Niall knew that I liked him. I mean, sure, I knew he was suspicious about me and Louis, but *this*? Was I really that obvious?

Snapping myself back to reality, I finally managed to close my gaping mouth. "I... shit," I said, running a hand through my curls. "Am I really that obvious?" I asked, looking at him desperately but at the same time worriedly. What if more people knew about it?

He tilted his head to the side, flashing me a small smile. "I guess you'd have to be observant, which I have been, but no, I don't think anyone knows."

I let out a sigh of relief. "Thank God."

He pursed his lips before raising his eyebrows at me questioningly. "So, does all this mean yes?"

My eyes widened all over again as I shook my head frantically. "No!" I burst out. "I mean, no, there's nothing going on between me and Louis," I said, a crease forming between my eyebrows as I thought about our kiss.

Definitely nothing going on between us.

Niall narrowed his eyes in suspicion, making me look away from him while biting my lip. Before he could open his mouth to ask me another question, I beat him to it. "Are you okay with me uh... me liking Louis?" I wondered. It felt weird to talk about this with Niall. Hell, it still felt weird to talk about my infatuation with Louis with *anyone*.

He furrowed his eyebrows. "You mean if I'm okay with you liking a guy?" He wondered, and I shrugged my shoulders while nodding my head.

"Yeah, I guess?"

A genuine smile formed on his lips as he let out a light chuckle. "Of course, Harry. You could like whoever you want and I'd still be your friend... except for my mom, though," he said. "That's just a big no," he warned me playfully, making me crack a small smile.

"Thank you, Niall," I said honestly.

He rolled his eyes. "You don't have to thank me, Harry," he told me, patting me on the arm. "So, does Louis know how you feel about him?"

I blinked my eyes, swallowing hard. "Uh, no."

"No?" He asked me in shock.

I shook my head, averting my gaze. "He's straight, Niall. We all know he is."

He let out a scoff. "That's a lame excuse. I bet he would go gay for you, you irresistible son of a bitch," he smirked, making me let out a chuckle.

"You're an idiot."

Niall shook his head, smiling. "No, but really, Harry. You shouldn't waste your feelings. That would be really stupid, don't you think?" He said, raising his eyebrows at me.

I looked down at my shoes, shrugging my shoulders. "It doesn't really matter, though. I already know he doesn't like me," I muttered.

He tilted his head to the side. "Does this have to do with why you two are ignoring each other?" He asked, cocking an eyebrow.

The exact same second I opened my mouth to reply, the bell rang, which meant I didn't have time to answer his question. "I'll see you later, Niall. Thank you for... being accepting," I said, cracking a small smile.

He reciprocated the smile. "Of course."

And with that said, we both went out separate ways.

I spent the next couple of hours thinking about how everyone around me seemed to be so accepting of my sexuality. Part of the reason I never came out was that I thought the guys wouldn't understand. I thought they would mock me for not being like them, thinking and talking about big boobs and butts all the time. But maybe I was wrong? Neither Louis nor Niall judged me, rather the opposite. It made me feel happy somehow, even if happiness was the last thing I was expressing at the moment with everything else going on.

When it was time for lunch, I made my way to the cafeteria after getting rid of my books. I didn't meet any of the guys on my way there, but they were all sitting at a table in the crowded room when I got there, Louis included.

I tried not to look at him as I sat down beside Liam and Zayn, opposite him and Niall. I could feel Niall's gaze on me as I unwrapped my sandwich, but I avoided him too. Liam and Zayn instantly got suspicious, sensing the tension in the air.

"Alright, what is going on?" Zayn asked, looking between me and Louis, then at Niall who shrugged his shoulders. The black-haired boy let out a sigh, slumping his shoulders when he realized he wasn't going to get an answer.

Only a few minutes later, we were accompanied by Alice, Evelyn, the blonde-haired girl Louis had kissed at my birthday party, and another brunette. They all got a chair to sit on, Evelyn squeezing herself in between me and Zayn, the blonde girl next to Louis (obviously), Alice next to Liam, and the other girl beside Niall.

"Hey, Harry," Evelyn greeted, flashing me a small smile.

I turned to her, my lips curling slightly. "Hi, Evelyn."

Even if I wasn't feeling the best, I was happy to see her. It had been quite some time since I last talked to her.

"How have you been doing?" She wondered. "I've barely seen you since your birthday party, which was like two weeks ago."

I shrugged my shoulders, glancing at the feathery-haired boy across from me who was now talking to the blonde girl. I couldn't help the jealousy that welled up inside me. Why was it so easy for girls? Why couldn't it as easy for me to be like that with Louis?

Shaking myself back to reality, I turned to Evelyn who was looking at me questioningly. "I've been great. Been quite busy with soccer and work, though," I explained. "You?"

"I see. Well, I've been good too. I've mostly just been hanging with the girls and done my homework. I'm so glad we're graduating soon," she sighed in relief.

I nodded my head in agreement. "Yeah. It's going to be great not having to do any school work for a while."

She tilted her head to the side. "So, you are planning on going to uni then?" She assumed, a curious glint in her eyes.

I pursed my lips, shrugging my shoulders. To be honest, I hadn't really thought about it too much. The scholarship that Coach had brought up had barely even crossed my mind since that day, let alone another University. Nevertheless, I had always pictured myself going to uni after high school. "I don't know, but I guess so. Are you?"

Evelyn nodded her head with a smile on her face. "Yeah. I'm thinking of moving to Manchester... if I get in, that is. I've kind of always wanted to move there."

I understood where she got that from. Holmes Chapel was a tiny place in comparison to Manchester, and Manchester was the closest big city. So, if you didn't want to move too far, that was the perfect place to go.

"I love Manchester," I grinned, making a smile form on her lips.

"You should apply there too, then," she said playfully, nudging me in the side.

I let out a light chuckle, my lips twitching. "Yeah, we'll see."

It wasn't until then I could feel someone staring at me. When I looked up, a pair of ocean blue eyes that I had grown so fond of during the last couple of years locked with mine. His jaw was clenched tightly as this dark look in his eyes appeared. It made me want to look away.

Before I had time to do so, though, he got up from his chair with a loud screeching noise and left, not even bothering to push his chair back in as he stomped away without a word.

Chapter 24

When the last bell of the day rang, I wanted nothing but to go home. If I were to decide, I would have stayed home the entire afternoon, but I wasn't that lucky. I had soccer practice, and it was going to be Louis' first day back on the field. I wasn't really looking forward to having to be so close to him, so the thought of staying home, watching a rom-com with mom was very inviting right now.

With a deep sigh, I closed my locker. Louis had already left, and I knew this because the second I arrived at the lockers, I could see him walking towards the exit. It made me so sad. I hated how things were between us now. The silence was killing me. I wanted to go up and talk to him, make a joke to turn those lips into a beautiful smile just like I had been able to do just a couple of days ago.

"Hey, mate."

I turned around abruptly only to come face-to-face with Niall. "Hi," I mumbled.

He tilted his head to the side, pursing his lips. "Come on, let's go to the bus stop," he said, nodding in the direction of the exit.

I bit my bottom lip, letting out a sigh before agreeing with him. We started walking in silence until Niall decided to break it once we came outside. "I don't know what happened between you and Louis, and you don't have to tell me if you don't want to, but I think you should talk to him. I mean, it's obvious that both of you are bothered by whatever happened," he told me, glancing at the side of my face.

I furrowed my eyebrows, shaking my head. "I'm not going to talk to him, Niall."

He let out a sigh, running a hand through his blonde hair. "Well, one of you has to eventually because this is affecting us lads as well. I don't mean to sound selfish, but we're all best mates. If two of us refuse to talk to each other, things are going to be tense between us all," he explained.

I nibbled on my bottom lip, looking into the distance. After a while, I finally opened my mouth to reply. "He kissed me, alright? He kissed me and then told me that he shouldn't have done it. Do you understand why I can't speak to him now?" I blurted out.

His eyes widened in surprise. "Really?"

"I didn't want to tell you," I muttered. "I didn't want anyone to know because it's embarrassing since I know it meant so much more to me than it did to him."

He furrowed his eyebrows. "But why did he do it if he was only going to regret it afterward?" He wondered.

I turned to look at him. "That's what I'd like to know, Niall. He just asked me how I realized I was bisexual, and--"

"Wait, so you're like... into other guys as well? Not just Louis?" He asked me, cutting me off.

I looked at him for a second before answering. "Well, I mean, I've been with other guys, but I've never really liked anyone before Louis. He's the first person I've ever had these strong feelings for," I mumbled.

His mouth formed the shape of an 'o'. "And Louis knows you're bisexual then? How did he find out?"

I scrunched my nose up. "He saw me kissing a guy at my birthday party, so I couldn't exactly deny it when he asked me about it," I explained.

"I see," he mumbled. "Alright, keep going."

I took a deep breath. "Okay, so he asked me how I realized I was bisexual, and I told him the story about when I was younger and kissed this guy only to realize that I liked it. Then he just leaned in and kissed me."

Niall pursed his lips. "Alright, that sounds quite suspicious if you're asking me. I definitely think you should talk to him, Harry. You have to get answers as to why he did what he did. Otherwise, it's going to bug you forever. Besides, you two really have to sort things out. Your silence and behavior towards each other aren't healthy for either of you."

I let out a sigh, looking down at the ground. "I don't know, Niall. To be honest, I just want to dig a hole in the ground and bury myself alive. Things are just so awkward, and I'm not sure I'll be able to look him in the eye after what happened. It probably wouldn't have been so difficult if I didn't feel anything for him, but now I do, and I can't watch him when he tells me that he doesn't feel the same. I just can't."

Niall placed a hand on my shoulder, stopping me in my tracks. "Look, Harry, I understand that it's not easy, but think about it. Maybe it's better to talk to him so you'll know the reason he kissed you. I mean, he just got up and left the cafeteria earlier when he saw you talking to Evelyn. Obviously, he must feel something at least."

I bit my bottom lip, furrowing my eyebrows together. "I don't know," I mumbled. "I'll think about it."

A small smile formed on his lips. "Great."

Right then, my bus showed up around the corner, which made me start moving towards the bus stop again. Niall's was across the street, so we had to separate in order to get on the right vehicle.

"Wait!" He called out before I had even taken two steps.

I turned around, looking at him curiously. "Huh?"

His eyebrows were furrowed as he nibbled on his bottom lip. "Why did you never say anything about your sexuality?"

I was slightly taken aback by his question, my eyes widening. "Oh, uh..." I trailed off, scratching the back of my neck. "I didn't think you would... approve? I mean, all you guys basically do is talk about girls, and I thought you would think I was weird if you knew I was attracted to both sexes. I'm sorry," I grimaced.

Niall shook his head, a smile making its way to his face. "No, it's okay, I was just wondering. You do know you can tell me anything, though, right? I would never judge you."

I cracked a small smile of my own, looking at him sincerely. "Thank you, it means a lot."

"Of course," he replied, reaching out to pat me on the arm. "We're not best mates for nothing."

"I guess not," I grinned.

It wasn't until then I noticed that the bus had pulled over and people were entering it, only a few of them still standing outside. "Shit," I muttered under my breath. "I'll see you later, Niall," I called out as I started running towards the bus, hoping to God that I would catch it on time.

"Sure, bye!"

Luckily, I managed to get onto the bus just as the doors were about to close. It made me let out a sigh of relief, and I flashed the bus driver a small smile before moving down the aisle to find an empty seat.

I really hoped this day wouldn't get more eventful because I was positive I wouldn't be able to handle that.

During the short time I was home before leaving again for practice, I thought a lot about what Niall had said. I did want to get answers as to why Louis had kissed me, and our silence was killing me, but I didn't know how I would be able to look him in the eye again. I couldn't even picture it in my mind, let alone see it happening in real life.

I was glad to have such a supportive friend like Niall. I never imagined that his reaction to finding out I was bisexual would be this good. Sure, he had been my closest friend out of all four of them before Louis and I grew closer, but he was also so into girls that I never thought he would approve of me liking guys, let alone figure it out on his own. He proved me wrong, though, and I was nothing but happy about that.

When it was eventually time for me to leave for practice, I almost did as I previously wanted to do; stayed home to wait for mom to get here so we could watch a movie together, but I forced myself to get changed into my soccer gear and pack my bag instead.

I was just about to exit the house when the front door swung open from the outside, catching me off guard.

"Oh, hey, H. You heading to practice?" Gemma asked, raising her eyebrows at me questioningly.

"Hi. Uh, yeah. Don't want to miss the bus," I told her, trying to walk past her, but she stopped me by placing a hand on my chest.

"Not so fast," she said, narrowing her eyes at me. After a few seconds, her features relaxed and her narrowed eyes were soon replaced by a smile instead. Reaching her hand out, she tilted her head to the side. "You'll need this. Your hair is growing way too long, brother."

I looked at the hair tie in her extended hand, trying to process what she just said before taking it from her. "Thanks. But hey, there's nothing wrong with my hair. I like it this way," I pouted, making her roll her eyes.

"Bye!"

The pout stayed on my face as I said goodbye to her in return. I then finally left the house, jogging over to the bus stop that was on the other side of the street. While I waited for the bus to show up, I reached up to put the curls on top of my head in a little bun so they wouldn't get in my face while running around on the soccer field.

Once the bus showed up, I got on it and sat down in an empty seat. The bus ride lasted for about twenty minutes until it pulled over at the stop closest to the gym. There was still a five-minute walk there, but it wasn't that bad. Honestly, I wanted it to take as much time as possible because the last thing I wanted was to arrive so early that there was a possibility Louis and I could be the first people there. Immature, I know.

It turned out I wasn't the first person to show up in the locker room. Louis was there, but so were at least ten other people, which made me let out a sigh of relief as I made my way over to one of the benches where there was a lot of space.

I started taking off my jacket and shoes to put on my shin caps and cleats. As I did this, I could feel someone's eyes on me. I didn't have to look up to know who it was. My gut always knew when Louis was looking at me.

Hesitantly, I looked up at him, meeting his blue eyes with mine. We stayed like that for a short while, just looking into each other's eyes until I had to avert my gaze. It was *so* hard to look at him now after the kiss.

The next second, the door of the locker room swung open by Niall, Liam and Zayn. Liam and Zayn were laughing at something while Niall had a pout on his face.

"Hey, it's not my fault I was born with brown hair. I have no other choice but to dye it if I want it to be blonde."

Liam and Zayn rolled their eyes, sitting down on the bench next to Louis. Niall let out a huff, walking over to sit down beside me. "Are they making fun of your hair?" I asked raising my eyebrows at him.

"Yeah," he pouted. "They're saying that only girls dye their hair, fucking dickheads."

I let out a light chuckle, shaking my head. "Don't listen to them, Niall. They're only trying to mess with you."

He crossed his arms over his chest, glaring in their direction. "I know. They should be aware that they're going to get back for it, though."

The smile stayed on my face as I leaned down to tie my cleats. Soon enough, it was time to go out to the field, where Coach was waiting for us, his arms crossed over his chest.

"Alright boys, I hope you're all in a good mood and are excited about today's training. Tomlinson is now back on the field, which means he is going to be the captain of the next match," he explained, giving Louis a look, who nodded his head curtly. "Also, I want to remind you that if anyone breaks the rules about injuring someone on the team intentionally again, you're off, alright?"

We all nodded our heads, Ryan rolling his eyes as he did so. It made me feel a little uneasy because Ryan couldn't be trusted whatsoever. Only he knew what was going on inside that head of his. It didn't seem like anyone else noticed his actions, though, and we were all soon off to start warming up by running three laps around the field.

The first half of the training turned out quite okay. We mostly practiced long shots and dribbling, where Louis outshone as usual. He had always been the best on the team at making his way past players while controlling the ball.

"Alright guys, we are now going to play a match with seven people on each team where the first to score wins. Tomlinson, Styles, you make the teams," Coach announced.

I chose both Liam and Niall on mine while Louis got Zayn. Ryan was chosen last, which he could only blame himself for, and since I was the first one to start picking, Louis got him on his team.

When I watched Ryan walk over to Louis, I could see that he was pissed about being picked last, but he didn't make any comment about it. Instead, he just walked over to Louis' team, sending both me and Louis a glare. The action made me feel uneasy again, but I tried not to put too much thought into it. It wasn't like he was going to do anything now that he had already gotten so many warnings from Coach anyway.

We started playing after that, and it didn't take long after Coach blew his whistle that Niall snitched the ball from Trevor and dribbled past Tristan. He then looked up to pass the ball over to Eric. Eric started running towards the opponents' goal, so I made sure that I was free, hoping that he would see me and pass me the ball.

Unfortunately, Louis snitched it from him before he had time to look up, making me let out an exasperated sigh. Louis started running towards Liam with quick and graceful strides, no one having time to catch up to him until he was close enough to swing his leg back and kick the ball towards Liam.

The goalie caught it in his hands securely, though, and sent Louis a wink. In return, Louis sent him a glare before turning around and jogging back towards the centerline. Liam tossed the ball to Niall, who quickly passed the ball over to me. I started running towards the opponents' goal, my eyes so focused on what to do next that it completely caught me off guard when someone pushed me so hard that I flew forward and landed in a heap on the fake grass.

I grimaced at the pain that instantly made its way down my spine, rolling over to face the ground in order to not yell out.

"What the actual fuck?"

The sound of footsteps getting closer made me turn around to see what was going on. Louis was storming over to the person who had pushed me to the ground, and to no one's surprise, it was Ryan. Louis' eyes were dark with anger as he got into Ryan's face, pushing at his chest.

"I said, what the *fuck* do you think you're doing, huh?" He snapped.

Ryan stumbled a bit, but he didn't look scared at all. In fact, he was looking at him in amusement, which only caused Louis to get angrier. "Aw, are you standing up for your little boy? Isn't that cute? So you two are actually fucking now then?" He taunted, wiggling his eyebrows with a smirk on his face as he looked between me and Louis.

His comment made Louis see red. He swung his fist back, ready to beat the shit out of Ryan. Before he could do so, though, Zayn grabbed a hold of his biceps from behind and pulled him back. "Louis, he's not worth it," he tried to calm him.

Louis breathed heavily through his nostrils, his gaze flicking between me and Ryan with a frown between his eyebrows. He inhaled a deep breath, wriggling out of Zayn's hold before stomping away without looking back.

"Ryan, get over here!" Coach called out sternly, making the said boy roll his eyes before doing as told.

Once I had processed what had just happened, I noticed that a hand was extended right in front of me. Blinking my eyes, I looked up to see Niall's blue eyes staring down at me, a sympathetic look on his face. "You okay, Harry?"

I looked at his hand for a couple of seconds before taking it in mine and letting him help me to my feet. He dusted off my shoulders, sending me a small smile.

Honestly, I couldn't feel any pain anymore, and I wondered if that was because I had been so shocked by the scene that had just played out in front of my eyes. "I'm uh... I'm okay," I mumbled, looking over his shoulder to see if Louis was still on the field or if he had left altogether.

"He went to the locker rooms," Niall said, as if reading my mind.

I swallowed hard, my eyes finding their way back to his face. He sent me a reassuring smile, patting me on the arm softly. "I think what just happened only added to the list of why you guys need to talk to each other, Harry. You should really take my advice."

Letting out a sigh, I nodded my head. "Yeah," I mumbled. "Maybe you're right."

Chapter 25

As soon as practice was finished, we all headed to the locker room. Louis hadn't shown up again after the incident, which made me a little confused. Was he really that upset about what Ryan said? I mean, sure, it was made as an insult, but was the idea of us together so disgusting that he couldn't even stay on the field? Okay, so the answer to that question was probably yes. I mean, he did regret the kiss, after all, so of course the thought of us being together didn't sit well with him.

Niall noticed that I was being quiet when we got to the locker room, but he didn't say anything. He just gave me another sympathetic smile and patted me on the shoulder reassuringly.

It took some time for me to shower and get changed because I didn't feel like hurrying. I figured I would probably miss the bus I usually took and would have to wait for the next one to arrive, but I couldn't care less.

Once I was finished, I noticed that I wasn't the last person to leave the locker room even if I had taken my time, but Niall, Zayn and Liam were all gone. Niall had made sure to ask me if it was okay for him to leave without me, to which I had just waved a hand in dismissal. I was sure his company wouldn't make things better at the moment anyway.

I slung my heavy bag over my shoulder before leaving the gym, running a hand through my damp curls. It wasn't as freezing outside now that it had been on my birthday, so my hair didn't freeze to ice the second I exited the gym, but it wasn't exactly warm either, so I made sure to hug my winter jacket closer to my body.

I was just about to pass by the parking lot when I noticed an oddly familiar car parked there. There weren't many cars around, so it wasn't hard to point it out. Squinting my eyes to get a better look at it, I noticed that someone was sitting in the driver's seat. Why the hell was he still here?

Instantly feeling a knot form in my stomach, I contemplated what to do. Should I go over, take Niall's advice and talk to him, or should I leave it to another day? Would he even want to talk to me if I tried to?

I really wanted to chicken out, but I couldn't bear the thought of being like this with him one more day, so I made my mind up and started walking towards the familiar black sports car. My heart was thumping loudly in my chest, and the thumping only increased the closer I got to the vehicle. The second I reached out to grab the door handle of the passenger door, I almost turned around and ran away, but I forced myself to open it and slide into the seat, dropping my bag on the car floor.

I felt sick to my stomach as I turned my gaze to look at Louis. His face had snapped in my direction the second I opened the door, and his mouth was now hanging open. However, he quickly composed himself and replaced the shocked expression with a frown.

"What are you doing here?"

I took a deep breath, trying to swallow down the lump I had in my throat. "I... We need to talk."

The crease between his eyebrows deepened at my words, and he turned in his seat to face the windshield. "We do?"

His answer almost made me angry. "Yes, Louis. We do."

He let out a sigh, closing his eyes for a few seconds before opening them again. "Alright, go on," he muttered, making me swallow hard.

He wanted me to talk when he was the one being secretive here? I wanted to know why he kissed me. I wanted to know why he regretted it, and I wanted to know why he had stood up for me against Ryan. What did I have to explain?

Biting my bottom lip, I turned in my seat so I was facing the windshield as well. Then I said the words that I had secretly been wanting to say to him all day.

"I... I miss you."

He snapped his head to me again, looking at me in slight shock. He searched my face for something I didn't know, but his gaze kept wandering over my features until he let out a sigh, running a hand through his fringe. "I'm sorry I fucked things up," he mumbled, turning back to face forward.

I took a deep breath. "You didn't fuck things up, Louis. I just... I just want to know why you did it," I mumbled.

My heart started thumping in my chest again, but this time it was because I was nervous about what he was going to say. Did I even want to know what was about to escape his mouth?

He bit his lip, looking out the side window before turning to look at me. "I... I don't know. It was stupid. I really shouldn't have done it."

I could feel my heart drop to the pit of my stomach.

I shouldn't have done it.

Of *course* he was going to repeat the sentence that had broken me three days ago. It wasn't enough to break me once, he just had to do it twice.

Looking down at my lap, I nodded my head slowly. I didn't say anything because I didn't know what to say. What *could* I say? That I wished he would have wanted to kiss me? No. He would never want to be in my company again.

"Can't we just forget it happened? I hate how things are between us now, and I... I miss you too," he admitted, looking me in the eye pleadingly.

Did he think I never wanted that kiss to happen? Or why did he make it sound like that? Maybe he just wanted us both to forget about it so we could go back to how we had been before the incident.

Knitting my eyebrows together, I nodded slowly. "Yeah... uh, sure," I muttered, avoiding eye contact. There was no way I could look him in the eye while telling him it was okay for me to only be friends with him.

"You don't sound convincing," he pointed out, and I could see him fiddling with his fingers through the corner of my eye.

I bit my bottom lip, looking out the passenger window. "I do mean it. It's just... I don't want you to feel like it ruined things between us if you think that, because it didn't, alright?"

Once I had finished the sentence, I turned to look at him only to notice that he was looking at me as well. A small smile broke out on his face at my words, his eyes glowing from the few lights in the car.

"It didn't?"

I shook my head, flashing him a small smile of my own. "No."

"So we're friends?" He questioned hopefully, making me grimace inwardly.

Niall's words went on repeat in my head. The way he had told me not to waste what I felt for Louis, that I should confess my feelings for him. But I couldn't do it. If the only way for me to be close to Louis was to be his friend, then I was willing to go along with it because I just couldn't picture my life without him.

I could tell that my silence made him uncomfortable because he started squirming in his seat with an evident frown on his face.

"Yeah, we're friends," I said, cracking a smile.

His eyes widened a little, but he quickly composed himself. "That's... great. That's awesome," he smiled, this time genuinely.

Even if his words made my heart hurt, his smile made my insides melt. I had missed that smile so much during the last couple of days. I think it was safe to say that I basically lived for that smile gracing his pink, beautiful lips.

"Alright, I should probably drive you home now. It's getting pretty late after all," he said, turning on the engine.

I didn't expect him to drive me home when I first decided to get into his car, but now I was nothing but thankful that he offered because I was sure I had missed the next bus by now as well.

"So, how's your back?" He asked me after a few seconds of silence, glancing at the side of my face.

At first, I was confused by his question, but then I remembered that Ryan had pushed me to the ground during practice. I really couldn't feel any pain at all anymore. "Oh, that. It doesn't hurt anymore," I said truthfully.

He raised his eyebrows at me in surprise. "Really? It looked pretty bad when it happened," he frowned, biting his bottom lip.

I shrugged my shoulders. "It hurt at the moment, but it disappeared pretty quickly," I admitted, remembering how the pain had disappeared as soon as Louis had caused that scene with Ryan.

"That's good," he mumbled, gripping the wheel tightly.

We were quiet for the next five minutes, and during that time, I contemplated whether I should ask him about the incident or not. Then I realized he wouldn't answer me if he didn't want to. "Why did you do it?" I asked him, turning to look at his profile.

I could see his jaw clench for a few seconds until it relaxed. "What do you mean?"

He knew what I meant. It wasn't hard to tell by the look on his face, but I decided to explain anyway. "Why did you stand up for me?"

Louis turned to meet my gaze before looking back at the road. "Ryan's a sick fucking idiot," he muttered.

I rolled my eyes at his comment. "I could have handled it, though."

He gritted his teeth, clenching his hands around the wheel again. "It doesn't matter."

Furrowing my eyebrows together, I looked at him in confusion. "What do you mean 'it doesn't matter'?" I wondered.

He turned to meet my gaze for a few seconds before shaking his head and facing the windshield again. "I couldn't help it."

"You couldn't help it?" I repeated in confusion because I didn't understand what he was getting at.

Letting out a deep sigh, he swallowed hard. "I couldn't fucking watch you be pushed like that without doing anything about it," he blurted, running a hand through his hair in frustration.

My mouth fell open in shock. Did he really mean that? He had actually gotten riled up because Ryan had hurt me specifically? Did that mean he wouldn't have done it if it was someone else?

"Oh," was the only thing that left my mouth, too shocked to say anything else.

Louis snapped his head to see my reaction, knitting his eyebrows together. "You think that's weird?"

I shook my head vigorously. "No, I'm just surprised, is all. I feel honored if anything. However, I am still sure I could have handled it myself," I said, a smile threatening to take over my features.

He raised his eyebrows at me. "Really now? You do know you were lying on the ground, right? You were at a disadvantage there already," he pointed out.

"Heeey," I whined, crossing my arms over my chest. "That doesn't mean I couldn't have handled the situation. I'll have you know I'm quite strong."

"Yeah?" He asked in amusement, his eyebrows arched. "Is that a challenge?"

I looked him up and down, knowing very well that he was stronger than I was even though I was taller than him, so I shook my head and stuck my chin out. "No, it is not."

He let out a loud bark of laughter, throwing his head back against the headrest. "That's what I thought."

I sent him a glare. "Oh, shut up."

He smirked at me, shaking his head in amusement.

After that, we were quiet for another while. I felt giddy about the fact that we were talking and getting along again, so I couldn't help it when I reached out to turn the radio on. I felt Louis glancing at me through the corner of my eye the entire time.

The first song that came on was 'Girls Just Want To Have Fun' by Cyndi Lauper. My eyes widened as I felt excitement well up inside me. Without hesitating, I turned the volume up so it was blaring through the speakers. It was so loud that I was sure people could hear it from the outside.

"Oh daddy dear, you know you're still number one, but girls, they wanna have fun. Oh, girls just want to have... That's all they really waaaaant, some fuuuuuun. When the working day is done. Oh, girls, they wanna have fun. Oh girls just wanna have fun," I screamed out with a smile on my face, doing a little dance with my arms.

I glanced at him through the corner of my eye to see his reaction only to notice that he was giving me a fond smile while shaking his head in amusement. It made the smile on my own face widen, and my arm movements escalated.

As soon as the song was over, I turned the volume down and looked at him again. "And here I was, thinking you hated loud music," he chuckled.

I tilted my head to the side. "You also thought you could make good sandwiches, but I guess you are wrong about many things," I joked, making him let out a gasp.

"Hey, there's nothing wrong with my sandwiches," he whined, sticking his bottom lip out.

I let out a snort. "You literally dropped the ham to the floor, Louis. You screwed up there already."

He rolled his eyes, shaking his head. "That was just bad luck."

Tilting my head to the side, I let a smile form on my lips. "You wish. That sandwich wasn't edible, and you know it," I said, crossing my arms over my chest.

"I ate it," he stated, shrugging his shoulders.

I cocked an eyebrow. "Only because you didn't want to admit defeat."

He raised his eyebrows at me. "If I remember correctly, you ate it too."

"Because I was hungry and I didn't want to seem rude. Besides, I only ate half of it," I reminded him.

Louis rolled his eyes, turning to face the road with a smile on his lips. "I have a feeling you won't stop until you win this argument," he chuckled.

My lips twitched at his words. "You're right, I won't."

Right then, Louis turned the corner to my street and pulled over outside the blue house. The second the car came to a halt, I turned to look at him, noticing that he was biting his bottom lip. I opened my mouth to ask him what was on his mind, but he beat me to it.

"I'll pick you up tomorrow morning, yeah?"

I felt butterflies erupt in my stomach at his words, and I let a smile spread on my face. "If you insist."

The corners of his lips twitched. "I'm going to show you what real music is then because whatever that was you played before is not called music compared to mine," he winked.

I scrunched my nose up. "Well, I'm sure I'm definitely going to be awake after that."

He let out a chuckle, pulling his bottom lip between his teeth. "I promise it's not that bad."

"We'll see about that."

With that said, I opened the car door and was just about to close it behind me when he stopped me in my movements.

"Oh, and Curly?"

I leaned down to get a look at his face. "Yeah?"

"Goodnight," he smiled, making my heart flutter in my chest.

"Goodnight," I replied breathlessly before shutting the door behind me.

I almost sprinted up to the porch, my bag slung over my shoulder as I heard him speed off in the distance. That boy really knew how to get to my heart. The funny thing about it was that I was positive he didn't even have to try because just the simplest things made my heart go crazy.

The second I entered the house, I noticed that Gemma sitting in the living room, her legs propped up on the coffee table as per usual.

"Where on earth have you been? I've tried calling you like five times," she burst out, looking at me with wide eyes.

I bit my bottom lip, walking further into the room to sit down at the edge of the couch. "Um, I kind of missed the bus because I stayed behind to talk to Louis," I explained, scratching the back of my neck.

Her mouth fell open in shock. "You talked to Louis? Did you sort things out?"

Averting my gaze, I let out a sigh. "I... Yeah, kind of."

I was happy that Louis and I were talking again, I really was. However, somewhere deep inside me, something was telling me that no matter how many times I tried to convince myself that I would be fine with being his friend, I knew that I would always want more. It was easy to say that I would be okay with it when the options were either talking to him or not talking to him at all, but if I really thought about it, I knew that I would never be able to watch him be with someone else while being stuck in the friendzone.

She furrowed her eyebrows together. "What do you mean 'kind of'? How can you 'kind of' sort things out?" She asked in confusion.

"We uh... we agreed on forgetting the kiss ever happened," I said, looking down at my lap.

She inhaled a deep breath, scooting over to place a hand on my thigh. "H, look at me," she insisted.

It took a while until I finally did what she said, turning to meet her brown eyes. "I know what you're thinking, alright? But maybe things are not that black and white. You don't know if he just said that because he wanted to save what you two have. I mean, there must be a reason why he kissed you, right?" She frowned.

Her words reminded me of the way he had asked me the question in the first place. How he had pleaded with me to forget about the kiss because he missed me. Then how he reacted when I told him that it didn't ruin anything between us. He had seemed so relieved. But then again, it could just be that he had missed me as a friend and thought he had ruined our friendship by kissing me. Also, he might just have wanted to find out whether he liked guys or not. It didn't necessarily mean he had actually wanted to kiss me but thought he had ruined everything by doing so.

Letting out a sigh, I ran a hand through my still slightly wet curls. "I don't know, Gems. I should have probably asked him about it, but I was just so happy that he was talking to me again that I didn't want to ruin anything. At the moment, I actually told myself that I would be happy to be his friend if it meant we were on speaking terms," I mumbled.

She pursed her lips, rubbing my thigh reassuringly. "And that just proves how much you love him," she smiled faintly. "But now that you know you are on good terms again, the thought of wanting more comes back, doesn't it?" She guessed.

I nodded my head sadly.

"And that's understandable. Honestly, I don't think you'll ever be able to be just friends with him. It's going to eat you up eventually."

Letting out a sigh, I averted my gaze again. She was right. I knew she was right.

The sad part about it was that I didn't know what to do because I realized then that if I would never get him to like me back, I would lose him one way or another.

Chapter 26

The next morning, I found myself stuffing my mouth with cereal at a quick pace. I had slept through my alarm and didn't wake up until half an hour later. Therefore, I was now in a hurry, and the fact that Louis was going to pick me up stressed me out even more since I knew he hated waiting for me.

It didn't take long until I could hear a car honk outside, and I knew it was Louis without even checking. I shoved the last couple of spoons of cereal into my mouth before hurrying to the sink to dump the bowl there. I then ran to the entryway to slip my black boots on, grab my bag and throw my winter jacket over my shoulder.

The second I had locked the front door, I ran over to Louis' black sports car, seeing how he was fumbling with the radio through the window. Opening the door, I threw my bag on the floor before getting inside. I turned to him, noticing that he was now looking at me.

"Good morning," I greeted.

His gaze wandered upward, and he instantly quirked an eyebrow. "What happened to your hair?" He questioned instead of greeting me in return.

I reached my hand up to touch my brown curls, realizing that I never had time to fix them because I was in such a hurry. "Um, I kind of overslept, so I never had time to fix it," I explained, biting my bottom lip.

He arched his eyebrows at me, an amused smile making its way to his face. "Really?"

"Yeah," I sighed, pulling down the sun visor to check my reflection in the mirror. Damn, he was right. My curls were literally sticking out in every direction.

Louis started driving to school as I tried to fix my hair. After running my hand through it a couple of times, I turned to him again. "Is it better now?"

He glanced at me, his gaze settling on my curls. "Yeah, much better," he smiled.

My lips twitched at his comment. "Oh, by the way, you don't happen to have a piece of gum, do you? I didn't have time to brush my teeth either," I grimaced, making him let out a chuckle.

"Really now? You could have just told me you needed more time. I could have waited, you know?"

I cocked an eyebrow at him. "You waiting? Can those two words even go in the same sentence?" I snorted, but a smile was threatening to take over my features.

He opened his mouth to protest, but he shut it again, which made the smile break out on my face. "That's what I thought," I laughed.

He muttered something under his breath as he kept his eyes on the road. However, he did reach out to open the glove compartment, taking out a package of gum. "Take as many as you want."

My face lit up. "Thank you."

There was just something about it when we were like this that made me forget about the problems that I thought about otherwise. I just couldn't think of serious things when I was on such good terms with him. Therefore, it didn't cross my mind that I had come to a somewhat realization about him yesterday. Also, I was known for living in the present and not thinking about the future too much.

"So, what song were you going to play for me?" I wondered, glancing at his profile as I started chewing my gum.

A smirk made its way to his face as he reached out to take his phone from between our seats. He then unlocked it while still keeping his eyes on the road, glancing down every two seconds to see what he was doing. "Alright, here it is. You'll love it, Curly," he promised me with a smug look on his face, pressing his thumb against the screen.

It didn't take long for me to realize that it was a rock song. I had already assumed so much beforehand, so it didn't take me by surprise. However, what did take me by surprise was that I didn't dislike it. It was actually quite good.

Louis bobbed his head to the loud music, drumming his palms against the wheel. "Jealousy, turning saints into the sea, swimming through sick lullabies, choking on your alibis, but it's just the price I pay. Destiny is calling me. Open up my eager eyes, 'cause I'm Mr. Brightside," Louis sang with a smile on his face.

His singing voice caught me off guard. It was so beautiful and angelic that I swore I could listen to it all day. It wasn't too easy to hear anything but the singer in the band since it was an uptempo song, but Louis had such a nice high tone that it could be heard over the loud music, and I couldn't help the way my lips twitched. Was there anything not to love about this boy?

A few seconds later, Louis turned the volume down, looking at me with the same smug look as before. "You have to admit that it's not bad," he said, raising his eyebrows at me.

I pursed my lips, trying to make it seem like I was hesitant about it. "Well, honestly..." I trailed off, biting the inside of my cheek. "Okay, I'll admit it, it's not bad. It's not bad at all actually. I honestly didn't expect that," I confessed, making his smile widen.

"See, I told you so," he winked, making me let out a light chuckle.

"Oh, shut up," I grinned.

He turned back to the road, the smile never leaving his face. His playlist was still on, and I didn't complain about it because he kept it at a low volume. However, the next couple of songs weren't even half as good as the first one, and something was telling me that it was all on purpose. He knew exactly what song to play to make me agree that it wasn't bad, that tosser.

"So, you wanted to ask me something," he stated after a while, turning to look at me.

I cocked an eyebrow, glancing at him. "I did?" I asked in confusion. I didn't recall wanting to ask him anything.

He knitted his eyebrows. "Yeah. Uh, that time when I wanted to ask you something first, you know? At your house," he explained, and when it finally clicked in my head what he was talking about, I understood why he found it so difficult to talk about it. It was the same day he had kissed me.

"Oh," was the only thing that left my mouth.

To be honest, I had almost forgotten about that whole thing. It seemed like ages ago when Lottie had entered the diner and told me that Louis usually didn't join family dinners and that he had a good reason not to, especially after something he had found out about recently.

I had been so eager to find out what that was all about at the time, but now that Louis and I hadn't talked for a couple of days due to the kiss, it had completely slipped my mind. It just hadn't been what concerned me the most anymore.

"To be honest, I had almost forgotten about it," I admitted.

He raised his eyebrows. "You did? So it was nothing important then?" He wondered curiously.

I bit my bottom lip, thinking about it. I mean, it was important - very important even, but now wasn't really the best time to talk about it. I was quite sure it was something he wouldn't be too keen on talking about either, especially not when we only had a couple of minutes until we would arrive at school. Besides, as mentioned before, we hadn't talked in three days, and I didn't want to throw that in his face the first thing I did.

"It's not that it's not important. It's just not the right time to ask you about it," I tried to explain.

He furrowed his eyebrows, and I could tell that he was suspicious. "Is there something I need to be worried about?"

I shook my head with a small smile on my face. "No. I'd just rather ask you when we have more time to talk," I told him.

He nodded his head in understanding. "I see."

Not long after that, we arrived at school, and Louis parked the car in an empty spot. We both got out of the vehicle, slinging our bags over our shoulders before making our way towards the entrance. We walked next to each other, easily falling into step with one another.

"So, how long have you been planning on studying in Manchester?" Louis asked me, kicking a rock on the ground.

My eyebrows rose in surprise. "Were you listening to my and Evelyn's conversation yesterday?" I gaped.

He pursed his lips, his eyes on the rock. "It doesn't matter," he muttered. "You didn't answer the question."

Letting out a sigh, I ran a hand through my curls. "Well, I'm not really planning on it. I haven't exactly thought about it, which you might have heard too. And as you probably know by now, I don't really like to think about the future. However, I guess if I don't get the scholarship, Manchester is probably going to be my first choice, yes."

"Why?" He wanted to know, making my face turn into a scowl.

"Um... Manchester has always been close to my heart. I spent a lot of time there as a kid, and it's not that far away either. I'd like to stay close to mom and Gemma if I don't get the scholarship."

He hummed in understanding, nodding his head thoughtfully. "I guess that's a fair point."

"What about you?" I asked him, curiosity lacing my voice.

He shrugged his shoulders. "I haven't really thought about it either, but if I don't get the scholarship, I'll probably stick to something close to Holmes Chapel as well."

It was as if I hadn't thought about the fact that we were going separate ways after high school until then because his words really hit me. It made me so extremely sad to think about it, so I guess that was why I always tried not to.

I could tell he noticed that I was concerned about something by the way he was looking at me. "Something's on your mind, Curly?" He wondered.

I looked up to meet his gaze. "I just... I don't like thinking about what's to come, you know? I can't really picture us guys going different ways," I mumbled, leaving out that separating from him specifically was what bothered me the most.

He furrowed his eyebrows together. "Yeah, I know. I don't like thinking about that either," he muttered.

"I mean, one of us two is going to move to London in just a matter of months," I mumbled, looking up at the grey sky.

He stayed quiet, not commenting anything about it. It made me wonder if it was bugging him as well. Did he feel the same way about us going separate ways? I hoped so because then it meant I at least meant *something* to him.

"Let's talk about something else, shall we? There are still a few months until then after all," he reminded me, trying to lighten the mood.

I nodded in agreement. "Yeah, you're right."

We started talking about soccer instead, and it didn't take long until we arrived at our lockers after that. Niall, Liam and Zayn were already there, chatting about something that made them all have smiles on their faces. The second they noticed us approaching them, their eyes almost bulged out of their sockets as their jaws dropped.

Liam was the first one to compose himself by inhaling a deep sigh of relief. "Thank heavens you two are talking again. I was getting so tired of having to choose whom of you to hang with," he said.

I cocked an eyebrow at him. "Liam, you only had to go through it for a day. Why are you making it sound like it was for a month?" I chuckled, an amused smile gracing my lips.

He pouted his lips, letting out a huff. "Well, it felt like a month. Yesterday was a tough day."

I rolled my eyes, glancing to my right to see Louis doing the same thing. Niall was the next one to compose himself, and he didn't hesitate to take a step forward and grab a hold of my forearm. "We need to talk."

With that said, he pulled me to the other end of the hallway, not letting go of me until we were out of the other lads' sight. He then raised his eyebrows at me questioningly.

"Tell me what happened," he demanded.

I inhaled a deep breath. "We just talked it through," I shrugged.

He narrowed his eyes at me. "And what? You know why he kissed you now? And if he feels the same way? What exactly did you talk about, and why are you acting like nothing happened?" He blurted.

I let out a sigh, running a hand through my dark curls. "I didn't really find out about any of those things. We just agreed that we would forget about the kiss," I explained, looking down at my boots.

He inhaled a deep breath. "Damn, Harry. That's not the way to go. You can't just go around ignoring such important stuff and try to be friends with him. It's not going to work."

I furrowed my eyebrows, pinching my bottom lip with my forefinger and thumb. "I just don't want to lose him, Niall. I'm already anxious about us going separate ways in just a few months. Besides, he was the one who wanted to forget about it. I couldn't just force him to explain himself then," I mumbled.

He pursed his lips, looking away from me for a second. "He's not playing fair, you know? He does exactly what he wants with you and you don't even question his actions," he huffed.

I bit my bottom lip, shaking my head. "That's not true. I... I do not let him do what he wants," I frowned.

Niall cocked an eyebrow. "So you think it's okay for him to kiss you and then not even explain himself? And you think it's okay for him to ignore you whenever something happens, then all of a sudden pretend that it never did? Because it seems like he does this a lot. Damn it, Harry. You're better than this."

To be honest, I had never thought about it like that. Maybe he was right. I mean, for example, Louis never told me the reason he was being distant the week after my birthday. Now I was fairly positive it had to do with his family, but that was beside the point. If he considered us close, then I would be one of the first people he told, right?

The crease between my eyebrows deepened at his words. "He is a little secretive at times, but I'm sure he has a reason for it," I mumbled, not really liking the fact that Niall was talking about him like this, even if I understood where he was coming from.

Niall rolled his eyes. "You're so gone for him, Harry, I swear."

I shot him a glare. "Whatever," I muttered, walking away to join the other boys again.

He let out a sigh before following me. He didn't say anything, though, so I assumed he understood that he wasn't going to get anything else out of me right now.

"What was that all about?" Louis wondered once we were standing in front of them, raising his eyebrows at me.

I glanced at Niall quickly before looking back at him. "Nothing important. He just wanted help with a math problem," I shrugged, making Louis narrow his eyes a little. He didn't seem convinced, but he accepted the explanation.

"On a completely different note, Alice is throwing a party on Friday and she told me to invite you all," Liam informed us.

Zayn let out a snort. "Well, I sure hope she did. We are her boyfriend's best friends after all," he said.

Liam rolled his eyes, punching him on the arm. "Oh, shut up."

Zayn let out a chuckle, sending him an air kiss.

"Should I take that as a yes?" Liam wondered, his eyebrows raised.

Zayn continued to laugh. "You can definitely count me in."

"Niall?" Liam went on, and the blonde-haired guy smiled at him. "For sure."

"Louis and Harry?"

To be honest, I wasn't sure if I wanted to attend this party because nothing good ever came out of them. I mean, at my birthday party, I had kissed my co-worker only because I had been so jealous about Louis kissing that girl. And sure, Emily's party didn't turn out that bad considering he ended up sleeping at my house, but he got hurt, and he did sleep with said girl, so I didn't know if I really wanted to attend another party.

"Sure, why not?" Louis smiled, shrugging his shoulders.

I swallowed hard, looking at the feathery-haired boy as he smiled at Liam. He probably didn't notice that I was staring at him because he didn't turn to meet my gaze, so I let out a deep sigh, knowing I couldn't say no when no one else did. "Okay," I mumbled.

Niall shot me a look, narrowing his eyes in suspicion. He knew something wasn't right.

"Great. I'm sure Alice will be delighted to hear that you're all going to be there. I can assure you that there are going to be a lot of girls as well," he smirked.

Zayn wolf-whistled while Niall clapped his hands together excitedly. I didn't do anything, and when I looked at Louis, he didn't seem to react much to this news either. He just gave Liam a nod with a small smile on his face, but nothing more than that. Somehow, it made me relax a little. Maybe this party was going to be different from all the other ones?

Before either of us could say something else, the bell rang, and we all went our separate ways... or so I thought. It turned out Louis caught up with me as I walked through the hallway, so he was now walking right beside me. I glanced at him in surprise, only to notice that he was smirking at me.

"You don't remember that both our classes are this way?" He asked, raising his eyebrows at me.

I couldn't help but smile at his words. "Yeah, I do. I even know you have Drama," I chuckled, making his mouth fall open in fake surprise.

"What? Are you some kind of stalker now?"

"You'd like that, wouldn't you?" I teased, making him laugh.

He didn't know how much of a stalker I actually was. I kept track of all his classes, and I had done so during the last couple of years. He didn't need to know that, though.

"Yeah, actually. It's nice knowing I have an admirer," he joked, nudging me in the side playfully.

Since when were our conversations this flirty? I didn't know, but I did know that I enjoyed it. If I knew he wouldn't find it weird, I would be flirting with him more often, although this was only in a teasing way.

We arrived at Louis' stop right then, and we said goodbye to each other before I hurried to my classroom, knowing I was probably running a little late.

During the entire hour, I thought about what Niall had told me earlier. He said that Louis did whatever he wanted with me, as if I was wrapped around his finger. I wasn't. I was just afraid of losing him and having him not like me. That was why I never pushed him to explain himself. I mean, after that time when he snapped at me in the hallway, I had felt like I had to be careful with what I said around him so I didn't do anything else that would upset him. And whenever he was secretive, he had made it pretty clear that he didn't want to talk about whatever the topic was, so I never pushed him to.

On the other hand, I guess Niall was right when he said that I couldn't go on like this. Louis was one of my closest friends now, so I shouldn't be afraid to ask him things. Sure, I had been about to ask him why he had been distant that week after my birthday twice now, but there was no denying that I was always a little afraid that he would react negatively and run away when I did. But I had to realize that if he didn't want to answer, he wouldn't, and I was sure he wasn't going to just leave if I did.

We were closer than ever, and we had been through so much during the last couple of weeks, so if he didn't want anything to do with me, he would have left a long time ago, right?

So, maybe asking him about it wouldn't be so bad? Maybe I had just built up the situation worse than it was? I knew that he didn't want to talk about it at the time, but maybe it wouldn't be so bad now that things seemed to be better?

That was how I came to the conclusion that I was going to ask him about it after school, and there was no turning back this time.

Chapter 27

When the last bell of the day rang, I made my way to my locker. All of the guys were already there, shrugging on their jackets and grabbing their bags while chatting with each other.

I hadn't talked to either Louis or Niall separately since this morning because whenever I had met them during the day, Liam and Zayn had been there too. Now, I didn't exactly know if Niall wanted to talk to me again, but I knew I wanted to talk to Louis.

"Hey guys," I greeted as I opened my locker, shoving my books into it.

Liam turned to me, a smile on his face. "Hey, Harry. Do you have work today?" He wondered.

I knitted my eyebrows together. "Yeah, I do. Why?"

By now, Zayn, Niall and Louis were listening to our conversation as well. Liam shrugged his shoulders. "Evelyn is joining me and Alice to this café in the city, so I just wanted to ask you if you wanted to come too. It's okay, though. I don't think she'll feel like she's third-wheeling."

My mouth formed the shape of an 'o'. "I would have loved to come if I didn't have work. I'm sorry," I apologized.

"No need to apologize, mate, I understand. I was ninety percent sure you had work anyway," he assured me.

Before either of us could say anything else, we were accompanied by the two girls Liam had mentioned just a minute ago. Alice didn't hesitate to walk up to Liam and wrap her arms around his waist from behind, pressing a light kiss to his neck.

Evelyn, on the other hand, walked over to me with a bright smile on her face. "Fancy seeing you here," she smiled joyfully.

I let out a light chuckle. "My locker is right here, so you shouldn't be surprised," I said, feeling a pair of eyes staring at the side of my face.

She shrugged her shoulders. "It didn't make me any less happy, though."

I just shook my head with a smile on my face.

"So, are you joining us for coffee at the café?" She asked hopefully, nodding towards Liam and Alice.

Letting out a sigh, I gave her an apologetic look. "I can't, I'm sorry. I have work today, unfortunately."

She pouted her lips. "That's too bad. It would've been nice to have you there with me," she said, looking at the loved up couple.

I glanced at them too, noticing that Liam had now turned around to look at his girlfriend. Their faces were close as they talked, smiles on their lips. Yeah, I was definitely jealous of their relationship.

"I'm sure you'll be fine," I reassured her, making Evelyn's lips twitch as she turned back to face me.

"I hope so."

I was just about to turn to my locker and grab my jacket when she started talking again. "Um, you don't want to uh... have coffee with me some other time?" She wondered, biting her bottom lip hesitantly.

My mouth fell open in surprise. However, it suddenly hit me that I shouldn't be because Liam had warned me about this. He had told me that Evelyn was planning to ask me out, but that she probably hadn't found the courage to do so yet. It just never registered in my mind that she would actually do it.

"I uh--"

Suddenly, I could feel someone wrap an arm around my shoulders, pulling me to their side. "Sorry to disappoint you, love, but Harry here doesn't date."

I snapped my head to my right, seeing Louis flashing Evelyn a fake smile with his head tilted to the side. To say I was shocked would be an understatement. I was beyond shocked. I didn't expect him to interfere with our conversation, and especially not like this.

While I tried to register what was happening, I noticed that Evelyn was surprised by Louis' actions as well, judging by the look on her face. Her eyebrows were almost reaching her hairline and her eyes were wide open. However, she composed herself before I had found the ability to talk.

"Oh, I... I'm sorry. Is that... is that true?" She wondered, turning to me.

I swallowed hard, glancing at Louis only to see that he had clenched his jaw while practically glaring at the black-haired girl.

"I... No, it's not exactly true, but it's not a lie either," I said, furrowing my eyebrows because what the hell was I saying? What did I even mean by that?

She seemed confused too as she bit her lip hesitantly. "Oh. Um... I'm sorry I asked. It's okay if you don't want to consider it a date. I... I just thought it could be nice to have a chat," she shrugged, looking down at the floor.

God, I felt so bad for her. She didn't deserve this. She was such a nice girl that didn't deserve anything bad, yet here I was, basically throwing it in her face that I didn't want to go out with her. Sure, *I* didn't exactly do it, Louis did, but I didn't exactly make things better either.

I could feel Louis' hold around my shoulders tighten as I flashed her a small smile. "I agree," I replied, making her look up at me with an almost hopeful smile. It made Louis grit his teeth.

"We can talk about it some other time, yeah?" She suggested, glancing at Louis quickly.

I nodded my head. "Sure."

With that said, she said goodbye before walking over to Liam and Alice, who were now talking to Zayn and Niall. As soon as she was gone, I unwrapped Louis' arm from my shoulders and looked at him with a frown on my face.

"That wasn't really necessary, was it?" I muttered, making him let out a snort.

Without a word, he turned to my open locker and grabbed my bag before walking away, heading towards the exits. I let out a groan, shutting my locker before going after him, knowing I needed my bag to get home since my bus pass was in it.

I finally caught up with him as soon as we were outside, and I didn't hesitate to grab a hold of his forearm, stopping him in his tracks. He turned around to face me, his features showing no emotion whatsoever.

"If you want me to apologize for what I did, I'm sorry to disappoint you because that's not going to happen. At least I'm not leading anyone on here," he muttered, making me want to snort.

Yeah, right. Says the one who goes and fucking kisses their best friend who's had feelings for them for three years only to regret it afterward.

If anyone was leading anyone on here, it was him. He just didn't know it. "I'm not leading her on," I mumbled. "She just looked so sad... I just didn't want to hurt her."

He rolled his eyes, shaking his head. "That's like the whole point of turning people down, Curly. You can't expect her to be happy when you tell her you don't reciprocate her feelings."

I knitted my eyebrows together. "But I don't want her to hate me. She's nice, and I don't want to lose her as a friend."

He looked up at the sky for a few seconds, letting out a sigh. "You can't be friends with someone who has feelings for you. It's not fair to them."

As if I don't already know that. It hurts like a bitch, Louis. You know that?

With a glare, I reached out to snatch my bag from his hand before stomping away, heading towards the bus stop. He seemed taken aback by my actions because it took a while until I could hear his voice behind me.

"Hey, where are you going?" He called after me.

"Home," I said monotonously, not really wanting to be in his presence probably for the first time in my life.

I could hear him let out a sigh as he jogged up to me, only slowing down when he was right beside me. "Come on, Curly. Is this because I interfered with the conversation? Fuck, I'm sorry, but I just didn't want you to get her hopes up," he tried to explain. It didn't really make any sense, though. Why would he care if I got her hopes up? This was between me and Evelyn, not him.

"I don't care about that," I muttered because I didn't. Sure, he could have been nicer to her, but that wasn't the main reason I just wanted to go home right now. His previous words were.

"Then what is it?" He pleaded, giving me puppy eyes, and no, damn it. I couldn't resist those beautiful, ocean blue eyes even if I wanted to.

I let out a loud groan. "It's nothing, alright? I shouldn't have to explain myself when you basically never do," I replied, making his face turn into a scowl.

"What are you talking about?"

I turned to meet his gaze. "I've been thinking about asking you something all day... or more like for two weeks now."

He seemed even more confused by this. "Then why haven't you just done so?"

"Because," I said, running a hand through my curls while inhaling a deep breath. "Because you wouldn't have answered me."

He furrowed his eyebrows. "How do you know that when you haven't even tried?" He asked, looking me in the eye.

I swallowed hard, averting my gaze. "Because you always get so secretive when we talk about certain things," I explained.

He bit his bottom lip, looking at something behind my shoulder. I doubted it was anything specific, though. "Well, you can always ask, you know? There's no harm in that," he shrugged, turning to look at me again. "Is this about what we talked about in the car this morning?"

I met his gaze, staring into his blue eyes for a couple of seconds until I let out a sigh. "Yeah, it is," I admitted. "And I guess you're right. I've been trying to tell myself that there won't be any harm in asking, but I guess I was just afraid that you would shut me out if I threw all these questions at you that you didn't want to answer."

He flashed me a small smile as he shook his head. "I guess I understand where you're coming from, seeing as I've been like a rollercoaster lately, but I can promise you that you don't have to worry about it. You know, you ain't getting rid of me that easily," he joked, and if his intention was to lighten the mood, he succeeded.

I let out a light chuckle. "Good to know."

His lips twitched at my comment. "Come on. I'll drive you home so you can finally ask me what you've been wanting to for so long," he suggested, giving me a look of expectation as he started walking towards the parking lot.

I didn't know whether I was supposed to hesitate or not, but I didn't. If Louis was asking me to come with him, I couldn't say no. My heart would never let me even if I wanted to. So, I followed him to his black sports car and slid into the passenger seat once he had unlocked it.

"Alright, shoot," he said as he turned on the engine and pulled out of the parking space.

Inhaling a deep breath, I turned to look out the window. How should I begin? And with what?

"Um, so you remember how I met Lottie at my work the other day, yeah?" I finally settled with, biting my bottom lip hesitantly.

He took it the wrong way and instantly turned to stare at me with this warning look on his face. "Curly, if you're going to tell me that you actually did try something with her, I don't have any other choice but to strangle you."

"Why do you always assume I've been hitting on your sister whenever I mention her? Damn, I thought I told you that I would never do that," I said, rolling my eyes.

He pursed his lips, knitting his eyebrows together. "Okay, go on."

I let out a sigh. "So, she told me that you usually don't join your family dinners and that she understood why, especially after something you had found out recently. She wouldn't say what it was, but something is telling me that it has to do with the way you were acting so off during the week after my birthday. Now, I know there's probably more to it... or at least why you were ignoring me, seeing as you seemed pretty upset about the fact that I told you we aren't close," I explained.

Louis stayed quiet for a long time, so long that I was getting more and more certain he wasn't going to say anything. However, he proved me wrong when he eventually ran a hand through his fringe and opened his mouth to start talking.

"Yeah, you're right. A lot of things happened at the same time, and I didn't really know how to handle it all, so I distanced myself from everyone."

Knitting my eyebrows together, I looked at him, noticing that he seemed a little nervous. When was Louis Tomlinson ever nervous?

"Um, can I ask what you found out? Or is it too personal?" I questioned him hesitantly.

The muscles in his face softened a little by my words, but he was biting his lip so harshly that I was almost certain it was going to draw blood. Again, it took ages until he opened his mouth to speak, and when he did, he let out a sigh. "I... I don't know about you, but I consider you one of the closest people to me now, and I feel like you are not going to spread this around to anyone, so uh... I'll tell you because I think you deserve to know why I acted the way I was, and why I'm still acting the way I am," he muttered. "But, I want to show you something first. It's going to be easier for you to understand then."

I didn't know how to react to what he just said. First of all, I was so happy that he considered me one of the closest people to him and that he felt like he could trust me. Words couldn't describe just how glad that made me feel. However, I was also confused by his words. What exactly did he want to show me?

"What do you mean 'I want to show you something first'?" I wondered.

A faint smile formed on his lips as he looked at me. "Are you free tomorrow after practice?"

I was even more confused by this. "Uh, yeah, I guess?"

"Then I'll bring you to my house. You're going to understand exactly what I mean then," he explained.

"Oh, um... okay," I frowned.

With his hands gripping the wheel, he glanced at me questioningly. "Was that all you wanted to ask me or is there more?" He wondered.

There were probably plenty of things I wanted to ask him about, but I couldn't remember them all at the moment. Everything was just blank in my mind right now.

"Uh, not that I can think of right now, no," I said, scratching the back of my neck.

He let out a light chuckle. "Alright, Curly."

During the next couple of minutes, I thought about what he had just told me, and honestly, I couldn't believe that he hadn't made more protest. I didn't expect this at all. It definitely took me by surprise.

The fact that I was going to find out what was going on in the Tomlinson household tomorrow made me both nervous and excited. Nervous because I didn't know what to expect although I knew it couldn't be anything good. Excited because I had been wanting to know for such a long time now. I was finally going to find out why Louis acted the way he did.

"How did you and Lottie even get into talking about all that?" He asked me after a while with a hint of amusement in his voice.

I turned to him, my lips twitching. "When she entered the diner, I remembered that your family ordered the chicken stew last time they came to pick up food, and since you told me you had never tried it before, I asked her if you usually ate the food they ordered from us," I shrugged.

His mouth formed the shape of an 'o'. "I see. Well, I must say that was actually pretty clever of you. Wouldn't take you as a smart guy," he joked, giving me a cheeky smile.

"Heey," I whined. "What's that supposed to mean?" I pouted, making his smile widen.

"It means exactly what it sounds like."

I leaned over to hit his arm, but not too harshly considering he was driving. "Says the one who had to repeat a school year."

His mouth fell open. "That had nothing to do with my intelligence, thank you very much," he huffed.

I rolled my eyes. "Okay, so what was it about then?" I wondered, raising my eyebrows at him.

He stuck his bottom lip out. "I was just unmotivated, is all. I didn't attend classes and I hung out with people who'd rather call in sick just to spend the day playing video games. Now that I think about it, it was actually a good thing that I had to repeat that year. Otherwise, God knows what would have happened to me," he said, shaking his head.

God knows what would have happened to me either.

Would I even have fallen for him if he never repeated that school year? I mean, I barely even acknowledged him when he was in the year above me, but as soon as he started hanging out with us lads, I just started falling for him more and more. Each day, I used to find something new about him that made me realize just how beautiful he was inside and out.

"Well, you wouldn't have known me," I reminded him, making him glance at me.

A smile crept to his lips as he nodded his head. "That's true."

A few minutes later, we arrived at my house, but before I had even made a move to open the door, Louis turned so his body was facing me. "Look, about the whole Evelyn thing... I'm really sorry, alright? I shouldn't have interfered in your conversation like that since I realize now that I didn't have anything to do with it. I just... I couldn't help myself," he apologized, biting his bottom lip.

I furrowed my eyebrows. "It's okay. I was just shocked, and I didn't want to hurt her feelings. But I guess you were right about the fact that it was probably for the best that she found out I'm not interested, even if it hurt her," I said, pursing my lips.

He nodded his head slowly. "Maybe I shouldn't have been the one to tell her, though."

I shrugged my shoulders. "Honestly, I don't think I would have been able to tell her myself, so you kind of did me a favor although you could have been a little nicer," I explained, the corners of my lips twitching, which he noticed.

He cracked a small smile of his own as he let out a light chuckle. "I'll keep that in mind till next time."

"Next time?" I frowned.

His smile turned into a look of amusement. "Well, you are an attractive lad, Curly. There are going to be more people trying to hit on you, so I might as well start preparing myself for letting more people down," he said, making my heart pick up its pace.

Did he just call me an attractive lad?

"How do you know I won't want them to hit on me?" I wondered, raising my eyebrows.

He shrugged his shoulders with a determined look on his face. "I'll make sure of that."

Chapter 28

When practice rolled around the next day, I found myself almost biting my nails in anticipation. I hadn't been able to stop thinking about the fact that I was actually going home with Louis after practice. Honestly, I couldn't remember the last time I was there. It must have been months ago, and whenever the guys and I were over, his parents weren't there. His sisters were the only ones who used to be home, and this fact made me more nervous, yet excited at the same time because I assumed I was going to meet his parents for the first time today.

"Alright, boys. That was all for today. Great job everyone," Coach announced, pulling me out of my thoughts.

We all walked off the field to head to the locker rooms. I felt someone bump their hip against mine on our way there, making me snap my head to the source. Niall was flashing me a lopsided smile, his head tilted to the side.

"You okay, mate?" He asked.

I furrowed my eyebrows. "Yeah, everything's fine. Why?"

He shrugged his shoulders, turning his gaze forward. "I just couldn't help but notice that you seemed a little off, so I was just wondering if something's bugging you?"

It was almost creepy how easy it was for Niall to read me. It was like he acknowledged every thought in my mind by just studying me. I really hoped no one else had the same ability as him because that would be embarrassing.

I looked around to make sure Louis wasn't in sight before letting out a deep sigh. "It's nothing to worry about. I'm just nervous because I finally talked to Louis and he's going to explain things after practice," I told him.

Niall looked surprised by this. "He's going to tell you why he kissed you? Why couldn't he have just done that right away?"

Honestly, that question had totally slipped my mind yesterday. I did mention that everything went blank after Louis had started explaining himself and said that he was willing to tell me the reason behind his behavior, but I never thought I would forget to ask him one of the most important questions. However, I still wasn't sure whether I actually wanted to know why he decided to press his lips to mine that afternoon.

"No, it's not about that. It's about something else that he has been keeping to himself," I explained, making his mouth form the shape of an 'o'.

"Oh. Well, at least you are heading in the right direction. I'm proud that you finally decided to man up and ask him things you've been wanting to know," he smiled, giving me a pat on the shoulder. "Maybe I was wrong. Maybe you don't let him do whatever he wants with you."

I shook my head. "It was never my intention, but you made me realize that it was kind of a problem and that I had to take matters into my hands and do something about it. So, thank you, Niall."

"No problem," he smiled.

When we reached the locker room, we went our separate ways. I sat down on the bench where I had my bag, not wasting a minute until I started stripping out of my dirty gear. I had only gotten my shirt off when I could feel someone staring at me. My heart started racing in my chest, and it wasn't because of the fact that someone was looking at me itself, but because I knew who it was without having to check.

When I snapped my eyes up to meet those ocean blue eyes, I felt my breath hitch because Louis was sitting on the bench in front of me, his gaze glued to my stomach. For a second, I thought something was wrong, that I had dirt on me or something, but when I looked down, I could only see my pale skin, my butterfly tattoo, my fern leaves tattoos and abs. Did that mean he was checking me out?

When he noticed that I had caught him staring, he immediately averted his gaze, not daring to look me in the eye as he hurriedly stripped off his gear and headed for the showers. I could only stare at his figure as my mouth fell open. Did that just happen?

It took me a few seconds to pull myself together before I continued stripping out of my clothes. The second I entered the showers, Louis left, walking past me quickly. I decided not to put too much thought into it, even if I was kind of freaking out on the inside. Him looking at me didn't need to mean anything, though. It could have just been a mistake, just like everything else he ever did.

Once I had finished showering, I got dressed in my black sweats and purple hoodie, keeping my eyes away from Louis during the time I did so. Not that I felt his eyes on me again, but because I didn't want things to be more awkward than they were.

I didn't look up at him until I had zipped my bag, knowing I would have to talk to him in a matter of seconds since I was leaving with him. It turned out that was a mistake, though, because suddenly, I was the one staring at him. He was wearing his green Adidas hoodie again, and I just couldn't describe how much I loved it on him. Couldn't I just cuddle with him already while having his arms wrapped around me?

"It's not nice to stare, Curly."

I blinked, looking up at Louis' face to see him smirking at me. Wait, what? Did he really just say that? Who did he think he was, pointing me out when he had been doing the exact same thing just a few minutes ago? "At least I'm not staring at someone's naked torso," I stated, raising my eyebrows at him knowingly.

He pressed his lips in a thin line, turning around to face the door. Most of the lads had already left by now, so no one was really acknowledging our conversation. "The car's leaving in five," was the only thing he said before walking out the door, leaving me to shake my head in disbelief after him.

I would have given everything to read his mind right now, but when would I not? He was so secretive sometimes that he made me want to be Edward in fucking Twilight, that wanker.

I grabbed my bag from the bench, slinging it over my shoulder before walking out of the locker room as well. To my surprise, Louis hadn't gotten far. In fact, he was leaning against the brick wall of the building when I got outside.

Raising my eyebrows at him, I watched him pull himself off the wall to join me. "I thought you wouldn't wait for me."

He shrugged his shoulders, a smile creeping to his lips. "I only said the car's leaving in five," he said, making me roll my eyes.

When we arrived at the parking lot, Ryan, Tristan and Derek were there, each with a cigarette between their fingers while probably waiting for their ride to show up. They were chatting with each other, laughing at something they had just mentioned.

I looked away from them quickly, hoping they wouldn't see us because I was getting sick and tired of Ryan's attitude and behavior. Of course we weren't that lucky, though, because right then, Ryan caught sight of us, his lips instantly turning into a smirk.

"Aw, if it isn't it the faggy little boyfriends I see," he sniggered, tilting his head to the side.

Louis hadn't noticed them until Ryan's words hit his eardrums, and he instantly turned to face the source. "The fuck did you just say?" He snapped, coming to an abrupt halt.

Before I knew it, he was stomping over to the brown-haired boy who still had that ugly smirk on his face. Louis' jaw clenched as he got in Ryan's face, gritting his teeth. "You wanna repeat what you just said, huh?" He challenged him, raising his eyebrows in expectation.

Ryan rolled his eyes, taking a step back. "I'm not afraid of you, Tomlinson," he laughed, tossing his cig to the ground before stomping on it.

Louis let out a scoff, narrowing his eyes at him. "You're just jealous."

This made Ryan let out a loud bark of laughter, throwing his head back. "Me, jealous? Yeah, right. As if I would be jealous of having a boyfriend."

Louis rolled his eyes. "I'm not talking about that, you stupid idiot. You're jealous because I took your title of being captain," he sad knowingly, and judging by the way Ryan's jaw clenched, he was most likely right about his statement.

"You know nothing, Tomlinson. You're just a spoiled little brat who gets whatever you want," he seethed, scrunching his nose up in disgust.

Louis swallowed hard. "You know fucking nothing about me either, you shit. And you know what? Doing everything you can to hurt me and Harry is not going to lead you anywhere. Coach will never let you be captain again," he spat before turning on his heel to walk away from him.

On his way back, he placed a hand on the small of my back to guide me forward. Wolf-whistles were heard from behind us then, but Louis just flipped them the finger without even turning around to look at them.

The second we were both sitting in the car, I let out a deep breath while running a hand through my damp curls. When I turned to look at Louis, I noticed that he was staring out the windshield with an unreadable look on his face. It made me nervous because I had no idea what he was thinking about after what had just taken place.

"I'm sorry," I mumbled, biting my bottom lip.

He snapped his head to look at me, his eyebrows furrowing together. "Why are *you* sorry?"

"I just... I'm sorry for what he said," I mumbled.

He rolled his eyes, shaking his head. "I don't give a shit about what he said. He can say and believe whatever he wants. I just don't tolerate his fucking attitude and that stupid tone he always uses."

I swallowed hard, averting my gaze from him. To be honest, I hadn't expected that. I thought he cared more about what people thought about him, but maybe I had gotten that wrong?

"So, you don't mind that he called us boyfriends?" I wondered hesitantly, feeling my heart race in my chest.

He shrugged his shoulders, facing forward again. "We both know that it's not true anyway."

My heart sunk to the pit of my stomach, feeling like a heavy rock that had just hit the bottom of a lake. "Yeah..."

With that, Louis turned on the engine and left the parking lot along with the three guys who were still standing there, waiting for their ride to pick them up. The drive to Louis' house only lasted for five minutes since he lived much closer to the gym than I did, but it was silent five minutes.

All the nerves about finally meeting his parents came back in the snap of the fingers, swimming around in my stomach in an almost teasing way. I felt like throwing up, especially since Louis and I didn't talk during the entire ride. It didn't exactly make me relax.

When he parked his car in their massive driveway, he turned off the engine before turning to me. He instantly noticed that I was nervous judging by the way his facial expression softened. "You okay?" He asked, his eyes scanning my face.

I pulled my bottom lip between my teeth. "Yeah, I just don't know what to expect," I told him honestly, making a faint smile appear on his lips.

"I understand, but don't worry. Just... just remember to not take offense at anything, alright?"

My face turned into a scowl by his words. What did he mean by that?

Before I had time to question him, he got out of the car. He opened the backseat door to grab his bag before shutting it again. When he noticed that I still wasn't moving, he walked over to tap my window.

"Come on, Curly," he mouthed with a wink.

It made my heart flutter, and I reluctantly grabbed the handle to open the door. I let out a sigh once I was outside and shut the door behind me. My bag was still in the car because I figured I wouldn't need it until I was going home anyway.

The second Louis reached out to open the front door of the massive, white house, I grabbed his forearm to stop him. "Louis, I never brought a change of clothes," I almost panicked, looking down at my attire that consisted of my sweats and hoodie.

He rolled his eyes. "Believe me, they won't care about that," was the only thing he said before finally opening the door.

He made sure to let me in first before closing it behind himself, instantly shrugging his winter jacket off. I did the same, and it wasn't until we had hung them up that I noticed the sound of utensils scraping against plates from the kitchen. Muffled voices could also be heard over the screeching sound.

I turned to Louis questioningly. "Are they already eating?"

He shrugged his shoulders. "Yeah, they never really wait for me. Not that I usually join them anyway, but you already know that."

Yeah, I did, but I thought things would be different today when I was coming over, but apparently not. "So, what exactly do you want to show me?" I asked, feeling confused all of a sudden. I thought it had to do with his family, so why weren't we joining them for dinner?

"Come on," he said, grabbing my forearm to pull me forward.

The house was massive, just like I already knew. I had been here before, but it never failed to amaze me just how beautiful it was. Everything was white except for the floor and decorations. The floor was made of dark brown wood while most of the decorations were either grey, beige or black. There were not many rooms on the bottom floor, but they were so big that I was positive you couldn't hear that a person was talking to you from the other side of it.

The kitchen was next to the living room, and you had to walk through it to get there. Louis pulled me that way, and together, we walked past the big, white leather couch and the most gigantic flat screen that I had ever seen on the wall opposite it. The second we reached the kitchen, the sound of utensils scratching against plates faded, and so did the voices.

Jay and Mark were sitting at the kitchen table along with all of the girls, even the twins. They were all staring at us as if we were two ghosts appearing out of nowhere.

Lottie was the first one to compose herself, and a smile instantly broke out on her face. "Harry!" She called out.

The lump that had formed in my throat when we arrived outside the house only grew bigger at the sight in front of me. Sure, Lottie's reaction helped a little, but not much because the rest of the family was still staring at us wide-eyed.

"Uh... hi, Lottie," I greeted, forcing a smile on my face. She returned it, her lips still curled up.

Louis cleared his throat as he walked over to pull out two plates and two glasses from the cabinets. He placed the items on the table, looking over at me quickly before grabbing some utensils from one of the drawers. He then sat down in the seat next to Lottie, leaving the one opposite him beside Fizzy empty for me.

"Come sit down, Curly," he said, looking over at me almost apologetically.

I swallowed hard, noticing that Jay and Mark had turned their attention back to their food, not even opening their mouths to say anything. Weird. I thought they would at least say hi to me, but apparently not. It made me furrow my eyebrows as I walked over to the empty seat, pulling it out.

The tension in the room could be cut with a knife. It was so thick that it made my sickness come back all over again. This must be the most awkward situation I had ever been in by far, and the only question that kept repeating itself in my head was; Why on earth were Louis' parents acting this way?

"Hey, Harry," Fizzy greeted once I had sat down beside her, flashing me a small smile.

"Hi," I grimaced, feeling so out of place that I wanted to run straight out the door Louis and I had just walked in through.

Across the table, Lottie and Louis were whispering something to each other while Jay and Mark had now fallen into a conversation of their own. I tried to flash Louis a confused look, wanting to know what the hell was going on, but he didn't notice it as he was focusing on what Lottie was saying to him.

"So, how was school today, girls?" Mark asked, breaking the awkward silence that had occurred.

The twins immediately spoke up while Fizzy's eyebrows pulled together. Lottie and Louis stopped talking as soon as Mark opened his mouth, but their faces remained neutral.

"It's been great, dad. Daisy and I got to make this painting during lecture," Phoebe, I assumed, explained, giving her father a toothy grin.

Mark's face lit up. "Can I see it?"

Phoebe shook her head. "No! It's not finished yet, daddy," she whined, her lips in a pout.

Jay shot the twin a smile, reaching out to run a hand through her brown hair. "You can bring it home once it is then, yeah?"

Phoebe nodded her head vigorously. "Yeah, of course, mommy."

Louis' lips were pressed in a thin line as he reached out to plate some food. By the looks of it, it seemed to be some meat stew with rice. While he did this, I could see Mark's eyes following his movements, an unreadable look on his face. It was almost as if he was conflicted about how to react to Louis putting food on his plate.

Louis didn't seem to notice this, though. He just put his plate back on the table before meeting my gaze, nodding towards my empty one. I immediately understood what he meant, but I felt hesitant about giving it to him. I got the feeling that Mark didn't want us to eat the food, which only made the sickness in my stomach intensify. I wanted to get out of here, and that was now.

However, I didn't want to draw any attention, so I handed Louis the plate and let him put some food on it before he gave it back. I could feel both Jay's and Mark's eyes on us as he did this, but I tried my best not to think about it. It only made the situation worse than it already was.

"So, what about you, Fizzy and Lottie? How was your day?" Mark continued, clearing his throat.

His question made my face turn into a scowl. Why did he make it so obvious that he didn't care about how Louis' day had been? First, he said the word 'girls', and now he specifically asked Fizzy and Lottie about their day, leaving Louis out of it completely. It made me even more confused than I already was.

"Um... It's been great, dad. Thanks for asking," Lottie grimaced, biting her bottom lip.

Fizzy nodded her head in agreement. "Yeah, my day's been good too," she mumbled, looking down at her plate.

The kitchen went silent after that again. Louis started eating his food, but he didn't seem hungry judging by the small bites he brought to his mouth. I, on the other hand, couldn't even bring myself to start eating. I wanted to throw up, not get anything *down* my system.

Mark and Jay fell into a conversation with the twins, but the rest of us stayed quiet. After five minutes, Louis noticed that I hadn't touched my food and wasn't planning on doing so either, so he glanced at his parents quickly before giving me a pointed look towards the doorway. Fucking finally.

We both got up from the kitchen table and dumped our dishes in the sink. Mark and Jay didn't even seem to notice it, seeing as they were too caught up in their conversation with the twins. Or, they just wanted to make it look like it. I couldn't care less, though. I just wanted to get out of here.

"Come on, Curly. Let's head up to my room," Louis said monotonously, not even looking at his parents as he did so.

However, I could see Jay pulling her bottom lip between her teeth, but Mark didn't so much as move an inch by his words, much less look up at him. It made my heart almost drop because what the hell was this?

Louis swallowed hard as he turned around, walking out of the kitchen. I followed him quickly, not wanting to be in that room for a second longer. We walked up the stairs in silence. I didn't know why he didn't say anything, but I knew that I didn't because I was still in shock after what had just taken place.

Something was definitely wrong, and I couldn't wait for Louis to explain it all to me.

Chapter 29

The second we reached Louis' room on the top floor, I could feel my eyes widening because damn, his room was massive. I had never been here before. Whenever the boys and I were over, we only just hung out in the living room downstairs.

The walls were dark grey while the floor was of the same brown wood as downstairs. There was a big, black king-sized bed in the middle of the room, and a huge flat screen on the wall opposite it. Above the headboard, there were different posters of soccer players such as Messi and David Beckham. Otherwise, the walls were clean.

He had a closet that took up half of the wall on the left side of the bed, and next to it and the closet, there was a black full-length mirror. On the right side of the room (in front of the door), he had a white desk that was so clean I doubted he had ever even touched it.

What took me by surprise was that the room was so neat. I had not taken Louis as a neat person, rather the opposite. Then again, his parents probably had maids cleaning his room every day, which was probably the reason for how clean and organized it was.

While I examined Louis' room, he sat down on the edge of his king-sized bed, looking down at the floor. I stayed in the door frame, my eyes on his figure. "You told me I didn't have to worry," I mumbled, knitting my eyebrows together.

He snapped his head up to look at me. "I uh... I didn't realize it was going to be that bad," he grimaced.

Letting out a sigh, I walked over to sit down next to him. "What happened?"

He reached up to run a hand through his fringe, turning to look out the window in front of us. "Things haven't always been *this* bad, but... do you remember how I once told you that I would switch places with you any day when you said that you couldn't afford everything you wanted?" He wondered.

It was the day before my birthday party, of course I remembered. I probably remembered every moment of the time we had ever spent together. "Yeah," I breathed, realizing now what he had meant back then.

"I just... I would because I don't really care about money. You have a family who cares about you, who loves you, and that is everything I have ever wanted. The only reason my family even gives me money is that they don't want people to get suspicious, and they also want to show off just how wealthy we are. They don't do it because they love me. Fuck, they don't even give a shit about me," he said in frustration, pulling his bottom lip between his teeth.

I didn't know how to react, but I felt so much compassion for him although I couldn't picture having my parents not caring about me like that. My mom had always been there, caring for and loving me whenever I needed it. My dad was too before he left and started a new life.

"I... I don't know what to say, Louis. I... I'm so sorry," I said, making him shake his head.

"Please, I don't need your pity. This is my life, and it's always been this way. I'm used to having them not caring about me," he muttered, turning his body away from me.

I let out a sigh, running my hand through my curls. "I'm not saying it out of pity, Louis. Damn it, I don't know if you still don't believe me, but I do care about you, and no one deserves to have parents who don't give a shit about their child."

He turned his head to look at me, his eyes showing nothing but sadness. "That's kind of the reason why things are worse now."

"What do you mean?" I frowned, not catching on.

He closed his eyes for a few seconds before opening them again. "It was the day before your birthday. I was just looking for my favorite pair of jeans, but I couldn't find them anywhere, so I went to check the other closets in the house, thinking the maids had mistaken my jeans for someone else's. So, when I got to my mom's, I was surprised when I started lifting her pants only to find a picture frame," he paused to inhale a deep breath, looking down at his lap.

"It was a picture of my mom with a man who had his arm wrapped around her, and I was on their lap. What caught me off guard was that the man in the picture wasn't who I had come to know as my dad. It wasn't... it wasn't Mark. This man was a complete stranger to me, and it all just started falling into place in my head. How Mark never looked at me the same way he looked at the girls, how he never treated me the same way he treated them, and how he never cared for me as he did for my sisters. It was all because he isn't my real dad. My mom was in a relationship with another man and had me before she met Mark and got pregnant with Lottie."

He shook his head, biting his bottom lip harshly. "I just... I just realized why they always treated me differently than the girls. I was never meant to be part of the family, Harry. They never wanted me to be here. I just... I was probably not even meant to be born. I was just a... a mistake. A fucking mistake."

With that, he got up from the bed at a quick pace only to kick the leg of it harshly, making the bed screech a little. He had this look in his eye that told me he was ready to punch something, so I got up too to take his hand in mine, squeezing it gently.

"Louis, look at me," I said softly.

I didn't know if it was my touch or what I said that made him turn his face to look at me, but it worked because the muscles in his face relaxed within a second. "It's okay to cry. You don't have to feel like you need to hold it back," I told him, making him furrow his eyebrows.

"I'm not going to fucking cry," he muttered, averting his gaze.

I let out a sigh, looking down at his hand that was still in mine. I felt ecstatic about it, but I had to force my feelings down right now because this was about Louis. So, I did the only thing I knew would help in this situation; I took a step forward and wrapped my arms around him, pulling my hand out of his in the process. I leaned my head against his shoulder as he stood there, frozen in place.

It took at least ten seconds until he finally gave in and wrapped his arms around me in return, bringing my body even closer to him. He clutched the fabric at the back of my purple hoodie as he let out a quiet sob, burying his face in my shoulder. His grip on my sweater tightened while the sobs continued, filling the silence in the room.

We stood there for a few minutes, wrapped up in each other while Louis let out small sniffles until he pulled away, looking down at the floor with his face red from crying.

He started shaking his head, running his hands through his hair furiously. "Fuck, I can't believe I just did that. I don't... I don't fucking cry."

"It's okay, Louis," I told him, making him knit his eyebrows together.

"No, it's not okay. Nothing is fucking okay. I don't even care about all this. I don't care that Mark isn't my fucking dad because he has never cared about me anyway. I'm just... I'm just mad that they never told me. It's been eighteen years, and they never once thought of telling me that I have another man's blood running through my veins."

He angrily wiped his damp cheeks, striding over to sit down on the edge of his bed again. He buried his face in his hands, letting out a loud groan. "I don't even know who my fucking dad is. I've never even met him. Hell, I didn't even know he existed. Do you know what that feels like, Harry?"

I was so caught up in the moment that I didn't even acknowledge the fact that he was calling me by my real name. Honestly, it was the last thing I was thinking about right now.

"No, I don't," I said, shaking my head. "I can't put myself in your situation even if I wanted to. Yes, my dad left me and our family just like I believe yours did too, but I've always known he existed and I know he loved me back in the days even if he decided to leave and start over. I... I'm so sorry all these things happened to you. I never... I never realized you were keeping so much within you. How did you manage to do so over all these years?" I asked him, my eyebrows furrowed in concern.

He shrugged his shoulders, avoiding eye contact. "My life has always been the same, except when I found out about the dad thing, so there was really nothing for you guys to notice."

I sat down beside him on the bed again, slumping my shoulders a little. "So when you told me that you didn't like it when people felt the need to care about you...?"

"It's because I have always taken care of myself. I don't need anyone else to do it for me," he muttered. "There was one exception, and it was the day after Emily's party when I woke up on your couch. I was about to head home when Gemma offered to give me some painkillers and a glass of water. I just... I just wanted to be taken care of for once. You had already helped me, and it felt like I was living some kind of dream, so I decided to let it continue for a while." He paused to shake his head, a small smile playing on his lips.

"Whenever I'm around your family, I see everything I don't have, everything I've always wanted to have. It makes me envy you so much, but it also makes me happy because I realize that there is another side of how a family can be."

I started feeling tears welling up in my eyes by his words. It was just so heartbreaking to hear him explain all this. "Mom and Gemma really like you, you know? They actually even wanted to invite you over for dinner a few days," I said, chuckling with glossy eyes.

He turned to me, a look of hope in his eyes. "Really? Why would they want to do that?"

Because they know how much you mean to me.

"Because they have noticed how much I seem to enjoy being in your company, and they really like you, as I just said. You've always had Gemma on your side, and you really stole mom's heart when you came over that one time only to throw me over your shoulder, although she's always liked you too," I explained, making him shake his head in disbelief.

"Your family is really something. I'd love to go over there sometime," he said, cracking a small smile.

"You're always welcome," I promised him, giving his thigh a light squeeze. It made him turn to look at me, his lips twitched slightly.

"So, there was actually another reason why you were acting the way you were on my birthday. You told me you had a bad day in general, but I didn't realize it was this bad," I frowned.

He inhaled a deep breath. "I just didn't want anyone to know, so it was a good thing that I had other stuff to blame my behavior on. I mean, I was a bit disappointed that you never told me that you were bisexual, but now that I think about it, I had no right to say that. I've been keeping secrets from you guys about my family for years, so why couldn't you? And some people have a hard time talking about their sexuality. I just... It just felt like we had grown closer, you know? And at the moment, I felt disappointed that you couldn't trust me with something like that. It's ridiculous, I know," he muttered, looking away from me.

I shook my head. "No, it's okay. I was stupid for saying the things I did about us not growing closer, which I've already explained to you. I regret it so much. I just... I was never comfortable with telling any of you about my sexuality because I thought you would judge me. All you guys do is basically talk about girls, and I thought you wouldn't accept the fact that I find guys attractive too, you know? Maybe it's immature, but I never felt the need to tell you about it."

Plus, I was afraid you would realize I had feelings for you.

"It's not immature. I just didn't realize how personal it is to talk about your sexuality. It was stupid of me to get upset with you for not telling me," he said, his eyes directed at his lap. "And I would never judge you or anyone, alright? It doesn't matter who you like. Besides, you can't really decide it yourself anyway."

I wondered if he would say the same thing if he knew he was the one I was head over heels for. I doubted that.

I cracked a small smile, biting my bottom lip. "Thank you, Louis."

He turned to meet my gaze, a smile gracing his lips too. "No problem."

We were quiet for a while then, just taking in everything that had happened and everything we had said. It was nice and comfortable, something people probably wouldn't understand if they weren't in the room with us.

"Did you... did you ever tell your mom that you found the picture?" I wondered, making his head snap to me.

He nodded his head slowly. "Yeah, the day after that, during breakfast. Chaos erupted the second I let the words fall from my lips. Mom started crying and Mark started yelling. I don't think they ever planned on telling me. They wanted me to live a lie throughout my entire life and never find out why they always treated me differently. It makes me sick just thinking about it," he breathed heavily.

I looked down at my fiddling fingers on my lap, just now realizing why Louis had brought up my dad that time in his car. He had asked me how I had coped with him leaving. Of course he did. His dad had never wanted to be a part of his life, and he had only found out recently. Of course he had a hard time taking it all in. He probably didn't know how to handle the situation.

Feeling even more for the guy sitting next to me, I decided to lean my head against his shoulder, feeling his muscles through his hoodie against my curls. "I'm glad you told me all this," I whispered, and I could feel him tense for a second until he visibly relaxed.

It took a while until he replied, though. "I'm glad I did too. It feels nice to talk about it to someone apart from Lottie and Fizzy. They are the only people I have ever spoken about it to."

I looked up from his shoulder to meet his eyes with mine. "I feel honored," I smiled faintly, and he returned it.

A few minutes later, he got up from the bed to walk over to the bedroom door, opening it slightly. "I don't want to sound rude, but I'd better drive you home now. It's getting late and you haven't eaten anything after practice," he told me.

I pulled my bottom lip between my teeth, nodding my head slowly. Truth be told, I didn't want to go home. I didn't want to leave him. I wanted to stay here and watch him while he fell asleep just to make sure that he was actually going to fall asleep. I wanted to make sure he was treated the way he should be because I knew he wouldn't by anyone else in this house apart from his younger sisters.

"Okay," I said reluctantly, getting up from the bed to follow him out of the room.

We walked down the stairs in silence, him a few steps in front of me. He quickly slipped his shoes on, throwing his jacket over his shoulder as soon as we reached the entryway. When he noticed that I wasn't even halfway done yet, he tilted his head to the side. "I'll go heat up the car," he announced, and I just nodded my head, knowing I didn't have to worry since I was leaving soon too.

However, before I had time to exit the open front door, I could feel a presence behind me. I expected it to be Lottie or Fizzy since they were the only people I actually knew in the family, so I was nothing but surprised to see Jay standing there, a sad smile on her face.

She didn't say anything when the sad smile turned into a look of apology, and I didn't have time to acknowledge more until she walked away, leaving me to stare wide-eyed at the empty spot where she was just standing.

I pulled myself together when I heard a car honk, and I quickly left the house to sprint over to Louis' black sports car in the driveway. Opening the passenger door, I slipped inside before shutting it behind me.

Louis was turned to me when my eyes fell on him, a questioning look on his face. "What took you so long?" He wondered, making me knit my eyebrows together.

"I just forgot I left my bag in here, so I started looking for it in the entryway," I shrugged, making him narrow his eyes at me in suspicion.

He decided to drop it after a few seconds, though, and pulled out of the driveway to start heading in the direction of my house. I reached out to turn on the radio at a low volume, making the atmosphere in the car a little cozier.

"I'm sorry for putting you through all that tonight. I honestly didn't expect things to be that bad," he grimaced.

I shook my head slowly, giving him a reassuring smile. "You already apologized for it, and it's okay. I get that you wanted me to see it for myself to really understand the situation. There's no way I would have thought things were that bad otherwise."

He bit his bottom lip, looking out the windshield while gripping the wheel tightly. "I'm sorry anyway," he muttered.

We were quiet for the rest of the ride, which I didn't mind at all. My head was still spinning from all the new information I had taken in tonight, but I was also getting a bit tired, which was probably because I had practiced soccer for an hour and a half, and because I hadn't eaten anything afterward. The hunger was starting to kick in now.

The second Louis pulled over outside my blue house, I turned to him. "Thank you for the ride," I told him. "See you tomorrow, yeah?"

He flashed me a half-hearted smile as he nodded. "I'll pick you up."

My heart fluttered in my chest at his words, my lips curling.

I then opened the car door to hop out, grabbing my bag in the process to sling it over my shoulder. Before I closed it behind me, though, I found myself hesitating.

"Oh, and Lou?" I said, leaning down to look at him. "Don't ever think you were a mistake, okay? You were not. You were meant to be born and be here today. Please don't ever think otherwise."

Without waiting for an answer, I finally shut the door behind me and walked over to the porch of my house, feeling warmth spread through my chest because wow, I just said that directly to his face.

Chapter 30

"So, do you wanna come over for dinner tonight?" I asked Louis when we were walking towards the school building the next morning, our hands almost brushing together.

As soon as I had told mom that Louis would love to come over for dinner after he had dropped me off yesterday, she clapped her hands together excitedly and told me to invite him as soon as possible. As if on cue, my boss had called me just half an hour later, informing me that I didn't need to come into work today, so it was the perfect opportunity to invite him over tonight already.

Although I spoke to my mom about Louis yesterday, I didn't say anything else to her about what he and I had talked about during the evening, and I wasn't planning to either. That was something that I would keep to myself forever if Louis didn't tell me otherwise.

"Tonight?" Louis gaped, and I could see his eyes widening from the corner of my eye.

"Yeah? If you want to, of course," I said quickly.

He shrugged his shoulders, a small smile making its way to his face. "Yeah, sure. Why not?"

My heart swelled in my chest, my lips twitching. "Great."

It didn't take long until his face turned into a scowl, though. "But don't you have work today? It's Thursday," he wondered, glancing at the side of my face.

I shook my head, my lips still turned into a smile. "No, Richard called yesterday to inform me that I don't have to come in today, so I'm free," I explained, making the crease between his eyebrows disappear.

"Well, then I'd love to come over. I bet dinner at your place is going to be a hundred times better than at mine," he grimaced, repositioning the bag on his shoulder since it had been about to slide off.

I rolled my eyes, biting my bottom lip. "Don't be so sure of that," I muttered under my breath, so quietly that I doubted he heard it.

I was actually quite nervous about him coming over, even if I was happy about it too. I mean, both mom and Gemma were going to be there, and they both knew that I had feelings for Louis. They were not exactly good at keeping these kinds of things a secret, although they had promised not to expose me. I just hoped that they would keep that promise tonight. Otherwise, I wouldn't know what to do with myself.

A few minutes later, we arrived at the lockers, where Liam, Niall and Zayn were already standing, chatting with each other. The second they noticed us, I could feel Niall's gaze on me, studying my features. Right. He knew Louis was going to tell me something yesterday, and now he was probably curious about what it was about.

"So, we were thinking of going to Niall's place before the party tomorrow. Are you guys in?" Zayn asked, making me take my eyes off the blonde lad.

"Sounds great," I shrugged. To be honest, I had pushed the party to the back of my head because I wasn't really looking forward to it, but I couldn't really say that.

Louis nodded his head in agreement, opening his locker to shove his bag into it. "Who's fixing the alcohol?"

Niall tilted his head to the side. "Have you already forgotten that I have an older brother, Tommo?" He asked, raising his eyebrows at the feathery-haired boy.

Louis' lips twitched into a cheeky smile. "Nope, I just wanted to point out the fact that you haven't turned eighteen yet," he winked, making Niall grit his teeth together.

"You little fucker," he muttered, turning on his heel to walk away. "Harry, I want to talk to you later," he called out so all of the people in the entire hallway could hear him as he disappeared around the corner with his head held high.

"He's such a drama queen," Zayn chuckled, shaking his head in amusement.

I, on the other hand, was thinking about Niall's last words. I didn't want to talk to him because there was nothing I could tell him. There was honestly not a single thing of what Louis had shown me yesterday that was okay for me to tell him, and I knew it was only going to make him frustrated.

"Come on, Curly. We're going to be late."

I snapped back to reality by Louis' voice, my eyes falling on him. He was facing me, his head tilted to the side with a smile on his face. "You're thinking too hard."

Rolling my eyes, I grabbed my books from my locker before shutting it. Liam and Zayn had already left, leaving me alone with Louis and the other people in the hallway.

We started walking to our classes side by side, and I was almost too aware of how close we were. Had we always walked this close to each other, or was I just more aware of his presence after the moment we shared at his place yesterday?

We small talked the entire way to his classroom, and I was so caught up in it that I almost didn't notice that he had stopped outside his door. However, I quickly came to a halt and watched how he placed a hand on the doorknob.

Before he entered his classroom, he turned to look at me. "Make sure to stay focused during class, alright? I mean, it would be a shame if you got so lost in your thoughts that you don't learn anything, now wouldn't it?" He joked, making my mouth fall open.

I was so surprised that I didn't have time to come up with a comeback before he had opened the door. "You-- Fuck, you'll get back for that later," I called after him before walking down the hallway to my own classroom.

I couldn't believe he just teased me. It felt like ages ago since last time, but it had only been a day since we were in the locker room after practice and he had teased me for staring at him. It must feel so long only because so much had happened yesterday evening.

I did as Louis told me during the next hour, though, and stayed focused on what the teacher said. Not that I did because he told me to, but because I was already planning on paying attention in the first place. I was honestly shocked when the bell rang an hour later, signaling the end of the class because it felt like no time had passed at all.

I made my way back to my locker with my books pressed to my chest. I was feeling a little happy, having come up with a good comeback to Louis and all. However, that was until I found Alice and her friends hanging around our lockers with the rest of the boys.

A lump formed in my throat at the sight of that blonde-haired girl clung to Louis' side, her hand grasping his bicep as she was flirting with him. The only thing I could picture in front of me when I saw them together was the way they had been making out against the wall at my birthday party. It made my stomach turn, and I could instantly feel how the smile fell from my face.

For some reason, I was even more bothered by the two of them now than I usually was, and I had a feeling that was because it felt like Louis and I had grown even closer now. We knew so many things about each other that no one else did, and it felt special. Therefore, I found it so hard to watch him get along with a girl so well.

I put the combination in before opening my locker, shoving my books into it without even looking at the people around me. I was so caught up in my thoughts that I barely noticed the hand on my shoulder, wanting me to turn around.

When I finally did, I found myself staring back into a pair of blue eyes, but not the blue eyes I had fallen in love with. "Hi, Evelyn..." I trailed off, our last conversation making its way back to my mind.

She tilted her head to the side, a small smile on her lips. "Hey, Harry. How are you doing?" She wondered.

I shrugged my shoulders, feeling an urge to just turn back around to face my locker again. I wasn't in the mood to have a conversation with anyone right now. "I'm okay, I guess. You?"

"To be honest, I'm a little sad for being turned down by you yesterday, but otherwise, it's okay," she half-joked, but you could hear the seriousness behind her words.

I let out a sigh, running a hand through my curls. "I'm sorry about that. I didn't mean to come off so rude," I apologized, but she shook her head vigorously.

"No, don't apologize. It's okay. I just... It would be nice to go out for a coffee someday anyway if that's okay with you, of course. I kind of like hanging out with you," she blushed a little, averting her gaze.

A faint smile made its way to my face as I nodded my head. "Yeah, why not?"

My eyes flickered to Louis and the blonde girl, whom I still didn't know the name of, noticing that Louis was staring right back at me now, the girl looking a bit confused as he was doing so. He had pulled his bottom lip between his teeth and clenched his jaw tightly.

"See you later, yeah?" I said to Evelyn, who nodded with a smile on her face.

"Of course. Bye, Harry."

With that said, she walked away, and the blonde girl followed her, probably because she didn't have Louis' attention anymore. The second they were gone, I turned back to face my locker, but it didn't take long until I heard a voice behind me.

"Why are you keeping her hopes up?"

I pressed my lips together as I spun around to face Louis. "I'm not," I muttered, still upset about what I had witnessed when I first came here.

He rolled his eyes, letting out a snort. "Keep believing that, and the next thing you know, she'll be kissing you."

Slamming my locker shut, I could feel my nostrils flare. "And so what? Maybe I've changed my mind and want to give her a chance? What would be so wrong with that?" I hissed. I only said that because I was upset. I didn't really mean it.

He pulled his eyebrows together, the muscles in his face hardening. "So, you mean you've changed your mind over a day, is that it?" He asked me, his voice cold.

I let out a sigh, closing my eyes for a second. "No, I just... She knows I don't feel the same way. She even told me so herself, and if she still wants to hang out with me, then it's up to her," I explained. "Why were you even listening to our conversation? You seemed pretty busy talking to that girl."

He shook his head. "Vanessa was just asking me if I was coming to the party tomorrow. It wasn't like she was asking me out or anything."

It was still bad enough. She had been touching his bicep in a not so ordinary way if you asked me.

I bit my bottom lip. "Well, it doesn't matter. You shouldn't care what Evelyn and I are talking about anyway," I muttered, knowing I was being a hypocrite. I mean, I cared about what he and Vanessa had been talking about.

"Yes, when you're making decisions that shouldn't be made. I'm your best friend. I'm just trying to look out for you," he said, his eyebrows furrowed.

"Well, I can take care of this myself, thank you very much," I muttered, making him sigh.

Right then, the bell rang, signaling it was time to head to our next classes. Louis glanced at me, his lips pursed. His jaw had gone slack and he didn't seem to be thinking as deeply anymore. Instead, he almost looked apologetic.

"See you later, yeah?" I wondered, forcing a smile on my face.

He nodded his head, looking down at the floor. "Of course."

Before I knew it, the last bell of the day rang. Honestly, I wasn't ready to go home. Louis and I hadn't really talked after that encounter before second class. It wasn't like we were arguing, we had just avoided having a conversation with each other. Nonetheless, it hurt. I hated not being on good terms with him.

What made me not being ready to go home was that I knew I had to face Louis and talk to him. He was coming over for dinner tonight, and we had barely even talked about it. I mean, we hadn't even set a time yet.

When I had gotten rid of my books and shrugged on my winter jacket with my bag slung over my shoulder, I could hear a loud laugh behind me. It was Niall, which reminded me that I hadn't talked to him either. It made me want to let out a deep groan. I didn't want to deal with all this.

Once I turned around, I noticed that all four of the guys had joined me at the lockers, and Liam and Zayn were in a conversation while Louis had just said something that made Niall laugh. At least those two were on good terms again...

"Harry, do you have a minute?"

I turned around, my eyes clenched shut. "Actually, Niall, there's not really much to talk about," I grimaced, opening them to meet his gaze.

He was standing right in front of me, Louis at his side. His eyes flickered to the feathery-haired boy next to him before looking back at me, his eyebrows pulled together. "I'm sure there is," he insisted.

Shaking my head, I shifted my weight from one leg to the other. "No," I denied, noticing that Louis had narrowed his eyes at us in suspicion.

Niall let out a sigh, running a hand through his blonde hair. "I'll let it slip for now, but you're going to tell me another time, okay?"

I pulled my bottom lip between my teeth. "I... Sure," I finally said, although I had no intention whatsoever to tell him about what Louis had confessed to me yesterday evening. No way that was going to happen. I only said it to make him drop the subject, which it turned out he did because he left not even a second later to go to his own locker.

I could feel Louis' eyes on me then, and they were still narrowed. "What was that all about?" He wondered.

I met his gaze, swallowing hard. "Nothing. He's just curious about unimportant stuff all the time," I explained, waving it off.

He still seemed a little suspicious but decided to drop it. "About earlier, I'm sorry about all that... again. I just can't stop myself sometimes," he apologized, looking down at the floor.

I shook my head. "No, I'm the one who's sorry. The way I acted... It wasn't my intention to be so rude. I was just a little upset, I guess, and I took it out on you," I sighed, running a hand through my curls.

He pulled his eyebrows together for a second before his face relaxed. "So, let's put all that behind us then, shall we?" He suggested, looking at me hopefully.

I nodded, a smile creeping to my lips. "That sounds great."

With that said, Louis grabbed his jacket and bag from his locker, and we both started heading towards the exit after saying goodbye to the lads. When we got outside, we noticed that it had started raining, so we both pulled the hood of our jackets over our heads before sprinting towards Louis' car. Thank God his ankle was healed by now. Otherwise, this would have been a nightmare.

I didn't even think twice when I headed to Louis' car, and maybe that was because I was getting so used to him always driving me to and from school nowadays. Well, at least whenever we were on good terms. He always insisted on driving me, so I no longer doubted that he wanted to.

"I fucking hate the weather in England sometimes," Louis groaned once we had shut the doors of his car behind us.

He threw his bag in the backseat while I put mine on the floor at my feet. I pulled my hood off, shaking my curls before running a hand through my fringe. It wasn't until I was finished with my movement that I noticed Louis was looking at me. When I turned to meet his eyes, he instantly looked away and turned on the engine of the car.

He pulled his own hood off as he reached out to turn the heat up. Once he had pulled out of the parking space, he cleared his throat. "So, have you stopped looking at cars altogether now, or how's that going?" He asked me, glancing at the side of my face.

"I'm looking every now and then," I shrugged.

Truth be told, I hadn't looked much into it at all. Louis was like my private driver these days, and I liked spending time with him like this, so I didn't really see the rush to buy a car of my own.

He raised his eyebrows at me, studying my face for a couple of seconds until he had to face the road again. "I have a feeling you're lying," he smirked, making me bite my bottom lip.

"Maybe I haven't looked too much into it, but you basically drive me everywhere anyway, so it hasn't really crossed my mind," I admitted.

I could see him tilting his head to the side, his smile growing wider. "Maybe I should stop then. Seems like it has a bad effect."

My eyes widened at his words. "What do you mean bad effect? I'm making the environment a great favor here," I gaped. "Besides, I'm saving a whole lot of money."

He threw his head back in laughter. "I should definitely stop driving you then. We can't have you save the planet and money at the same time," he chuckled, shaking his head in amusement.

"Heey," I pouted, crossing my arms over my chest. "That's not fair."

He turned to give me a wide smile, the crinkles by his eyes showing. "Life isn't fair, Curly."

I just rolled my eyes, staring out the door window with a smile on my lips. I loved him. I loved him so much it hurt. I just couldn't see my life without him in it somehow. It was just impossible.

A few minutes later, Louis pulled over outside my house, turning off the engine of the car as he did so. He then turned to me with a questioning look on his face. "So, what time should I come over?"

I bit my lip as I stared down at my lap. "You can... you can come with me now if you want? Then you don't have to go home in between," I suggested, looking up to see his reaction after a few seconds.

He had pulled his eyebrows together, and I wondered if he was thinking about the same thing I was. Last time I had asked him to come inside, he had ended up kissing me. Was he contemplating it because he was afraid it was going to happen again?

"I mean, you don't have to. You can always come later and--"

He cut me off by shaking his head, a smile making its way to his face. "I'd love to come with you now."

My heart stopped beating for a couple of seconds until it started racing, my face lightening up. "Great."

Chapter 31

The second Louis and I had gotten rid of our outdoor clothing, I asked him if he wanted something quick to eat since it had been a few hours since we had lunch in school. He turned to me with narrowed eyes, and I knew exactly what he was thinking.

"No, we don't have to eat my sandwiches, but we're not eating yours either," I said, shaking my head in amusement as his lips formed a pout.

"They aren't even that bad," he disagreed.

"Yes, Louis, they are," I said matter-of-factly as we made our way to the kitchen.

I opened the fridge, eyeing its content while Louis sat down at the kitchen table. "You're mean, Curly," he pointed out, and when I looked over my shoulder, I could see that his lips were still in a pout.

"I'm just being honest. I thought you liked honest people?"

He went quiet then and only let out a huff because he must have realized I was right. I felt proud of myself for having the last word. It happened so rarely that I felt like celebrating. However, I settled for a wide smile instead.

"I have cereal. Does that work for you?" I wondered, raising my eyebrows at him questioningly.

He pursed his lips. "Depends on what brand you have."

I rolled my eyes, opening the cabinet to check because I had no idea. Gemma was usually the one eating cereal in this household. "Coco Pops?"

His eyes instantly lit up. "Give them to me already," he said eagerly as if he was just about to open his presents on Christmas day.

I shot him a confused look, but he ignored it as I brought the box of cereal to the table along with the milk, two bowls and two spoons. He instantly reached out to fill his bowl with cereal and milk before shoving a spoonful of it into his mouth.

"I fucking love Coco Pops."

"I can tell," I chuckled, unable to hide the fond look on my face. He was just so adorable.

He tilted his head to the side, a smile forming on his lips. "I'm that obvious, aren't I?" He chuckled.

"Yep," I grinned.

Once we had finished eating (Louis ate two full bowls), we headed to my room across the hallway. Neither of mom nor Gemma was home yet, so it was just the two of us. Nonetheless, it just felt natural to go to my room even if we were all alone.

When I had closed the door behind us, silence filled the place. Louis was staring at my bed while biting his bottom lip. So he *was* thinking about the same thing I was. I mean, there was no other explaination as to why he was staring at my bed that way, was there? His mind was most likely replaying what had happened the last time we had been here together. When he had kissed me, to be more specific.

The tension only got worse as we stayed on our spots, not moving a muscle. To break it, I eventually cleared my throat, walking over to sit down on the edge of my bed. "Are you excited about the party tomorrow?" I asked him out of the blue, just to make conversation and try to get him on other thoughts.

The crease that had formed between his eyebrows disappeared as he looked at me. "The party? Oh, um, yeah, I guess. Aren't you?"

I shrugged my shoulders, looking down at my lap. "To be honest with you, not really," I admitted.

Louis raised his eyebrows in curiosity as he decided to make his way over to sit down next to me, leaving some space between us. "Why's that?"

"I just... They all just end up the same, don't they? You get drunk and then you wake up with a killer headache only to find out you've done stuff you regret."

That wasn't entirely my thought on it. The main reason I didn't like parties was that I hated seeing him flirt with different girls, but I couldn't exactly say that.

He thought for a second before letting out a light chuckle. "I've never actually thought of it like that, but I guess you have a point, although you're forgetting to mention the fun part of it. The feeling of letting loose just makes it all worth it."

He had a point as well. It was nice to let loose, but with the constant reminder that he was with someone else in the back of my head, it was hard to do so completely. He was always on my mind one way or another.

"Yeah, maybe you're right," I muttered.

He glanced at me, studying my face for a few seconds until he decided to drop it. I couldn't tell whether he believed me or not, but he didn't comment on it. Instead, he changed the topic completely.

"About earlier when Niall wanted to talk to you... I've been noticing that he's done this quite a lot lately, and I have a feeling that it is about me, am I wrong?" He wondered, his eyebrows pulled together.

I could feel a lump form in my throat by his words. "I uh... No, you're not completely wrong," I finally said after trying to find the right words. I couldn't lie to him in this situation because I knew he would get pissed at me if I tried and it turned out he could see right through me.

"What do you mean 'completely'? You haven't mentioned anything about what I told you yesterday, have you?" He asked me, his face turning void of emotions.

My eyes widened as I shook my head vigorously. "No, of course not! I would never do that," I said quickly before letting out a sigh and running a hand through my curls. "He knew that you were going to explain something to me yesterday, but not what it was about. So, he wanted to know what you told me, but you were there when I said that there was nothing to talk about."

He nodded his head slowly as if thinking about it. "Okay, I believe you. I mean, we have both told each other stuff that we don't want anyone to know before, and we've kept it to ourselves, so I believe that you won't tell anyone now either," he smiled faintly.

I felt the same happiness explode inside me as the last time he had told me he trusted me. I couldn't put into words how much it meant to me. What I could do, though, was to feel how my chest swelled with warmth because of it. "Thank you," I replied sincerely, making his smile widen.

We were quiet for the next minute, so I decided to lie down on my back, letting my head land on my pillow while Louis stayed seated at my feet. "Now that we're talking about yesterday, have you spoken to your mom lately?" I couldn't help but ask, remembering the look she had given me before I left that evening.

He glanced at me with a frown on his face. "No, why would I?" He huffed.

I pursed my lips, shrugging my shoulders. "I don't know, I just... Do you remember how I stayed behind while you went out to start the car up?"

He nodded slowly. "Yeah?"

"Well, she joined me in the entryway and gave me this smile as if she was apologizing for what happened in the kitchen. I just thought you should know. I mean, she might want to talk to you about something," I explained, biting my bottom lip softly.

He snorted, shaking his head firmly. "That's just a bunch of bullshit. You probably mistook the look she gave you for something else. My mom has never and won't ever care about me nor anything that has to do with me. End of story."

Letting out a sigh, I sat up to look at the side of his face, seeing his prominent cheekbone up close as he clenched his jaw. "I didn't mistake it, Lou, but I understand what you mean. If I were you, I'd probably never expect my mom to do something like that either if she had never shown that she cared about me before," I said, flashing him a sympathetic smile.

He went silent after that, and I started getting worried that I had said something wrong. That was until he suddenly scooted closer and lied down on the bed next to me. I looked down at him from my sitting position, feeling my heart race in my chest. He was *so* close, and he was lying on my *bed*, looking as beautiful as ever with his brown fringe swept to the side and his hands entwined on his chest. I wanted to touch him, feel his skin underneath my fingertips as I caressed his flawless features.

Louis snapped me back to reality by asking me a question and turning to meet my gaze. "Have you ever been in love?"

Yes. Right now, at this very moment.

He said it so innocently, his eyes looking deep into mine as he waited for my reply. I could feel my heart beat in my ears from how fast it was racing, and I had to swallow hard before I could answer him. "Yeah," I breathed.

His eyes widened a little, but his lips were formed into a smile. "Yeah?"

I nodded slowly, still lost in his beautiful eyes.

"How does it feel?" He wondered, his eyes full of curiosity.

I had to look away in order to faint because it was so overwhelming to look into those eyes for too long, especially when we were talking about something like this. I was positive my heart wouldn't be able to another few seconds.

"It's the best feeling in the world," I said truthfully, glancing at him quickly to send him a smile.

He returned it before looking away thoughtfully. "I've always wondered, you know? I've never been in love myself," he mumbled, mostly to himself. "How did you know you were in love?"

His question made a feeling of déjà vu erupt inside me because it reminded me so much of when he had asked me how I realized I was bisexual. However, there was a much easier answer to this question.

With a shake of my head, I let my lips curl. "You just know, Lou. You don't really have to question it because you can tell when a person is your entire world. It's when you can't stop thinking about them, when everything revolves around them and you want to be with that person all the time," I explained.

He turned to meet my eyes, a smile making its way to his face. "I see," he said, holding my gaze with his.

After a short while of silence, I decided to lie down next to him, staring up at the ceiling. "You know... I really like it when you call me Lou," he mumbled.

I glanced at the side of his face, but he refused to look back at me. "Yeah?" I breathed, feeling my cheeks heat up a little.

He nodded his head, finally turning to meet my eyes. "Yeah," he confirmed with a smile. "It makes me feel special somehow. No one really calls me that," he shrugged.

I could feel my lips curl. "For your information, I kind of like it when you call me Curly too."

"Really?" He chuckled. "I thought it annoyed you."

I shook my head. "No. It makes me feel important to you, and I like that," I admitted, feeling proud of myself for saying something like this to him. I felt brave for the first time ever around him.

He was just about to open his mouth and say something when there was a knock on the door. A second later, mom poked her head in the room.

"Hi, boys. I'm sorry to bother you, but dinner's ready in five minutes," she informed us, her lips curling at the sight in front of her.

How long had we been in here? I hadn't even noticed that she had come home. Was Gemma home as well? Honestly, it felt like it had been ten minutes since we had entered the room, but it must have been at least an hour.

"Hi, mom. Uh, great, we'll be there," I promised.

She nodded her head before closing the door behind her, leaving me and Louis alone once again. The second it clicked shut, I turned to Louis who looked a bit surprised.

"Did you realize it was already so late?" I couldn't help but ask.

He shook his head, turning to meet my gaze. "I had no clue at all," he replied, amusement making its way to his face.

We both got up from the bed a minute later to leave the room and join mom in the kitchen. It turned out Gemma was home as well because she was sitting at the kitchen table when we got there, scrolling through her phone while mom was standing at the stove.

The second we entered the room, they both looked up, immediate smiles forming on their lips. "Hi, Louis," Gemma greeted.

My mouth fell open. "What about me? I'm here too," I pointed out, faking offended.

She rolled her eyes. "I can see that, H."

Letting out a huff, I pouted my lips as Louis let out a chuckle. "Hi, Gemma," he greeted, making the brown-haired girl grin.

Mom turned around with a pot in her hands and walked over to place it in the middle of the table. I didn't even have to look, I immediately recognized the delicious smell of the food. "No way! You made Pasta Alfredo?" I gasped, literally giving the pot heart-eyes.

"Look who's excited about food now," Louis chuckled so only I could hear.

I nudged him in the side with my elbow. "Shut up," I whined before walking over to the kitchen table, sitting down on the empty chair opposite Gemma.

"I know it's your favorite, so I thought 'why not make it when my son's best friend is coming over?'" Mom explained, making me flash her a toothy grin.

"Thank you, mom."

Louis sat down in the seat next to me only a few seconds later, mom taking the seat next to Gemma. We all plated some food before we started eating in silence. I was so caught up in how delicious it was that I almost didn't hear mom opening her mouth to talk.

"So, how's your day been today, boys?" She asked, her eyes flicking between me and Louis.

Louis' mouth fell open in shock, his hand stopping mid-air from where he had been about to bring the fork to his mouth. It was probably the first time he had ever had that question directed at him, and it made my stomach knot. It wasn't fair how cruel he had been treated during his whole life.

"My day's been alright, thank you, mom," I replied while Louis tried to compose himself.

"Uh, yeah, mine's been alright too," he coughed.

"That's lovely to hear, boys," mom replied, flashing us a smile.

I could tell that Louis was still a bit tense, so I reached over to pat his thigh in reassurance, letting him know that I knew what he was thinking and that I was there.

When I glanced at the side of his face, I could see that the corners of his lips were twitched into a small smile. It made butterflies erupt in my stomach because I loved it when I was the reason for his smiles. It just made me so happy.

I could suddenly hear someone clear their throat, and when I turned to the source, I noticed that Gemma was sending me a knowing smile. It made me pull my eyebrows together. Was I really that obvious with my staring?

"When is your next game? Was it next Friday?" Mom asked, completely oblivious to what was going on.

Louis had fully composed himself now and nodded his head. "That's correct. We're going to Manchester to play actually," he explained, making mom's smile widen.

"Really, now? Harry, you never mentioned that," she accused me.

Mom loved Manchester, and she had always done so. When Gemma and I were kids and dad was still in the picture, we used to go there at least once every month. We either went to the zoo, the carnivals, or other stuff like that. We used to visit our grandparents too when they were still alive because the main reason mom loved the place so much was because she was born there.

During the years she had brought me and Gemma to the place, I had grown pretty attached to it. That was why I had never really pictured myself going to any uni apart from one in Manchester. I knew mom wanted me to go there too... if I got in, that was. My grades weren't the best, but I at least hoped they were good enough for me to get into uni in Manchester. However, that was if I didn't get the scholarship, then I would have to leave for London.

"It slipped," I apologized.

She let out a snort, turning back to Louis. "So, I heard you and Harry are competing against each other for a scholarship."

Louis nodded his head, swallowing hard. "We are. It's always been a big dream of mine to play for a professional club," he said, cracking a smile. "But I bet that's one of Harry's biggest dreams too."

He was right, it was a dream of mine, but seeing Louis get disappointed if it turned out I got it and he didn't would be devastating. I wasn't sure if I could handle that, especially now that I knew how much it meant to him.

"So, you really want to get it then, yeah?" Mom wondered.

"Yeah, but I'd never try to do anything unfair to get it. I've already told Harry that I want it to be a fair game between us, and I wouldn't want it if I don't deserve it," he explained, making my chest swell with warmth. Why was he so perfect?

"That's so sweet," mom beamed, flickering her eyes between the two of us.

It made Louis blush a little as he brought his fork of spaghetti to his mouth. He chewed on it slowly, his jaw following his movements. I could feel myself staring again, but I couldn't care less. It was impossible not to stare at this beautiful creature.

I could feel someone kick me in the shin, and I didn't even have to look to know that it was Gemma. However, I decided not to care about it and grabbed my own fork to bring some food to my mouth instead.

"Thanks again for making this dish, mom. It's sooo good," I complimented her, making everyone at the table chuckle.

"Indeed it is. It's much better than your sandwiches," Louis joked, nudging me in the arm playfully.

I let out a gasp. "I can't believe you out of all people just said that. Your sandwiches have to be the worst of them all," I snorted.

"I'm just saying, Curly," he shrugged, a smirk playing on his lips.

Crossing my arms over my chest, I let out a huff. "I bet you have never even cooked a meal before."

"Maybe I have, maybe I haven't," he shrugged. "I'm actually pretty good at making noodles," he bragged, making me burst out laughing.

"The fact that you're bragging about that is pretty sad, Lou."

He tilted his head to the side, the smile never leaving his face. "I'll have you know my noodles are actually pretty damn delicious," he said, crossing his arms over his chest.

I arched my eyebrows at him. "Is that so? How about you make me some noodles next time then, so you can prove yourself?" I suggested.

He let out a light chuckle as he nodded. "Deal."

When I looked over to the two people sitting across from us, I was a little taken aback to see the looks on their faces. Gemma was smiling smugly at us while mom seemed close to burst from how happy she was. I'd probably never seen a smile so wide on her lips before.

She cleared her throat, her lips still curled. "If you two are finished, you're free to go do whatever you want," she said, flicking her eyes between me and Louis.

I glanced at the feathery-haired boy only to notice that he was already looking at me. "You finished?" I asked him, to which he nodded.

I bit my lip. "So, do you wanna watch a movie?"

"Sure, why not?" He grinned, the crinkles by his eyes showing.

We both got up from our seats to bring our dishes to the sink before turning to walk out of the room. Before we could do so, though, Gemma interrupted us when we were in the doorframe.

"Oh, and Louis?"

He turned around to face her. "Yeah?"

"Harry likes to cuddle and have someone card his hair while watching movies. I just thought you should know," she informed him, sending him a wink.

I started coughing while my eyes widened in absolute fear. "Gemma!" I exclaimed as Louis burst out laughing.

"Come on then, Curly. Let's go cuddle."

Chapter 32

Louis and I did end up cuddling on my bed, and honestly, I couldn't be happier. I wanted to thank Gemma just as much as I wanted to slap her across the head. What she said was uncalled for, but she did me a favor.

We laid there next to each other on my bed, my laptop on our thighs with our shoulders touching as we watched a random movie. It didn't take long until Louis wrapped an arm around me, and I leaned down to rest my head on his chest while facing the screen.

Only a matter of minutes later, his other hand found my curls, and he started running it through them slowly. The feeling made me almost purr, but I held it back and kept my mouth shut as best as I could.

We stayed like that during the rest of the movie, and honestly, I had never felt so content in my entire life. I wanted to stay like this with him forever.

Once the movie was finished, we decided to turn on another one, both of us too comfortable and lazy to get up. Sometime during the second movie, we lost track of time and everything else that had to do with real life. Or, I did at least because all I could think about was Louis' hand in my hair, his arm around my body, and his chest against my cheek.

I didn't know when, but at one point, my eyelids started getting heavy, and it didn't take long until I could feel myself drift off to sleep, everything going completely black around me.

When I woke up, it was by the sound of something hitting the floor. My eyes snapped open at the loud thud, but the first thing I noticed wasn't what caused the loud noise, but the fact that I wasn't alone in my bed. Scratch that. I wasn't even *in* my bed, I was lying on top of the covers with someone's arms wrapped around me, my head resting against their chest.

"Uggghhh... what was that noise?" The person grumbled, and my muscles froze at the sound of that voice.

My heart started racing in my chest when I realized that Louis was the person lying next to me with his arms wrapped around my body. Oh, God, we must have fallen asleep while watching movies. Fuck. What time was it?

It took a few seconds until my vision became clear and I could see that my laptop was what had caused the noise. Louis must have kicked it off our thighs because it was on his side of the bed and not mine. I also noticed that the sun was shining through the window, which meant it was morning.

"You knocked my laptop to the floor," I muttered, moving so I was lying with my head on my pillow beside him instead of on top of his chest.

I could suddenly feel Louis' body tense up too, and I had a feeling it was because he realized he wasn't alone.

The next second, his eyes snapped open. "Oh, shit. Did we fall asleep while watching movies?" He gaped, unwrapping his arms from my body, much to my disappointment.

"Yeah," I nodded. "I guess so."

He ran a hand over his face. "Fuck. What time is it?" He yawned.

"I have no idea," I mumbled, reaching down to grab my phone that was still in the back pocket of my jeans.

The screen lit up and the time read 7:30, meaning that we only had ten minutes until we had to leave for school if we wanted to get there on time.

"Shit," I muttered. "It's seven-thirty."

He let out a loud groan, covering his face with both of his hands. "Can't we just skip school? I'm too tired to bother with this."

I tilted my head to the side, shaking my head. "You know what they say, Lou. No school, no having fun, meaning that you can't go to the party tonight if you don't go to school."

He pulled his hands down, looking at me with a scowl on his face. "You sound like a mom," he scoffed, making me chuckle.

"Well, someone has to knock some sense into you," I smirked.

He rolled his eyes but hoisted himself up to get out of the bed. "Alright, I'll go to school, but promise me not to act like a boss again. It doesn't suit you," he joked, reaching his hand out for me to take.

I let out a huff, looking at his extended hand before taking it skeptically, letting him pull me up from the bed. I bent down to pick up my laptop from the floor to make sure it was still working after the fall. When I realized it was, I pushed it under my bed before turning to Louis who was watching me with his hands in the front pockets of his blue jeans.

"You want to borrow some clothes?" I wondered, biting my bottom lip.

He looked down at his outfit before looking back at me, eyeing my body. "Um, I honestly don't think your clothes will fit me," he said almost sheepishly.

I couldn't help but let out a bark of laughter. "It can't be easy to be so small," I joked, walking over to pat him on the shoulder.

He let out a huff, smacking my hand away from him. "I'm not small. You're just a tree," he muttered, making me chuckle.

"Yeah, right."

"I'll have you know I'm 5'9," he stated with a nonchalant look on his face, making me raise my eyebrows at him.

"5'9? More like 5'7," I chuckled, earning a glare from him.

"Watch it, Styles. If you keep going, you'll have to take the bus to school," he threatened, pointing a finger at my chest.

I rolled my eyes. "I'm doubting you'd let me do that," I smirked.

He let out a snort. "Don't be so sure of it."

My eyebrows shot up in amusement as I tilted my head to the side. "Is that so? Then why do I have the feeling that I can be?" I wondered, crossing my arms over my chest, the smile never leaving my lips.

He looked me in the eyes, the glare disappearing by the second as he did so. He took a step forward, reaching up to flick me on the nose. "See you downstairs, loser!"

With that said, he left my room, leaving me to shake my head to myself with a smile on my face. Words couldn't describe that boy, he was just one of a kind.

Somehow, Louis and I ended up arriving at school on time. However, we had to stuff our breakfast into our mouths to do so... or Louis did while I brought my sandwich into his car and ate it on my way to school. I bet he was secretly mad that I could take my time while he had to hurry, but he didn't say anything about it.

The school day flew by in the blink of an eye, so it didn't take long until I was home again after Louis had dropped me off. He was going home to get changed, and I was too before we were all going over to Niall's place before the party.

Speaking of Niall, he had kept sending me glances the entire day, and I was pretty sure he still wanted to talk to me about Louis, but I had tried to ignore him as best as I could, just like yesterday. I should probably just tell him that I couldn't say what Louis had told me, but I was afraid he wouldn't accept that. It wasn't like he had any other choice, though.

I was currently standing in front of my closet, trying to find something to wear for the party. I spent five minutes looking for a good enough outfit until I had enough and let out a frustrated groan. "Gemma, can you come here for a second?" I called out.

It didn't take long until my bedroom door opened and my sister came in. "What's the emergency, H?" She asked me, popping her hip out while placing her hand on it.

I bit the inside of my cheek, scanning the clothes in my closet. "I don't know what to wear for the party, and you helped me out last time, so I'm wondering if you can do it again?" I asked her hopefully.

She reached up to tap her chin with her forefinger thoughtfully. "Let me think... Of course I'll help you," she said, a smile forming on her lips.

Walking over to where I was standing, she started going through my clothes, looking for the perfect outfit. She hummed, tilting her head to the side and shaking her head at one of my button-ups. "Oh, yes. This is the one!" She said excitedly, pulling out a bright yellow, short-sleeved button-up.

My eyes widened at the piece of clothing. "Do you want everyone to look at me?" I gaped, to which she rolled her eyes.

"Louis' going to absolutely love this on you. I'm sure he won't be able to look away the second he sees you in this," she promised me.

Letting out a snort, I shook my head. "He's not going to love it. I'm sure he won't even pay attention to me..." I trailed off, averting my gaze.

I could still see the scowl forming on her face, though. "What do you mean?"

Letting out a sigh, I looked back at her. "He basically never pays attention to me at parties. Sure, he sang happy birthday to me last time, but that was about it. Otherwise, he's always too busy finding a new girl to hook up with," I huffed.

Gemma crossed her arms over her chest. "Well, that was before you two got this close. I mean, you are practically inseparable when you are on good terms. You seriously can't get enough of one another. You're just too blind to see it yourselves," she said, shaking her head in disbelief. "But I'm not here to tell you how stupid you two are. Hopefully, you're going to figure it out on your own soon enough."

I furrowed my eyebrows together. "Wait, what?"

She let out out an exasperated sigh. "Come on, just put this on. You just have to trust me on this."

Pouting my lips, I eventually agreed and stipped off my black t-shirt to replace it with the yellow button-up, leaving the top four buttons undone so part of my chest was on display. I then pulled on a new pair of black, skinny jeans.

Once I was finished, Gemma eyed me with a content smile on her face. "I knew it would be perfect."

I walked over to my full-length mirror to have a look. It wasn't actually that bad, although I was sure I would get more attention drawn to me than necessary because of the color. "It's not actually that bad," I reasoned, twirling around to see my behind as well.

"See, I told you," Gemma smiled, putting her hand on her hip again.

She was just about to leave the room when I stopped her. "What did you mean when you said that Louis and I are too blind to see it?" I asked her.

She rolled her eyes. "You're too blind to see how much you like each other." With that said, she finally left the room, closing the door behind her.

I sat down on my bed, staring into space as I thought of what she had just said. Could she be right? I mean, I knew for sure that I liked Louis, but could he actually have feelings for me? I had never really let myself think about it because let's face it; he was most definitely a ladies' man, and he had kissed me only to tell me how stupid he had been for doing so *twice* afterward.

But then again, he did stand up for me against Ryan when we weren't even on speaking terms, and his only excuse was that he couldn't help it, just like he couldn't help it when he had interfered with my conversation with Evelyn when she asked me out. He had told me he did it because he was looking out for me, but could it actually be because he was jealous?

Now that I thought about it, he had been checking me out in the locker room just the other day, and that must mean something, right? But, he had also told me that we were just friends only minutes later when Ryan called us boyfriends.

So, the final question was; Why was he giving me so many mixed signals? How was I ever going to know whether he actually liked me or not when he one second made me think he had feelings for me only to deny everything the other?

Letting out a frustrated groan, I ran my hands over my face. Why couldn't things just be easy and simple?

Before I had time to think more about it, a car honked outside. I didn't have to check to know it was Louis, so I instantly got up from my bed to head out of my room and to the entryway.

"Bye, Gemma!" I called out once I had put on my black coat and brown boots.

"Bye, H. Enjoy the party!" She replied cheerfully.

I exited the house and ran over to Louis' black sports car, noticing that Zayn and Liam were in the backseat, so I didn't hesitate to slide into the front next to Louis, closing the door behind me.

"Hey, guys," I greeted, running a hand through my hair.

Louis was already looking at me when I turned to him, a smile playing on his lips. "Hi, Curly."

Liam and Zayn greeted me too before Louis stepped on the gas pedal and sped off towards Niall's house. During the entire ride, he made sure to drive at a safe pace. Honestly, he always did when I was in the car with him nowadays, so I never really had to remind him anymore.

Only five minutes later, Louis parked the car in Niall's driveway, and we all headed inside the white house without bothering to knock, knowing Niall was alone in the house anyway.

"Nialler, you here?" Zayn called out, and it didn't take more than five seconds until Niall emerged from the living room, a smile on his face.

"Hey, guys. Come on in, come on in," he urged us.

It wasn't until we had gotten rid of our jackets that I really got to see Louis' outfit and let me tell you, it would probably be best if I didn't see it because damn, he was so *hot*. He was wearing a navy blue, short-sleeved button-up with a pair of black jeans that were unfolded at the ankles. His hair looked so perfect, the way his fringe was swept to the side and the rest of his locks sticking out just in the right places. How did he do it? I just didn't understand.

I didn't notice I was staring until I could feel his gaze on me as well, wandering up and down my body until it stopped at my face. A small smile broke out on his lips, and I could feel myself instantly returning it without even thinking about it.

"Guys, are you coming?" Liam asked, standing in the doorframe.

Looking at my surroundings, I noticed that the other guys had already left and Louis and I were the only ones who were still in the entryway. I scratched the back of my neck, feeling my cheeks heat up a little. "We're coming," I mumbled, clearing my throat awkwardly.

Zayn and Niall were already sitting on the couch, a beer can in their hands as they were chatting away. The second we entered the room, their eyes fell on us. "What took you so damn long?" Zayn questioned, his eyebrows arched.

"Nothing," Louis muttered, avoiding my gaze.

We all sat down on the couch, Louis on one of my sides and Niall on the other. I reached out to grab a beer from the coffee table as well and popped it open. "So, how are you feeling about tonight?" Niall asked me while Louis fell into a conversation with Liam and Zayn.

I shrugged my shoulders. "I don't know, to be honest," I admitted, biting my bottom lip.

Niall pursed his lips, looking over my shoulder. I didn't have to think twice to know he was glancing at Louis. "Is this about a certain someone?" He wondered.

"Maybe," I muttered, averting my gaze while taking a swig of my beer.

He nodded his head slowly, his eyebrows knitted together. "About that, can you please tell me what he said to you the other day? I've been dying to know," he pleaded, sticking his bottom lip out.

It was a good thing he was keeping his voice so low because I was sure Louis would've heard him otherwise. Letting out a deep sigh, I closed my eyes for a couple of seconds before opening them again. "Niall, I'm sorry to tell you this, but I can't say anything. It's not my place to tell. If you want to know, you'll have to ask him yourself," I apologized.

He seemed confused about this. "So, you're telling me he's hiding something?"

"I'm not telling you anything," I muttered, and the tone I was using made him shut up, which was my intention. I just wanted him to stop asking me about the subject once and for all.

"What are you guys whispering about?" Liam wondered, raising his eyebrows at me and Niall curiously.

Louis and Zayn turned to us as well, Louis sending me a suspicious look. "We were just talking about the party and how awesome it's going to be," Niall explained.

Liam and Zayn bought it, but Louis didn't, and I understood why. Just yesterday, I had told him that I wasn't really excited about the party at all, so he knew it wasn't the truth. However, he also knew that Niall had been curious to find out about his secret, but I had told him that I wasn't going to say anything, so there was really nothing for him to worry about.

"How about we play some Fifa? I mean, it never gets old, does it?" Niall suggested, which we all agreed to.

During the next hour, we took turns playing, and somehow, Louis and I ended up playing on the same team just like the last time. It wasn't like I minded. I was nothing but happy about it because that meant we had to interact, and every additional interaction with Louis was a good thing.

"Harry, have you heard anything from Evelyn yet?" Liam asked out of the blue, making my muscles freeze, and judging by the way Louis stopped moving, I assumed his did too.

"I... yeah. She asked me out the other day," I explained, biting my bottom lip while looking down at my lap.

Zayn let out a wolf-whistle. "Well well, look at that. Way to go, Harry."

I looked back up, my gaze flicking between Liam and Zayn. "I actually turned her down. She's a really nice girl and all, but I'm just not interested," I explained, making their jaws drop.

"The hell, man?" Zayn gaped while Liam just looked utterly confused.

Louis decided to step in then, throwing an arm around my shoulders. The gesture made my heart flutter in my chest. "Come on, lads. There's nothing wrong with not being interested in someone. Just because he thinks she's a nice girl doesn't necessarily mean he wants to be involved with her romantically, so chill out," he said, rolling his eyes.

Zayn's jaw dropped once again as he stared at Louis. "You *too*? What happened to 'wanting to get laid' and 'hooking up with different girls'? When did all this change?" He gasped.

Louis let out a humorless laugh, unwrapping his arm from around my shoulders, much to my disappointment. "It hasn't changed, Zayn. I was just saying that you aren't attracted to everyone, and Harry here just so happens to not want to be with Evelyn, and that's okay, so just drop it, alright?"

Zayn muttered something under his breath, sending me a look of suspicion before taking a large swig of his beer. I could feel Niall pat me on the thigh then, and when I turned to him, he looked at me reassuringly. It actually helped because he was the only one who actually knew the real reason I turned down Evelyn.

Right then, a car honked outside, and that could only mean one thing; Our ride was here. We all got up from the couch, Niall muttering something about not being drunk enough yet while Zayn and Louis went to the entryway. Liam and I grabbed the empty cans of beer and bowls of snacks to bring them to the kitchen, cleaning the coffee table up as best as we could.

Once we were all finished, we left Niall's house before heading over to the familiar car. Danny was driving us again. I sort of felt like calling him 'Danny the driver' because he was always the one who drove us to parties. Louis must be happy to have a friend like him.

Thankfully, Alice didn't live that far from Niall, so it didn't take long until Danny pulled over outside her house. "Have fun tonight, lads, and don't get too wasted," Danny warned us when we were getting out of the car.

"Thanks, man. Drive safe," Louis replied, reaching out to fist-bump him.

With that, Danny drove off, leaving the five of us to stare at the beautiful grey house that belonged to Liam's girlfriend. "Are you guys ready to party?" Zayn asked, a smile playing on his lips.

No...

"Hell yeah!"

Chapter 33

The second we stepped into the house, loud music hit my eardrums. It could already be heard on the outside, but the volume was at another level in here. It almost made me want to press my hands to my ears, but I wasn't going to be that that person, even if I wasn't really in the mood for all this.

As soon as we had gotten rid of our jackets, Zayn and Liam disappeared into the house, Liam probably to go find Alice and Zayn to find some girl. It surprised me a little that Niall and Louis lingered because they usually followed Zayn's actions, but apparently not tonight.

Niall flicked his gaze between me and Louis before he stopped at me. "You going to be okay?" He mouthed, reaching out to touch my arm.

I nodded, plastering a smile on my face. I wasn't going to ruin his night only because I wasn't excited about the party. He deserved to have fun and let loose.

He shot Louis another look before returning my smile sympathetically. "Bye, guys!" He shouted over the music, and then he was gone too, which left me alone with Louis.

"Come on, Curly. Let's go find something to drink," he announced, grabbing my forearm to pull me into the living room.

I wasn't going to lie, I was shocked. He had never paid attention to me like this at a party before. My birthday party might have been an exception, but it was my birthday. If he didn't pay any attention to me then, he would have been a shitty best friend.

Now, this was a completely normal house party, and the way he was acting now was not the way he usually acted. The memory of him opening the door of Emily's kitchen when I had been talking to Evelyn entered my mind, and I could still remember how he had searched the room for her only to notice me standing there. When he had asked me if I knew where she was and I had told him I didn't, he had just turned around and slammed the door shut without another word. That was the perfect example of how he usually treated me at parties, so it wasn't weird that I was surprised.

The living room was crowded with people dancing and chatting over the loud music that was blaring through the speakers. It was so dark that I could barely make out any of their faces, but I knew that most of them were from school since the majority of the people Alice knew went there. There was no doubt that Evelyn was one of them. However, not to be rude or anything, but I didn't want her to notice me because I didn't want to argue with Louis about her yet another time. We had already had more arguments than necessary about her.

Louis didn't let go of me until we found a table full of different drinks and alcoholic beverages. He didn't hesitate to fill two shot glasses with tequila, which made my eyes widen. "We're going to start with tequila?" I gaped, making him roll his eyes.

"You've already had a few cans of beer, Curly, so this is no biggy," he reminded me.

"Speak for yourself," I mumbled, but he couldn't hear me over the loud music.

"You were saying?" He asked, arching an eyebrow.

Without meeting his eyes, I snatched the shot glass from his hand. "Just give it to me."

I downed the whole thing in one go, grimacing at the strong taste. Louis was watching me the entire time with widened eyes. "Woah, where did the eagerness come from? What about the salt and lemon, huh?"

"Not necessary," I shrugged, making him let out a light chuckle.

"Well, then," he said, taking his shot without the salt and lemon as well before slamming the empty glass on the table.

"You want another one?" He wondered, glancing at me.

I shook my head. "Nah, I'm good. I'm just going to grab a beer," I told him, doing just that and popping the can open before taking a swig.

I thought Louis was going to follow my actions, but instead of grabbing a beer, he picked up a glass of vodka mixed with coke and took a sip of it, a grimace instantly taking over his features.

"What?" I chuckled, finding the expression on his face cute somehow. "Was it too strong?"

Without saying a word, he extended his hand with the drink to me. "Have a try yourself," he said, raising an expectant eyebrow at me.

I studied his features for any sign that he was just joking with me, but I couldn't find one, so I took the drink from his hand and brought it to my lips to take a sip. I ignored the fact that Louis' lips had touched the rim of the glass just a few seconds ago and focused on the taste instead.

It was strong, I wasn't going to lie. It almost felt like there was more vodka than coke in it, and I started wondering if Alice wanted everyone at the party to get drunk off their asses because I was sure that by just downing one of these drinks, anyone would get intoxicated.

"Judging by the look on your face, I'll take it you understand what I was on about," Louis chuckled, taking the drink back when I held it out to him.

"We should go find Alice and ask her if she wants to poison everyone at the party," I joked, making his lips twitch into a smile.

During the next half hour, Louis and I stayed there, talking to each other while sipping on our drinks. It was nothing like I had thought this night would turn out to be. It was much better. Spending time with Louis always made me happy, and this night was no exception.

"So, you think Zayn's going to find any girl tonight?" Louis asked me, a beer in his hand. He had placed the drink back on the table, not caring that both of us had already taken a sip of it and that other people didn't know that.

Neither of us was drunk, but we weren't exactly sober either. I was a little lightheaded, and judging by the slur in Louis' voice, I assumed he was as well.

"Zayn always finds someone," I said, rolling my eyes.

Louis let out a chuckle, nodding his head. "You're right about that," he agreed.

You do too...

The thought made my heart hurt because I wasn't sure if Louis actually wanted to be here with me, or if he just felt sorry for me since he knew I wasn't very excited about the party. I didn't want him to be here just because he felt like he had to, although I didn't exactly want him to run off to chase some girl either.

"Come on, Curly. Let's go dance," Louis suggested, interrupting my thoughts completely as he grabbed a hold of my forearm and started pulling me forward again.

I followed him reluctantly, not really feeling like dancing, but I wasn't sure if I actually had a choice because Louis seemed quite determined about it. There were a lot of people dancing, jumping and singing to the music that was blaring through the speakers. Some of them were even making out, something I found a bit odd because an uptempo song was playing at the moment, making it just look a bit weird if I were being honest.

As soon as Louis had found an empty spot on the dance floor, he let go of me and started dancing along to the music, his body turned to me so he could see my every move. A smirk made its way to his face as he noticed my discomfort, and he didn't hesitate to grab my hands, pulling me closer to him.

"Come on, Curly. Let loose," he shouted in my ear, his breath tickling my skin. It made me shiver involuntarily, a tingling feeling making its way down my spine.

It didn't make matters better that he didn't let go of me but instead kept our bodies close, his arms wrapped loosely around my waist as he swayed to the music, bringing me with him. I wrapped my arms around his neck, having no idea where else to put them since it felt weird to just let them hang at my sides.

As if on cue, a slower song came on, making my heart race in my chest because everything suddenly felt a lot more intimate between us. Louis' arms tightened around my waist, pulling our bodies even closer together, making my breath hitch.

Looking him in the eye, I noticed that he was already studying my features, his lips twitched into a small smile. "You're quite beautiful, you know that?"

His words made my eyes widen, and my heart stopped beating altogether. Did he just call me beautiful? No, there was no way that my crush since three years back just said that he liked my features. There was no way.

But as he kept looking at me with that fond smile on his lips, I started realizing that yes, he did just say that. It also made me think of what Gemma had told me earlier. Was there a possibility that Louis actually did reciprocate my feelings? I mean, you didn't go around calling your friends beautiful, now did you?

"I... Uh, n--"

"There you are, Harry!"

Evelyn's high-pitched voice cut me off, taking both of my and Louis' eyes off each other to face the girl who was now standing beside us. A hesitant smile formed on my lips, my heart now beating like crazy in my chest by what Louis had just said.

"Hi, Evelyn," I greeted, my voice laced with a bit of panic.

Her eyes fell on Louis for a split second before looking back at me. "Do you wanna dance?"

Through the corner of my eye, I could see Louis clench his jaw, but he kept quiet as I bit my bottom lip. I didn't want to say yes because I was more than happy to already be dancing with Louis, but I had a hard time turning people down, and this was no exception.

"I... yeah, why not?" I said, and I was sure I wasn't smiling but more like grimacing at her. "If it's okay with Louis."

The feathery-haired boy was looking down, but at the sound of his name, he looked up, the crease between his eyebrows smoothening out. "Uh, yeah, sure. I was actually just about to head to the toilets anyway," he smiled, and it actually seemed genuine, something I wasn't quite prepared for.

We had now let go of each other and were standing a few feet apart, and I couldn't help but miss the warmth of his body against mine already. The fact that I knew he was about to leave in just a matter of seconds didn't make me feel any better either.

Before he did so, though, he turned to me, the genuine smile still spread on his lips. "I'll see you later, Curly, yeah?"

There was something in the way he looked at me that told me he wanted me to be careful, though, and I understood what he meant by it seeing as Evelyn had feelings for me that I didn't reciprocate. I had to be careful in order to not fuck things up.

"Of course," I smiled, this time whole-heartedly because it was directed at him.

After that, Louis left us, making his way through the crowd towards the bathroom. It hurt to see him leave. I wanted him to stay by my side, keep me company during the entire night because we had been having so much fun. I didn't want it to end.

Evelyn wrapped her arms around my neck, making me look at her instead of the direction Louis just disappeared in. When our eyes met, she let out a sigh. "He's the reason you turned me down, isn't it?" She asked me, making me furrow my eyebrows.

"What do you mean?"

She shook her head, a faint smile forming on her lips. "I don't mean that he told you to do it because he doesn't seem to like me. What I mean is that he's the reason you didn't want to go out with me."

I swallowed hard at her words as I averted my gaze. "I, uh... that might be the case."

She nodded, the faint smile never leaving her face. "You don't have to be Einstein to put two and two together, you know? I can see the way you look at him, and the fact that he has interfered with our conversation twice when we've been talking about going out just shows how jealous he is about it," she explained, making my eyes widen slightly.

First Niall and now Evelyn. Was there anyone else who had noticed the way I looked at Louis or was it just these two people at school? I was actually starting to fear how obvious I was, but since Louis hadn't said anything about it, I must be safe, right?

And about Louis being jealous. The thought had crossed my mind, but I wasn't sure whether he had actually been jealous or if he was just looking out for me. However, hearing Evelyn agree with my assumption made it feel like it could actually be true, though.

"I uh... I'm sorry," I sighed, looking at her apologetically.

"Don't be," she said. "I'm the one who should be sorry. I shouldn't have asked you out when I had a feeling you were going to say no anyway. It was always pretty clear to me that you only saw me as a friend, but I wanted to give it a try, you know? I'm sorry I ruined things between us," she apologized.

"No," I said, shaking my head. "You didn't ruin anything. I'd still like to be your friend... if you want me to of course. I don't want you to feel like you have to if it hurts to be around me," I grimaced.

"I'd love to be your friend," she smiled, this time genuinely. "I mean, it's just a silly crush anyway. I'll get over it," she chuckled, waving her hand in dismissal before placing it on the back of my neck again.

My lips twitched at her words, happy that she seemed so okay with it. I didn't want to hurt her in any way, so if she had told me otherwise, I would have never forced her to be my friend.

"So, how're things going with Louis then?" She wondered, raising her eyebrows at me.

I let out a humorless chuckle, shaking my head. "There's nothing going on between us."

She let out a snort. "Yeah, right."

My eyes widened at her words. "I'm telling the truth. I mean, I know that I have feelings for him, but I don't really know how he feels about me," I explained, biting my bottom lip.

She cocked an eyebrow at me. "So, you haven't talked about it? What are you waiting for, Harry? He's right there, and it's obvious that you have feelings for each other. Why don't you just tell him?"

A scowl formed on my face. "I'm afraid I'll lose him," I muttered, ignoring the fact that she just told me it was obvious he felt the same way. I didn't know for sure, and I couldn't take any risks.

She let out a sigh. "You won't, Harry. Trust me."

I looked into her eyes, seeing that she was telling the truth... or at least what she thought was the truth. "I'll think about it," I muttered.

She nodded. "I just... I reckon you tell him sooner rather than later, before you lose him to someone else," she told me, looking me deep in the eyes.

Her words stung because I didn't want to picture him with someone else. The thought alone hurt bad enough. What would happen if I had to witness it in real life?

I let out a hum, looking down at the floor.

"Go find him, Harry. He said he was going to the bathroom. Just go look for him," she suggested, and when I looked up, I noticed that she was smiling at me.

I felt a little reluctant about telling him about my feelings tonight. However, it didn't matter whether I decided to do it today or not because I wanted to go look for him anyway. I didn't know for how long he had been gone now, but it was definitely longer than what a visit to the toilets should be.

"You're okay with me leaving you?" I wondered, to which she rolled her eyes.

"Just go," she chuckled, and I didn't need to be told twice.

I started making my way through the crowd, bumping into people's shoulders, which almost got me stuck, but I eventually managed to make it out of the living room and into the hallway where I knew the bathroom was.

A smile started making its way to my lips, knowing I would be seeing Louis in just a matter of seconds. It was crazy how fast I started missing him. He had barely been gone for twenty minutes, and yet here I was, almost running to him.

The smile instantly dropped from my face at the sight I was met with outside the bathroom, though. Louis was there, but he wasn't alone. Vanessa was pressed against the wall by his body, her head thrown back as he was pressing kisses to her exposed neck, all the way up to her jaw.

Even though it wasn't a kiss on the lips this time, I couldn't help the tears that welled up in my eyes. Just the sight of him with someone else made my heart break into pieces. It didn't matter what kind of affection it was, all that matter was that this girl was someone that wasn't me.

And here I was, thinking he had actually caught feelings for me. For a second, I had actually *thought* that he liked me back. How stupid could I be?

The gasp made its way past my lips before I could prevent it, and the sound made Louis pull away in an instant, his head turning to look at the source. When his eyes met mine, I could see his face fall, and he didn't waste a second until he took a step in my direction.

"Harry, I..."

I shook my head vigorously, taking a few steps backward before turning around to sprint back to the living room, making my way through the crowd much quicker this time, until I was in the entryway. Luckily, I found my coat after only a few seconds, and I didn't hesitate to swing open the door and leave the house.

With tears rolling down my cheeks, I started running towards what I thought was the direction of my house, but to be honest, I had no idea of where I was going. I didn't recognize these streets at all, and the possibility of getting lost right now was probably more likely than me actually finding my way home.

"Harry, wait!"

The voice made me almost come to a halt because I was taken aback that he had actually decided to follow me, but I composed myself enough to make my legs keep moving forward. I wasn't very quick, though, because one, I didn't know where I was going, and two, my entire body felt like crumbling down after what had just happened. I just couldn't make myself move faster.

So, it didn't come as a surprise when I could feel Louis' hand on my shoulder, making me come to a stop. I felt nothing but defeated when I turned around, wiping my cheeks feverishly so he wouldn't see that I had been crying. I had a feeling he could see it anyway, though.

"I'm so done with this," I breathed, squeezing my eyes shut for a second. "I'm so fucking done thinking that I will ever have a chance with you. I thought... I thought we had grown closer, Louis. I thought we were actually going somewhere. Fuck, I thought you actually *liked* me!" I paused to run my hand through my curls in frustration, feeling new tears build up in my eyes.

"I can't believe I was so stupid. Why would Louis Tomlinson, the boy who hooks up with different girls at every party he goes to ever fall for a boy like me, his best *friend*? How could I be so stupid to think that? I'm probably just that boy you feel sorry for because I'm fucking poor and have to work to be able to afford things. Is that why you hang out with me? Because you feel sorry for me?"

He didn't move an inch as he stared at my face, his mouth agape. The sight made me let out a humorless laugh. "Do you know how long I've felt this way for you, Louis? Three years. For *three* fucking years have I witnessed you being with different girls, and do you want to know something? It hurts. It hurts like a fucking bitch every single time I see you with them, but I never said anything because I was afraid you would be disgusted with me if you found out the truth. But I'm sick and tired of this. I don't care anymore. I don't care if you'll think I'm disgusting for having feelings for you, I couldn't fucking care any le-- mmpf."

I was interrupted by the impact of his lips on mine, almost knocking the air out of my lungs because his entire body collided with mine in the process. I was so caught off guard that I couldn't get my head around what was happening as his lips moved with mine so desperately, as if he was afraid I would let go.

After a few seconds, I could feel my own lips starting to move against his, my brain still not working as it should. I only knew one thing, and it was that I loved the feeling of what his lips did to me. My entire body exploded with pure satisfaction because this was what my body craved the most; his skin on mine, and especially his mouth.

He cradled my head in his hands, his mouth feeling like electricity against mine as he pulled my body even closer to him.

It wasn't until he parted his lips to let his tongue lick my bottom lip that I finally realized what was going on, and I instantly pushed at his chest to get him away from me.

I started shaking my head vigorously again, feeling new, hot tears roll down my cheeks. "N-no, you don't have the right to do that. You're just going to... you're just going to regret it like last time. You're going to tell me that it was stupid, that it meant nothing. You can't... I can't let you do that to me again," I let out between sniffles, squeezing my eyes shut because everything just *hurt* so much right now.

I didn't know what to do, so without looking at him, I turned around and ran away again. And this time, he didn't follow me.

Chapter 34

I didn't sleep very well that night. To be honest, I didn't even know how I managed to find my way home, but I did somehow. How I then opened the front door and made my way to my room without waking up either of mom or Gemma was still a mystery to me, but I managed to do that as well.

It wasn't until I laid there in my bed, staring up at the ceiling that I finally let myself think of what had taken place just an hour ago. It was painful. It hurt so much to even imagine myself standing there, right in front of Louis while confessing my feelings for him. The memory was still so fresh. It was like he was standing in front of me right now, and I was repeating the same words to him over and over again. It all made me want to curl myself into a ball and cry.

Would I ever be the reason for the beautiful smile that made the crinkles by his eyes show again? Would I ever be sitting in Louis' car while he drove me to and from school again? And would I ever hear him tease me for something stupid that would make me feel all fussy inside ever again?

I probably wouldn't, and that fact made new, silent tears roll down my cheeks. What was even going to happen now? Because there was no way all five of us would be able to hang out with each other again. Louis wouldn't want that after tonight. He probably never wanted to see me again after what I confessed.

Squeezing my eyes shut, I let out a quiet sob, hugging the covers close to my body. I was going to miss him so much. How was I going to survive without having him near me? How was I going to survive seeing him at school without being able to be close to him, *talk* to him? And those soft, pink lips... Fuck, I would never get to feel them against my own again.

The thought of kissing him made me reach my hand up to run my fingertips over my lips. They were still tingling from the feeling of having his lips pressed to them, and honestly, I never wanted the feeling to go away because that was the only trace I had left of him.

Thinking about the kiss made me wonder why he had done it in the first place. It was just like the first time, only that I had been the one pulling away now. Did he really feel so sorry for me that he wanted me to feel better about the situation? Did he honestly think kissing me would make me feel better when I was so upset? Sure, it would have been more than okay if I knew he reciprocated my feelings, but he had just kissed a girl's neck right in front of my eyes, so what were really the odds of that?

I didn't know what time it was when I finally fell asleep, but I knew that my cheeks were still damp and my nose stuffy from all the crying I had done when blackness took over.

I didn't know what time it was when I woke up, but I could tell that it was pretty late because the sun was shining through my window. I had forgotten to shut the blinds last night, which didn't exactly surprise me. I was more surprised about the fact that I had managed to get my clothes off my body.

It was just impossible for me to find the will to wake up this morning. Because if I did, I knew that I was just going to start thinking about what had happened last night, and I didn't want to do that just yet. If I could just erase the memory from my mind, I would be more than happy. Honestly, I just wanted to turn back time and have the entire night undone, but I knew that was impossible.

Rolling over to the other side of the bed, I buried my face in my pillow. I started getting more aware of the warm sheets against my bare stomach and the feeling of my eyes wanting to flutter open with every second that went by. However, it wasn't until I heard a thud against my door that I finally decided to fully wake up.

I opened my eyes before I had even rolled over to be able to see the door, but when I did, I was pretty sure I had a heart attack because someone was sitting on the floor with their back pressed against the door and their hands in their unruly hair. It wasn't just someone, though.

It was Louis.

The sight made me let out a loud gasp as I scrambled up to press my back against the headboard, hugging the covers close to my chest to shield my body. My eyes were wide open as I stared at the boy on the floor, his gaze already directed at me.

"What... what are you doing here?" I blurted. "How did you... how did you even get in?"

He ran his hands through his disheveled locks, his face showing no emotion whatsoever. "Your mom let me in," he mumbled, and *of course* she did. She had no idea what happened last night, after all.

Looking away from him, I bit my bottom lip. My heart was racing so fast in my chest. I couldn't believe he was actually in the same room as me after last night. What was he even doing here?

"Look, Harry," he sighed, trying to make eye contact with me. "I know you're mad at me for what happened, but I--"

I cut him off by shaking my head. "I'm not mad at *you*, Louis. I'm mad at myself for feeling this way about you," I explained, my eyebrows pinched together. "But that's not why I'm asking why you're here. I thought you wouldn't... I thought you wouldn't *want* to be here."

It wasn't until then I noticed that he was wearing the green Adidas hoodie that I loved so much, and the sight made a knot form in my stomach. For some reason, that sweater always made me want to have his arms wrapped around me while I nuzzled my nose into the crook of his neck.

He squeezed his eyes shut, biting his bottom lip harshly. He started shaking his head, letting out a deep sigh. It took at least ten seconds until he finally opened his eyes and replied to me. "That's where you've got it wrong."

The crease between my eyebrows deepened in confusion. "What do you mean?"

Without saying anything, he hoisted himself up from the floor and walked over to me. With every step he took, I could feel my heart beating faster in my chest, and it definitely didn't stop when he sat down on the edge of my bed, just a foot away from my body.

Pain filled his eyes when he reached out to take my hand in his. His gaze turned to our hands as he started running his fingers over mine, almost as if he was nervous. The touch made tingles shoot up my entire arm, which had me wondering if he knew of the effect he had on me. His touch just made me all warm and fussy inside.

"I... I don't know how to say this because I have a hard time admitting it to myself, but I can't escape it anymore. It's inevitable," he started without looking up to meet my gaze.

I took a deep breath in an attempt to steady my hammering heartbeat as he finally looked up to make eye contact with me. The look in his blue irises made my breath hitch, and I stopped breathing altogether.

"What I wanted to say to you yesterday is that I have feelings for you too, but I'm scared as fuck because I've never felt this way about anyone before, let alone a boy. And before you say anything, I want to assure you that I don't have anything against homosexual people. I meant it when I said I would never judge anyone for their sexual preference, but that doesn't include myself. I... I always thought I was only into girls. I always thought that when I finally felt that I wanted to settle down, it'd be with a girl," he paused to run the hand that wasn't holding mine through his fringe, inhaling a deep breath.

"Lately, though, I've come to realize that's not how things will turn out. I think it all began when we started hanging out more before your birthday party. I found myself wanting to spend as much time with you as possible without really knowing why. But it wasn't until I saw you kissing Lucas at the party that I first realized that something was about to happen to me. I've never been jealous before. I mean, I have never had a reason to since I never really had feelings for anyone, but when I saw you with Lucas, something just snapped inside me and I just got so angry."

He shook his head, squeezing my hand gently. "While I did my best to try denying my feelings for you, *that* happened with my family and I just thought it'd be best to distance myself from everyone. It worked quite well until I realized that I couldn't stay away from you. I always found myself looking at you, only to avert my gaze every time you caught me doing so. It was like my brain told me to stay away while my heart wanted to get closer to you." He let out a dry chuckle, glancing at me through the corner of his eye.

"I guess things only got worse after that. I found myself always thinking about you, whether I was in class, in the middle of soccer practice, or in my room after school. You were just everywhere. I even found myself wondering what your opinion would be in conversations I had with other people," he smiled faintly.

"So, it came to the point where I had to know whether my heart was just playing a trick on me or not. That is the reason I kissed you last week. I remember hoping that you had a relatable story of how you realized you were bisexual so I had a reason to actually kiss you. It worked out just fine until I realized that my heart wasn't in fact playing a trick on me. Because kissing you is the best thing I have ever experienced. Kissing you was so addicting that I never wanted to pull away, but my mind caught up with what was happening, and I panicked."

He looked down at our hands again, running his thumb over the skin between my thumb and forefinger. "I'm so sorry for everything I put you through. I never meant to play with your feelings like that. I didn't... I wasn't aware that you had such strong feelings for me, even if my heart always hoped you did. I had my ideas that you might like me more than a friend, but I wasn't sure since you never really made a move on me. However, with the way I was acting towards you, I shouldn't be surprised that you didn't. I was like a ticking bomb," he chuckled dryly, still avoiding eye contact.

"I'm not going to lie and say that I have accepted it all yet, but I'm working on it because I know that I can't stay away from you. My heart literally beats for you, and I don't even want to think of not being on speaking terms with you again. Whenever we haven't been in the past, everything just hurt so fucking much, which is why I'm here right now. I just couldn't risk going back to school on Monday having you ignore me, so I knew I had to fix things with you right away after you left yesterday."

The second he stopped talking, the room fell dead silent. I couldn't even begin to process everything he had just told me. It was just surreal, the way he had basically just told me everything I had ever wanted to hear. After all these years of liking him, thinking that he would never reciprocate my feelings, this was just unbelievable.

I didn't know what to say or do, so I just stared at him, my mouth hanging open while feeling nothing but speechless. I noticed that the longer I waited to react, the more nervous he got. His hand that was still tracing my skin started shaking slightly as it got a little clammy. He also refused to meet my shocked gaze, keeping his eyes on our hands instead.

"Please say something, Harry. Your silence is killing me," he pleaded.

I swallowed hard, trying desperately to find the ability to speak, but my brain wasn't working properly. I couldn't get my head around the fact that he had just confessed that he had feelings for me, it was just impossible.

So instead of replying to him, I laced our fingers together, giving his hand a gentle squeeze to let him know that everything was okay. It seemed like it did the trick because he looked up at me in just a matter of seconds, his lips curling hesitantly.

When I finally started processing it all, I inhaled a deep breath, closing my eyes momentarily before opening them again to look at his beautiful features. "I... I don't know what to say. You just... you just told me everything I've ever wanted to hear. How am I supposed to react to that?" I breathed.

The smile broke out on his face, and I suddenly felt the urge to reach out and touch the crinkles that formed by his eyes. "I don't know. You tell me," he chuckled softly, his thumb running patterns over my skin again.

It wasn't until then everything started getting back to me, and I realized something that made the smile drop from my face, my muscles tensing in my body. Louis seemed to notice this immediately by the way he stopped moving as well, his face turning alarmed.

Before he could ask me what was going on, I opened my mouth to explain. "If this... if everything you just told me is true, then why did I find you kissing Vanessa in the hallway yesterday?" I mumbled.

I suddenly wanted to pull my hand away, out of his hold, but I had a feeling he wouldn't let me. The frown was back on his face in a second, and he inhaled a deep breath. "Right. So, as you might have noticed, I stopped caring about flirting with girls all the time. Whenever Vanessa or Chloé was at my side, it was all thanks to them. I never intended anything. At first, I was mad at myself because of this, thinking that there was nothing or no one that could make me stop me from hooking up with girls, but then I realized that there was nothing I could do about it. You were all I could think about every time a girl tried flirting with me. I always glanced your way, trying to read your mind and find out what you thought about the situation. Did you mind that they were flirting with me, or did you not give a shit?" He paused to let out a dry chuckle.

"I never meant for anything to happen yesterday because honestly, I haven't even thought about hooking up with a girl in weeks. But when I came back from the bathroom after leaving you to talk to Evelyn, I saw your arms around her neck and you looked so happy around each other. It seemed like you were really enjoying your time together, and I don't know, but this anger built up inside me and I couldn't think clearly. I know you told me several times that you didn't have feelings for her, but seeing you two together like that made me think you had lied to me all along. So, I did the first thing I could think of to take my thoughts off you, but I regret it so fucking much now. I'm so sorry I hurt you," he apologized, looking at me with pain in his eyes.

I let out a sigh, my muscles relaxing as a faint smile made its way to my face. "She was telling me to make a move on you, you know? She said she could tell how much I liked you, and that she was sorry for asking me out when she had a feeling I was going to say no anyway. We were just coming clean, but I guess it might have looked different in other people's eyes. You should have just come over and asked me about it, though," I told him, my eyes boring into his.

He bit his bottom lip, nodding his head slowly. "Yeah, I realize that now. I just couldn't think clearly. I guess I was blinded by jealousy," he muttered, the pain remaining on his face.

I squeezed his hand gently, offering him a small smile. "I know what you're talking about actually, so I shouldn't blame you."

He pulled his eyebrows together. "What do you mean?"

Inhaling a deep breath, I sat up more properly against the headboard. "It was at my birthday party. I was looking for you because I wanted to confront you about singing to me. It had also been quite some time since I last saw you and I was pissed drunk, so when I found you making out with Vanessa, every common sense just left my body and all I knew was that I needed a distraction," I mumbled, averting my gaze.

His eyes widened in realization. "So you kissed Lucas," he breathed.

I nodded my head, letting out a sigh. "I couldn't help myself. It just hurt so much to see you with someone else, and it's been like that for years. It was worse that night, though, because I really wanted you to pay attention to me, not anyone else."

Louis looked at me for a few seconds, studying my face intently before boldly lifting his hand to touch my cheek with his fingertips. He started running his fingers gently against my skin, making goosebumps appear on my entire body.

"I can't believe how much pain I've put you through all this time. Is this the reason why you were never really excited to go to parties? Because you knew you'd witness me with someone else?" He asked me, his eyes filled with pain.

I nodded my head slowly, looking away from him while biting my bottom lip.

"Oh, God," he breathed, brushing a few curls from my face before looking down in shame. "I'm so fucking sorry. I didn't know, Harry."

"Hey," I said, now realizing that he had moved a lot closer. He was almost hovering over my body, his face no further than a few inches away from mine. "Don't blame yourself for this. You didn't know, Louis. It's okay," I tried to reassure him, but a crease formed between his eyebrows anyway.

"It's okay? You think it's okay that I hurt you?" He asked incredulously.

I let out a sigh. "You didn't know, alright? So don't blame yourself for it."

He was silent for a long time, his blue eyes studying my face. I felt so exposed when he did this. I was lying in my bed, with barely any clothes on, and he was mere inches away from my face, looking at me so intently that I almost had to look away. My heart was thumping in my chest, and it didn't make matters better when his fingers moved from my cheek to my lips, his thumb running over my bottom lip slowly.

His eyes turned to my mouth for a split second, his lips parting slightly before looking back into my eyes. "Can I?" He asked, his breath fanning my face, smelling of mint.

I knew my breath was not nearly as fresh as his, but I couldn't begin to care when he was this close to me, asking me if he could kiss me. There was no way I was going to pass up on this opportunity, so I nodded my head slowly, my eyes stuck on his beautiful features.

He didn't hesitate to lean down and seal our lips together, his hand now cupping my cheek again. The thrill that went through my body by his lips on mine made me let out a gasp, and I couldn't help myself when I let go of his hand to grip the back of his neck, bringing him even closer.

This kiss was nothing like the other ones we had shared. It was filled with passion and love while the first one had been hesitant and the second almost desperate. I just couldn't get enough of him. I wanted him even closer although his chest was pressed to mine, his nose digging into my cheek while his lips worked absolute magic.

His lips were so addictive, the way they massaged my own but at the same time moved so passionately that I found it hard to breathe. I didn't know how he did it, but I knew that I didn't want it to stop. Honestly, I didn't know what could possibly make us pull away this time because this kiss was amazing and neither of us had any reason to do so.

When he sucked my bottom lip into his mouth, running his tongue along it, I let out a soft whimper, leaning my head back against the headboard to create a small distance between us. He let out a low grunt at this and didn't waste a second to put his legs on either side of my hips so he was straddling my waist. He then leaned in to connect our lips again, making me shudder. The only thing that separated us was his layer of clothes and the blankets that were still covering my body.

"Louis," I breathed when he licked my bottom lip again, clearly asking for entrance.

"What?" He asked in a muffle, his lips still pressed to mine.

"Morning... fuck, morning breath."

He pulled back a little, our faces still so close that our noses were brushing. A frown was apparent on his features as he shook his head slowly. "I couldn't care less," he muttered before connecting our lips again, almost bruisingly.

It made me gasp, and he took that opportunity to slip his tongue inside my mouth, rubbing it against my own. The feeling made my knees go weak, so I was nothing but thankful that I was lying down because otherwise, I would have been putty in his arms right now, and probably fallen to the floor.

He let his hands wander to my hair, lacing his fingers through my curls while pulling me impossibly closer to him, our breaths mixing together by the second. After a couple of minutes, we were mainly just breathing into each other's mouths, too out of breath to be able to have them connected.

He pressed one last kiss to my lips before moving to my jaw, leaving small kisses all the way down to my neck and collarbone. "So fucking beautiful," he mumbled against my skin, pressing his lips to my pulse point. "I literally can't get enough of you, Harry."

When he eventually pulled away, he rolled over on the bed so he was lying next to me on his side. He ran his forefinger from my jawline, down to my neck, and it was so feathery light that I couldn't help but shiver.

I had a hard time taking in what had just happened, so I lied there, facing the ceiling while trying to process it all for at least a minute until I turned to face him, my arm tucked under my head. His eyes were shining as he examined my features.

"It feels weird hearing you call me by my real name," I couldn't help but say. "But I quite like it."

An almost cheeky smile spread on his lips. "Yeah? No more Curly then?"

My lips formed a pout at his words because no, I didn't want him to stop calling me that.

He let out a chuckle at my facial expression, leaning in to kiss my pout away. The action made my lips tingle. "I'm just kidding. You'll always be my Curly," he smiled, making my heart flutter.

My Curly. *My.*

"So, you finally realized I actually meant it when I said I care about you then?"

He sent me a small smile. "I realized it the second you mentioned that you helped me at the party and stopped me from punching Ryan that time in my car. I know I told you that you just did because you had to, but I knew that you were telling the truth. To be honest, I think I only wanted an excuse to say you didn't care at the time. Even though my heart ached for it, my brain hated the idea. Besides, everyone I've ever wanted to care about me never did, so it felt so surreal, you know?"

I returned his smile. "I understand, especially now that I know about your family situation. I get that you have a hard time believing people care about you since the people closest to you never did."

He nodded his head, and we fell silent after that, just looking into each other's eyes.

It was the sound of my stomach grumbling that interrupted our staring, and a smirk made its way to his face. "I see someone's hungry. How about I make you some breakfast?" He offered, the smirk never leaving his face.

My eyes widened as I started shaking my head. "No. Nope, just no. I don't want to get food poisoning after a day of drinking. I need to keep the food in my system," I said, half-teasingly and half-seriously.

He tilted his head to the side as he let out a chuckle. "You haven't even let me try. I made you what? A sandwich, where luck wasn't on my side. It was one time. Who says I haven't improved since then?"

I raised an eyebrow at him, letting out a snort. "I highly doubt that."

He huffed. "Well then, I hope you still have some Coco Pops in your cabinet because this boy is not going to accept anything else," he sassed, flicking his none existent hair from his shoulder.

His comment made me lean in to nuzzle my face into his neck, nosing at his warm, soft skin. It was something I had wanted to do for a very long time now, and especially when he was wearing this hoodie.

With an arm wrapped around his waist, I pulled his body closer to me, loving the fact that I didn't need a reason to do this anymore.

"Good thing I made mom buy a new box just for you then."

Chapter 35

The second Louis and I entered the kitchen, we noticed that mom and Gemma were already there, both of them munching on a slice of toast. Mom was the first one to look up when we showed up, and a smile instantly formed on her lips.

I had pulled on a pair of black joggers and a white t-shirt before exiting my bedroom with Louis, and unlike the first time he had been in my room when I got dressed, he had now eyed my body from head to toe. I could still remember how he hadn't even paid attention to me that morning after Emily's party. Oh, how the tables had turned.

"I see you finally woke up, Harry."

I nodded my head, flashing mom a smile. To be honest, I hadn't been able to stop smiling since Louis confessed his feelings for me. I was just so happy that I couldn't.

"Have you been crying?" Gemma blurted, a suspicious look taking over her features.

I could feel Louis shift his weight from one foot to the other, running his hand through his fringe in discomfort. He knew he was the reason that my face was still a bit swollen and red from the crying I had done yesterday.

Biting my bottom lip, I shook my head. "No, I just slept very deeply."

She didn't seem to buy that answer at all, but she didn't question me about it. Instead, she turned to Louis with a small smile on her face. "It's nice to see you again, Louis, although it hasn't been more than two days since last time."

He let out a chuckle. "It's nice to see you too, Gemma."

She turned back to mom after that, and I took that as my cue to grab a bowl and a spoon for Louis before pulling out the Coco Pops from the cabinet. The milk was already on the table, and so was the butter, so I just put a slice of bread in the toaster for myself before sitting down at the table.

Louis joined me in a matter of seconds, thanking me for the bowl and cereal. I flashed him a smile in return, reaching over to give his thigh a little squeeze.

The touch made his lips twitch as he poured some cereal into his bowl. Gemma cleared her throat, earning both of my and Louis' attention.

"What?" I asked her.

She shrugged her shoulders, an obvious smile forming on her face. "So, what were you doing before coming here? It's been quite some time since I heard mom let Louis in," she asked, and judging by the look on her face, she had a very good idea of what had happened.

I could feel my cheeks heat up as I looked down at the surface of the table. "I was sleeping, Gemma," I mumbled, refusing to meet her gaze.

Mom decided to interfere then. "Gemma, darling, don't be nosy. It's none of our business what they were up to." She paused to turn her head to us. "But it melts my heart to see you two so happy, boys."

I almost choked on my own spit by her words, my eyes widening. I could feel Louis tense beside me, and it reminded me of what he had told me about the fact that he still hadn't fully accepted that he liked a guy. So, having people speak so openly about us being romantically involved with each other probably made him uncomfortable.

I didn't want to take it to heart, but I couldn't deny that it hurt a little, the fact that he probably wouldn't admit to anyone that something was going on between us. I understood that it was hard for him, though, and I would never pressure him into something he wasn't comfortable with.

Louis cracked a smile before turning his attention to his bowl of cereal. I decided to step in by taking his hand in mine and lacing our fingers together, hoping that it would soothe him and nothing else.

He surprised me by squeezing back and turning to look me in the eyes. I wanted to reassure him that it was okay, that he didn't have to worry about anything because this was my family, and they loved him to pieces.

For some reason, though, I was pretty sure that wasn't the problem. He didn't care about what other people thought, he had made that clear many times before. I had a feeling it was more about how everything became so real for him when other people were around and pointed out that he was romantically involved with a guy. His own thoughts were the problem, no one else's.

"Mom, please," I whined, finally turning to meet her eyes.

She tilted her head to the side, her gaze flicking between the two of us. "I mean it," she clarified, and to my surprise, Gemma nodded her head in agreement.

"I've been waiting for this moment way too long now. I'm nothing but happy for you," she smiled genuinely, flashing me an obvious smirk.

I wanted to run my hands over my face because this was just too embarrassing right now. Louis and I had basically come clean to each other just a few minutes ago, and here they were, practically congratulating us for admitting our feelings for each other. I was not ready for all this yet.

Thankfully, my toast popped right then, turning my attention away from the two women I called my mother and sister. I got up to fetch it, letting go of Louis' hand in the process before quickly going back to sit down again. It wasn't until I was spreading butter on my toast that I realized just how quiet Louis was. He was never this quiet otherwise.

Glancing at the side of his face, I noticed that he was caught up in his food, chewing ever so slowly on his Coco Pops. It was as if he could feel me looking at him because he instantly turned to meet my eyes, a smile forming on his lips.

Somehow, the smile took my breath away. He was just *so* beautiful, and he liked *me*? I was still pretty sure I was dreaming because this couldn't be real. Louis Tomlinson, the boy I had been crushing on for three years, reciprocated my feelings? Yeah, right. Maybe in another world.

As soon as Louis and I had finished eating (I ate as quickly as possible because I couldn't stand all the looks mom and Gemma threw at us), we went back to my room after putting our dishes in the sink. Mom told us she would take care of them later.

I let out a sigh of relief when I shut the door behind us, running a hand through my curls. "I'm so fucking sorry about them. I swear, if I knew they were going to act that way, I wouldn't have suggested eating with them," I apologized, pulling my bottom lip between my teeth.

He turned to face me, taking a step forward to wrap his arms around my waist. The gesture made me all warm and fussy inside, and I couldn't help but place my hands on his shoulders as he looked me in the eyes.

"Don't apologize, Harry. I'm the one who should be apologizing for reacting that way. It's just..." He paused to suck in a deep breath. "This is so fucking hard because I'm not used to this... any of it. It doesn't only have to do with the fact that you're a boy. It's also about the whole settling down thing. This is all new to me, and it's going to take some time to get used to. When we're alone like this, I don't even think about it, but as soon as there are other people around that remind me of it, it's a different story. I'm so sorry," he said, sadness filling his eyes.

I pulled his body close to me, wrapping my arms entirely around his shoulders to give him a tight hug. "It's okay, Lou. I understand that things are difficult. I've never been with anyone the way I want to be with you either, so the idea of settling down is new to me too. We're in this together, and I don't mind taking things slow. I'd actually prefer it over anything else because I've never been one to rush into things. I mean, the fact that it took us this long to admit our feelings for each other kind of speaks for itself," I chuckled, pulling away to get a look at his face.

The corners of his lips curled as he tilted his head to the side, a fond smile taking over his features. "Have I ever told you that you're pretty damn amazing?"

I flicked my curls nonchalantly. "You haven't, but of course I am. Why would you ever think otherwise?" I joked, making him roll his eyes.

"Shut up," he chuckled, reaching up to ruffle my curls.

"Heeey," I whined, fixing them after the mess he just made. "Don't touch my precious curls, you twat."

He threw his head back in laughter. "Oh, don't you even try telling me that you don't love having my hands in your hair," he said cheekily, making me let out a gasp.

"Woah, slow down there, you dirty-minded tosser," I smiled, reaching out to place a hand on his chest.

He put his hand on top of mine, lacing our fingers together. "I think you secretly love my dirty mind," he mumbled, leaning closer so our noses were touching.

I raised my eyebrows at him, feeling my heart race in my chest at his proximity. "Is that so?" I breathed, and he nodded his head, dropping our hands to the side.

"Yeah."

He leaned in all the way to close the gap between us, placing his delicate lips on my own. The feeling was just as exhilarating as every other time we kissed, goosebumps rising on my body as shivers ran down my spine.

This time, Louis didn't waste a second to run his tongue over my bottom lip, asking for entrance. I still hadn't brushed my teeth, but we had both just eaten breakfast, so neither of our breaths would smell of fresh mint. Therefore, I didn't hesitate to part my lips, letting his tongue slip into my mouth to swirl with my own.

The kiss was slow, yet passionate. It made me want him even closer to me, even if our chests were already pressed together. Louis placed a hand on my cheek, his thumb caressing the skin on my chin as his other hand wandered up the back of my t-shirt until his palm was pressed against the small of my back to pull me, if possible, even closer to him.

The feeling of our groins pressing together made me let out a gasp, and my grip on his shoulders tightened. "Fuck, Louis."

He pulled back then, wiping his lips that were wet with my saliva with the back of his hand. "I knew you loved it," he winked.

My mouth fell open, and I didn't hesitate to put my hands on his hips to push him down on my bed. Since he was still holding me, I fell right on top of him, making our chests collide, which sucked the air out of our lungs.

"What was that for, Curly?" He groaned, looking at me through his long eyelashes.

I let out a groan myself as I tried inhaling new air into my lungs. "It's not my fault you didn't let go of me," I accused him.

"Oh, shut up. Why did you even push me to begin with?"

"Because you're mean," I pouted.

He tilted his head to the side, a smirk making its way to his face. "I'm not mean. I'm super sweet, kind and good-hearted. I'd never do anything bad."

I let out a snort, rolling my eyes. "Heey," he said, reaching up to grip my chin to make me look at him. "I'm telling the truth."

"Sure you are," I smiled, flicking him on the nose.

Louis let out a gasp, pushing me off his chest. "You're the only one who's actually mean here," he accused me, pointing a judging finger at me where I was now lying next to him on the bed.

"In your dreams, Tomlinson."

He shot me a glare, crossing his arms over his chest. "Are you ever going to stop?"

"No," I beamed.

He let out a sigh, wrapping his arms around my body in a side-hug and leaning in to bury his face in my neck. "You're going to be the death of me," he mumbled against my skin, making me shiver.

"I-I think you're actually going to kill me first," I said breathlessly.

Chuckling against my neck, he tightened his hold around my body. "See you in hell then."

I raised my eyebrows although he couldn't see me. "What makes you think we're going to hell?"

He pulled away to look at me, a small smile gracing his lips. "I was just kidding."

His words made me relax a little, but I couldn't help but wonder if he actually thought we were going to hell. But why, if so?

We laid there for a few minutes, just enjoying each other's company before an idea struck me. "You wanna watch a movie?" I suggested hopefully.

He glanced at my face, his eyes narrowed in suspicion. "So you can have me card your hair with my fingers again?"

"I wouldn't say no to that," I smiled toothily. "But you have to promise me not to push my laptop off the bed this time, alright?"

He nodded with a wide grin on his face. "I promise, Curly."

We stayed inside during the entire day, only going out of my room to get some food once in a while. It was nothing but cozy, and I loved every second of it. We didn't even bother to move when it turned dark outside, so Louis ended up sleeping over with his arms wrapped around my body.

I had to go to work on Sunday, which meant he only stayed the morning before he left the house. It felt lonely the second he closed the front door behind himself after kissing my lips sweetly. It was the first time I was alone after he had told me he felt the same way about me, and I didn't know what to think of it. I knew I was being overdramatic, but I felt empty without him.

Unfortunately, Lucas wasn't at the diner that day, which made the time pass by slower than it would have otherwise. There weren't any fun customers either, so it was a relief when I finally got home that evening. I took a long, hot shower before heading to bed, missing the warmth of Louis' body during the entire night, and not to mention his warm hands on my stomach.

When it was time to go to school the next morning, I found myself standing in front of my closet, contemplating what to wear. For some reason, it mattered more to me this morning than any other day, and maybe that was because of a certain someone. Even though I knew Louis didn't care about what I was wearing, I wanted to look good for him.

I pursed my lips, my eyes landing on a dark grey, checkered button-up that I hadn't worn in a while. It was a favorite of mine, so I didn't hesitate to take it off the hanger and shrug it on. I buttoned it up, leaving only two buttons undone since I was going to school. I didn't want any teacher scolding me for not dressing properly.

After pulling a pair of black, skinny jeans on, I glanced at myself in the mirror and ruffled my curls. It would have to do.

Not long after that, I could hear a car honk outside. So, with a smile on my face, I skipped out of my room and hurried to slip my brown boots on. I then grabbed my winter jacket and bag before leaving the house, almost forgetting to lock the door behind me in my hurry.

The second I opened the passenger door of Louis' car, I dropped my bag on the car floor and sat down in the seat. I closed the door behind me before finally turning to look at the boy sitting behind the wheel. Louis was already looking at me, his lips spread in a wide smile.

"Morning, beautiful," he greeted, making my heart flutter like crazy in my chest.

I could feel my cheeks heat up as I bit my lip. "Morning, Lou."

With a light chuckle, he stepped on the gas pedal and started driving off towards school. "So, how was work yesterday?"

I shrugged my shoulders. "It was okay, but it could've been better. Lucas wasn't there and the customers were boring," I explained.

He raised his eyebrows, glancing at the side of my face. "So, things are better when you work with Lucas?" He asked me with a flat voice.

His tone made me turn to meet his gaze, noticing that the smile had now dropped from his face. Realization hit me like a slap in the face. "That's why you don't like him," I gaped.

He knitted his eyebrows together in confusion. "What do you mean?"

I inhaled a deep breath. "You just never seemed to enjoy his company, and Lucas reminded me of that every time you were around, but you never mentioned it, so I didn't give it much thought. Now it all makes sense, though."

He gripped the wheel tightly, his knuckles turning white. "It's not that I don't like him..." He trailed off. "I just... I just didn't like the fact that he had a chance with you. I mean, you kissed him, and I was jealous, so of course I wasn't the happiest person around him."

His words made me reach out to place a hand on his thigh, and he instantly loosened the tight grip he had on the wheel. "I understand where you're coming from, but you seriously have nothing to worry about. I never had feelings for him. The only one I've ever felt this way about is you. Even when I kissed him, you were the only one on my mind."

The corners of his lips twitched, but he also scrunched his nose up. "But you thought of me kissing a girl that time, which makes it a lot less cheesy than what you made it sound like."

I let out a gasp, letting go of his thigh to hit him on the arm lightly. "You just ruined the entire moment."

A chuckle escaped his lips as he reached over to take my hand in his, lacing our fingers together. "I'm sorry, princess," he said, bringing our hands to his mouth so he could press his lips to my knuckles.

I stared at him for a few seconds, trying to take in what he had just done before clearing my throat. "I'm not a girl, Louis," I mumbled.

"No, but I know how much you love it when I call you that," he smirked.

My lips formed a pout although I knew he was right. There was no denying the skip in my heart whenever he called me 'princess'. It made me feel so special and important to him somehow.

He took my silence as a sign that I didn't disagree, which made a smug smile form on his pink lips. We were now parked in an empty parking space outside of school, the engine turned off. Neither of us had made a move to get out of the car, though, and I knew that we would be running late if we didn't get going, so I reached out to open the car door.

Before I had managed to do so, though, Louis pulled me back by his hold of my hand, raising his eyebrows at me. "No kiss?" He pouted.

My gaze fell to his lips, feeling a blush making its way to my cheeks. How did he make me feel this way?

Without a second thought, I leaned in to press my mouth against his, letting my lips massage his soft ones. The kiss was sweet and innocent, just perfect for a moment like this. It made butterflies erupt in my stomach and shivers run down my spine, and I absolutely loved it.

When we pulled away a few seconds later, a smile was playing on both of our lips. It took another few seconds until we could look away from each other and finally got out of the car.

During our walk to the lockers, the back of our hands brushed together, but nothing more than that, and that was absolutely okay with me.

Chapter 36

"Zayn can't know about us."

Those were the last words Louis said before we joined the boys at the lockers. It made me very confused because what did he mean by that? That it was okay for the other boys to know, just not Zayn? But why was he an exception?

I didn't have time to question him about it until it was too late, though. Liam, Niall and Zayn were already turned our way, smiles forming on their faces upon seeing us. "Morning, guys."

"Good morning," Louis and I replied in unison as we opened our lockers.

Through the corner of my eye, I could see them exchanging glances with each other. "So, where did you disappear to at the party? We were told you two hadn't been seen in hours when it was over," Liam wondered, his eyebrows furrowed.

"We went home. No offense to your girlfriend, Liam, but the party wasn't very fun," Louis shrugged as if it was no big deal.

Liam quirked an eyebrow, glancing at me. "Well, I had fun, and so did you Niall and Zayn, didn't you?" He asked them.

Before they had time to answer, I opened my mouth to explain. "I didn't feel great, is all. I wasn't too excited about the party to begin with, so Louis offered to take me home. That's why we left pretty early."

Liam pursed his lips in thought but slumped his shoulders after a few seconds. "You could have just told us, Harry. We wouldn't have forced you to go if you weren't feeling well."

I waved a hand in dismissal, just wanting this conversation to be over. "It's alright, don't worry about it," I promised, flashing him a small smile.

Zayn turned to Louis. "So, you gave up finding a girl for the night to bring our friend Harold here home then?" He asked, his eyebrows raised so high that they were almost touching his hairline.

I felt uncomfortable having their eyes directed at us while they interrogated us about what had happened the other night. I just wanted to escape the situation, but it didn't feel like they would drop the topic anytime soon. Hearing Zayn ask Louis about girls didn't exactly make me less uncomfortable either.

"Yeah, I wasn't really feeling it," Louis said, shrugging it off and trying to be nonchalant about it.

Zayn was suspicious, though. He didn't buy the fact that he would just leave a party like that without getting any action first. I understood where he was coming from since Louis would have definitely not left a party a couple of weeks ago just to take someone home... if it wasn't a girl, that was.

Thankfully, we were saved by the bell that went off right then, signaling it was time to head to first class. Liam and Zayn disappeared quickly while Niall lingered, his eyes turned my way. He glanced at Louis quickly before looking back at me.

"So?"

I swallowed hard, turning to Louis who had furrowed his eyebrows before glancing back at the blonde guy. "What?"

Niall opened his mouth to continue, but Louis grabbed my forearm to pull me away from the blonde-haired boy. "See you later, Niall!" He called out.

When we started walking towards our classrooms, I could feel the confusion return to my body, and even more so now when Louis had pulled me away from Niall. "Hold up," I said, stopping in my tracks.

Louis came to a halt as well and turned to me. He had pulled his lip between his teeth and was avoiding eye contact. The hallways were now empty since all students were already in class. I couldn't care less about being late, though. Having this conversation was more important.

"I'm sorry," he said before I could say anything myself.

"For what?"

I wanted to know specifically what he was referring to because I was at a loss right now. I knew he had a hard time accepting everything that was happening between us. I understood that. Everything was new to me too. It was a huge deal to settle down, and especially if it was with someone that was the same gender as you when you had never had feelings for a guy before, but why was it so necessary that Zayn out of all people couldn't know about us? And what was his deal with Niall?

He ran a hand through his brown hair. "I'm sorry for being confusing, I guess," he explained, slowly turning his gaze to meet mine. "I just... Does Niall know about us?"

I let out a sigh, shaking my head. "No, he doesn't. He knows that I have feelings for you, and he's been encouraging me to tell you how I feel."

Louis seemed a bit surprised by this, his eyes widening in realization. "Oh," he said. "So that's why he has been pulling you away to talk lately?"

"Exactly," I nodded. "Did you think I had already told him that we have something going on?"

He shrugged his shoulders, averting his gaze.

Letting out another sigh, I took a step forward to place my hands on his shoulders, making him look me in the eyes. "Look, I know what you told me on Saturday. I know this is difficult for you, and I agreed that we should take things slow. I wouldn't just go around telling people about us without your knowing, alright?"

A smile formed on his lips as he nodded his head. "I'm really sorry, Harry. I wish I wasn't so... on edge about it all. I wish I could just accept it and show you off to everyone."

I shook my head, letting my fingers play with a few strands of his hair. "It's still new, Louis. We'll get there one day. There's no need to hurry."

He closed his eyes for a couple of seconds, the smile never leaving his face. "I don't deserve you, you know that?"

Letting out a light chuckle, I wrapped my arms around his neck, realizing that I could basically do whatever I wanted since there was no one around. "Of course you do. You're amazing," I grinned, pulling him close to give him a hug.

He let out a snort but decided to return the hug anyway by letting his arms go around my waist.

"There's one thing that I'm still confused about, though," I said, pulling back to look at his face. "Why did you tell me that Zayn specifically couldn't know about us?"

He pulled his eyebrows together, looking away from me. "It's uh... it's nothing, really. I just don't want him to know, is all."

I looked at him suspiciously, not buying that excuse at all. Before I could ask him further about it, though, he took a step back and started heading for the door that led to his classroom. "I'll see you later, Curly," he said, sending me an air kiss before opening the door and going inside.

Although my heart fluttered at the sweet gesture, I couldn't help but let out a sigh. He was hiding something, there was no doubt about it. I just wondered what it was and what Zayn had to do with it.

When lunch break rolled around, I wasn't surprised to see that the hallways were packed with people. I tried my best to make my way through the crowd, but it took at least ten minutes until I finally got to my locker to get rid of my books. The boys weren't there, so I assumed they had already gone to the cafeteria.

It turned out I was right because the second I entered the crowded room, I spotted my four best friends at our usual table. However, I also noticed that they weren't alone. Alice and her friends were there as well, and that included both Evelyn and Vanessa.

I could feel a knot form in my stomach at the sight of the blonde-haired girl sitting next to Louis. The last time I had seen her, Louis had his lips pressed to her neck. It was an image I wanted to be removed from my mind, just like the image of them making out at my birthday party.

Once I had bought my lunch, I walked over to the table almost reluctantly. This must be the hardest part of not being able to show everyone that Louis and I had something going on. Anyone could flirt with him, and I couldn't do anything about it. I just hoped that Louis would think of me and try his best to avoid Vanessa's obvious affection.

The only empty seat at the table was next to Evelyn and Niall, so I plopped down on the chair, trying to draw as little attention to me as possible. Louis and Vanessa were sitting right in front of me, which I wasn't very happy about, so I tried my best to keep my eyes on something else instead.

"Harry," Evelyn greeted, pulling me out of my thoughts.

I turned to her, noticing that her lips were twitched into a smile. "Hey."

She tilted her head to the side, glancing at Louis through the corner of her eye. "So, did you find Louis at the party? Have you told him how you feel?" She asked me curiously.

I was a bit surprised that she seemed so unbothered by the topic since she told me just a few days ago that she had a crush on me. I was nothing but happy that she took it so well, though. Maybe she was right when she said it was just a silly crush that she was going to get over, and maybe being friends with her would be easier than I first thought.

Biting my lip, I shrugged my shoulders. "I did find him, and we went home not long after that. We've also talked about a few things," I explained, trying to make it sound like it wasn't a big deal. I wasn't going to tell her that he had told me he reciprocated my feelings and that we now had something going on.

Her eyes lit up with curiosity, and I knew then that she wouldn't stop asking me questions until she knew everything. Therefore, I raised my hand when she was about to open her mouth again. "I really appreciate your support and all, but can we please talk about something else instead?" I pleaded, giving her the best puppy eyes I could manage.

She seemed a bit surprised about this, but she nodded her head anyway. "Yes, of course."

We started talking about uni, and again, she told me how excited she was about going to Manchester and encouraged me to apply there as well. "You said you liked the place too, and it would be so much fun to go there together," she said with a hopeful voice.

I couldn't help but think about Louis and the scholarship, though. What would happen to us after high school? What if Louis got the scholarship and I went to Manchester? Would we still stay together? I mean, I would love to go with him, but I was sure I wasn't going to get into a University in London. My grades were nowhere near that good. And for all I knew, Louis might not even want me to move to London with him.

My head kept spinning during the next ten minutes, making it impossible to hear what Evelyn was talking about. It wasn't until I could feel someone kick me in the shin that I finally snapped out of my thoughts and looked up to find the source. I was a bit surprised to see Louis looking at me from across the table with a concerned look on his face.

"You okay?" He mouthed.

I cracked a small smile and nodded. Vanessa was still sitting next to him, her body turned his way. Yet, he was focusing on me, and I couldn't be happier about that.

He shot me another worried look before turning back to Vanessa who had been trying to get his attention during the entire time he was looking at me. I let out a sigh, only now realizing that they must have been talking during the entire lunch break when I was chatting with Evelyn.

Even if I tried going back to talk to Evelyn during the rest of the break, I could feel myself glancing in the direction of two people sitting opposite me almost too often. I didn't want to be jealous, but I couldn't help myself when I saw Louis listening to what the blonde-haired girl was saying, sometimes even trying to stifle a laugh. It felt like a stab in my heart.

Didn't he realize how much it hurt seeing him get along with the girl he had been romantically involved with just a couple of days ago? She was the girl who had made me so upset that I had admitted my feelings for him. How could he even think that wouldn't affect me?

And sure, I was talking to Evelyn, but I had told him that she knew how I felt for him, that she even encouraged me to tell him about my feelings. He knew that she wasn't trying to make a move on me anymore, but things with Vanessa were entirely different. She didn't know shit about us, and she seemed determined to get something out of Louis judging by the flirtatious look on her face. I wanted to throw up.

Thankfully, the bell rang only a minute later, and I didn't hesitate to stand up from my seat and leave the cafeteria. So much for thinking Louis was actually paying attention to me. I thought he was so aware of me that he noticed when I got upset earlier. Yeah, right. It was probably just a coincidence that he had caught the sad look on my face and asked me if I was alright.

"Hold up, Curly."

The sound of that nickname made a jolt go through my body and I couldn't help but shiver. God, sometimes I hated the fact that he had such a big effect on me.

Closing my eyes momentarily, I turned around to face the brown-haired boy. "What is it?"

He looked in the direction of the bathrooms. "Can we talk?"

I bit my bottom lip, my eyes following the people who were walking past us. "I'm going to be late for class," I mumbled, not knowing if I really cared about that. I just wanted an excuse not to go with him.

He took a step forward, looking me deep in the eyes. "Please."

Letting out a sigh, I started walking towards the bathroom, not looking back to see if he was following me. Since he was the one who wanted to talk in the first place, I figured I didn't need to check, though.

The second I entered the bathroom, I checked the stalls so no one was there. When I realized they were all empty, I turned around to face the person who had followed me into the room. Louis's face was in a scowl as he was staring at the floor in front of his feet.

"You're upset with me, aren't you?" He wondered, looking up to meet my gaze.

We walked further into the bathroom so we were standing a few feet away from each other. I was leaning against the sink while Louis was now standing with his back pressed against one of the stall doors. "I... Well, I can't say I'm happy with you," I admitted.

He took a step closer to me, but still kept a fair distance between us. "Is it because of Vanessa?" He guessed, his eyes boring into mine.

It was because of Vanessa, but it was also regarding the fact that even after everything we had gone through the last couple of days, he was still hiding something from me, and I didn't like that. We weren't supposed to keep secrets from each other... or at least in my opinion.

"Partly, yes."

He let out a sigh, running a hand through his brown fringe. "You know, I was pretty upset too. You kept paying attention to Evelyn, not even realizing that I was looking at you for two minutes straight. I wanted to talk to you, but you didn't even notice me."

"So you decided to be a child about it and do the same thing to me? How mature of you," I snorted, averting my gaze.

He shook his head, the scowl remaining on his face. "That wasn't it at all. I was genuinely concerned about you when you started closing in on yourself. I noticed how you stopped responding to Evelyn, and it worried me. When you told me everything was fine, I went back to talking to Vanessa, and yes, she might be a bit too much, but you know that I don't have any feelings for her," he explained, trying to get me to look at him.

"It doesn't matter that I know you don't feel anything for her. You have kissed her, and the last time was just a couple of days ago. Forgive me for not liking the fact that she's practically flirting with you right in front of my eyes. I think I have the right to be upset about it, don't you?" I fired back, my voice cold.

The scowl deepened on his face. "Evelyn was talking to you too," he muttered, crossing his arms over his chest.

"Exactly, Louis. That's the difference. She was *talking* to me. She knows that I have feelings for you. She fucking knows that it's never going to be us. Does Vanessa even have a clue that you don't want to be with her? No, she doesn't," I retorted, glaring at him.

He let his arms drop to his sides as he inhaled a deep breath. "Okay, so maybe you're right about that, but I can't just stop talking to her out of nowhere. People will get suspicious, and that's the last thing we want."

I let out a sigh, running a hand through my curls. He was right about that. People would get suspicious if Louis just stopped talking to Vanessa or any other girl that tried to get into his pants, but that didn't mean I liked it. "Can't you just... can't you at least try to show her that you're not interested?" I pouted, looking down at the floor.

Within a matter of two seconds, he moved forward to place his hands on my hips. "For your information, my dear friend, I'm not flirting back with anyone. I'm just being civil. I could never flirt with anyone now that there's only one person on my mind, and this person is the only one who gets to receive my charms."

I couldn't stop my heart from racing in my chest by his words. It still amazed me that these words were coming from him, the boy I had dreamed of being with for three years now. It was just surreal. "Since you just called me friend, I take it you're not talking about me," I joked, but I kept a straight look on my face in an attempt to seem serious.

He rolled his eyes, leaning in to brush his lips against mine. "No, it's definitely not you. Are you really that full of yourself?" He mumbled, taking my bottom lip between his teeth to pull at it teasingly.

I let out a gasp, reaching up to place my hands on his neck. "S-shut up."

He chuckled before finally leaning in to press his lips against mine in a proper kiss. I couldn't help but moan at the feeling, and I just wanted him closer to me, even if our chests were pressed together. I had noticed this was a common thought that appeared in my mind whenever we kissed.

The kiss was both passionate and eager as our lips worked with each other. Louis' hands were still placed on my hips, but he didn't waste many seconds until they found their way under my dark grey button-up so they were roaming my bare back instead. Meanwhile, I pulled at his feathery-brown locks, loving the feeling of them between my fingers.

Things only escalated when Louis licked his way into my mouth, his tongue finding mine in just a few seconds. It wasn't like I was stopping him. I didn't even stop him when he gripped the back of my thighs to pull me up on the sink, spreading my legs so he could stand between them.

I didn't hesitate to wrap my ankles around his waist, pulling him even closer to me. Everything was just so hot and messy at the same time, and I loved every second of it. It made my mind go blank to the point where I wasn't thinking anymore. The only thing I could focus on was Louis' lips against mine and his hands that were now trailing up my back under my shirt.

It was the sound of the bathroom door swinging open that made us jump apart. Louis didn't hesitate to pull me with him into one of the empty stalls, shutting the door behind us quickly. I was breathing heavily after our make out session, and so was Louis, but we did our best to keep quiet.

We could both hear how someone entered one of the other stalls and started taking a piss. I squeezed my eyes shut because I knew that if I kept them open, I would expose us by bursting into laughter.

I couldn't help but find the situation funny, and if I looked at Louis, I wouldn't be able to stop myself.

After hearing the person flush the toilet and leaving the stall and bathroom altogether, I let out a sigh of relief before finally letting out my laughter. Louis did too, which made me laugh even harder. It was quite difficult to do so in the small space we were in because our chests were almost touching from how close we had to stand, but we managed somehow.

As soon as our laughter died down, Louis looked down between our bodies. "I can't believe I'm still hard after that," he said, shaking his head in disbelief.

I cocked an eyebrow at him, bucking my hips to meet his. He hissed at the contact, placing his hands on my hips. "You're standing literally an inch away from the person who caused it in the first place. Why are you so surprised?" I chuckled.

He reached up to tap my nose. "Aren't you just the bluntest person out there?"

I tilted my head to the side, shrugging my shoulders innocently. "I'm just stating facts."

Louis let out a snort. Without saying anything, he moved the hand that was on my hip to touch the front of my pants, putting pressure on my obvious boner. I let out a loud gasp, reaching out to grip his bicep.

"Looks like I'm not the only one who's affected by the situation, eh?" He said, smiling cheekily at me.

"Fuck you," I muttered under my breath.

He leaned in to ghost his lips over the shell of my ear. "I'll gladly have sex with you sometime in the future, Curly."

With that, he pulled away and opened the door to exit the stall. I could feel myself losing the ability to stand up, so I leaned back against the wall of the stall, letting my back slide down it until I was sitting on the floor with my hands in my hair.

The only thing I could think was; what the *hell* was that?

Chapter 37

The rest of that day flew by in the blink of an eye. I didn't talk to Louis about what happened in the bathroom after that, and Niall never got an opportunity to interrogate me about what he wanted to say in the hallway that morning either.

Later in the evening, I found myself in my bed after an hour and thirty minutes long soccer practice. It should have probably been easy for me to fall asleep after that, but for some reason, my mind was spinning like crazy.

The first thing people would probably assume that kept me awake was the image of me and Louis kissing while being naked on my bed, but it wasn't. It wasn't even the image of him talking to Vanessa that did. She had left my mind the second Louis had made me go so weak in the knees that I had to sit down on the dirty bathroom floor. No. It was the fact that Louis had told me that Zayn specifically couldn't know about us that kept me awake.

It was something about the way he said it that made it impossible for me to stop thinking about it. He had said it with panic in his voice. When we talked about taking things slow and not telling people about us before, it was nothing like this.

It all made me start thinking about other situations when he had acted this way, and it didn't take long for me to realize that it had only happened when it had to do with his family. He had panicked when I almost followed him to his front door that time he was using crutches, afraid that I would find out about his family situation. He had panicked whenever one of us guys asked him if we could come over to his place when his parents were home. He had also panicked when he was afraid that the boys would find out that he got hurt at Emily's party.

And it was the last out of these three incidents that made me realize that this whole thing actually did have to do with his family. I could remember that I had asked Louis why the boys couldn't find out about what happened, and his answer was; *"You know that Zayn's parents work with mine, right?"*. Then he had told me that he didn't want his parents to find out about it.

So, that could only mean one thing; He didn't want Jay and Mark to know about us. Now, that didn't surprise me since they had never really cared about him in his entire life, so why would he want them to know? But there was something about the way he was panicking about it that made me think that there was more to it. It wasn't just because he didn't want them to know, it was something else.

I didn't figure it out that night. Instead, I finally managed to fall asleep, and if I did dream about Louis and I having sex on my bed, it was only for me to know. However, the dream continued after that. We stayed cuddling on my bed, our limbs tangled together while talking to each other. It reminded me of when we had cuddled on my bed only a couple of days ago after I had pushed him down on it and landed on his chest.

In a matter of seconds, the dream started changing, and I soon realized that it wasn't a dream anymore, but a memory.

"You're going to be the death of me," he mumbled against my skin, making me shiver.

"I-I think you're actually going to kill me first," I said breathlessly.

Chuckling against my neck, he tightened his hold around my body. "See you in hell then."

See you in hell then.

With a jerk, I woke up, snapping my eyes open. There was no way. There was no way it could be what I thought it was. I mean, Louis would have told me if that was the case, wouldn't he?

Suddenly feeling alert and more than ready to face the feathery-haired boy to get some answers, I scrambled out of bed and stumbled over to my closet to grab a black t-shirt and a pair of dark blue jeans. I rarely wore these pants. My go-to was black, skinny jeans, but I felt like trying something new today.

Thankfully, I was home alone. I was happy about it because mom and Gemma would have asked me why I was acting so weird. So, I went over to the fridge to pull out the butter and milk. After that, I put a slice of bread in the toaster before patiently waiting for it to pop.

I didn't know why (because I wasn't in a hurry), but I found myself stuffing my mouth with my breakfast, wanting Louis to get here as quickly as possible. The second I was finished, I noticed there were at least ten minutes until he would show up, so I went to the bathroom to fix my curls and brush my teeth, not wanting to have Louis point it out yet another time.

I was just finished putting my outdoor clothes on when a car honk was heard outside, so I didn't waste a second until I exited the house, locked the door behind me, and sprinted over to Louis' car with my bag slung over my shoulder.

Once I was sitting in the passenger seat, Louis turned to me, a look of confusion taking over his features. "What's got you in a hurry? Did you oversleep just like that other time?" He asked me, his gaze wandering to my hair.

When he noticed that it looked alright, a frown made its way to his face. I shook my head, letting a smile form on my lips. "No, I didn't oversleep. I woke up right on time actually."

"Then why were you just sprinting out of the house?" He wondered.

His words made me go silent because I didn't know how to confront him about what I had realized last night. How would I ask him without him getting all defensive? "Uh... I couldn't fall asleep yesterday because I was thinking of something..." I trailed off.

He seemed even more confused about this. "What does that have to do with you sprinting out of the house?"

I wanted to roll my eyes at him, but I decided not to. "If you had just let me finish, I would've gotten to that."

He pouted his lips, turning on the engine to start driving towards school.

"So, what I was saying is that I couldn't fall asleep because I was thinking of what you told me yesterday about you not wanting Zayn to know about us. I know you said that there was no specific reason behind it, but it reminded me of when you told me that you didn't want him to know that you had been hurt at Emily's party. It was because you didn't want your parents to know." I paused to see his reaction, noticing that he had tightened his grip on the steering wheel.

"So, I came to the conclusion that it was the same case now. You don't want your parents to know about us."

He opened his mouth to say something, but I held my hand up. "Let me finish first."

Closing his mouth, he pursed his lips, keeping his eyes on the road.

"I realized pretty quickly that there was more to it, though. You wouldn't just panic like that without a good reason, so I figured it couldn't just be because you don't want them to know. There's a reason you don't want them to find out, and I think I realized it when I was asleep."

I turned to him, looking at the side of his face. "You told me you'd see me in hell if we died."

He swallowed hard, nodding his head slowly.

Hesitantly, I inhaled a deep breath. "Is there... did... did your parents tell you that?" I asked very timidly, afraid he would get upset.

To my surprise, he only let out a sigh, loosening the tight grip he had on the wheel. "I didn't want you to know..." He trailed off, refusing to meet my gaze even for a second. "I didn't want you to know because I was ashamed."

I knitted my eyebrows together. "What are you ashamed of?"

Running a hand through his fringe, he bit his bottom lip. "I'm ashamed of myself for still listening to Mark's words when I know he's just a piece of shit," he explained, still not looking at me.

I reached over to take one of his hands in both of mine, squeezing it tightly. "Don't put yourself down for that, Lou. He's one of the people who brought you up, so of course you listen to what he says. That's what every son and daughter's mind is born to do. What about your mom, though? Doesn't she have the same mindset?" I couldn't help but ask because I was curious.

He shook his head with a grimace on his face. "Mom never spoke a word about it. Now that I think about it, she's been quiet almost my entire life. She's always followed Mark's orders, though," he huffed.

I pursed my lips, the scene of Jay showing up in the entryway at his house when I was just about to leave playing through my mind. Something was telling me she had wanted to say something but that she was afraid to do so.

"What exactly did he say to you?" I wondered, almost afraid of hearing the answer. If he mentioned people going to hell, then it couldn't be good.

Many seconds passed by without Louis saying anything. I assumed it was because he didn't know how to say it, but I wasn't sure. When he finally opened his mouth, he let out a deep sigh. "It's bad, Harry. He told me and my sisters that... that if we didn't find a partner of the opposite gender, bad things would happen to us. People would look down at us, they would find us disgusting and they would hate us. He also told us that we would end up in hell." He paused to finally look me in the eyes, pain filling his blue irises.

"I was ten when he told me this. Lottie was seven and Fizzy was five. I don't think Fizzy remembers it, but *I* recall it so clearly that I can hear his voice in my head, repeating those awful words over and over again. I know that's why it took so long for me to accept that I have feelings for you, and the fact that I still can't fully accept it kills me."

He looked down at his lap for a couple of seconds before looking up at the road. I squeezed his hand in mine, feeling nothing but sorry that he had to go through all this. "Please don't say that, Lou. It's okay. I understand why things are difficult for you, more so now than ever. Why didn't you just tell me?"

He shook his head with a grimace on his face. "I guess you know that I'm a person who likes to keep things to myself by now. That's one of the reasons. Another one is that I am ashamed, as I mentioned before. I'm so ashamed of myself that his awful words still affect me, that I still listen to them. I usually don't care about people's opinions, so it's embarrassing that such a sick person as Mark has managed to get through to me. That's why I never told you, Harry. I'm sorry," he apologized, squeezing my hands back.

I looked at him with a sad smile on my face. "Don't apologize for that, Lou. I get that it's difficult to talk about it, especially since I know about your family situation. I'm just happy that I finally know. It's so much easier for me to understand now that I know why you feel the way you do. And, I would never do anything you're uncomfortable with. You know that, right? You mean way too much to me," I said honestly, looking at the side of his face.

He turned to meet my gaze, a smile creeping to his lips. "Really?"

If only you knew.

"I am most certainly not lying to you right now if that's what you think."

He let out a light chuckle, shaking his head in disbelief. "I'm so happy that I managed to shake most of Mark's words out of my head because damn, I feel like the happiest human being sitting here with you right now," he breathed.

I couldn't help but smile at his words, feeling my heart flutter in my chest. "Don't go all sappy on me now, Tomlinson."

Letting out another chuckle, he brought my hands to his mouth, pressing a kiss to every knuckle on my hands. "I mean it."

I rolled my eyes, but couldn't help but love his affection. If we could be like this for the rest of our lives, I would die happy.

Not long after that, we arrived at school. Louis reached behind us to grab his bag from the backseat before we both got out of the car. We started walking to the lockers in silence, the back of our hands brushing together just like yesterday.

"So, what happens now?" I asked.

Louis looked at me in confusion. "What do you mean?"

I ran the hand that wasn't brushing against Louis' through my hair. "I just... I understand that you don't want Zayn to find out since there's a risk his parents will find out about it, but would it be okay if I told Niall? I know he is dying to know what's going on between us, but I also noticed how scared you were when you thought he knew about it yesterday."

He was quiet for a few seconds until he let out a sigh. "I... I wouldn't mind if you told Niall, I guess. I was just being paranoid, thinking that if he knew, he could have easily told Liam and Zayn as well. I was just afraid that everyone would find out, and if Mark knew what is going on, I don't know what would happen. I mean, sure, he already dislikes me, but if he found out that I like a guy, he would kick me out without a doubt. I would have nowhere to go, and I don't want my sisters to witness their dad doing something like that. Lottie and Fizzy are aware of how he treats me, but the twins are oblivious," he explained.

I moved my hand so it touched the back of his hand. No one would notice it if they looked, but Louis could feel it, and that was what mattered. "I understand, Lou. I'll make sure that Niall won't tell anyone, and I trust him. He found out about my sexuality, and he didn't tell a soul about it that I know of."

Louis nodded his head, sending me a small smile. "Yeah, you're probably right. Niall's not one to spread things around if he's been told not to," he agreed.

I nodded my head, feeling relieved that things had gone so smoothly. I was afraid that he would be more reluctant about explaining it all to me, but I should probably know by now that it never hurt to ask. Louis had even told me so himself. I guess I was just afraid he would get mad at me.

We had just entered the school building when Louis pulled me to the side where no one could see us, pressing my body against the wall. His action caught me so off guard that I could feel myself let out a loud gasp as I tried to register what was happening.

Before I had time to come to my full senses, he leaned in to seal our lips together, pressing his soft ones against mine in a sweet kiss. It took a moment for me to react, but when I did, I didn't hesitate to curl my arms around his neck, and he reached up to cup my cheeks.

After a few seconds, he pulled away with a wide smile on his lips, his ocean blue eyes gazing into my own. My brain was barely working as I stared at him, completely stunned by his actions. "What... what was that for?" I asked breathlessly.

His smile turned into a smirk as he tilted his head to the side. "I never got my morning kiss earlier, so I figured I'd have it now."

My mouth fell open as I stared at him in disbelief. "Why didn't you... you could have just asked me," I said, still breathless from his actions. He was just too much for me to handle.

"This was a lot more fun, though," he chuckled, and with that, he left me standing there with my back pressed against the wall, trying to get my brain to start working normally again, but it was hard since the boy who had caused me to feel this way in the first place was all I could think about.

It wasn't until lunch break that same day I finally caught Niall alone at the lockers. I had just left class and was planning to get rid of my books when I saw him standing there, his back facing me.

"Hey, Niall," I greeted, making him turn around to face me.

His mouth formed the shape of an 'o' when he saw it was me, his eyebrows shooting up. "Harry. I didn't expect you out of all people to talk to me," he replied, shutting his locker behind him.

I furrowed my eyebrows together. "What do you mean?"

He shrugged his shoulders, averting his gaze. "It just seems like you've been avoiding me lately," he mumbled.

Letting out a sigh, I bit my bottom lip. "I'm sorry, Niall. It wasn't my intention. I just... I have something to tell you actually, and I think it's something you'd like to know."

His face lit up at my words and he instantly turned to meet my gaze. "Really? You're finally going to give me some answers?"

I felt bad for treating Niall this way. We had talked about Louis a lot before things eventually started happening between us, and now that they did, I had pretty much ignored him. It wasn't fair to him, and if there was someone who deserved to know what was happening, it was him. I mean, I would probably not know half of the things about Louis today if it wasn't for this boy.

I searched my surrounding to make sure that no one was listening before I opened my mouth to explain. "Yes, but you have to promise not to tell anyone, okay? Not even Liam and Zayn."

He seemed confused about this but nodded his head anyway. "Of course, I promise. But what's so secret that they can't know about it?"

Inhaling a deep breath, I ran a hand through my curls. "Louis and I kind of have something going on?" I explained, but it came out more as a question than a statement.

His eyes widened in surprise as his jaw dropped open. "What? Harry... why didn't you tell me?" He gaped, staring at me in shock.

I let out a sigh, pursing my lips. "It's new, very new. It only happened this Saturday," I explained, meeting his blue eyes.

He seemed even more surprised about this. "But it's Tuesdays today! You've had what? Three days to tell me now," he whined, his lips forming a pout.

I couldn't help but chuckle at his reaction. "I'm sorry, Ni. I told you now, though, didn't I?" I said in an attempt to cheer him up.

It worked because his pout was gone in the next second, replaced by a small smile. "Well, I guess. How did it happen, though? Was it at the party? You have to tell me *everything*, alright? You're not getting away this time, Harry."

And so I did... almost. I didn't tell him everything. I left out the parts about Louis' insecurities and everything that had to do with his family. I told him how I had seen him with Vanessa at the party, how that made something snap inside me, resulting in me confessing how I felt for him. I told Niall how I had run away after Louis kissed me, how I eventually found my way home and thought I had ruined everything. I also told him that Louis surprised me in the morning by sitting on the floor at my bedroom door, ready to tell me that he felt the same way.

By the time I was finished, we were in the cafeteria, ready to buy our food. "Oh my God, that is so cute. He was actually in your room when you woke up?"

I nodded with a smile on my face, feeling giddy just thinking about the memory of seeing him the first thing I did the morning after I thought I had ruined everything. It must be one of the greatest surprises I had ever experienced.

"I can't believe two of my best friends are dating," he gushed, fanning his face with his hand as if it would help him understand it better. "This is fucking gold."

I couldn't help but laugh at him. "You can't tell anyone, though, okay?" I told him, raising my eyebrows.

He sipped his lips shut with his fingers. "I won't tell a soul, I promise."

But even if he promised not to tell anyone, it didn't stop him from throwing me and Louis suggestive glances during the entire lunch break. And, I was sure it didn't go unnoticed by Louis because he kept giving me looks of confusion, probably wondering what the hell was going on.

So, if I hit Niall across the head once we had left the cafeteria, no one had to know.

Chapter 38

The days went by, and things didn't change very much. Louis and I still kept things a secret although he got more and more affectionate in public every day. I was surprised every time he discretely patted me on the bum when I was about to walk away, or when he leaned in to whisper things in my ear when the boys were around.

I didn't mind, though. If anything, it made me happy. It made me feel like he really liked me because if he even went so far as to show me affection in public when he had told me he was afraid that Mark would find out about us, then it must really mean something. Plus, I had a feeling it was also because he was starting to warm up to be with me in public.

Niall wasn't being very subtle either. Even if he had kept his word about not telling anyone, he kept teasing us when only we were around. It made me want to hit him. Not because he was being too obvious, but because it was embarrassing.

The funny part was that Louis didn't mind. A few days after I had told him the reason Niall had kept giving us suggestive looks that time in the cafeteria, he started playing along with Niall. If he didn't flash him a wink in return, he would prove his point by doing something to me, like wiggle his eyebrows, pat my thigh under the table or send me a knowing look. These gestures only added to the list of reasons I was sure Louis really liked me. Not that I doubted it, but it made me feel warm inside.

It was Friday today, the day we were going to Manchester to play a soccer game. We had just finished school, and the whole team was gathered in the parking lot, waiting for the bus that would take us there to arrive.

Since we were going directly after school, we had to bring our soccer gear with us in the morning, which would have been a pain in the ass if it weren't for the fact that I had a personal driver nowadays, so I could keep my bag in Louis' car during the school day. I was sure it would have never fit in my locker.

It was late February, meaning that it was still chilly outside. Even though I had my winter jacket on, I couldn't help but shiver as we stood there, waiting for the bus to arrive. Louis was right by my side, but so were the other boys. Judging by the concerned glances he kept sending me, I had a feeling he wanted to wrap his arms around me and keep me warm. It was just sad that he couldn't.

Thankfully, the bus showed up just a few minutes after that, and I didn't hesitate to hop on as soon as it pulled over and the doors opened. Louis told me he would put my bag in the luggage compartment so I could get into the warmth as quickly as possible. I definitely didn't turn down that offer.

I sat down in the middle of the bus, choosing the window seat because one, I really wanted to sit there, and two, so it would be easier for the person who would choose to sit with me to settle down. I crossed my fingers that Louis would get here before anyone else.

Thankfully, Liam, Niall, Zayn and Louis were among the first people who entered the bus after me, and they all walked over to where I was sitting.

"Can I ask you why you decided to sit down in the middle of the bus out of all places?" Zayn asked, raising an eyebrow at me.

I pouted my lips. "I like the middle, Zayn."

He arched his eyebrows. "Really? Because you never want to sit in the middle of the backseat in the car."

"Oh, sod off, Zayn. That's not even the same thing. If Harry wants to sit here, then so be it. It's just a seat anyway," Louis butted in, not hesitating to plop down next to me.

I gave him an appreciating smile while Zayn looked at Louis weirdly. "Where the fuck did you even come from?" He huffed, turning around to sit down in the seat in front of us. Liam and Niall had already settled down beside us, ignoring Zayn's complaints.

Thankfully, the black-haired boy kept quiet after that, plugging in his earphones to shut every sound out. I turned to Louis who was scrolling through his phone and nudged him lightly in the side to gain his attention. He looked up, shooting me a small smile.

"You still cold?" He wondered, eyeing me.

I shook my head but decided to snuggle into his side anyway. "No, but you're really warm," I sighed happily.

He let out a chuckle, wrapping his arm around my waist to pull me even closer to him. It was a good thing that there was no handle between us. Otherwise, it would have been crushing my hip right now. "You wanna listen to some music?" He offered, pulling out his earphones from the pocket of his jacket and plugging them into his phone.

"Sure, but only if I get to choose a few songs," I said cheekily, making him raise his eyebrows at me.

"Last time I checked, it's my phone and earphones. Also, I'm the one who asked in the first place, so shouldn't I get to decide what music we're listening to then?"

I tilted my head to the side, pinching my chin with my forefinger and thumb as if thinking about it. "Let me think... No."

He rolled his eyes, handing me his phone in defeat. "Fine, but only because I'm kind," he smirked.

I cocked a knowing eyebrow at him as I took the phone from his hand. "You would have never agreed if I was someone else, would you?"

He pursed his lips for a few seconds. "Probably not, no," he chuckled, making my lips twitch.

"I knew it. I can't believe Louis Tomlinson has a weak spot for me," I gushed, fanning my face with my hand dramatically.

He rolled his eyes. "Just choose your damn songs before I change my mind."

With a content smile on my face, I did as told. While I scrolled through his Spotify playlists to find some good songs, none other than Ryan, Derek and Tristan decided to walk by. Ryan caught sight of us immediately and scrunched his nose up. "Disgusting," he muttered, and I could instantly feel how Louis tensed beside me.

To my surprise, he relaxed the second I placed my hand on his arm in reassurance. However, his calmness only lasted for a second until he clenched his hands into tight fists. "Shut the fuck up, Ryan," he fumed, making Ryan roll his eyes.

Thankfully, no more words were uttered after that, and Ryan, Tristan and Derek continued walking to the back of the bus. Louis only relaxed when they were entirely gone, leaning his head back while exhaling a deep breath.

"Don't listen to him, Lou. He's just trying to provoke you," I said, rubbing his thigh reassuringly.

I was glad that no one could see us. Niall was the only one who was able to watch our every move since he was sitting in the seat next to us (only the aisle in between), but he was too busy scrolling through his phone. Besides, if he was the one who saw us doing something we shouldn't in front of people, it wouldn't be the end of the world. Other than him, only people who walked by could see us, and since no one was doing so at the moment, I felt as though I could touch Louis' thigh without having to worry about it.

"I know," he mumbled, staring at the seat in front of him. "I just fucking hate his attitude."

I let out a sigh. "Yeah, me too, but I've come to realize that there's nothing to do about it. I mean, I'm pretty sure there's nothing that will make him change anyway."

He was quiet for a few seconds, keeping his gaze on the seat in front of him. It wasn't hard to tell that he was lost in his thoughts, probably thinking about what I had just told him and about Ryan and his behavior.

Meanwhile, I decided to keep looking for some good songs on Louis' phone. It took me a while, but when I was finished, I picked up the earphones that were scattered across our laps, handing him one of the buds while putting the other in my ear.

When he didn't react, I let out a sigh, nudging him in the side once again. "Come on, Lou. Stop thinking about him. He's not worth it."

He turned to meet my gaze, a small smile forming on his lips as he took the bud in his hand. "You're right. He's not worth it."

I flashed him a smile in return, pressing play once he had put the bud in his ear too. I had barely acknowledged the fact that the bus had started moving, but when I found myself drowsing in my seat, I could feel the tires bumping against the asphalt.

Only minutes after that, I was falling asleep, and the last thing I remembered was how my head fell on Louis' shoulder.

The ride to Manchester only lasted for forty-five minutes, so it wasn't long until the bus came to a stop and I woke up with a jerk. We all exited the bus and grabbed our bags from the luggage compartment before heading into the gym. We were still playing indoors, but on fake grass, which was a relief since I didn't like the cold very much.

Once the entire team was in the locker room, we started changing into our gears while Coach was sitting on the bench in one of the corners, going through his papers. It wasn't until we all had changed that he got up, pacing the small space in the room.

"Alright, boys, we have an important game today. This team is the only one above us in the series, so if we win today, we're going to surpass them. Therefore, I expect you all to play your very best this evening, alright?" He said, his eyes flicking between every player on the team.

"Yes, Coach," we all replied in unison.

"Great, and I don't want to see anyone misbehave out there today. If you play unfairly, I won't hesitate to kick you off the team, and I mean it this time," he continued, his eyes boring into Ryan's pointedly.

"Okay, boys. I want you all to be out on the pitch in five minutes. See you then."

With that said, Coach left the locker room after closing the door behind him. The second he was gone, people started getting up from the benches to chat with each other. Louis was sitting beside me, but we didn't utter a word until Niall walked over with his phone in his hand.

"Guys, I need to show you this," he smiled fondly as he squeezed himself in between us.

I was a bit confused about what he was talking about, but the second I saw the screen of his iPhone, it all made sense. It was a picture of me and Louis that he had taken on the bus. My head was on Louis' shoulder and my legs were thrown over his lap while he had his arms wrapped around my waist securely.

What made the entire thing even cuter was that we were both sleeping, unaware of what was going on. The only thing I recalled was falling asleep with my head on his shoulder, not that I had pretty much been lying on top of him.

"Aww, look at that. Don't we look cute, Curly?" Louis gushed, taking the phone from Niall's hands to inspect the picture closer.

I didn't have time to say anything until he opened his mouth again, his eyebrows in a frown now. "You were the only one who saw us like this, though, right?" He looked at Niall who waved a hand in dismissal.

"Of course. I think pretty much everyone fell asleep on the bus except for me, so don't worry about it. Besides, no one was sitting around us except for Zayn and Liam, and they were both sound asleep," he promised.

Louis nodded his head, the smile returning to his face.

"Alright, Louis, I need my phone back," Niall said, trying to take the device from the boy's hand, but Louis held it out of his reach.

"Wait, I'm just going to send it to myself first," the feathery-haired boy objected.

I could feel my lips curl at his words. It made me all warm and fussy inside, knowing Louis liked the picture so much that he wanted to have it on his phone. It seemed like Niall could sense my joy because he nudged me in the side with his elbow teasingly while wiggling his eyebrows.

I rolled my eyes at my friend, elbowing him back, but harsher than he had done. It made him let out a wince, rubbing the sore spot on his ribcage through his jersey. "Damn, Harry. Couldn't you have been a little gentler?" He whined.

"You're such a wimp, Nialler," I chuckled, getting up from the bench to leave the locker room. I could hear him huff behind me on my way out, and I couldn't help but shake my head in amusement.

I could hear Niall trying to get his phone back from Louis once again, and when he finally did, they both followed me to the pitch along with all the other boys on the team.

The opposing team was already warming up when we got there, but by the looks of it, they had just started doing so. Seeing the pitch, the opponents and the bleachers right before my eyes instantly made excitement well up inside me. This was one of the greatest feelings in the world; the adrenaline running through your body before a soccer game.

We started warming up as well, and I could feel myself getting more and more pumped the more time that passed by. I could tell Louis noticed it judging by the way he raised his eyebrows at me, but I decided to only shoot him a smile in return.

The game kicked off soon enough, and just like the game we had played a few weeks ago, I could feel the same energy among the team. Everyone was excited, and we all really wanted to win. Only this time, Louis was playing with us too.

Manchester was great, there was no denying it. They scored the first goal only ten minutes into the game, the people on the bleachers going crazy while the players hugged the guy who had scored the goal. Some people would probably think that would make us lose the energy we had going on, but it had the opposite effect. It only made us want to score a goal of our own.

And so we did. Niall passed the ball to me, and I started running towards the opponents' goalkeeper, dribbling past a guy who tried to slide tackle me. Looking up, I noticed that Louis was free on the other side of the pitch, so I didn't hesitate to kick the ball over to him. He easily received it, looking up towards the goalkeeper that was only a few yards away before swinging his leg back to shoot.

Score.

My heart fluttered in my chest in both pride and happiness, and I wasn't the only one who ran over to congratulate him. I made sure to give him a tight hug before pulling away to run back to my position.

Sadly, things didn't go quite as well after that. Manchester scored two goals and we none before the referee blew his whistle to signal that the first half of the game was over.

Coach was not happy when he entered the locker room, his eyes traveling between each player of the team. "I'm not proud of you this evening, boys. They're great, but I know you can do much better than this. I saw the energy in your eyes during the first fifteen minutes, but then it just vanished. What happened, guys? Don't you want to win this match?"

We were all quiet for a few seconds until we muttered; "Yes, we do, Coach."

"Then go out there and show me how much you want this because you are not proving it right now."

We hummed in reply, and I could feel myself looking down at the floor while pursing my lips. What happened to the excitement? What happened to the adrenaline? And what happened to having fun?

Louis got up from the bench then, turning to look at us. "Coach is right, guys. We're not playing our best. I've seen us do way better than this, and the last time was in the game only a couple of weeks ago. Don't you remember the feeling of having fun while doing what we all love? That's what we need tonight, guys. We need the adrenaline, we need the motivation, and we need the desire to win. That's what's going to turn this game around. If we go out there with all these things in our minds, there's no one stopping us from winning tonight. What do you guys say?"

The smiles that broke out on our faces were proof enough that Louis succeeded in his speech and the loud cheers that erupted added to it.

It was at that moment I realized just how much Louis deserved the scholarship. He was made to do this, play soccer while bringing his team to the top. He was just amazing, and I was nothing but proud of him. What only added to it all was the wide smile on his lips at this very second because anyone could tell just how much he loved doing this. It was his dream, and I could no longer see why I would get the scholarship to play for Arsenal instead of him, why I *should* get it because I had never seen myself as a professional soccer player in my future. Don't get me wrong, I loved the sport to bits, but I had never really pictured myself playing in a big stadium with thousands of people on the bleachers cheering for me and my team. I was sure Louis had, though.

A few minutes later, we exited the locker room to go back to the pitch. I could see Coach shooting Louis a smile when we left, and I could tell he was impressed. I was too, so it didn't surprise me.

What did surprise me, however, was that Louis patted me on the bum when we separated to leave for our positions. It made a blush form on my cheeks because we were right in front of so many people. What in the world made him do that?

Before I could think more about it, the referee blew the whistle to start up the game again. The atmosphere among the team had changed drastically. Everyone had gained a fighting spirit, and I could tell by the way we were all radiating it.

As soon as the opponents had the ball, a guy on our team was there immediately to steal it, and when they succeeded, we all started moving towards their goal with adrenaline pumping in our veins.

It was only five minutes into the second half of the game that we scored a goal, Zayn kicking the ball right into the net behind their goalie. And ten minutes after that, it was Trevor's turn to do the same thing, which meant it was now 3-3.

Manchester started getting back on track after that, and they got a lot of chances to score on Liam, but he saved all of the shots that were aimed at him. It was now only five minutes left of the game, and it was still a tie.

Ryan snitched the ball from one of the opponents, and we all started running towards their net. He passed the ball to Tristan, who dribbled past a guy easily before kicking the ball over to Niall who was closer to the opponents' goal. The blonde-haired boy received it with a light touch, looking up to see what his next move should be.

I was standing in the target area, trying to stay away from the opponents as best as I could, and Louis was on the other side, doing the same thing. When Louis made sure he was free, Niall passed him the ball. Meanwhile, I ran closer to the goal, signaling that I was free to head the ball into the net.

Louis noticed this and didn't waste a second to kick the ball towards me. I fought my way through the guys that were trying to block me and jumped just as the ball came flying towards me. With a lot of determination, I headed the ball, turning my head to send it towards the goal.

The goalie tried to reach it as best as he could, and it touched his fingertips, but he couldn't save it. The ball went right into the net, causing loud cheers to erupt behind me. I looked up only to see my team celebrating by hugging each other. Niall came running towards me, enveloping me in a tight hug.

"You fucking made it!" He screamed in my ear.

It wasn't until then it dawned on me what had happened, and a wide smile broke out on my face while my body exploded with exhilaration. When Niall let go of me and I could see Louis smiling at me not too far away, I couldn't help myself. Without thinking twice, I ran up to him and jumped, hugging him tightly with my legs wrapped around his waist.

He didn't hesitate to grip my thighs to hold me up, chuckling against the skin on my neck. "I'm so proud of you, babe."

If my body wasn't already filled with joy, it definitely was now. Babe. He called me *babe*.

With my arms around his neck, I hugged him tighter, burrowing my nose in his sweaty, feathery hair. He smelled absolutely amazing. I was sure this boy couldn't smell bad even if he wanted to. There were just no words that could describe how much I loved him. I would scream it out right now if I could, but that would be a very bad idea, which hugging him like this probably was too.

But, I couldn't bring myself to care because I never wanted to let go of him.

Chapter 39

It surprised me how oblivious Liam and Zayn seemed to be about me and Louis. Actually, it surprised me how oblivious *everyone* seemed to be about us considering we were a bit more touchy than just two friends, but no one had commented on it. Well, no one but Ryan, Niall, Gemma and mom, and Ryan had pointed it out long before we were even a thing.

Louis slowly but surely started warming up to my family. He didn't find it as hard to show affection towards me when they were around anymore, and maybe that was because they didn't point it out every time they saw us in the same room.

But even though he was warming up, he would still get a bit edgy if they or anyone else commented on us sometimes, but I didn't expect anything else. These things took time to get used to and accept, especially if you had been taught that homosexuality was wrong right from the start.

It was now Thursday, almost a week after the game in Manchester, and Louis and I were just about to enter my house after a day at school. I was going to work in just a short while, but we both wanted to spend some time together before that, so I suggested going to my place and eat something before he drove me to the diner.

I kicked off my shoes and shrugged off my jacket in the entryway, noticing that Louis was doing the same thing out of the corner of my eye. I kept glancing at him as he struggled to get his shoe off, hopping on one foot while pulling at it.

I couldn't help but burst into laughter, muffling it the best I could with the back of my hand since he was shooting me a glare. "Don't laugh at me, you curly-headed wanker," he whined, finally managing to get the shoe off.

"I'm sorry, but that must be the funniest thing I've ever seen," I laughed, dropping my hand from my mouth. It was a Vans shoe, a fucking Vans shoe, and he couldn't get it off.

He narrowed his eyes at me, and before I knew it, I was lifted into the air and thrown over his shoulder. I let out a loud squeal at the sudden action while he held my legs in a tight grip. It wasn't until then I opened my eyes and was met with quite the sight; his butt. "Why thank you for this beautiful view," I chuckled, smacking his bum pointedly.

"Heeey," he warned. "Don't touch the most precious part of my body."

"Why, though? I quite enjoy it," I said, tapping one of his ass cheeks.

"Harold Styles, don't you dare."

Chuckling, I finally dropped my hand, and we entered the kitchen. Since I couldn't see anything but Louis' behind, I didn't know why he came to a sudden stop until another voice was heard. "Honestly, guys, I think I'm in love with your relationship. Can I have it?"

Louis relaxed just a second after Gemma had spoken and let out a chuckle. "We're not exactly in a relationship yet, so that would be pretty sad for you," he said, and I could practically see Gemma roll her eyes.

Yet.

I didn't know if that word was supposed to make my stomach erupt with butterflies, but it did.

"Louis, would you please put me down? I'm quite positive my head's getting too much blood," I pointed out, reaching under his black t-shirt to pinch the skin at the bottom of his spine.

He winced slightly and instantly put me down on the floor. "Damn, you didn't have to pinch me to make me listen to you," he whined, making me raise an eyebrow at him.

"So you mean you wouldn't have protested at all?"

He nodded, a smirk playing on his lips. "Of course not."

I rolled my eyes, turning to Gemma who was still studying us from the kitchen table. "Hey, Gems," I greeted, a wide smile breaking out on my face.

"Hi, H," she smiled back.

I turned around to pull out two packages of noodles from the cabinet when she suddenly said; "Hey, Louis. Did you know that Harry used to think you had a crush on me?"

I turned around just in time to see amusement take over her features. "Gemma!" I gasped.

"What? It's true," she chuckled, turning to see Louis' amused face.

He glanced at me, the smirk never leaving his lips as he wiggled his eyebrows teasingly. "You actually thought I was crushing on your sister? I thought you were only joking that time."

I pulled my eyebrows together, a pout forming on my lips. "It wasn't even weird for me to think so. She actually made you change your mind about not wanting to go home that morning after Emily's party," I muttered, looking away from his intimidating blue eyes.

He reached up to pinch my cheek. I didn't know how or why, but I couldn't help but love it. "Aw, sweet little Curly thought he wasn't my first choice," he joked, making my pout only grow.

But then I remembered that he shouldn't be one to talk. "Hey, you thought I was crushing on Lottie too," I pointed out, the pout instantly leaving my face to be replaced by a cheeky smile.

He pursed his lips, looking away from me. The action made it obvious that my words were true (which I already knew), and I couldn't help but nudge him in the side teasingly. "Seems like you shouldn't be one to talk, eh?"

He rolled his eyes while Gemma shook her head in disbelief but also amusement. "You guys are really something. For all I know, you could have still been going around thinking that the other didn't have feelings for you. You must be the most oblivious people I've ever met."

With that said, she got up from her chair and walked over to put her tea mug in the dishwasher before leaving the kitchen. I turned to Louis with raised eyebrows only to notice that he was already smiling at me.

"Let's make some noodles."

My shift at the diner was pretty okay, and it was all thanks to Lucas and the fact that we barely had any customers. It made it possible for us to talk much more than we would have otherwise.

"Did you see his face?" Lucas laughed, his eyes widened in amusement. "He looked like he wanted to be anywhere but with that girl. What if it was a set-up? What if their parents forced them to go on a date together?"

We were standing behind the counter, and since we had nothing better to do, we had been inspecting the customers. There was a young couple who had been sitting at the windows, and the boy had been staring at anything but the girl while she had been talking nonstop. Maybe that was the problem, but who knew? They had just left the diner, thus why Lucas had started talking about them.

"I have no idea, Lucas, but I'm pretty sure it won't last," I chuckled, and he nodded his head in agreement, the smile never leaving his face.

"You think she was talking about herself and didn't listen to what the boy had to say? I swear that's like a common issue these days. One of the two in the relationship is too self-centered, and that's when it all goes downhill," he said, shaking his head with a faint smile.

I couldn't help but think about me and Louis, and how this couple was far from how we were. The thought of listening to what he had to say wasn't even something that crossed my mind. It just came naturally because I cared so much about him.

Before either Lucas or I could say anything else, the doorbell went off, signaling that a new customer had just entered the diner. The second I looked up, I could feel how every muscle in my body went rigid, my eyes widening.

Lucas noticed my reaction and furrowed his eyebrows. "Do you know that woman?"

The closer the brown-haired female got, the clammier my hands went. What was she doing here? She never visited the diner, or not that I knew of. I had only ever seen her kids here.

Her blue eyes that were so familiar I couldn't help but gulp stared into my own, a small, hesitant smile making its way to her features. She seemed nervous, and honestly, I felt the exact same way.

"Harry," she said, her voice soft and her eyes twinkling slightly. "I'm so glad to see you. I was hoping you'd be here."

I opened my mouth to reply but nothing came out. I squeezed my eyes shut and swallowed down some saliva before trying again. "Johannah," I croaked. "I... Why would you want to see me?"

She looked down at the floor, her eyelashes fluttering. "I'd like to talk to you... about Louis."

I had a hard time processing everything that was going on, but what was the hardest to register was that she was actually here. Sure, I had caught the apologetic look on her face when I had been about to leave their house that evening, but I never expected this to happen. Why did she want to talk to *me*?

Looking around at my surroundings, I caught Lucas sending me a small smile. "It's okay, Harry. We barely have any customers, so I'm sure we'll manage without you for a while," he reassured me.

Johannah flashed him an appreciating look before turning to meet my gaze. "Only if you're okay with it, though, Harry."

I nodded my head slowly, averting my gaze from her. I didn't want to come off as rude, but knowing the way she had treated Louis his whole life made it hard to be entirely nice to her. However, I had a feeling she was hiding something, and I'd felt this way ever since she joined me in the entryway that evening.

We made our way to the secluded table that Louis usually sat at when he was here and settled down opposite each other. She folded her hands on the table, looking down at them with pursed lips. Her brown hair was falling down her shoulders perfectly, looking as though she had just been to the stylist. All in all, she radiated poshness, which wasn't surprising considering I knew how rich she was.

I swallowed hard, furrowing my eyebrows. "How did you know I work here?" I asked, still taken aback by the fact that she was actually here.

Her lips formed a faint smile. "I asked Lottie. She's had a crush on you for ages, so I figured she'd know things about you," she explained, looking up at me.

The crease between my eyebrows deepened. "But why? Why do you want to talk to me?"

She inhaled a deep breath, fiddling with her fingers on the table. "I... First of all, I wanted to apologize for the way we treated you when you were over at our house. It was extremely disrespectful of us, and I'm really sorry. I..." Her face turned into a scowl. "I guess you took us by surprise. Louis' never... he's never brought a friend over before, not when we've been around. You know that, right?"

I nodded, swallowing hard.

Her lips curled as she looked down at her hands. "I'm so happy he found you, Harry. When you were sitting there at the kitchen table, I noticed the way Louis was looking at you, and it warmed my heart. Ever since he was a little kid, all I've ever wanted is for him to be happy because he deserves the world." She paused to shake her head, fighting back tears. "He's my baby, my firstborn. He'll always have a special place in my heart even if he doesn't think so."

Jay wiped the few tears that had fallen from her eyes, laughing dryly. "God, I'm sorry about this, Harry. I didn't mean to come here and cry. I just... I know that Louis doesn't think I love him because I've been an awful mother to him ever since he was a kid, but I didn't mean for things to turn out this way. I swear I didn't."

I reached over to place a reassuring hand on top of both of hers, giving them a light squeeze while sending her a small smile.

She returned it through her tears. "You know about our family situation, don't you?"

I nodded, looking down at the surface of the table.

"I figured. If he went as far as to bring you to our house when we were home, I assumed he had told you. So, you know that Mark isn't Louis' real father then, yeah?"

"Yeah," I breathed, my gaze meeting hers.

She let out a sigh, sending me a painful look. "I didn't know Mark had anything against Louis until a few years after we got married and Lottie was born. When I noticed, it was already too late. I just... I couldn't just leave and start over all over again, and with two kids this time. Troy ruined me when he left me and Louis, so when I found Mark, I thought everything was finally going to be alright. I *wanted* things to be alright. I guess I was blinded by that, the image of wanting everything to be perfect. I was so blinded by it that I didn't notice the way my husband treated my own son."

She inhaled a deep breath. "He didn't... he didn't like the fact that Louis wasn't his. He told me after a few years when I confronted him about it. I didn't know how to react because Louis was my treasure, my sweet little creature that I first didn't expect but made my life so much better. I don't think I would have ever managed the loss I felt when Troy left me just a week after he was born if it wasn't for him and the joy he brought me. It killed me when Mark said he could never like Louis because he wasn't his, but I couldn't bring myself to end things with him," she sniffled, reaching up to wipe the tears that were rolling down her cheeks.

"I've hated myself for it every single day ever since. And believe it or not, but things only got worse after that. Mark made sure I treated Louis the same way he did because he didn't want Louis to feel like he was part of the family. I just... I can't believe I went along with it all these years. My little Louis... he never deserved any of it."

Jay looked me in the eyes, her own ones red from crying. "That's why I was so happy when I saw you with him, Harry. I'm so glad he found you, and I am sure you care about him just as much as he cares about you because Louis wouldn't tell all this to anyone. I hope you realize how much you mean to him."

I let out a shaky breath, feeling my heart pound loudly in my chest. "I... He means a lot to me too," I told her honestly.

She sent me a small smile. "I noticed that during the dinner too, and if you're more than just friends, I'm only happy for you guys. All I've ever wanted is for Louis to find someone he loves and someone who loves him just as much in return. Mark has another view on it, but I never cared. Love is love."

My heart nothing but exploded in my chest because those were the exact same words Louis had told me when I admitted that I was bisexual to him. This woman in front of me was definitely the lady who had brought Louis up, and even if she wasn't in the picture during the majority of his life, she had been there at the start, and I was certain Louis knew that. Somewhere deep down, he must know that his mom loved him.

I shook my head in disbelief, feeling speechless by everything she had just confessed to me. Was this woman the same one who had been sitting at the kitchen table that evening? Because this woman was so different from her. I mean, sure, I had been positive that she was hiding something, but I didn't expect this. This was huge.

"Yeah, I guess," I finally said, not wanting to admit anything because I knew Louis would kill me, even if she wouldn't tell Mark.

Jay inhaled a deep breath, taking my hand that was still on top of hers to squeeze it. "I'm sorry that I just came here and threw all this at you. I just... I just had to tell you how happy I am that he found you, that he finally has someone who cares for him the way he deserves to be cared for when I... when I couldn't be that person."

She looked down at the surface of the table with tears running down her damp cheeks. I could feel my own eyes well up at her words, my heart breaking in my chest. It was so sad, the way things had turned out. If only Jay would have found a man who wasn't such a heartless human being, things would have been completely different now.

Louis wouldn't have a hard time believing that people cared about him, he wouldn't distance himself from everyone when he didn't want anyone to find out about something, and he wouldn't have felt as though he was doing something wrong when he started falling for me.

I wiped my cheeks with the hand that wasn't in between Jay's. "I've cared for Louis ever since we became friends, and I'm not planning to stop doing so anytime soon, I promise."

She sent me a sad smile, giving my hand another squeeze. "Thank you, Harry."

I shook my head, furrowing my eyebrows together. "No need to thank me, Jay. It's just come naturally to me. However, I think Louis would appreciate it if you told him the truth. He deserves to know that you never stopped caring about him, that Mark is the devil here and not you," I said.

Looking down at our hands, she nodded slowly. "Yeah, you're right. I've always been afraid that Mark would find out, which is why I never told him the truth. Lately, though, ever since Louis found out that Mark's not his real dad, I've had this longing to tell him everything because he deserves to know, and I *want* him to know. Mark will get mad if he finds out, but I can't bring myself to care anymore. Louis is an adult now, and he might be leaving the house in just a matter of months. I just... I can't let him leave without him knowing the truth. And if Mark leaves me, then I guess I will have to deal with that then. I just want my baby back before it's too late."

I sent her a sad smile, understanding that things were difficult for her. It was either Mark, the husband she had come to love over fifteen years ago, the man she thought she would share the rest of his life with, or Louis, her son, the boy who was her own flesh and blood. Sure, Mark was a horrible man, but if Jay had been willing to put up with him all this time, she must really love him, and I couldn't blame her for that.

"Do what you feel is the right thing to do. I understand that it's hard for you, and no one else can make this decision, Jay. It's up to you, although I'm sure Louis would love to know the truth."

She nodded, her lips curling slightly. "I'm glad I came here, Harry. You're good for him, I know you are. Whatever happens, promise me you'll always be there for him, please."

I gave her hands a squeeze. "I promise, Jay."

Her lips spread into a whole-hearted smile. "Alright, I probably shouldn't hold you up anymore. You've got a job to return to," she said, nodding in the direction of the counter pointedly.

I waved my hand in dismissal. "Oh, don't worry about that. I'm happy you came here and told me all this."

She shook her head. "It was a pleasure. I am so happy he found you, honestly. Take care of him, Harry, yeah?"

Smiling, I nodded. "Always."

Chapter 40

I didn't know what I expected when seeing Louis the next morning, but I certainly didn't expect him to be staring out the windshield with a clenched jaw. When I greeted him, he didn't even turn to look at me. He just mumbled a quiet 'morning'. It made me feel uneasy, to say the least. I mean, when he had dropped me off at the diner yesterday, things had been great. Nothing but absolutely great.

The entire car ride was quiet except for the music that was blaring through the speakers. Louis had turned the volume up pretty high, but I was too taken aback by his behavior to complain about it.

Once we arrived at school, I was staring out the door window with a beating heart. I didn't know what I had done wrong, but it was certainly something judging by the way he was acting towards me. I wanted to confront him about it, but when I turned to him, he was already out of the car.

I closed my eyes, slumping back against the seat. What the hell was going on? Why was he acting this way? As far as I knew, things were going great, nothing but absolutely fantastic. I didn't understand anything.

I got out of the car eventually, not even caring about the fact that it would stay unlocked since Louis had already left and he had the key. It was his car, and if he didn't want to wait for me, then it was his fault if the car was stolen by the time school ended.

Slowly but surely, I made my way into the school building, dragging my feet against the hard concrete with my head facing the ground. Niall was the only one at the lockers when I arrived there, which I was thankful for. He was the only one besides Louis that I wanted to see right now.

"Harry," he greeted with a smile, but it dropped as soon as he caught the sad look on my face. "What happened?"

"I don't know, Niall," I muttered. "That's the thing. I don't fucking know what happened."

He furrowed his eyebrows together. "What do you mean 'you don't know'? Is it something between you and Louis? Did you guys fight?" He wondered.

I opened my locker, throwing my bag on its floor before taking off my jacket. "We didn't fight. Things were going great. As far as I know, things are still going great, but when I entered his car this morning, he wouldn't even look at me. The only thing he's said to me today is 'good morning'," I explained, running a hand through my curls frustratingly.

Niall seemed even more confused about this. "Wait, what? So nothing happened? He just started treating you like this out of nowhere?"

"Yes," I said, turning to stare into his eyes. "I wanted to ask him what was wrong, but he had already left the car when I was about to do so. Did you see him before he left for his class?"

He shook his head, looking at me sympathetically. "No, he must've already left when I got here. What do you think it is about then? I mean, since nothing happened between you two, it must be because of something else, right?"

He was right. Louis usually acted this way when something bad had happened. It was his way of dealing with things. And since nothing had happened between us two that I knew of, there must be something else.

Then it hit me.

What if Jay had already decided to talk to him?

My mouth formed the shape of an 'o', which Niall noticed immediately. "You just realized something, didn't you?"

Pulling my eyebrows together, I grabbed my books from my locker. "Yeah, maybe, but I don't know for sure. I'll have to ask him about it," I mumbled.

Niall tilted his head with a proud smile on his lips. "This is the Harry I have always known. Talk things out is what solves everything. I was afraid I had lost you there for a second when you refused to confront him about important stuff, but you proved me wrong. I'm glad," he said, patting me on the shoulder.

I rolled my eyes, letting out a light chuckle. "Such a sap, aren't you?"

He hit my arm. "Hey, I mean it," he pouted.

"Okay, then," I said, shaking my head in amusement. "I'm glad I made you happy."

He crossed his arms over his chest with a content smile on his face. We didn't have time to talk more than that because the bell rang. Niall grabbed his own books before we went our separate ways, leaving each other with a 'see you later'.

During the next couple of hours, I tried to come up with a plan to make Louis talk to me because it turned out I wasn't the only one he wasn't speaking to. He was distancing himself from everyone, just like he had done after he found out Mark wasn't his real dad. It was kind of a relief because that most likely meant his behavior wasn't because of me. However, I had wished he would have told me if something was bugging him. I thought we had come to that stage now, but apparently not.

I noticed that Liam and Zayn seemed confused about Louis' behavior as well. They would flick their eyes between me and the feathery-haired boy, wondering if something had happened between us. It was actually a little funny because only a couple of weeks ago, it was the exact opposite. They couldn't picture us together without being shocked, and now they couldn't picture us without each other.

When lunch rolled around, Louis was already in the cafeteria with Liam and Zayn when I got there. They were chatting about something that made them laugh, but Louis wasn't involved in it. Instead, he was picking off pieces from his uneaten tuna sandwich absentmindedly while staring into the distance.

I sat down in front of him, trying to catch his attention by clearing my throat, but he didn't even move an inch. Letting out a sigh, I kicked him in the shin lightly, and this time, he turned to meet my eyes. His face still showed no emotion whatsoever, though.

"You okay?" I mouthed.

A wave of déjà vu hit me because I realized this was exactly what had happened a week ago when I had been the one staring into the distance while he asked me if I was okay.

He nodded his head curtly before averting his gaze again, making my heart ache in my chest. Why couldn't he just tell me what was bothering him? He should know that he could talk to me now, seeing as I knew pretty much everything about him, but no, he apparently still felt like he couldn't.

Things didn't end up getting better when the girls decided to join us at the table. Vanessa didn't waste a second to sit down next to Louis, putting on a flirtatious look on her face the moment she did so. It made me want to roll my eyes, but I contained myself, keeping my jealousy within me instead.

It wasn't like Louis was very responsive to her attempts at flirting anyway. He just nodded his head and cracked a small smile every once in a while, but he didn't say much. Sometimes I even caught him glancing at me, and if that made me feel warm inside, no one had to know.

Evelyn wasn't with them today, which I was actually a little relieved about because she had been dying to know what was going on between me and Louis, but I had refused to tell her. It wasn't that I couldn't trust her, I just knew that it was best that she didn't know because the fewer people who knew about us, the better, and I knew Louis agreed with me on that.

When we exited the cafeteria, I made another attempt at trying to get Louis' attention and ask him if we could talk, but he managed to slip away from me before I had time to do so. It made me frustrated. Was he avoiding me intentionally or did I just have really bad timing? I didn't want it to be the first option, but I was afraid it was.

It wasn't until school was over that I finally got my chance to talk to him. We were all standing at the lockers, shrugging on our jackets and grabbing our bags. Liam had kept giving me questioning looks the entire day, clearly wondering if something was going on, but I had avoided it. I didn't want to talk to people about what was happening when I didn't even know myself.

Louis was just about to turn around and walk away when I decided to make my move. I walked up to him with determination, my face void of emotion. "I'm going with you," was all I said, and I had a feeling he couldn't find it in him to say no because he clenched his jaw with a curt nod.

I didn't know if he had expected me to take the bus home, but since he had been about to leave without even saying a word to me, I assumed so. The realization made my heart ache, and sadly, it wasn't the first time it had done so today. This day had just been a total mess.

We started walking in silence, Louis' gaze turned towards the floor while I thought of how I was going to start the conversation.

The second we came outside. I inhaled a deep breath. "What happened?" I asked bluntly, jumping right to the point because I was sick and tired of always being afraid that he was going to run away.

I could see him furrow his eyebrows through the corner of my eye. "Nothing," he muttered.

Letting out a humorless laugh, I shook my head. "Nothing, you say? Then why haven't you spoken a single word to me today? And why have you been shutting yourself out? I just... I'm sick and tired of you always distancing yourself like this. Why can't you just talk to me about it?"

When he didn't say anything, I let out a sigh, running a hand through my curls. "Look, I'm sorry. I didn't mean to get upset with you, I just... I thought you knew that you can tell me when bad things happen to you. I thought you would *want* to tell me when things happen to you, but right now I don't get the feeling that you do," I muttered. "It's... It's not something I did, is it?"

By now, we were standing at his car that hadn't gotten stolen during the day even if it was still unlocked. He climbed into it, which resulted in me doing the same thing. The second I got inside, I could see him slump against the seat with his hands covering his face.

It took at least a minute until he finally dropped them and opened his mouth to talk. "No, you haven't done anything, I promise," he replied, still looking ahead of him and not turning to meet my gaze.

"Then what is it?" I asked, this time softly since the adrenaline had left my body.

Hesitantly, he turned to meet my gaze. He studied my features closely before letting out a sigh. "Fuck, I'm sorry. I know I shouldn't have distanced myself like that. I just... I can't help it. I've always reacted this way when something happens. It's just my way of dealing with things, I guess," he explained with pain in his blue eyes.

I reached out to place my hand in between us on the center console with my palm facing upward in an invitation. He looked down, a small smile creeping to his lips as he slowly moved his own hand to put it in mine, lacing our fingers together. The gesture made my heart flutter in my chest, and I couldn't help but return his smile.

"I know, and I get that. You've never thought anyone really cared about you, so whenever something happens, you distance yourself from everyone. I just wish you wouldn't shut *me* out because you know I care about you, and I want to be there for you when these things happen, alright?"

He nodded, looking down at his lap. "I'm sorry."

I gave his hand a squeeze, cracking a small smile. "It's okay. Just... Would you please tell me what's been bugging you all day? I hate seeing you like this," I mumbled, glancing at the side of his face hesitantly.

It took a few seconds until he opened his mouth to reply. "It's about my mom and Mark. They were fighting yesterday, screaming at each other so harshly that I heard the twins cry in the other room. I decided to go make sure that they were okay, but when I left my room, I heard what they were fighting about," he paused to bite the inside of his cheek, looking out the side window.

"It was about me. I couldn't really make out what exactly they were saying, but I heard my name several times, so instead of going into the twins' room, I decided to go downstairs. I figured if I was the topic they were arguing about, I would be able to stop it. However, when I got to the bottom floor, the front door slammed shut, which made me confused. I then walked into the living room to see what was going on. Mom was the only one there, her eyes red and her cheeks damp with tears."

He looked down at his lap, pulling his eyebrows together. "I didn't know how to react because I have never seen mom so upset and sad before, and we have definitely not had a relationship where we talk about emotional stuff. So, I considered going back upstairs and was about to do so when she stopped me. She... she told me to join her on the couch because she wanted to tell me something," he mumbled, looking up to meet my gaze.

"I hesitantly did so, and then she told me that she didn't mean for things to turn out this way. She said that if she had been the one to decide, I wouldn't have been treated any differently from the girls. She... she actually apologized," he grimaced, inhaling a deep breath while running a hand through his hair. "She apologized for treating me the way she has during all these years. I just... I didn't know how to handle the situation. Hell, I didn't even know if she was telling the truth or if it was all a lie, but when I looked into her eyes, I just knew that she meant it, and that fact scared the hell out of me."

He looked up to meet my eyes again, pain still evident in them. I squeezed his hand reassuringly, indicating for him to go on. "I didn't know what to do, so I did the first thing I could think of. I ran. I ran up to my room, locked myself into it, and stayed there for the rest of the evening. It was just so hard for me to process everything she had just told me. I... I needed it to sink in."

"Have you talked to her since then?" I couldn't help but ask with a soft voice.

He nodded his head slowly. "Yeah. She was in the kitchen when I went down to eat breakfast this morning. The girls weren't there, so there were just the two of us because I noticed that Mark never came back the night before. We just stared at each other without saying a word for a minute until she finally did, but I never thought she would utter those words in my entire life.

"What did she say?" I wondered, feeling both curious and nervous at the same time.

With a grimace, he shook his head. "She said that she and Mark are getting a divorce because he apparently can't stay with her now that she decided to tell me everything. But she said that it doesn't matter anymore because she has realized that finally being able to show how much she loves me means more to her than he does."

Louis looked up at the ceiling of the car, blinking back the tears that had welled up in his eyes. I felt a sudden urge to comfort him, and I didn't see a reason not to, so I climbed over the center console to straddle his lap, my knees on either side of his waist. I then took his head in my hands, tilting it so he was looking into my eyes.

His blue irises were glossy with unshed tears, pain written all over his features. I brushed some loose strands of hair out of his face, not breaking our eye contact even for a second. I then leaned in to press a feathery-light kiss on his pink lips before pulling back to rub my nose against his.

"It's okay to cry, Lou. For all I know, you can cry your eyes out if you want because you're allowed to express your emotions. You don't have to... you don't have to feel like you need to keep them within yourself. Not with me. *Please,* Lou, not with me."

He let out a breath, reaching up to tuck a stray curl behind my ear. "What did I ever do to deserve you?"

A few tears rolled down his cheeks, so I wiped them away with my thumbs, giving him a sad smile. "You didn't have to do anything. I've been here, waiting for you for three years," I said in an attempt to lighten the mood a little.

His lips twitched slightly at my words, the crinkles by his eyes showing. "I can't believe you never told me."

"I was afraid you'd hate me," I mumbled, looking down at his collarbones.

He tilted my face up by placing a finger under my chin. "I could never hate you, Harry. Not in a million years. You mean so much to me, you know that?"

Biting my bottom lip, I let a sheepish smile form on my lips. "I do?"

He nodded. "Yes, more than you think. I may not always be the greatest at showing it, but you really do mean a whole lot to me. You would have never been here now otherwise because no one else knows about my family situation apart from themselves. You're the only one I've ever felt comfortable sharing it with," he told me, looking me deep in the eyes.

I moved my hands so they were gripping the back of his neck, the smile never leaving my face. My heart was beating like crazy in my chest, and it was all thanks to this boy. He made my insides literally explode by just the smallest things.

"You mean a whole lot to me too," I whispered, but since we were so close, he could hear me perfectly.

"I'm glad," he breathed, his hands now placed on my hips to keep me steady on his lap.

I looked down at his irresistible, pink lips for a second before looking back into his eyes. "Are you okay? With what your mom told you and about the divorce, I mean?" I asked him.

He pursed his lips, shrugging his shoulders. "I don't know, to be honest. It hasn't really dawned on me yet. Right now, I'm just trying not to think about it although I haven't been able to stop doing so the entire day. I just can't believe she's kept it to herself all these years without saying anything thanks to that awful man. I still have a hard time believing it's true because she never even gave me a clue except for the fact that she never intended anything herself. She always just did whatever he told her to do."

I nodded, fiddling with some locks at the back of his neck. "She came to the diner yesterday and explained all this to me, you know? She told me how much you mean to her, and I encouraged her to tell you because I thought you'd want to know," I explained, not daring to look him in the eyes.

His mouth fell open in shock as his body tensed up against me. "You can't be serious."

I didn't know what to say, so I let him process what I had just told him for a few seconds until he opened his mouth to talk again. "She... she really did that? But why? Why would she come talk to you?" He frowned, relaxing a little bit.

"That's what I didn't understand either, but she told me it was because she was so happy that you had found someone who cared for you the way you deserved to be cared for, and she wanted me to know that. I didn't understand how she could know this by only having seen us together once, but she said she saw it in our eyes," I explained, feeling a blush coat my cheeks.

If Louis wasn't shocked before, he certainly was now. "Are you sure it was my mom? It sounds like you're talking about a stranger," he gaped, making my lips twitch a little.

"I couldn't believe it either," I said. "But I can guarantee you that it was her. You have her eyes," I chuckled, making him roll his eyes.

"Well, I don't know what to say other than the fact that I'm shocked. I literally don't know what to think of all this. It's all just... it's all just so much to take in. I have to process it," he said thoughtfully.

I nodded. "I understand. If all I'd ever known was that my mother hated me, I'd be surprised if I found out eighteen years later that she never did too. Just take your time, Lou. No one's expecting you to process it all just like that."

He flashed me a small smile, reaching up to touch my cheek with his fingertips. He ran them along my cheekbone softly, making goosebumps appear on my skin. I couldn't help but lean closer to him, so close that the tips of our noses were touching.

"Would it be very bad if I wanted to kiss you right now?" I whispered.

He looked at our surroundings, probably noticing that his car was the only one left in the parking lot since we had been here for quite a while because he shook his head, his lips twitching.

"You kind of already did earlier anyway," he pointed out with a chuckle.

I leaned in even more, ghosting my lips over his almost teasingly. "So, is that a yes?"

I could hear his breath hitch as he nodded his head slowly, his eyes flicking between my lips and eyes.

"Yes, please."

Chapter 41

"Can I come over tomorrow? I'm bringing a surprise."

Those were the last words Louis spoke before I left his car to go into work on Saturday afternoon two weeks later. I didn't know how to react because he said it with such a smug look on his face. Did that mean what I thought it did or was I just imagining things? No matter what, I couldn't help the race and beating of my heart.

The thought never left my mind during the rest of that day, and it didn't make matters better that I didn't get to talk to him. My shift didn't finish until ten in the evening, so we only texted each other to say goodnight before we went to bed, which was absolutely fine, but his words still lingered in my head.

It was only eleven in the morning when Louis texted me on Sunday to say that he was on his way. I was surprised because I didn't think he was going to show up until a few hours later, but I was nothing but happy that he was going to be here so soon. It had almost been twenty-four hours since I last saw him, and I already missed his beautiful face.

My mom had left for work an hour ago, so it was only me and Gemma at home. She was in her room watching series, which she usually did on Sundays. I just hoped she wouldn't be a burden like she usually was when Louis was around.

I was currently lying on the couch in the living room, looking through my social media on my phone to kill some time until Louis would be here. After going through Twitter, I went onto Instagram, getting more and more bored by the second. I had just enough time to check my feed until the doorbell went off in the entryway.

I didn't waste a second to get up from the couch, shove my phone in the pocket of my joggers, and sprint to the front door. And there he was, in his forest green Adidas hoodie and a pair of black joggers. His fringe was perfectly swept to the side while the rest of his hair was sticking out in the hottest way possible. What surprised me, though, was that he didn't come empty-handed. He was holding a grocery bag.

"Why did you ring the doorbell when you decided to go inside anyway?" I asked him, amusement lacing my voice although my eyes were stuck on the plastic bag in his hand.

Was this the surprise he had been talking about yesterday? For some reason, I couldn't help the disappointment that erupted inside me. I was hoping he had been talking about something completely different.

He shrugged his shoulders, a smile forming on his lips. "I did before I could think about it, but then I figured I could just go inside because this feels like my second home these days."

My heart fluttered in my chest at his words, my lips twitching. "I'm glad you feel that way. What's with the bag, though?" I wondered, nodding towards the said item.

His eyes traveled down to the bag before moving back up to meet mine, a grin now evident on his face. "You like chicken, right? I mean, your favorite dish is Pasta Alfredo and you made it pretty clear that the chicken stew is your favorite dish at your work, so I got the feeling that you don't hate it at least."

I squinted my eyes at him in suspicion. "I love chicken, but why?"

Louis reached the bag up and pointed at it. "I was thinking we can cook some chicken with some mash potatoes since it's a favorite of mine," he smiled, showing off his white teeth.

My jaw dropped in surprise. "Wait a second. Are you saying that you were planning this all along? I thought you hated cooking," I asked incredulously.

He rolled his eyes, shaking his head. "It's not like I hate it. I'm just not very good at it, but since you're going to be with me, I'm sure it'll be fine. Besides, my noodles weren't that bad, were they? I'm honestly quite proud of how they turned out," he bragged, putting a hand on his popped-out hip.

I snorted, raising my eyebrows at him. "It was noodles, Louis. They are either edible or not. It's not like they taste better depending on who makes them. Besides, I'm quite sure you would have overcooked them if I hadn't been there."

He waved a hand in dismissal. "Let's not be like that. Come on, this will be fun," he promised, flashing me a wide smile as he took a step forward to bump my hip with his.

Shaking my head in amusement, I followed him to the kitchen. Before we could reach it, though, Gemma emerged from her bedroom with a look of surprise on her face. "Oh, hi, Louis. I didn't know you were coming over."

Louis glanced at me, raising his eyebrows before looking back at her. "Really? Harry and I made plans yesterday," he explained.

I bit my bottom lip, feeling Gemma send me a pointed look. "You don't need to know everything, Gems," was the only thing I said, making her roll her eyes.

"Whatever, H. I'm heading to Melissa, so I guess you'll have the house to yourselves for a couple of hours. Make sure not to burn it down until then. Oh, and please don't have sex on the kitchen table. I want to be able to eat again without getting any images," she said, scrunching her nose up.

My mouth fell open in shock, and so did Louis'. He was the first one who managed to compose himself by letting out a laugh, though. "Funny, aren't you, Gemma? I promise we won't do anything like that. We're just going to cook a meal together," he promised.

She shrugged her shoulders. "Well, I'm just saying. It's better to take those things to the bedroom, you know?" She winked, making me want to smack my hand over her mouth. Couldn't she just shut the hell up?

"Alright, thank you very much for your beautiful speech, Gems. You are very welcome to leave the house now," I said, moving so I was standing behind her before putting my hands on her shoulders and guiding her to the entryway.

Louis was still laughing at Gemma while I found the situation nothing but humiliating. I was sure my face was as red as a tomato by now.

Thankfully, Gemma left the house not only a minute later, so I walked back to Louis who had now entered the kitchen to unpack his grocery bag. He was standing at the counter, placing the food on the surface of it with his back facing me.

I walked up to him while letting out a sigh, running a hand through my curls. "I'm so sorry about that. I swear I didn't know she was going to make that comment," I grimaced.

He turned around to send me a smile, his head tilted to the side. He then reached out to wrap his arms around my waist, pulling me close to his frame. "It's okay, I promise. It was actually kind of funny," he told me, glancing over my shoulder towards the kitchen table. "It does look pretty inviting now that I think about it, doesn't it?" He wiggled his eyebrows at me, making me almost choke on my own saliva.

"What? No! Louis, you can't just say things like that," I whined, leaning in to hide my face in the crook of his neck.

Chuckling, he tightened his hold on my waist and leaned down to press a kiss to my hoodie-clad shoulder. "I'm just kidding, babe. Our first time is not going to be on a kitchen table, I promise."

I could feel myself blush at his words, and I slowly pulled back to get a look at his face. Talking about this made me think about what I had thought the reason he wanted to come here today was. I wouldn't have minded that at all. To be completely honest, I had been looking forward to it ever since the words left his mouth.

"So, are we going to get started? I have a feeling making this meal is going to take a while," I said, raising my eyebrows at him.

He nodded, leaning in to press his lips against mine quickly. "Sounds like a perfect idea, love."

Love, babe... what was this? My birthday? What had I done to deserve being called this?

The smile wouldn't leave my face during the entire time we cooked the meal. Being called 'babe' and 'love' was only part of that reason because cooking with Louis was just a lot of fun in itself. Not because it was enjoyable (even if it was), but because he was such a bad chef. He barely knew that the potatoes needed water to boil. He was also very clumsy, dropping the spatula on the floor at least three times while flipping the chicken in the pan.

In the end, I ended up in front of the stove while he settled down on the counter next to me, dangling his feet back and forth in the air. "So, have you been talking to your mother recently?" I asked, turning to glance at his face.

He pursed his lips while nodding slowly. "Yeah. I talked to her yesterday after I dropped you off."

"What did she say?"

Shrugging his shoulders, he averted his gaze. "We mostly talked about the divorce. Everything is still pretty stiff between us, but I'm slowly warming up to her," he explained, turning back to give me a smile.

I returned it before looking down to flip one of the two chicken fillets in the pan. "I'm glad. What did she say about the divorce then?"

He reached out to stir the gravy, taking a little time to reply. "She's moving out in a few weeks because she can't afford to keep the house herself. She wanted to ask me what I want to do about the situation, if I want to come with her or if I want to stay."

He looked up to flash me a small, hesitant smile. "And I told her I want to come with her. There's literally nothing that's holding me back in that house. Besides, I'm probably moving out in a few months anyway, so I might as well get used to it now."

I tilted my head to the side, reaching out to squeeze his hand that was on his lap. "I'm so happy that you've handled all this so well. Your life has literally been turned upside down in a matter of a few weeks, yet you're ready to take that step. I'm proud of you," I told him.

He shook his head, letting out a light chuckle. "There's nothing to be proud of, really. I just... I guess you were right about her. You saw that she was hiding something by just one look she gave you while I straight off refused to even acknowledge it, let alone believe your words. I'm sorry," he apologized.

"Don't be. I'm just glad she decided to finally tell you. You deserved to know the truth."

With a smile, we dropped the subject and started talking about other stuff instead. It wasn't long until the meal was finished. Louis set the table while I placed the pan and pots on it, making sure to be careful not to drop anything now that it was finally finished after an hour and a half.

The meal was delicious. I could really tell why Louis liked it so much. "This is so good, Lou. Does it have a name or something?" I asked him while we were eating, glancing up at him.

He shrugged his shoulders. "Nah, not really. I usually just call it chicken stuffed with mozzarella cheese, wrapped in parma ham with some homemade mash and some gravy on the side."

I arched an eyebrow at him. "So, if I ever want to look the recipe up, I'll have to type all that in the search bar?"

He fluttered his eyelashes, shaking his head with a chuckle. "This recipe can't be found on the internet, I'm pretty sure."

With a pout, I looked down at my plate and brought another forkful of food to my mouth.

"I could always write it down for you, though," he smirked, making my face light up.

"That'd be great," I smiled brightly, sending him a look of appreciation.

Once our plates were empty and we had put all the dirty dishes in the dishwasher, Louis crossed his arms over his chest, looking at me with squinted, suspicious eyes. The action made me feel a bit uneasy because I could tell he was thinking about something specific, but I had no idea what.

"Tell me what you actually thought when I asked you if I could come over," he ordered, tilting his head to the side.

He was leaning against the counter while I was leaning against the kitchen table across from him. His question caught me off guard, and I had to swallow hard to be able to answer him. "I, uh... nothing? I had no idea what your intention was," I replied, feeling my cheeks heat up and knowing they were giving me away. Fuck.

He arched his eyebrows, an amused smile taking over his features. "Really now? Because I am pretty sure I saw disappointment cross your face when I said that we were going to cook a meal together."

A new lump formed in my throat, which made me have to swallow thickly again. "I wasn't disappointed," I mumbled, refusing to meet his intense gaze that I could feel on me.

He took a few steps forward so he was now standing right in front of me, his hands on the table on either side of my body. "You can just tell me, love. I promise I won't laugh," he whispered, leaning in so close that our noses were touching.

My heart started racing in my chest at his proximity, and not to mention at the topic we were talking about. I couldn't tell him what I had been thinking. It would be embarrassing, especially since it hadn't been his intention whatsoever. There was just no way that was happening.

When I didn't say anything, he raised an eyebrow at me, a smile making its way to his lips. "Come on, tell me," he encouraged me, reaching up to cup my cheek while running his thumb over my chin slowly.

I bit my bottom lip, inhaling a deep breath. "It's too embarrassing," I finally mumbled with my gaze turned towards the floor.

I could still feel him staring at my face, though, and the fact that he was so close didn't make things better. "If I tell you that you were right, that my intention was something completely different than making lunch with you, will you tell me then?"

My jaw literally dropped by his words, my eyes widening. He chuckled at my reaction, leaning in to press soft kisses to my neck, moving all the way from the point where my neck met my shoulder up to just below my ear. It felt so good that I couldn't help but close my eyes while tilting my head to the side to give him more access.

After repeating the same action at least three more times, he pulled back to look at me expectantly, his lips now puffy. "Tell me, Harry," he breathed, leaning in to run his nose along my cheekbone to press a kiss to my jaw.

I swallowed thickly, trying to get my heart to beat at a normal pace again, but it was impossible when he was doing this to me. Goosebumps were covering every little piece of my body while shivers were running up and down my spine. I was pretty sure this boy was going to be the death of me.

I leaned in to close the gap between our lips because I literally couldn't take it anymore, but he pulled away with a smirk on his face. "Tell me, then you can kiss me," he promised.

Why was he suffocating me like this? Why was it so necessary for him that I explained what I thought he had intended by coming over? Couldn't he just drop it and let our actions speak for themselves instead?

With a groan, I squeezed my eyes shut before opening them again. I refused to look at him, though. "Fine. I thought... No, I was hoping you wanted to have sex with me. There, I said it. Are you happy now?" I blurted, scrunching my nose up in embarrassment.

A smirk made its way to Louis' lips as he nodded. "Yes, very happy. You wanna know something?"

I pursed my lips, barely daring to look at him while mumbling a 'sure'. He cradled my face in both of his hands, his fingers brushing a few strands of curls out of my face. "It *was* my intention, but I didn't want to seem pushy, so I decided to cover it up a bit," he admitted, making my breath hitch.

"Really?" I whispered, reaching out to wrap my arms around his waist.

He looked me in the eyes, his blue irises twinkling from the lights in the room with a smile on his face. "Yes, really."

With that said, he closed the space between us and sealed our lips together in a firing kiss. He didn't waste a second to lift me onto the kitchen table and spread my legs to stand between them, so close that our chests were pressed together. I could feel my breath hitch as his lips moved passionately against mine, his hands traveling up the back of my hoodie.

"Jesus," I breathed against his lips, making him chuckle.

Locking my ankles around his waist, I experimentally swiped my tongue along his bottom lip, asking for entrance. He decided to be a tease at first by refusing to part his lips, but when an embarrassing whine escaped my mouth, he finally let my tongue slip into his mouth to meet his own.

I could feel myself getting worked up by the situation, my breathing strained and my heart pounding in my chest while blood was rushing to my lower region by the second. Kissing Louis like this just had this effect on me, and I didn't mind it one bit right now. I wanted to feel everything that this boy was able to do to my body.

My hands eventually found his brown locks as our tongues swirled together, creating a hot mess. It wasn't until Louis started pulling at the hem of my hoodie that I pulled away from him, but only for a second until my lips nudged against his again.

"Not here," I mumbled against his mouth that was wet with a mixture of our saliva.

A smile made its way to his face as he nodded quickly, not even hesitating before lifting me off the table with a tight grip on my bum.

I let out a squeal at the sudden touch and movement, our teeth clashing together, which almost caused him to bite my bottom lip.

"Careful," he breathed, placing a sweet kiss on my lips while carrying me through the house to my bedroom.

Somehow, Louis managed to pull my purple hoodie off on our way there, and his green Adidas one was halfway off too. I was roaming his bare chest with my cold fingers when he kicked my door shut and headed for my bed. He carefully laid me down on my mattress before tugging off his hoodie that I had only managed to pull up to his chin. He then climbed on top of me, settling between my parted legs with a smirk on his face.

"Couldn't even pull off a hoodie, huh? How is this going to end?" He joked, leaning in to kiss the tip of my nose.

"Oh, shut up," I huffed, pinching his bare hip.

He let out a gasp, looking at me with wide eyes. "Did you just pinch me?"

An obvious smile formed on my lips as I tilted my head to the side. "Yes. What are you going to do about it?"

He squinted his eyes for a second as if thinking about it. "In any other situation, I would have tickled you, but that won't be the case this time."

My mouth formed the shape of an 'o'. Before I could ask him what he was planning to do, he dove down to press his soft lips against my chest, leaving kisses all the way down to my navel, where he let his tongue slip past his lips to lick around it. I had to inhale a deep breath, feeling shivers run down my spine by the pleasure that was quickly entering my body.

He chuckled against my skin, moving back up to press several kisses to my neck before hovering above my face with a soft smile on his face. "You're so beautiful, Harry."

I could feel my cheeks heat up as I bit my bottom lip. "Shut up, Lou."

He shook his head as he leaned down to press his lips against mine. "Never," he mumbled, reaching down to fumble with the hem of my joggers. "You sure you want to do this?"

Did I just hear him correctly? If *I* wanted to do this? I had been waiting for this to happen for years now, of course I was wanted to do it. If there was anyone to be uncertain, it was him since he had only started accepting the fact that he was into a guy a month ago.

"Yes," I breathed, reaching up to run a hand through his hair. "Are you?"

He nodded, sending me a smile. "One hundred percent."

Feeling my heart flutter in my chest, I pulled him down so our lips could meet once again. It didn't take long after that until he managed to slip my joggers and boxers off in one go, leaving me completely naked underneath him. I didn't waste many seconds to pull the rest of his clothes off too since I didn't want to be the only one completely bare here.

It wasn't until then it actually dawned on me what we were about to do, and I couldn't help the excitement that erupted inside me. I wanted him as close to me as humanly possible, and I didn't want to wait one more second for it.

I could feel his erection against my lower abdomen as he thrust his hips to meet mine, causing us both to release soft moans. My hands found their way to his back and started moving down towards the back of his waist, making him shudder involuntarily.

He had his face buried in my neck while leaving kisses there but pulled back to get a look at my face. "Do you have lube and a condom?"

I nodded, reaching out to open the drawer of my nightstand to grab the said items. Considering I couldn't see what I was doing since I had an entire person on top of me, it was pretty difficult to do so, though. Louis noticed my struggle and let out a chuckle while reaching out to help me pull out the items.

He leaned down to press a delicate kiss to my lips before getting to work. He coated his fingers with lubricant before reaching down to circle his index finger around my rim. I let out a hiss at the cold touch, arching my back off the bed.

"Jesus. We have barely even started, yet you already react like this. I can't wait to see what you will do when we get to the real thing," Louis joked, sending me a cheeky smile.

"Heey," I gasped. "It's been a long time since I did this, alright?"

He arched a curious eyebrow at me. "How long?"

"Almost a year, I think? I barely even remember it. I wasn't exactly sober," I mumbled. "To be completely honest, I have never had sex with anyone without having consumed alcohol, so you should feel honored."

A wide smile formed on his lips. "Oh, I do, believe me."

With that said, he slipped his index finger into my heat, making me squeeze my eyes shut at the stretch. "Fuck," I breathed.

I mean, I knew I would be tight, but I didn't think I would be *this* tight. I was probably not going to be able to walk tomorrow, especially not judging by the size of him.

He circled his finger inside me while leaning down to seal our lips together. It took my mind off the pain at least a little, and it was nothing but a nice distraction.

The second he added another finger, I arched my back off the mattress again, my chest colliding with Louis' as a gasp made its way past my lips. "I'm sorry," he mumbled against my mouth, moving down to press soft kisses along my jawline down to my neck.

I shook my head with my eyes squeezed shut. "No, no. It's... it's okay."

"Yeah?" He asked, pulling back to get a look at my face, I assumed.

"Yes," I confirmed, cracking a smile.

A few seconds later, he started scissoring his fingers to stretch me out even more, and I had to bite my lip not to let out any sound. He reached down to wrap his other hand around my length, dragging it up and down in an almost teasing manner, and I couldn't bite back the moan that slipped past my lips this time.

"Fuck, I'm ready, Lou. I'm... God, I'm ready," I panted, my eyes squeezed shut in pleasure.

"You sure?" He whispered, rubbing his nose against mine lovingly.

I opened my eyes to meet his gaze, sending him a smile. "I'm sure."

With that said, Louis pulled his fingers out and picked up the condom that he had placed on the bed beside us. He ripped the foil open before rolling it on his erection. He then settled between my legs, lining himself up while looking me in the eyes.

The second I could feel the tip of his length against my entrance, I squeezed my eyes shut again to prepare myself for the pain. With a gentle thrust forward, he entered me, sinking into my warmth. We both let out loud gasps at the feeling, mine a little more pain-filled than his, but nonetheless, the feeling that I could tell erupted in us both by being connected like this was mutual.

He eased himself in inch by inch, trying his best not to hurt me. The second he bottomed out, I was breathing heavily, trying to catch my breath and get used to the stretch of his dick.

Louis leaned down to press a soothing, yet sweet kiss on my lips. "I'm sorry for hurting you, love," he apologized, and you could hear the concern in his angelic voice.

It made my heart swell with warmth and love for this boy. I loved him so much it hurt, more than the physical pain I was feeling right now. "Don't be," I breathed, reaching out to wrap my hands around his neck, letting my thumbs caress the skin on his jaw.

The pain slowly started subsiding after that, and I nodded in confirmation that he could start moving. And so he did. He was very conscientious, though, going slow yet passionate at the same time.

The drag of his length against my walls made pleasure explode inside of me, and I couldn't help but wrap my legs around his lower back while arching my back to meet his thrusts.

When he noticed that the pleasure was taking over my body, he started moving faster, every thrust getting more and more firm and determined. He leaned down to connect our lips at one point, but it was almost impossible to kiss him while doing this because we were both breathing heavily, and the movements we were making made our teeth clash together instead of our lips.

"Fuck, you feel so good, Harry," Louis moaned, his hands gripping my shoulders tightly as he thrust into me, his hips working absolute magic.

Right then, he hit one specific spot that made my toes curl, and I almost screamed out his name. "Shit, yes! Right there, Louis. Fuck, right there."

He seemed determined to aim at the same spot with every thrust after that, and it had me writhing underneath him. I could feel my nails claw at his back as he hit my prostate over and over again.

"I'm... shit, I'm gonna come, Harry," he panted in my ear. I could feel myself getting close too, a bubbly feeling building up in my lower abdomen.

Even if he said he was getting close, he didn't slow down. If anything, he went even faster, which had me throwing my head back in pleasure, my hands now gripping the sheets tightly. However, with one final thrust, he released his load into the condom, coming with a cry of my name.

It was the sound of his angelic voice and the feeling of him coming that brought me over the edge as well, and I shot my load onto our chests, seeing fucking stars as I did so. Louis rode out of his orgasm while I tried to catch my breath, my chest moving up and down at a quick pace.

Once we had both calmed down, Louis collapsed on top of me, his face nuzzling into the crook of my neck. I could feel his soft lips against my skin as he left small kisses there.

"I love you, Harry," he whispered, making every muscle in my body go rigid.

Did he just say what I thought he said? Did he actually just say the words I had been dying to hear for so long?

He pulled back to glance at my face, and when our eyes met, I couldn't help the wide smile that spread on my lips. "I love you too, Louis, more than you can ever imagine."

His entire face lit up at my words, and he didn't hesitate to press his lips against mine, sealing everything together perfectly.

Chapter 42

Louis and I ended up staying in bed for the next couple of hours. We barely moved an inch. He just pulled out of me, got rid of the condom, and cleaned our chests with a wipe before we both got under the covers to cuddle. Our naked limbs were now tangled together as I was resting my head on his muscular chest, and he was carding his fingers through my curls.

I didn't recall that I had ever felt this content before. It felt like I was on cloud nine, my entire body filled with pure satisfaction. I loved it. I never wanted to move. I wanted to stay here with Louis for the rest of my life, just lying intertwined like this.

"I think I'm ready."

I glanced up at his face when he said this, my eyebrows pulled together in confusion. "What do you mean?" I asked him softly.

He looked down to meet my gaze, a lazy smile gracing his puffy lips. "I think I'm ready to come out. I mean, there is no threat anymore. Mark can't do anything now that I'm moving out with mom, so it doesn't matter if Zayn tells his parents," he explained.

My eyes widened slightly at his words. "But... but are you ready? I mean, you said that it was going to take a while for you to accept the fact that you like a guy, and what about the whole settling down thing? Are you really sure you want to do it?"

The smile remained on his face when he let out a soft chuckle. "We just had sex, Harry. So, it'd be pretty sad if I wasn't ready to accept the fact that I fancy a boy, don't you think? And about settling down, I have come to realize that I don't want to do any of the things we just did with anyone else. I only want you, and I think that speaks for itself. I'm nothing but ready to accept everything."

My breath hitched in my throat as I blinked at him, barely comprehending that those words just left his lips. I opened my mouth to reply, but nothing came out. Instead, I could feel my eyes getting glossy with tears. The feelings that welled up in my body by his confession were just too overwhelming.

He noticed this and reached out to caress my cheek gently, running his thumb right under my eye. "Harry Styles, would you do me the extreme honor of becoming my boyfriend?" He asked me, looking deep into my eyes.

"Oh, God," I managed to let out, my hand covering my mouth in shock while the tears were now threatening to leave my eyes.

"Is that a yes?" He chuckled, arching his eyebrows at me.

I nodded vigorously with a smile on my face, dropping my hand from my mouth. "Yes, yes, yes, a million times yes. I'd love to be your boyfriend, Lou."

He leaned down to press his soft lips against mine in a sweet kiss before pulling back to send me a smile. "Thank you," he breathed, wrapping his arms around my body to give me a tight hug.

I nuzzled my face into his neck, inhaling his inviting scent while nosing at his skin. "I should be the one thanking you. You don't know how happy I am right now. I never thought this would happen to me. You were that friend who was just too beautiful, too amazing to be true. I never thought you would like me back. It was just impossible," I said, shaking my head in disbelief because it still felt so surreal to me. For three years, I had thought it was unthinkable for him to have feelings for me, yet here we were now, confessing our love for each other. Was it okay to cry out of happiness because of that?

He let his fingers caress the skin on my chest slowly. "It wasn't impossible. I always saw you differently than the other guys. There was just something about you that made me want to tease you all the time. I loved seeing your reactions, and I loved having you give me comebacks. Maybe my subconsciousness always knew you were special, only that it took ages for my mind to realize it since it had been damaged by my asshole of a stepfather."

I pulled back from his neck to look at his face. "It doesn't matter. The fact that we are here right now makes up for it. I'm just glad that you have realized your feelings because I have honestly never been happier than I am now."

His lips curled at my words, and he tightened his hold on my body. "I'm happy I realized my feelings too. Otherwise, I would still have no idea of what being in love feels like."

My heart fluttered in my chest, and I couldn't help but cradle his face in my hands to pull him down for a kiss. He instantly reciprocated it, one of his own hands coming up to rest on my neck.

When I could feel his tongue licking my bottom lip, I opened my mouth to allow him access, but right then, Gemma's voice boomed through the house. "What is your hoodie doing in the hallway, Harry?"

Louis and I barely had time to separate before there was a knock on the door. Not even a second later, she turned the handle and poked her head into the room. She didn't even seem surprised at the sight of us under the covers, a smirk only making its way to her face.

"Well, at least you made it to the bedroom."

Louis ended up staying the night, which I was nothing but happy about. I had probably never slept so well before, having his arms wrapped around my naked torso while my cheek was resting against his chest. I just felt so safe and comfortable, and I silently wondered why we hadn't spent the night like this with each other before. We had only slept in the same bed twice, and one of those times was before we had confessed our feelings for each other. It couldn't even compare to how amazing it felt now. I just loved it.

When Louis drove us to school the next morning, I could feel myself getting nervous. It wasn't until now that he had told me he wanted us to come out that I first realized that I was anxious about it. I had always told myself that all I ever wanted was to show everyone who I loved and be proud of it, but now that I was about to do it, I felt nervous.

I mean, I had kept the fact that I was bisexual a secret from everyone. No one except for the people I had been with and my family knew that I was attracted to both sexes, and now everyone was going to know that I was even in a relationship with a boy. It wasn't that I was ashamed or anything, I was just a bit scared of how people would react.

Louis noticed that my foot was bouncing against the car floor, so he reached out to take my hand in his, giving it a reassuring squeeze. I wasn't sure if he knew the reason I was nervous, but somehow, it felt like he did, and maybe that was thanks to his next words.

"Harry, love, we don't have to do this if you don't want to," he said, glancing at me to give me a soft smile.

My eyes widened as I shook my head vigorously. "No! I mean, no, I want to do this. It's just... I'm just a bit scared of how everyone's going to react," I admitted, biting my bottom lip.

He gave my hand another squeeze, the smile remaining on his face. "I understand. I'm honestly a bit scared of that too, but we're doing this together. We have each other, right? I mean, I know I want everyone to know that Harry Styles is taken so that they all can stop even thinking about trying to get with you, and I want everyone to know that I'm the lucky guy. I can't speak for how you feel, though."

My chest swelled with warmth at his words, and I couldn't help the curl of my lips. "If there's one thing I have wanted since we confessed our feelings for each other, it is to show everyone that you're mine and no one else's. I want them all to know that you're no longer available too," I confessed, tracing my thumb against the skin on his hand.

We exchanged a smile before silence fell between us, and the silence stayed during the rest of the ride. The second Louis parked the car in an empty spot, we both got out and grabbed our bags from the backseat before making our way towards the entrance of the school building.

My heart started pounding in my chest when Louis grabbed my hand to lace our fingers together, glancing at the side of my face to give me a reassuring smile. I returned it before turning my gaze forward to see where I was going. Considering what took place yesterday, I couldn't exactly walk graciously, though, because my limp was pretty obvious. However, I tried my very best to hide it.

Surprisingly, no one really seemed to pay attention to us when we made our way through the hallway. They were all too caught up in their own business to notice that two of the most popular guys at school were holding hands while walking to their lockers. It made my heartbeat slow down a little because maybe this wasn't going to be as scary as I first thought?

Louis and I let go of each other when we reached our lockers. I shoved my bag into mine before shrugging off my jacket. Neither of the boys was there yet, which made everything a little easier to handle too. So far, things were going surprisingly okay, but that was probably because no one had really noticed anything yet.

I was just about to close my locker when Niall's chirpy voice could be heard behind me. I turned around to see him walking over with Liam and Zayn hot on his tail with smiles gracing their lips. "Morning, guys!" Niall greeted, patting me on the shoulder when he walked by to get to his own locker.

"How was your weekend?" Liam asked, his gaze flicking between me and Louis.

I couldn't help the smile that made its way to my lips as I recalled what happened yesterday, and I could see through the corner of my eye that a smirk was playing on Louis' lips too. "Great," I replied, the smile never leaving my face.

Liam seemed a bit surprised, judging by the way his eyebrow arched. "Really? I thought you were working on Saturday?" He asked in confusion.

I shrugged my shoulders. "It didn't make the weekend worse."

Zayn decided to interfere then. "Alright, so what happened that made it so 'great' then?" He asked, his gaze traveling to Louis who was standing there with his hands in the front pockets of his jeans (he had borrowed a pair of mine and rolled them up at the ankles).

I glanced at Louis, suddenly feeling a lot more comfortable about the situation than I did when I entered the school building just a couple of minutes ago. It was like the nerves were leaving my body by the second.

He glanced back at me, the corners of his lips twitching. "Nothing," was all he said, turning back to look at Zayn.

"So, you guys spent the weekend together?" Liam concluded judging by the fact that Louis had just answered the question that was directed at me.

"Maybe," I shrugged, looking at Louis knowingly.

I could see through the corner of my eye how Niall tried his best not to say anything. He was grinning from ear to ear, probably knowing exactly what had happened during the weekend.

Before any of us could say something else, the bell rang. Liam and Zayn were looking between me and Louis suspiciously, probably sensing that we were keeping something from them. I tried not to think of it when I turned to Louis, who was already looking at me.

"I have to go talk to the school nurse about my injury. She said she wanted to have a follow-up with me after a couple of weeks, so I'll see you here later, yeah?" He smiled to which I nodded.

Then he did something that made everyone in the hallway that was looking stop breathing. He leaned in to press a soft kiss to my lips before departing with a cheeky smile. I could feel myself stop breathing too, but it was because of the butterflies that erupted in my stomach.

Before anyone found the ability to talk, Louis and I went our separate ways, leaving the people in the hallway to gape at the spot where we were just standing. Liam and Zayn's reaction was the best, though. Their jaws were dropped to the point where I thought their mouths couldn't possibly open any wider, and their eyes were bulging out of their sockets. Niall, on the other hand, just had the proudest smile playing on his lips, his eyes sparkling with happiness for the two of us.

I was floating on clouds throughout the next hour, my heart racing and fluttering at the same time because I was both excited and nervous. It was out there now. I could tell rumors about my and Louis' kiss were now spreading like a wildfire around the school without even having to make sure of it.

It all became obvious when I exited the classroom once the bell rang to walk to my locker too. As I made my way through the hallways, I could feel people following my figure with wide, curious eyes. I didn't know how to react, so I just kept my gaze forward while trying my best not to make eye contact with anyone.

Much to my relief, Louis and Niall were already at the lockers when I got there. The second I joined them, they turned to me, Louis' entire face lightening up. "Hey, babe," he greeted, reaching out to wrap an arm around my waist and pull me close.

I could feel my cheeks heat up as I looked into his ocean blue eyes, my breath hitching in my throat because we were in public, and I was not used to this at all. It felt good, though, exciting, yet scary at the same time.

"I'm so happy for you guys, you have no idea," Niall confessed, shaking his head in disbelief with a smile on his face.

"Thank you," I said, biting my bottom lip while glancing at Louis who was smirking slightly.

"How did things go at the school nurse? Was everything alright?" I asked curiously, pressing my books against my chest.

"Yeah, everything's fine. She said my ankle has healed perfectly. It's still a bit frail, though, so she told me to keep being careful with it," he explained.

I nodded. "That's great."

Before we could say anything else, Liam and Zayn joined us at the lockers. The second Zayn caught sight of me and Louis, he crossed his arms over his chest, looking at us with raised eyebrows.

"Care to explain what the hell is going on here?" Zayn wondered, motioning towards Louis' arm that was wrapped around my waist.

Louis cleared his throat. "Harry and I are dating if it isn't already obvious enough."

Zayn swallowed hard as he clenched his jaw. "Since when? And why didn't you say anything? We're your best friends for fuck's sake."

Niall's eyebrows pulled together, and he took a step forward to place a hand on the black-haired boy's shoulder. "Calm your tits, mate. Why are you reacting like this?"

I was honestly a little intimidated by him, and ever since he opened his mouth, I had visibly moved closer to Louis. Niall was right, though. Why was he reacting this way?

Zayn ran a hand through his hair, flicking his gaze between me and Louis. "I thought you guys were into girls. I thought you didn't want to be attached to someone, that you enjoyed having fucking fun. What happened to that?"

I had a scowl on my face as I looked at my supposed friend. "Liam is also in a relationship, and you never complained about that. Why is this any different?" I asked, my voice almost in a whisper because honestly, I was hurt. Zayn was supposed to be our friend and be supporting us in this.

He looked at Louis, searching his features for something I didn't know. When he couldn't find it, he squeezed his eyes shut in frustration. He then inhaled a deep breath before opening them again, now looking more relaxed. "Fuck, I'm sorry. I just... I never saw this one coming. I never thought you guys were into lads, let alone each other. I guess I just feel a bit betrayed because I thought you had the same mindset as me about relationships and partying, especially you, Louis." He looked at the boy standing beside me with pain in his eyes.

"You've been my closest friend for years, and I thought we would always think the same and look at things the same way. I guess it shouldn't matter to me this much, but it does. I'm sorry. But, I guess if you really like each other, I'm happy for you guys. You're my best friends, and I'll support you no matter what. You just took me by surprise," he apologized, biting his bottom lip.

Liam stepped in then, a smile forming on his lips. "I'm also happy for you. Just like Zayn, I was a bit surprised, but if being with each other is what you want, then I am here to support you too," he said.

I let out a deep breath that I didn't know I had been holding in. The nerves slowly left my body, and I could feel myself relaxing beside Louis. I wrapped the arm that wasn't holding onto my books around his waist, squeezing his hip. "He makes me really happy, for both of your information. Honestly, I've been pining after him for three years, but I was too afraid of what he would think if I told him about my feelings. So, I couldn't be happier when he confessed he has feelings for me too," I explained, flicking my gaze between Liam and Zayn, who were now smiling at us.

"Is that so?" Zayn asked, glancing at Louis before looking back at me. "Jesus, you must've gone through hell then, being friends with him when he was with all those girls. I can't imagine the amount of pain you went through."

Louis pulled his eyebrows together. "Stop reminding me of that, Zayn. It kills me to even think about it," he said, pulling me closer to his side.

Zayn bit his lip. "Sorry, mate. I'm just trying to see it from Harry's perspective."

Louis didn't say anything, he just kept me close to him. Liam, who seemed to have been deep in thought for a while decided to open his mouth. "Now that I think about it, you guys have been acting a bit different lately. Sure, you've grown closer during the past few months, but during the last couple of weeks, there was something else. You started getting more cheeky and touchy with each other. I mean, you even patted Harry on the bum a few times,

Louis. God, I should have seen the signs. Why didn't I do that?" He blamed himself, a pout on his lips.

Zayn placed a hand on his shoulder, chuckling slightly. "Well, in your defense, I didn't put too much thought into it either, Li. I just thought they were two great pals."

Niall decided to interfere then by rolling his eyes. "Jesus, guys. You were so blind. Did you never see the way Harry kept staring at Louis? It's been going on for years. It was so cute, the way he cared so much about him and always wanted to be on his good side. He was always afraid that Louis would turn on him if he said something wrong. It's nothing but really fucking sweet if you ask me," he said with a bright smile on his face.

I could feel my cheeks burn in embarrassment at his words. "Niall," I whined, making Louis chuckle.

"Aww, don't be embarrassed, love. I agree with Niall. It's super cute," Louis said, leaning in to kiss me on my flushed cheek, which didn't exactly make the situation better.

"So, you knew the whole time then?" Zayn asked Niall in surprise, his eyes wide open.

Niall shrugged his shoulders, looking at me with a smirk. "Nah, not the whole time, but I confronted Harry about it before they got together. I knew they had feelings for each other because it was obvious. You were just too blind to see it."

Zayn let out a scoff while Liam was still pouting.

The bell rang not long after that, so we had to separate to go to our second period of the day. Just like I had felt when I walked to the lockers after first class, people followed me closely with their eyes as I made my way through the hallway. The word was really going around, I assumed.

Once lunch break rolled around, I made my way to the cafeteria, trying not to catch anyone's gaze as I walked to the table where the boys were already sitting. Much to my delight, there was an empty seat right next to Louis, so I didn't hesitate to plop down beside him with a smile on my face.

The second we made eye contact, his lips curled and he leaned in to press a sweet kiss to my lips. "Hey, love," he greeted, making my heart flutter in my chest, especially while feeling all of the boys' eyes on us.

"Hi, Lou."

We all started eating, Liam, Niall and Zayn talking about the soccer practice we had this afternoon while Louis and I fell into a conversation.

"Has anyone said anything to you about us today?" He wondered, biting his bottom lip.

I shook my head. "No, they've just been staring... a lot, but it's been manageable. How about you?"

He shrugged his shoulders. "Not really. Some girls just walked up and asked me if it was true, and when I said yes, they asked me if they could be friends with me? It was super weird," he frowned.

I couldn't help but laugh. "They wanted to be your friend because they think you're gay. Never heard that some girls' biggest dream is to have a male best friend who's gay?" I chuckled, to which he arched his eyebrows.

"Really?"

I nodded with a smile on my face.

"Well, I probably crushed those dreams when I just looked at them strangely and walked away then," he laughed dryly.

I threw my head back in laughter, clapping my hands together. "Oh, God, I could have killed to see that. That's hilarious," I laughed.

He pouted his lips adorably, and I couldn't help myself when I leaned in to kiss it away. "I'm sure they'd forgive you, though," I smiled.

Before he could reply, Niall spoke up from across the table, looking at me and Louis with a smirk on his face. "So, how's the sex?" He asked, wiggling his eyebrows.

My mouth dropped open in shock as Louis let out a loud bark of laughter. "What? Not to be mean or anything, but your limp is pretty obvious, Harry," Niall winked, making me blush probably for the thirteenth time today.

I hid my face behind the palms of my hands, letting out a groan. "Oh, God."

"Don't be ashamed of it, babe. I quite honestly love your limp," Louis said, rubbing my back up and down slowly. I didn't know if he did it to tease me or reassure me, but either way, it didn't help.

"To answer your question, Niall, the sex is absolutely ama--"

My eyes dilated, and I instantly moved my hands from my face to reach over and clamp them over his mouth. "You are *not* telling them about our sex life, Louis," I gasped, looking at him with widened eyes.

He let out a chuckle behind my hands. "Whhhnnt?" He mumbled behind my hands, making me roll my eyes.

Liam and Zayn were also listening now, Zayn seeming amused while Liam was looking at me sympathetically. "Because it's private, you idiot. Oh, God. This is so embarrassing," I groaned, looking down at the surface of the table, my cheeks practically burning up.

Louis licked my palm to make me pull my hands away, and I dropped them within a second, scrunching my nose up in disgust. "Ew, now my hand is covered in your saliva," I complained.

He arched an eyebrow at me. "You certainly weren't complaining about my saliva yesterday when I--"

I let out a loud gasp, clasping my saliva-covered hand over his mouth again. "Louis, what the *hell*?" I whined as I looked at him accusingly. I wanted to hit him, so bad.

He chuckled against my hand, reaching up to pull it away from his mouth. "I'm just teasing you, love. I'm sorry," he apologized, but it didn't seem like he was sorry at all because the smirk was still playing on his lips.

I let out a huff, crossing my arms over my chest childishly. "Well, it wasn't funny," I muttered, refusing to look at him.

He tilted his head to the side, reaching out to pinch my thigh under the table. "Come on, babe, I'm sorry. I didn't mean to embarrass you, I promise," he said, and through the corner of my eye, I could see him giving me puppy eyes.

I finally turned to meet his gaze, my eyebrows pulling together. "Fine, I forgive you, but only if you promise not to tell them anything about our sex life or any other private things, alright?"

He reached his pinky out to me, and when I looked down at it, I couldn't help but let out a chuckle. Once he had pinky promised, I finally looked up at the guys to see their reactions, and it surprised me to see that they were all grinning at us from ear to ear.

"Well, I'm definitely supporting this relationship," Zayn said with an amused glint in his eyes.

Chapter 43

The rest of the school day turned out pretty okay. Neither of me and Louis received any hate from anyone. There were mostly people who were curious and came up to ask us if the rumors were true. Other than that, they all kept it to staring at us when we walked by in the hallways either alone or together.

Evelyn came up to give me a tight hug after lunch before letting go to congratulate me and Louis. The look on Louis' face when she did this was priceless. His jaw practically dropped to the floor in surprise, but I couldn't blame him. The last time he had listened to her talking to me apart from the party, she had been trying to take me out. So, this side of her was new to him.

Vanessa didn't so much as glance at us as she waited for her friends to leave with her, but I couldn't honestly care less about that. As long as she kept her filthy fingers as far away from my boyfriend, I was happy. Louis didn't seem to even acknowledge her, though, so it was all good.

I realized that there wasn't really a reason for me to be as nervous as I had been in the morning about the whole coming out thing. Sure, Zayn's reaction wasn't the best in the beginning, but he loosened up to the news pretty quickly.

However, I knew soccer practice was probably going to be a different story because it wasn't exactly a secret that Ryan didn't like the thought of me and Louis together judging by the way he had provoked us about it before. So, even if the day had gone well so far, I was still a bit nervous to see what his reaction would be.

Louis and I were currently sitting in his car on our way to the gym. Music was playing through the speakers, and even though he was the one choosing it today, he was nice enough to play more songs by The Killers. The song that was playing right now was 'Read My Mind', and I couldn't help but bob my head along to the music.

"The good old days, the honest man. The restless heart, the Promised Land. A subtle kiss that no one sees, a broken wrist and a big trapeze. Oh well, I don't mind if you don't mind, 'cause I don't shine if you don't shine. Before you go, can you read my mind?" Louis sang, drumming his thumbs against the wheel.

I glanced over at him when he did this, and I couldn't help the smile that formed on my lips. I loved it when he sang because his voice was so beautiful and angelic. I swear I would have fallen asleep to it in just a matter of seconds if I had been lying in my bed.

Once we arrived at the gym, we got out of the car and grabbed our bags from the backseat before walking over to the building, our joined hands swinging between us. The second we entered the locker room, the chatter that had filled the place disappeared in the blink of an eye, and it was suddenly so quiet that you could hear a needle drop to the floor.

I swallowed hard as everyone's attention turned to us, or more specifically our entwined hands. Most of them had probably heard the rumors that had been going around school the entire day, but some of them seemed shocked if the looks on their faces were anything to go by.

Louis cleared his throat and didn't hesitate to walk into the room with me, his head held high. "What are you staring at? It's as if you've never seen two guys holding hands before," he scoffed, and honestly, no words could describe how much I admired him for standing up for us, even if the tone he was using was a bit cold.

I squeezed his hand in mine in reassurance because I could tell he was getting riled up by the situation. Through the corner of my eye, I could see his body relax a little by my touch, and I could feel it through his hand as well.

We walked over to sit down on an empty bench, letting go of each other's hands as we did so. Meanwhile, the other guys in the room seemed to go back to what they had been doing before Louis and I made an entrance, as if nothing had happened. They didn't even utter a word to what Louis just said.

It turned out I spoke too soon, though, because the next second, I could feel the presence of a guy hovering over me and Louis. As if on reflex, I scooted closer to Louis, suddenly feeling my heart race in my chest because whoever the person standing in front of us was, he was intimidating.

"Look who we have here. Isn't it the two little love birds?" A familiar voice taunted, and I could actually feel chills running down my spine by it. I wondered if Ryan had the same effect on everyone or if it was just me.

Louis snapped his head up to look into Ryan's eyes, his eyes narrowing within a second. "Piss off, Johnson," he seethed through his teeth.

Ryan let out a loud, humorless laugh. "As if, Tomlinson. I'm surprised you didn't make it official until today. You two have been throwing your disgusting gay love right in our faces for long enough now," he said, making a gagging sound for more effect.

I could feel my stomach turn by his words. How could he be so cruel? I didn't understand how he had the heart to even say those words.

Louis scrunched his nose up. "If there's anyone who's disgusting here, it's you. How can you even look yourself in the mirror, you homophobic piece of shit? You should be fucking ashamed."

Ryan leaned down to grab the collar of Louis' shirt to pull him up to his feet. The action made my eyes widen in fear, and I instantly knew that this wouldn't end well. I wanted to pull Louis back down again and keep him away from Ryan, but I was sure that would be to no avail.

"The fuck did you just say? Ashamed? Really? If I were *you*, I would be ashamed. Have you never been taught how disgusting it is to be together with a fucking boy, huh? That it's a fucking sin? Or did you never have parents who taught you shit?" He spat while stepping far too close into Louis' personal space.

Ryan's words made my breath hitch because bringing Louis' parents into the picture was probably the stupidest move he could have ever made. He didn't know, but I did, and I knew this couldn't possibly end well.

Louis pushed at Ryan's chest, making him stumble backward a little, but he was quick to regain his balance. Louis was quick to follow him, though, and grabbed the collar of his shirt while backing him up against the wall of lockers across the room.

"Don't you fucking dare mention anything about my parents, you piece of shit. If yours taught you that homosexuality is wrong, then I feel nothing but fucking sorry for you because that only means they would never accept you for who you are. It wouldn't surprise me if you're actually into guys yourself," Louis snarled, his grip tight on Ryan's collar.

Ryan tried to break free, but it was to no avail because Louis was too strong. "I'm not fucking gay, you disgusting fag. I'd rather fucking die. It's nothing but pure disgusting the way you'd actually choose to fuck an ass rather than a vagin--"

He didn't get to finish that sentence because he was caught off by a fist connecting with his cheek. Louis was breathing heavily as he held his bruising hand in the air, staring at Ryan with a look so cold that I almost got scared.

I didn't notice that I had gotten up from my seat to follow the two boys across the room, but I caught myself suddenly standing right by their sides. I was just about to lay a hand on Louis' shoulder to calm him down when a new voice spoke up.

"That's enough!"

Everyone went stiff at Coach's stern tone as he walked over to us with quick and determined strides. He pulled Louis and Ryan apart, his eyes flicking between the two of them.

I had a feeling this couldn't be good for Louis. Things didn't look great at all, the way his fist was all bruised from hitting Ryan, and the way Ryan's cheek was flushed after the harsh impact. Louis had only been defending himself, but how was Coach to know that if he didn't see it all unfold?

"Ryan, pack your bag and leave. Now. I am not repeating myself. You crossed the line yet another time, and I do not accept homophobia on this team. If you have a problem with it, keep it to yourself instead of going around spitting it in people's faces like that. You're not welcome here anymore."

He then looked up to meet my gaze, and even if it was still ice-cold, I knew his anger wasn't directed at me. "Styles, I want to talk to you before practice begins. You can meet me in the locker room across from this one when you've changed into your gear."

With that said, Coach turned on his heel to exit the room, leaving the place so silent that you could hear every person in the room breathing. It took at least ten seconds until the first person moved, and to my surprise, it was Ryan.

"You deserve to fucking die, Tomlinson. First, you steal my title as captain, and now you're getting me kicked off the team," he seethed, backing away from Louis.

With that said, he went to grab his bag before storming out of the locker room, bumping his shoulder into Louis' on his way out. The second the door slammed shut again, the feathery-haired boy let out a deep breath before running his good hand through his fringe.

"Jesus Christ."

"I'd say the same thing," I breathed, swallowing thickly.

He turned to me, his lips curling into a faint smile. "I'm so sorry you had to see that," he apologized, reaching up his good hand to touch my cheek gently.

I shook my head, placing my hand on top of his and squeezing it. "It wasn't your fault. I'm so happy Coach actually saw what happened before you hit him, though. Otherwise, it might've been you walking out that door right now," I sighed.

He pursed his lips. "He had it coming. There have been way too many times he's slipped up during the last couple of months. This was just the icing on the cake. I'm glad he's finally gone, though."

I nodded. "Yeah, me too."

He flashed me a small smile, letting his fingers pinch the skin on my cheek playfully. "You should go change now. Coach's waiting on you," he smirked, making me roll my eyes.

"Yes, sir."

When I turned around, he went to pat my bum, making me let out a high-pitched squeak. "Louis!" I whined.

He let out a round of laughter as I turned around to glare at him. "You seriously have an obsession with my ass."

He shrugged his shoulders with a cheeky glint in his eyes. "I can't help it. It's just so perky."

I arched an eyebrow. "Well, it's nothing compared to yours."

His mouth fell open, and it wasn't until then we both realized that we were in a room with other people. Louis looked at our surroundings to see if anyone was listening to us, but they all seemed caught up in their own business. We weren't being very loud anyway.

"Get changed into your gear before Coach comes looking for you," he told me, ignoring my last comment.

I raised my eyebrows. "I will as long as you go wash your knuckles. That cut looks pretty bad."

It was as if he had totally forgotten that he was bleeding from the blow he had swung at Ryan because he seemed confused about what I was talking about at first. The second he looked down at his hand, though, realization struck his features. "Oh, I will."

Once I had changed and Louis had walked off to the bathroom, I exited the locker room to head into the one across the hallway. It wasn't until I cracked the door open that I could feel nerves erupting within me because why would Coach want to talk to me right out of the blue?

"Harry, sit down," he ordered from where he was already sitting on the bench across from me, nodding towards the one beside him.

I swallowed down the lump that had formed in my throat and nodded curtly before doing as told. I then looked up at him expectantly, my eyes focusing on his features. Unfortunately, they were impossible to read.

"First off, congratulations," he smiled, and when he noticed my confusion, he added; "On your and Louis' relationship. I managed to hear what Ryan said before I interfered earlier. I'm happy for you."

My eyes widened in surprise. Out of everything I ever expected, I never thought Coach out of all people would congratulate me on getting together with Louis. This was just surreal and weird at the same time.

"Uh, thanks, I guess," I said.

He flashed me another smile. "But, I didn't make you come here only to congratulate you on your relationship. I wanted to talk to you because I have something to tell you," he announced.

I could feel my heartbeat in my ears as he took his time to continue. Honestly, I wasn't sure if I wanted him to because this whole situation made me want to run.

"You've been accepted to the Arsenal Football Club Academy."

I didn't know how to react, so I just sat there, gaping at him for at least a minute. I then came to my senses and started shaking my head frantically while breathing heavily through my nostrils. "No, no, no, no, that can't be true. You must've gotten it wrong. I... Louis is supposed to have it, not me," I panicked, looking at Coach with widened eyes.

He let out a sigh. "Harry, I get that this is a tough situation for you, especially now that you and Louis are dating, but they chose you."

I furrowed my eyebrows. "What do you mean *they* chose me? I thought you would make the decision?" I asked him in confusion.

He shook his head, inhaling a deep breath. "I was supposed to, but then scouts came to watch the first game of the year, and they loved you. They've been keeping an eye on you ever since then, and they think you're an amazing player and good at reading the game," he explained.

"Wait, did you just say that they watched the first game of the year? Louis was injured that game. He didn't even play. This isn't fair if they didn't even see him on the pitch. How do they even know that they want me when they haven't even given him a chance?" I let out in frustration while pulling at the ends of my hair that wasn't tied up in my little bun on top of my head.

He let out another sigh. "I know, Harry. I mean, sure, they have seen him play considering they have been keeping an eye on you ever since that first game, but you're right. I'm pretty sure they never even gave him a chance. I know they like him too, but they want you, and even if I understand that it's hard for you, I think you should take the chance, Harry. Isn't this what you've wanted?"

Now that I really thought about it, no. This was not what I wanted. I wanted Louis to be happy, that was it. I should have never even agreed to make this into a competition between us. I should have just told Coach that the scholarship was Louis' already from the start.

I shook my head. "I can't do this, I'm sorry. I know how much this scholarship means to Louis, and I genuinely thought he would get it. I have barely even thought of getting it myself. I'm sorry, Coach, but I'm backing out. You can tell the people working at the university that I'm glad they thought so well of me, but I can't take the offer. Louis deserves it much more than I do."

Coach let out a hum, looking down at the tile floor with pursed lips. "Harry, I hope you understand what you're doing. If you say no now, you won't get another chance. Are you sure you don't want to think about it for a while? Let it sink in?" He questioned sincerely.

I shook my head. "No, I've had plenty of time to think this through, and I am one hundred percent sure that I don't want it if it means Louis won't get it," I replied determinedly.

He closed his eyes for a few seconds before opening them again. "I really hope you're not just doing this because of Louis. If you actually want the scholarship, I'm sure he's going to be happy for you, Harry. You have to think about yourself too."

I pulled my eyebrows together. "Well, I am thinking about myself because I know that I would never be able to live with the thought that I'm the reason his dreams are ruined. I know how much he wants this, and I know it's more than I have ever wanted it, so please, Coach, listen to me when I say this. Give the scholarship to Louis, okay? I beg you," I pleaded, looking him in the eyes.

He was quiet for a long time, probably an entire minute until he nodded curtly. "If that's your final answer, then I will inform Louis about the news after practice. Is that okay?"

A faint smile formed on my lips at his words. "Yes. Thank you, Coach."

He gave me another nod before telling me that it was okay for me to leave. When I went to turn the door handle, though, he stopped me by opening his mouth once again.

"I hope Louis knows what a wonderful boyfriend he has because there are not a lot of people who would do this for someone else."

I could feel a blush coat my cheeks as I bit my bottom lip. Looking back at him, I saw that he was sending me a smile, but I didn't say anything as I exited the room, closing the door behind me silently.

It turned out the other boys on the team were already out on the pitch warming up. Coach and I had been talking for longer than I thought. Even Liam, Zayn and Niall had joined them, and they weren't even here when I left the locker room.

Louis was quick to ask me what Coach wanted to talk about, but I just shrugged it off, telling him it was about what he wanted me to think about during the next game. He seemed to buy it because he didn't question me any further.

However, I was sure he noticed that I was a bit off because he kept giving me concerned glances, his eyes filled with worry. I wanted to reassure him that nothing was wrong because nothing *was* wrong. I was happy that he was getting the scholarship, so extremely happy.

It was just one thing that made my mood turn completely upside down, and it was the fact that being reminded that university was waiting for us right around the corner made me realize that there wasn't a lot of time left until we would be there.

Or to be more specific, until Louis and I would most likely have to go our separate ways.

Chapter 44

I didn't know what was worst; the fact that I had been right when I predicted how the future would turn out, or the fact that time seemed to pass by at a pace that didn't seem normal. It didn't matter, though, because both of them were just as bad.

It was now in the middle of June, and only a couple of weeks ago, a few days before graduation, I had been accepted to the University of Manchester. Unsurprisingly, it was the only one I had been accepted to, which meant that Louis was moving to London and I was moving to Manchester.

I couldn't describe how much pain this fact brought me, although I was happy for us at the same time. When Louis had emerged from the locker room after talking to Coach after practice that day a few months ago, he'd had the brightest smile that I had ever seen on his face, and knowing that *I* was the reason behind it made me nothing but extremely happy. He had told me that he was sorry that I didn't get the scholarship, but I had waved it off as if it was nothing because it *was* nothing. Seeing Louis so happy just made me realize even more that I had made the right decision.

If only my university wasn't so far away from Louis', things would have been amazing now. I would be the happiest I had ever been with the boy of my dreams by my side while studying for something I really wanted to become. But now things weren't like that. Louis was moving to a city that was miles away from where I was going to be. It would be hours separating us instead of minutes like it had always been before.

Quite honestly, I wasn't sure if I was going to survive without breaking. The longest Louis and I had been separated since we got together were four days, and it was because he had caught a cold and didn't want me to catch it as well. It had probably been the longest three days of my life. I could only imagine how long my days were going to be when I wouldn't be able to see him for weeks.

What made it all a little bit better, though, was that Niall and Evelyn would go to the same university as me, and Niall and I were even going to be roommates. So, even if Louis wasn't with me, I wouldn't be alone. Besides, Liam and Zayn were moving to Manchester as well, even if they were moving to the other side of the city, so things could have definitely been worse.

Louis wouldn't have anyone, but I was sure that his love for soccer would make things better. I knew how much he wanted to do this, and I was sure there was nothing that could really stop him from it. He had been glowing ever since he was told the news, and he really deserved it after everything he had been through during his entire life. He deserved every good thing that could happen to him.

However, I knew that he was just as sad as I was that we had to go our separate ways. He wanted me to move with him to London, and even if I would have loved to do so, I knew I couldn't. I needed an education, and since no university accepted me in London, I had no other choice but to move to Manchester.

Today was the day Louis would go to London. They were starting up earlier than other universities considering they had to be in good shape once the season began. Louis had slept over at my house like he did almost every day these days. Not that he despised living with his mother and sisters at her new apartment, but we always wanted to be as close as possible, and spending the night together was at the top of that list.

"Louis, you have to get up. Your train is leaving in only two and a half hours," I mumbled, trying to shake him awake gently where he was lying under the covers behind my back.

His face was buried in the pillow, and he had his arms sprawled out, one of them above his head and the other on my side of the bed. "Noo, I'm too comfortable right now."

I rolled my eyes, letting out a sigh while turning around so I was sitting beside him. I then took his hand in mine, lacing our fingers together. "It's not going to wait for you, you know?" I continued, drawing patterns on his soft skin with my thumb.

He grumbled in his sleep, turning his head to glance at me. "Is it bad that I don't want to go?"

I pursed my lips, averting my gaze. "I don't want you to leave either, but you have to, Lou. This is your dream," I told him, to which he sighed.

"I know."

We were quiet for the next couple of seconds, and during that entire time, I could feel him staring at the side of my face. Then, he all of a sudden grabbed my hips to pull me down on top of him, his arms holding me tightly to his chest. "My little, curly-headed boyfriend, I don't want to let go of you, ever," he muttered against the skin of my neck.

I could feel goosebumps form on my body at the touch as I let out a quiet chuckle. "I'm not little, you small bean."

He pulled away to look at me with wide eyes. "Did you just call me what I think you called me?" He said with a dark voice, but you could hear that he was only joking.

"Maybe," I smiled cutely, tilting my head to the side.

"Tosser," he muttered under his breath, but his lips were twitched into a smile.

"We have to get up, though," I reminded him, but when I made a move to get out of his hold, he tightened his arms around me.

"Not so fast, Curly."

And with that said, he pulled me down to press his lips against mine in a sweet kiss. His lips felt so soft against mine the way they moved so carefully yet passionately. One of his hands traveled up to my curls, and he laced his fingers through them while I placed my hands on each side of his neck.

The kiss was so filled with love and care that I could feel myself getting emotional because of it. Therefore, I pulled away after only a minute in order to not start bawling my eyes out right in front of him. That would have been a disaster.

Louis and I eventually got out of bed and started getting ready for the day, even if neither of us wanted to. He still had to go home to his mother and fetch all of his stuff that he would bring to London, which mostly included a suitcase.

We ate breakfast together before he left, though. Nowadays, he had his own box of Coco Pops at our house, and while he ate those basically every morning, I ate my famous sandwiches that *I* at least liked quite a lot.

Once we were finished, I followed him to the entryway and watched as he slipped on his black Vans. "You'll be back as soon as you've fetched the suitcase, right?"

He looked up at me, a smile gracing his lips. "Of course. I'm not leaving Holmes Chapel without saying goodbye to you," he promised, leaning in to give me a sweet kiss on the lips.

The reason I wasn't coming with him right away was that I wanted him to have his privacy with Jay, and I didn't want to pressure him by waiting for him in the car or something. I was sure Louis appreciated this as well. His relationship with his mom had grown quite strong during the last couple of months, so I knew he genuinely wanted to say goodbye to her.

"I really hope not," I said, biting my bottom lip.

He shook his head, the smile remaining on his lips. "I wouldn't dream of it. I'll be back in an hour, I promise."

With that said, he exited the house, leaving me in complete silence. Mom and Gemma were both at work, so I had to spend the next hour alone. It was a good thing that I had a few courses to do. Otherwise, I would have felt nothing but bored right now.

The first thing I did was to take a shower. My hair was turning greasy from not having showered in a while, and I wanted to be fresh when I said goodbye to Louis at the train station. I then took care of our dishes in the kitchen, putting everything in the dishwasher before turning it on.

My bedroom was quite a mess with different articles of clothes scattered everywhere. Most of them were Louis', but some of them were mine too, so I picked them up and put everything in the laundry basket in the bathroom. I then made my bed, making sure it was all neat and perfect before heading into the living room to throw myself on the couch.

I fished my phone from the pocket of my skinny jeans, noticing that it was still half an hour until Louis would be here. How on earth didn't it take longer to do all those courses? But then again, I was known for wanting to be done as quickly as possible with everything I did, so it probably shouldn't surprise me.

The next half-hour passed by way slower than the first, but the front door eventually opened in the entryway, and Louis' angelic voice was soon calling my name. "I'm back, Curly."

I instantly flew up from the couch to greet him in the entryway. He was standing with his hands stuffed in the back pockets of his black, skinny jeans while looking down at the floor with pursed lips. However, the second I arrived, he looked up to give me a sad smile.

I didn't hesitate to walk over and wrap my arms around him, letting him bury his face in the crook of my neck and inhaling my scent. "God, if it was this emotional saying goodbye to my mom, I don't even want to begin thinking of how I'm going to feel after saying goodbye to you," he mumbled against my shirt, tightening his arms around my body.

I didn't know what to say because I was sure I was just going to start crying if I decided to talk. So, I stayed quiet while comforting him, running my hands up and down his back while nuzzling my nose into his shoulder.

We didn't pull away from each other until we really needed to go. I slipped on my shoes before exiting the house with Louis, locking the front door behind us. We then got into his car to drive off towards the train station. The sad part was that it was only a ten minutes ride there, which meant that my time with Louis was running out.

I could feel a large knot form in my stomach at the thought, and I had to swallow thickly not to throw up. I didn't want to be present during the next hour of my life. I just wanted to skip it and return to my body after it had taken place because I didn't want to experience the heartache I knew I would be going through. However, I wasn't sure if skipping just the next hour would make me get away from it. I would still be sad after Louis was gone.

The car ride was silent until Louis decided to turn on the radio. I wish he hadn't, though, because the first song that came on was one that held a lot of memories between us.

"Coming out of my cage, and I've been doing just fine. Gotta gotta be down because I want it all. It started out with a kiss, how did it end up like this?"

I instantly tensed by the familiar lyrics of Mr. Brightside by The Killers. It was the song Louis played for me the day after I had confronted him about our first kiss. The first lyrics really fit our situation as well, which only added to the pain it brought me.

Through the corner of my eye, I could see Louis tense up too while gripping the wheel tightly, his knuckles almost turning white. I swallowed hard while looking up at the ceiling of the car, trying my best not to get emotional, but it was hard. It was *so* hard not to when the song reminded me of great memories with him.

The entire ride to the train station was silent. We didn't say a single word, which I was actually grateful about because I was sure I would only burst into tears if we did. I was sure just a single word between us was going to bring me over the edge.

It wasn't until we had exited the car, entered the train station, and come to a stop in front of the rail that the silence broke between us. We were now standing in front of each other, Louis gripping his suitcase in one hand while looking into my eyes. I couldn't help but avert my gaze because it was too painful to look into those beautiful blue irises right now.

"Harry," he breathed, making me squeeze my eyes shut while shaking my head.

I didn't want to believe that this was it, that we were now in the moment I had been dreading for the last couple of months. And even if I wanted to, there was no running away. I couldn't escape the situation because it was happening right now, whether I wanted it to or not.

I didn't move until I could feel the feathery light touch of his fingertips running against my cheek, making me flutter my eyes open. "Look at me, love," he pleaded, his eyes filled with pain.

Inhaling a shaky breath, I bit my wobbling bottom lip. "I don't want you to go," I whimpered, reaching up to wrap my hand around his wrist to keep his hand attached to my cheek. I never wanted him to let go. I wanted to feel his fingers against my skin forever.

The pain in his eyes didn't disappear as sadness took over his features. "And I don't want to leave you."

But we both knew that he had to. The words didn't need to be said, we just knew.

We stayed like that for a couple of seconds until he breathed out heavily. "I want you to have something," he said, and I reluctantly released the grip I had on his wrist so he could pull something out of the pocket of his jeans.

I pulled my eyebrows together, wondering what he could possibly want me to have that fit into his pocket. But when he held my hand out with the little item in his hand, I couldn't help but let out a whimper. It was his car key.

"No, Louis," I said, shaking my head frantically. "Please don't."

He inhaled a deep breath before looking me in the eyes. "I can't take my car with me to London, and I know that you've been wanting to buy one ever since you got your driver's license. I also remember how much you loved driving around in mine when I was injured, so please take care of it when I'm away. I don't trust anyone else with it but you," he pleaded, holding his hand out to me with the key.

I could feel my heart pounding in my chest when I looked down at it, my eyes watering by the second. "I can't take this," I told him, my eyes founding his. "It's too much. You can't... I can't..."

He shook his head. "It's not too much. You'll just take care of it when I'm away. I'm sure you're going to need something to drive around in when you're in Manchester anyway. Plus, you can go see your family more often if you have a car. Just please, Harry, take the key," he said, reaching it out further towards me.

I swallowed thickly as I hesitantly lifted my hand to take the key from his hand, gripping it tightly before sticking it into the pocket of my jeans. "You didn't have to do this, Louis. I would have managed fine without a car. I could have bought my ow--"

He cut me off by shaking his head again. "No, I want you to have it and no one else. See it as a goodbye present if you want," he smiled sadly.

A single tear left my eye, but he was quick to reach up and wipe it away. "I... Thank you, Lou. It's amazing. You really didn't have to, but I'm glad you feel like you can trust me with it."

"Of course," he said, letting go of his suitcase to cradle my face in his hands. "If there's anyone I trust in this world, it's you, Harry. You are the best thing that has ever happened to me. I don't even want to imagine how miserable my life would have been if I never got to know you. Everything was so bad until you came around and turned my life upside down, and for that, I am nothing but thankful. You've brought me so much joy and love, two things I never thought I would experience with my past. I'm so happy that I made you mine, and even if we're going to be apart for a while now, I want you to know that you will always be on my mind, alright?"

I nodded, feeling more tears leave my eyes as I sniffled. "You will always be on my mind too. I love you so much, Louis," I breathed, taking a step forward to wrap my arms around him in a tight hug.

As I felt his arms envelop me, I couldn't help but let more tears roll down my cheeks at a steady pace. This was too painful for me to handle. My heart was screaming at me not to let this boy leave my arms. It wanted me to hold on for dear life and make him stay with me forever. But all good things must come to an end, don't they?

We were cut off by a voice that was calling through the speakers that it was time for everybody that was going to London to start entering their train. We pulled away reluctantly but stayed so close that the only thing we could see was each other's eyes. I could feel his breath on my lips as I gazed into the eyes I was so in love with.

His gaze flicked down to my lips for a couple of seconds, and I could feel every fiber in my body wanting him to do just one thing at this moment. I nothing but craved it right now.

"Kiss me, please," I breathed, leaning in to ghost my lips over his.

He didn't hesitate to close the gap between us and seal our lips together in a kiss filled with passion and love. I reached up to grip the hairs at the back of his neck with one of my hands while I traced the skin of his jawline with my other. Meanwhile, he lifted his hands to cup my cheeks, being so gentle with me. It was as if he was afraid I was going to break into pieces at any second, and maybe, he was right about that.

Our lips moved in sync as I inhaled a deep breath, savoring the feeling of having his soft lips pressed against my own. I never wanted to forget how it felt to kiss him. I never wanted to forget how amazing he smelled, and I never wanted to forget how incredible it felt to have him this close to me. How was I even going to survive without it?

My cheeks were damp when we eventually pulled away, and I noticed that he hadn't been able to hold back the tears during our kiss either because his eyes were glossy and his cheeks rosy. "I'm going to miss you so much, love," he said, sending me a small, sad smile.

I didn't know how I was still able to keep my feet on the ground because it felt like I was losing control of every part of my body as I looked into those beautiful eyes. "Don't forget about me," I pleaded, biting my bottom lip with tears in my eyes.

He shook his head vigorously. "Don't ever think that I will. I love you so much, Harry, and I promise I'll call you as soon as I have arrived, okay?"

"Okay," I croaked. "I love you too."

As soon as he wasn't holding me anymore, I could feel myself wrap my arms around my body. Even if he was still standing there, right in front of me, I already felt so empty and lonely.

Before he left to enter the train, he sent me another sad smile. "I have something else for you in the backseat of my car. I couldn't give it to you personally because I knew it would hurt too much, but you can open it as soon as you get there."

I went to open my mouth and say something, but he had already left when I did so. Not once did my eyes leave his figure until he was out of my sight, and the last thing I saw was him waving at me through the train window with the same smile I had fallen in love with all those years ago.

Then he was gone.

I felt like crumbling to the floor the second I couldn't see him anymore, but I forced myself to keep my feet on the ground and start moving towards the exit. I didn't know how I managed to get out of there because my mind wasn't working properly and my vision was blurry with unshed tears. It was a wonder how I even managed to find my way back to Louis' black sports car, but I did eventually.

I got into the driver's seat and was just about to start bawling my eyes out when I remembered the last words he said. He had something for me in the backseat of the car. Turning around, I could see a blue box with a green ribbon on it. How could I not have noticed it before?

With shaking hands, I reached out to take it into my hands and put it on my lap. I hesitantly lifted the lid to see what was inside it, and I was positive my heart stopped beating altogether at the sight in front of me. No. No. No. There was no way. It couldn't be what I thought it was.

But after blinking my eyes at least ten times, I could still see the same thing in front of me, and I realized then that it was, in fact, what I thought it was.

His green Adidas hoodie.

I also noticed that there was a piece of paper lying on top of it, so I reached down to take it into my already shaking hands and read what it said.

I am aware that this isn't the most expensive thing I could have given you, but I know how much you love this hoodie, so I have a feeling it won't matter. I want you to have it so you can remember me as if I'm there with you, and it might even bring you back to one of the memories when you saw me in it. Until we meet again, I love you, Curly. You are always in my heart.

Yours sincerely, Louis.

And that was when I could feel myself breaking down to the point where I had no control over my body. The only thing I knew was that tears were being shed and that my heart was breaking into pieces.

Epilogue

Four months had now passed since Louis left for London, and to say that I was handling being apart from him well would be a lie. Niall and I had moved into our apartment in Manchester and university had started up two months ago. I couldn't really focus on my schoolwork, though, because I was still a total mess.

The first month without Louis had been the worst, but things were still far from good. I had spent the entire month in my room, lying on my bed with my phone in my hand, waiting for Louis to call or text me. I had refused to even move a foot from my room if it weren't to get food or using the toilet.

The boys had been worried about me, especially Niall. He came to check on me every other day, asking me how I was doing and making sure I stayed somewhat healthy while mom and Gemma were working. And even though I appreciated his concern, I couldn't help but find it a bit annoying. I didn't need anyone to look out for me. It wasn't like I was sick. I was just extremely sad, sad that my boyfriend had moved away from me.

Louis and I talked to each other every day, though, and things were alright between us. I just couldn't help but feel like talking, texting and even Facetiming him wasn't enough. I wanted to touch him, feel his soft skin underneath my fingertips. I wanted to feel his arms around me as I nuzzled my nose into his neck. But most of all, I wanted to kiss him. God, how I missed feeling those pretty lips pressed against my own. I couldn't even begin to describe just how much.

Mom and Gemma were worried about me when I left for Manchester. I could tell mom didn't want to let me out of her sight, but Niall promised her he would take care of me, which I didn't think was necessary, but it calmed her.

And Niall had been there for me ever since we moved into our apartment. He made sure I went to classes, ate at least three times a day and didn't stay in bed or on the couch all day. I felt bad for him, that he thought of it as his duty to take care of me, and I had told him several times that he should just leave me to handle it myself, but he refused. So, he could only blame himself that he still tried with me.

Things had gotten a little better during the last month, though. He didn't need to tell me to go to my classes and eat anymore. However, that didn't mean I could focus on anything the professors said. Even if my body was there, my mind was miles away from the classroom, and it made it impossible for me to keep up with anything school-related.

Today, it was exactly two months since I moved to Manchester, and I was lying on my bed with my back turned to Niall's side of the room. It was Wednesday afternoon, and I couldn't be bothered to do anything but sulk in the bedroom while Niall was out grocery shopping.

My thoughts were interrupted when the bedroom door swung open and my blonde friend walked into the room. "Jesus, Harry. You've seriously got to stop this. It's been what? Four months since Louis left for London, and you still haven't gotten any better. You haven't even broken up, for Christ's sake," Niall groaned.

I furrowed my eyebrows together. "I'm not that bad, Niall," I muttered, and I could see him roll his eyes.

"Not that bad? You're seriously cuddling his fucking hoodie as we speak. Yeah, right. Not bad at all," he snorted.

I looked down at the green Adidas hoodie that Louis had given me the day he left me four months ago. I was gripping it tightly with my hands while pressing it to my chest as if it was him and not his hoodie.

With a pout, I brought it to my nose, inhaling the fading scent of my boyfriend. I wish it wasn't fading away. I never wanted to forget how Louis smelled, and I never wanted to stop being able to inhale his amazing scent. God, I just wish he was here with me. Was that too much to ask for?

"His scent is starting to fade," I muttered, not looking up to meet Niall's eyes.

I could hear him let out a sigh, though. "Harry, I'm not saying this to be mean. I'm saying this because I care about you. Louis isn't dead. He's alive, and you talk to him every single day. He has a life in London without you, but he doesn't go around moping about it every second of every day. You have a life that needs to be lived too,

Harry. You can't go around wasting three years of your life grieving over someone you are going to meet again. I mean, Christmas is only two months away. You'll be able to see him for at least two weeks then."

I bit my bottom lip, finally looking up to meet his blue eyes. "I know. I just... I miss him, alright? I miss touching him, hugging him and kissing him. I just want to have his arms wrapped around me while watching a movie or sleeping or napping or anything! I just want to see his smile without it being through a fucking screen," I let out in frustration, running a hand through my curls.

Niall sent me a sympathetic smile, walking over to sit on the edge of my bed. "I understand that. I know how much you love him and how much he loves you, but now things are like this, and you have to accept that, even if it's hard. Look on the bright side. One day, you and Louis will be able to live together, and good things come to those who wait," he said in an attempt to cheer me up.

I returned his smile half-heartedly. "Yeah, maybe you're right," I mumbled.

"I know I am."

Before any of us could say something else, there was a knock on the front door. Niall and I exchanged a look before a chirpy voice could be heard in the apartment.

"I'm here, boys!"

A second later, Evelyn entered the room and instantly settled down on Niall's bed with a smile on her face. That was until she saw the look on my face. "Harry, honey. Are you still sad about Louis?" She asked me sadly.

Evelyn lived in the same apartment complex as us with another girl that went to our university. However, she spent more time at my and Niall's place, but since I hadn't been very social lately, she had gotten quite close to Niall. They were closer than she and I had ever been, but I didn't really mind.

I pulled my eyebrows together. "What do you mean 'still'? You were here yesterday. Did you think things would have changed over a day?" I asked incredulously.

She pursed her lips, shaking her head. "No, not really. That doesn't mean I didn't hope they would have, though. I miss seeing you smile," she explained.

"Well, I miss Louis," I muttered grumpily, letting my head fall to the pillow.

Both Niall and Evelyn let out a sigh, exchanging a sympathetic look before Evelyn continued talking. "We know you do, Harry, but you have to focus on school too. You're falling behind, and we only started university two months ago."

I didn't reply to her because I knew she was right. I knew I was falling behind because I couldn't focus on anything that was related to school these days. I knew I had to improve. I just had to find the willpower to do so.

Niall eventually joined Evelyn on his bed and they fell into a conversation with each other while I hugged Louis' hoodie tighter to my chest. After a while, I fished my phone from the back pocket of my jeans, a pout forming on my lips when I noticed that Louis hadn't replied to my text. It had been five hours and he never took this long to answer.

Feeling even more upset, I tossed the phone on the mattress at my feet and turned around to bury my face in my pillow. To be honest, I didn't know how I would survive being away from Louis for three years. I just couldn't imagine how I would be able to go through it. I could barely make four months, for God's sake.

I was so busy thinking and sulking that I barely heard the bell going off in the entryway, but when Niall told me to go look who it was, I realized that I heard right. I didn't really want to get out of bed, but I reluctantly did as told and dragged my feet against the floor on my way to the front door.

I probably looked like a mess in my purple hoodie and unruly hair that went in every direction, but I couldn't care less. It wasn't like I was expecting someone I cared about anyway.

The second I opened the front door and caught sight of who was standing in front of me, I was pretty sure I could hear my jaw drop. It wasn't possible. I must be hallucinating or something because it couldn't be true. There was no way that Louis Tomlinson, the boy I had fallen in love with three years ago and whom I called my boyfriend was standing right in front of me.

But there he was, with his famous smile on his lips that reached his eyes and made the creases below them show. His brown fringe was perfectly swiped to the side while the rest of his hair was covered by a grey beanie. He was wearing a black and red Adidas hoodie along with a pair of black Adidas pants. And even though he basically had the most comfortable clothes on, he looked amazing. He always looked amazing.

And just like that, I could feel myself letting out a loud gasp as my knees went weak. If it weren't for the fact that he reached out to grab my arms, I would have fallen to the ground. The feeling of his hands on my forearms made my heart start racing in my chest, and the fact that he was *so* close didn't make things easier for me.

"Am I dreaming?" I asked breathlessly, looking into his ocean blue eyes.

The angelic sound of his laughter hit my eardrums, and I could feel goosebumps form on my skin. I had missed hearing it in real life so much.

"No, love. I'm pretty sure you're not."

I blinked my eyes at him, trying to register that he was actually standing right in front of me and that his hands were gripping my forearms to keep my feet on the ground, but it was so hard because I hadn't seen him in so long. It had been four months since he left me at the train station.

It took a long time until it finally dawned on me that he was in fact standing here, outside my apartment in Manchester, but when I did, I didn't hesitate to throw myself at him. The impact was so harsh that he stumbled backward a little, but he successfully caught me in his arms and hugged me back tightly.

"I've missed you so much," I cried against his neck, feeling hot tears rolling down my cheeks as I inhaled his scent.

He pressed his lips to my skin, leaving a delicate kiss on the side of my neck. "I've missed you too, my beautiful, beautiful boy."

We stayed like that for so long that I lost perception of time, but eventually, we pulled away to look into each other's eyes. We remained close, so close that I could only see him and nothing else.

"What are you doing here?" I breathed. "Not that I'm not happy to see you. I couldn't be happier right now, but what about London? It's in the middle of the week. Don't you have soccer practice to attend?" I asked him incredulously.

To my surprise, a smile formed on his face as he shook his head. "No, not anymore."

I knitted my eyebrows together in confusion. "What? What do you mean?"

He tilted his head to the side, an amused smile playing on his lips. "I have transferred to Manchester United. I've been in contact with them during the last couple of weeks because I can't handle being so far away from you, and since they saw me playing at our game a couple of months ago when we were still in high school and thought I was great, they accepted me. So, here I am," he explained, spreading his arms out.

My mouth dropped open. He was moving here? As in Manchester? As in the place where I lived? What was this? Christmas? A dream? Because these were the best words I had heard ever since he confessed his love for me.

It wasn't until then I noticed that he had his suitcase with him, and I couldn't help but burst into tears as I flung my arms around him once again. "You have no idea how happy this makes me," I sobbed against his shoulder while hugging him so tightly that I was pretty sure it was hurting him, but I couldn't bring myself to care because I was *so* happy. Words couldn't describe it, but my heart was racing and fluttering at the same time while silent tears were running down my cheeks.

I lifted my face from his shoulder to look him in the eyes. The smiles that were on our lips were equally genuine and loving. He was my everything, my entire world, the reason I wanted to be alive. I loved him so much it hurt.

I broke our eye contact by leaning in to seal our lips together in a deep kiss. Our mouths fit like two puzzle pieces and moved like they knew each other inside and out, which they did. One of his hands traveled up to my cheek, massaging the skin tenderly while the other one settled on my hip.

My arms were still wrapped around his neck, but I moved one of my hands to pull the beanie off his head so I could run my fingers through his soft locks. "Mmhhmm," I hummed against his lips as he licked my bottom lip.

He let out a chuckle, leaning back to break the kiss, but he made sure to press two more kisses on my mouth before eventually pulling away entirely. I waited a few seconds until I fluttered my eyes open, feeling my stomach do somersaults by the feeling of finally kissing my boyfriend again after so long.

"I want more kisses," I pouted, making him let out another chuckle.

"I'll kiss you as much as you want if you would just let me inside your apartment. I'd rather not want anyone to see when I ravish you," he joked.

My eyes widened slightly, which he found absolutely hilarious because he let out a loud bark of laughter. "I'm just kidding, Curly, but I'd love to come inside instead of standing outside the door."

So, I reluctantly let go of him to let him walk past me and into my and Niall's apartment with his suitcase. He glanced around the place impressively while nodding his head. "This isn't bad. It's not bad at all, and it's big. I'm sure you were the one who decorated most of it, though. Something's telling me Niall doesn't really care about these kinds of stuff," he chuckled, turning around to look at me.

I nodded. "Yeah, it was mostly me, although I haven't put as much effort into it as I'd like to. I've uhh... I haven't really been at my best the last couple of months," I admitted with a grimace.

He eyed my body before tilting his head to the side. "Yeah, I can see that," he winked jokingly, making my mouth fall open.

"Heeey," I whined. "You're supposed to tell me how good I look, that it doesn't seem like I've been feeling bad at all."

He mocked my pout, taking a few steps forward so he was right in front of me. He then cupped my face in his hands, looking me deep in the eyes. We stayed like that for a couple of seconds, and I could feel my heart pounding in my chest at his proximity, wanting and expecting him to do something about the situation.

So, when he pulled away with an amused glint in his eyes and just flicked my nose without saying anything, I let out a loud gasp. He turned around to walk into the apartment, but before he had even taken five steps, I jumped on his back. It was as if he had predicted my action because he instantly grabbed my thighs to keep me in place as he laughed loudly.

"You should be happy I didn't knock you to the floor, you twat," I huffed into his ear, hitting him in the chest gently, so gently that he let out a fake gasp.

"Oh, I'm so scared. Harry Styles, as in the kindest person in the world is threatening me, his boyfriend to knock me to the floor. Oh, and let me remind you that he's currently hugging me too. Shouldn't I be scared shitless?" He joked, tilting his head so he could see my face.

I reached out to cover his eyes so he couldn't see anything and let out another huff. "You definitely should because once I'm done with you, you won't be laughing, I'm telling you," I tried to threaten him, but since he let out another laugh, I was pretty sure I failed.

"You're as scary as a kitten. You can't even sound threatening. I'm really sorry, princess," he chuckled, and I could feel my heart flutter at the nickname. It'd been ages since he last called me that.

I removed my hands from his face so he could see the pout on my lips. He was quick to lean in and kiss it away, though. I just couldn't help but smile when he kissed me. "I fucking hate you, Tomlinson," I muttered fondly, shaking my head.

He tilted his head with an amused smile on his face. "I love you too, sweetheart."

Right then, Niall and Evelyn decided to make an appearance, walking out of the bedroom to see me on Louis' back in the entryway. Their eyes widened at the sight, their mouths falling open.

"Louis?" Niall let out in surprise, a smile slowly forming on his lips. "Thank heavens you are here. I honestly thought I'd have to book Harry a train ticket so he could go see you. He's been miserable without you. Nothing but a total wreck, I'm telling you."

I could feel my cheeks heat up, and I instantly buried my face in Louis' shoulder in embarrassment. "Niall!" I whined. "You can't tell him that."

Louis let out a light chuckle and tilted his head to look at me fondly. "If it makes you feel better, my roommate wanted to kick me out because I couldn't stop talking about how much I missed you. So, I'm pretty sure I've been just as miserable as you."

My mouth dropped open. "And here you were, teasing me for looking bad because of our situation just minutes ago. How rude of you," I whined with a huff, sliding off his back so I could stand next to him.

He reached up to touch my cheek. "You know I was just kidding. I'm sure it's impossible for you to ever look bad. You were born with natural beauty."

I smiled at him, feeling my heart swell in my chest by his words. All I wanted was to kiss him right then and there, but I was interrupted by Niall who opened his mouth to talk again.

"So, should I take all this as though you finally told Louis that you gave up the scholarship because of him?"

I could feel every muscle in my body go rigid because no, fuck. Louis didn't know. He wasn't supposed to ever find out about it, and especially not now by Niall.

Louis looked at me alarmed. "Harry, love, what is Niall talking about?" He asked warily.

I could see a look of realization cross Niall's face, and he didn't hesitate to grab Evelyn's hand. "I think we should leave these two alone for a while. They probably have lots of things to talk about now that they're in the same room again," he said urgently, pulling Evelyn to the door, and they were out within a few seconds.

Louis flashed me a pointed look, putting a hand on his hip. I let out a deep sigh, biting my bottom lip. "Remember that day when Coach told you the news about the scholarship?"

He nodded in confusion. "Yeah?"

"Then you might also remember that he wanted to talk to me before practice. He uhh... he told me that there had been scouts from Arsenal at the first game, the game where you weren't present in, and he told me that they had been following me since then and wanted me to have the scholarship. I couldn't accept it, though. I knew how much you wanted it, and you also deserved it much more than I did. It was only because you weren't playing in that game. They never even gave you a chance," I explained, looking at him pleadingly. I didn't want him to be mad at me.

He pulled his eyebrows together. "Why didn't you tell me this?" He asked with a calm voice.

"Because I was afraid you wouldn't let me do it, and that you would go on about how you didn't deserve it if they wanted me. I know you were meant to have it. You were meant to play soccer in a stadium with thousands of screaming fans on the bleachers. Not me.

Please don't be mad at me, Lou," I pleaded, taking his hand in both of mine.

He shook his head, the frown remaining on his face. "I... I don't know what to say, Harry. I can't believe you actually turned down the offer. Why would you do that to yourself? I know how much you wanted it too."

I put my hands on his biceps to make him look at me. "No, I wanted you to have it more than I wanted it myself. You deserved it more than anyone else. I should have just told Coach that I didn't want it before they made the decision. Are you... are you mad at me?" I wondered, my voice small.

He let out something that sounded like something in between a snort and a laugh. "You may be the stupidest person in the world for turning down a scholarship, but I could never be mad at you. What you did for me... I don't know what to say. It's the most amazing thing anyone has ever done for me, but I shouldn't be surprised because it's you we're talking about. I really do have the most amazing boyfriend in the world, and you have shown me that so many times now. I love you so incredibly much."

I couldn't help the smile that spread on my lips, and I didn't hesitate to kiss his pink lips, throwing my arms around his neck. "I love you too, you sappy asshole," I chuckled.

He replied by closing the distance between us again and lifting me up by the thighs so I was straddling his waist. I let out a little squeal while lacing my fingers through his brown locks.

We kissed all the way to the bedroom where Louis laid me down on the mattress before climbing on top of me. "Is this my hoodie?" He asked, lifting the green article of clothing that was lying on the bed beside us.

I bit my lip while glancing at it. "Yeah? I uhh... I kind of cuddle it when I sleep," I admitted with a blush on my cheeks.

His lips twitched at my words and he leaned in to peck my lips sweetly. "I wish I had something that belonged to you too back in London. It would have saved me from many tears," he said, making my mouth fall open.

"You were crying over me?" I asked incredulously.

He looked at me as if I were dumb. "Only a couple of hundred times. I missed you so much, my curly princess. Leaving you is the worst thing I've ever had to go through. During the first couple of days without you, I couldn't get any sleep at all, and I walked around like a zombie. My teammates noticed it too and kept asking me if I was okay."

I nibbled on my bottom lip, letting a shy smile form on my lip. "If it weren't for Niall, I would have probably spent all my time sulking about you in this bed. I never left it if it weren't for him dragging me to the lectures where I couldn't even focus. You are all I have been able to think about since we departed."

He leaned in to rub his nose against mine. "I think this is enough proof that we are meant to be together and not supposed to spend time in two different cities that are miles away, or what do you say?"

I nodded, a smile gracing my lips. "I agree one-hundred percent."

He then kissed my forehead. "I'm so glad that I'm finally here with you, that I can finally kiss you, hug you and touch you again. I've missed you so much."

I wanted to say that I felt the same way, but he cut me off by kissing my lips, letting his lips linger for a few seconds. "I've missed *everything* about you. Your dimples," he whispered, leaning in to press his lips to the one on my left cheek. "Your nose," he said, pressing his lips to it too. "And the crease between your eyebrows that appears every time you think too hard," he continued, kissing the skin between my eyebrows. "Your gorgeous, green eyes." He kissed each of my eyelids before hovering a few inches above me. "And your pink, plump lips. You're so beautiful that it hurts, princess. I love you so insanely much," he whispered and closed the gap between our lips.

I was so taken by his words that I could feel tears pricking my eyes. He was just amazing. How could I have gotten this lucky? Who would have ever even thought that Louis would reciprocate my feelings? I sure didn't, but I was nothing but thankful for it because he had brought me so much love and joy. I never wanted to let him go again, and I had a feeling he would never let that happen either. We were finally back together, and nothing could ever change that, not even if anything or anyone wanted to.

"I love you too, Louis, more than anyone has ever loved another person."

He smiled at me, the crinkles by his eyes showing. "So, what do you say about kicking Niall out so we can live together?"

I let out a light chuckle. "I'd say it sounds like an amazing idea, although I'm sure Niall won't be as happy."

He tilted his head to the side. "You don't think Evelyn would let him stay in her apartment?" He wondered, raising his eyebrows in amusement.

I let out a loud fit of laughter as I nodded. "Yeah, I'm pretty sure she would."

"Then it's settled. You, Harry Styles, are no longer getting away from me, even if you ever want to. From now on, you're stuck with me for the rest of your life. I hope you know what you're getting yourself into," he grinned so wide that his teeth were showing.

I closed my eyes happily before opening them again. "That is most definitely the easiest deal I've ever had to agree on. I'm all yours, Lou, always and forever."

And with that said, we closed the gap between our lips to seal it all together with a kiss.

The End

BOOKS BY THE AUTHOR

The Kiss
You Think I Hate You?
When Hate Turns Into Love

Made in the USA
Las Vegas, NV
18 November 2024